I0665882

SUFFERED *from the* NIGHT

SUFFERED *from the* NIGHT

QUEERING STOKER'S *DRACULA*

EDITED BY STEVE BERMAN

LETHE PRESS
MAPLE SHADE, NEW JERSEY

Published in 2013 by Lethe Press, Inc.
118 Heritage Avenue • Maple Shade, NJ 08052-3018 USA
www.lethepressbooks.com • lethepress@aol.com
ISBN: 978-1-59021-399-5 / 1-59021-399-8
e-ISBN: 978-1-59021-498-5 / 1-59021-498-6

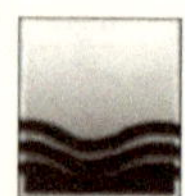

These stories and poem are works of original fiction. Names, characters, places, and incidents are products of the authors' imaginations or are used fictitiously.

Set in Agmena and Goudy Old Style.
Interior design: Alex Jeffers.
Spatter illustrations: Transfuchsian.
Cover artwork and design: Niki Smith.

Library of Congress Cataloging-in-Publication Data

Suffered from the night : queering Stoker's Dracula / edited by Steve Berman.
pages cm
ISBN 978-1-59021-399-5 (pbk. : alk. paper) -- ISBN 978-1-59021-498-5 (e-book)
1. Gay men--Fiction. 2. Dracula (Fictitious character)--Fiction. 3. Horror stories, American. I. Berman, Steve, 1968 editor of compilation.
PS648.H57S84 2013
813'.01083538086642--dc23

2013024728

Table of Contents

INTRODUCTION

BRAM Stoker was a fan of Walt Whitman. Does that seem odd? I am not suggesting that Stoker was himself attracted to other men. But his devotion cannot, should not, be ignored by critics:

"When he was twenty-two, Stoker read and fell in love with Walt Whitman's poetry, finding solace and joy between the covers of *Leaves of Grass.* And, like many fans, he wanted the connection that he felt to Whitman to be real. Late one night, cloaked in the comfort of darkness, Stoker poured his soul out to Whitman in a shockingly honest letter that described himself and his disposition. That letter, when Stoker finally mustered the courage to mail it, would begin an unexpected literary friendship that lasted until Whitman's death."[1]

Stoker's idolization of one of the most prominent and lasting homoerotic literary voices ever known did not begin with blind appreciation. Few copies of the unabridged *Leaves* were available to British readers. But Stoker's earlier dismissal of Whitman's verse gave way to insight and awareness of the poet's talent. To a government clerk with a fondness for literature, Whitman was mythical, supernatural, otherworldly. And seductive in his power.

Perhaps his appreciation became a direct influence on Stoker's desire to write (the short stories began in 1872). Whitman returned Stoker's letters (as mentioned in *With Walt Whitman in Camden*) with encouragement. At this time Whitman was no longer the vibrant man of his poems. He was more akin to the earlier views of the Count: aged but possessing an unmistakable

1 Meredith Hindley, *Humanities*, November/December 2012 | Volume 33, Number 6

charisma that demanded attention. Whitman's blatant homoerotic elements did not fare well with much of the establishment and certainly many reviewers.

Years later, Stoker, involved with his Lyceum tour in Philadelphia, did finally meet his idol in the flesh. Dennis R. Perry considered the link between Whitman and Stoker's most well-known novel in a 1986 *Virginia Quarterly Review* article. Most convincing to gay readers of both authors are the scenes from "Song of Myself" which may have influenced Stoker's image prey's mouth to the vampire's breast.

Did Stoker ever remark about Whitman being a "poof"? I have yet to read any disparaging remarks by him. I suspect his involvement in the theater inured him to homosexuality.

Stoker had a deep fondness for the romantic elements of Gothic literature. This part of his tastes may have made his fascination with both Whitman and Henry Irving, dramatic and imposing actor and manager of the Lyceum troupe, utterly natural. Dracula cannot be honestly termed the first homoerotic vampire; in the course of the novel, he never sinks his teeth into a male victim – but the reason for *Suffered from the Night* will soon be apparent after a brief discussion of more queer-themed undead.

Samuel Coleridge's "Christabel" is regarded as the first vampire poem in English literature...and its Sapphic elements cannot be ignored. Its influence on Sheridan Le Fanu's *Carmilla*, one of the most well-known homoerotic vampire tales ever written, cannot be denied and the story has not diminished in its allure despite the passage of over a century.

The first gay-male-themed vampire to survive the passage of time would be found in *The House of the Vampire*, a novella published in America a decade after *Dracula*. George Sylvester Viereck is probably more known today for his Nazi sympathies and his 1952 memoir of prison life *Men into Beasts* (which some consider among the first examples of the "gay pulp" genre) than for the verse that made him famous in the first two decades of the twentieth century or, indeed, his vampire novella. *The House of the Vampire*'s fiend, Reginald Clarke, preys upon the psyche of young artist Ernest Fielding, who is no stranger to a Hellenistic bond with men. Consider this exchange:

> The strange personality of the master of the house had enveloped the lad's thoughts with an impenetrable maze. The day before Jack

had come on a flying visit from Harvard, but even he was unable to free Ernest's soul from the obsession of Reginald Clarke.

Ernest was lazily stretching himself on a couch, waving the smoke of his cigarette to Reginald, who was writing at his desk.

"Your friend Jack is delightful," Reginald remarked, looking up from his papers. "And his ebon-coloured hair contrasts prettily with the gold in yours. I should imagine that you are temperamental antipodes."

"So we are; but friendship bridges the chasm between."

"How long have you known him?"

"We have been chums ever since our sophomore year."

"What attracted you in him?"

"It is no simple matter to define exactly one's likes and dislikes. Even a tiny protoplasmic animal appears to be highly complex under the microscope. How can we hope to analyse, with any degree of certitude, our souls, especially when, under the influence of feeling, we see as through a glass darkly."

"It is true that personal feeling colours our spectacles and distorts the perspective. Still, we should not shrink from self-analysis. We must learn to see clearly into our own hearts if we would give vitality to our work. Indiscretion is the better part of literature, and it behooves us to hound down each delicate elusive shadow of emotion, and convert it into copy."

"It is because I am so self-analytical that I realise the complexity of my nature, and am at a loss to define my emotions. Conflicting forces sway us hither and thither without neutralising each other. Physicology isn't physics. There were many things to attract me to Jack. He was subtler, more sympathetic, more feminine, perhaps, than the rest of my college-mates."

"That I have noticed. In fact, his lashes are those of a girl. You still care for him very much?"

"It isn't a matter of caring. We are two beings that live one life."

"A sort of psychic Siamese twins?"

"Almost. Why, the matter is very simple. Our hearts root in the same soil; the same books have nourished us, the same great winds have shaken our being, and the same sunshine called forth the beautiful blossom of friendship."

Ahh, "Indiscretion is the better part of literature" could have been spoken by Oscar Wilde.

Dracula conquered where so many other vampires (Polidori's Lord Ruthven, Southey's Oneiza, or even the infamous penny-dreadful Varney) faltered. Perhaps because Stoker's novel found an ideal *zeitgeist* in Victorian British xenophobia and fears of contagion brought by foreigners. Perhaps the medical elements introduced into a profoundly supernatural tale possessed the lure of sciencefiction to the turn-of-the-century reader. Perhaps the potency of the sexual imagery meant that none could resist the taboo images it brought to mind. And let us not forget that love so many of us feel when reading horror.

None of this has changed, even though some twenty-first century readers might be distressed by the epistolary style of the novel and those early elements of the vampire folklore that have been discarded from the canon by later films and fiction. Yet every day of the year some website is offering a daily excerpt from Stoker's book. Dracula does not die easily.

Beyond Viereck's Reginald Clarke, modern and contemporary authors have deepened the role of vampire in the queer bestiary. Ann Rice treats them with an almost religious awe. The lost Jeffrey N. McMahan still owes readers more stories, though it seems sadly unlikely we'll see them. Jewelle Gomez ensures that ethnicity is not forgotten. The author formerly known as Poppy Z. Brite created one of the most vocal and youthful fan bases. Jeff Mann has never felt tied to the smooth androgyny of any *bête noire*.

But back to the vampire proclaimed king of his kind by the entertainment industry. Stoker's novel has never been out of print, making it the second work of fiction to achieve this honor (the various permutations of the Bible being the first such work). More versions of *Dracula* have appeared in print, on the radio, on television programs and a commercials, and in cinematic and video releases than any other Western character, trailed only by that other Victorian creation, Sherlock Holmes (and how many times have these two figures meet on the page?). Dracula does not die easily.

So, after Lethe Press released an anthology queering Holmes (*A Study in Lavender*), I knew that we could not deny Dracula his due. I sought stories that would be interstitial, fill in the cracks in the original novel with gay themes. The sailors aboard the *Demeter* are no different than so many men who found comfort in the arms of each other. Mina and Lucy's friendship on Stoker's page is revealed to be more than sisterly. Not all the gypsies protecting the Count do so out of fealty; one among them succumbs to ardor. One or two authors went further, inspired by the effect Stoker's work had on the oeuvre of horror that just so happens to feature gay characters.

But I have begged your patience for too long. Night has fallen – somewhere in the world. Don't bother to bolt windows and doors or drape fragrant strands of garlic. If you are reading this anthology, your desire is to encounter nosferatu, the vampyre, *Homo sanguinus*. If you happen to get a paper cut while turning the page, do not forget to share the little crimson drops with someone who you cannot resist.

Steve Berman
Spring 2013

THE TATTERED BOY

Lee Thomas

W*e learn from failure and not success.*

I've offered those sage words more times than can be counted on the scarred fingers of a legion. I always believed it to be a brave statement, an optimistic salve for the disease of fear, with which all men are chronically afflicted. Like the rough handle of the axe, failure is the wounding that summons the ameliorating callus, and this callus reminds us of and protects us from insidious and redundant missteps. Perhaps lust is the exception proving my rule, or perhaps I am simply weak; few would doubt – particularly those of God's church – that I am of sin.

But speculating on the path of my soul illuminates nothing, as all that is to come is blackness, blinding and cold. Only in the examination of my skin and bone and damnable heart, can any light be found, and in using the word "light" I define this not by an airy, gay pleasantry, but rather a stark bath in keeping with the harsh cast of the surgeon's lamp, which is to say that much can be revealed, but for most, the grotesquerie cannot be borne.

The boy entered my life as I strolled through the walled city of Maastricht. I was in my forty-first year and had brought my wife and child to summer in the stone house that once served as home to a favored uncle, but which I now used for reflection, study, the writing of books and to some smaller degree, respite from my heart's home, Amsterdam.

To compare these cities is to compare shades of blue, for both are beautiful, warm of heart and exciting to the intellect. A framed map of Amsterdam, drawn by the skilled mapmaker Johann Murray, hangs on the wall of my study. My first impression upon seeing this artful rendering was that the outline of Amsterdam looked much like a bat, striking prey. Maastricht, to compare, more resembles a butterfly, with grand, blunt wings spreading out from the river Maas, as if taking fresh flight. Walls had been built over the centuries to protect this fragile butterfly-city, shielding her from the shifting aggressions and authorities of the ever changing European theatre.

Within these walls I strolled, enjoying a morning of crisp sun-brightened atmosphere as I passed the brick and whitewashed homes and shops, making my way to the grand gate, the Helpoort. Though many of the residences remained shuttered, the streets were busy as merchants prepared for the day, stacking loaves in fabric-draped windows and putting flame to wick so that their lamps burned in greeting.

As I approached the Helpoort, I paused to admire the fortress of stone that protected this small kingdom. The Helpoort gate, with its high arc and a depth of fifteen men, stands as one of the earliest city walls. For centuries it stood in wait and service, only relinquishing its guardianship when the Nieuwstad was itself walled in, sometime at the birth of the sixteenth century.

And there he stood, this tattered boy, his face pressed to the mortared stones, his black hair ragged and slicing the plane of his neck into a jagged ridge. From his clothing, I assumed him to be an apprentice, perhaps to one of the many potters or bead makers in the city, but as I approached this odd young man, I saw the looseness of his shirt's weave, worn holes and stains, which led me to believe he had no vocational standing in the least. The boy mumbled into the stones at his face, a prayer or jest I could not discern. A breath of wind rustled the serration of hair at his nape, and he craned his neck in its direction, at which time he noted my presence at his back.

Upon turning his full face to me, I discovered that while young and slight, he was not truly a boy. Though youthful, he was surely of university age, or nearly so. His eyes were of a unique blue, not quite sky but shimmering and rich like the surface of the river Maas. His face, spotted with smudges and (I saw with some distress) streaked by tears, was of cream and ivory.

This was not the type of face that I had grown accustomed to as a professor; my students wore a variety of masks, painted by the confidence of their social positions (their fathers' wealth), and experiences, though limited, with matters of the world. No. This striking face was free of guile, and I felt an instant paternity with its wearer. Seeking to ingratiate myself with a lightness of word, I asked, "And what does the gate tell you?"

I nodded my head toward the chipped surface of the Helpoort to indicate my meaning, and he looked at me then as if I wore a bonnet of tulips on my head. Certainly, he was unaccustomed to answering the rhetorical questionings of strangers. His river-rich eyes turned hard and judging-cold, and then broke and thawed.

No two men could have looked more opposite then, I'm certain. I in my proper jacket and pressed trousers, and he attired in little more than rags; I, wearing a wave of wisdom-bleached hair, while he remained coiffed in the deep hues of youth. I, assured and content. He, stricken and weighted.

"A gate is the most wonderful part of a wall," I told him. "Stone is unmoving and segregates without bias, while a gate can be locked or opened, depending on the needs of its keeper."

"Locked is safer," he told me.

"Indeed and without question. Perhaps you'll tell me what it is that you have locked out?"

"Who are you, sir?"

"Abraham."

"And where do these questions take us, Abraham?"

"As with all questions," I said, "they take us forward."

"And if I choose to go backward?"

"If any of us had that magic, God would certainly shrug his shoulders and depart."

"I think, sir, he already has."

Confounded by what I took to be no more than an innocent blasphemy, I found myself drawn deeper in my interest of this tattered boy. His proposition that perhaps God had left us behind intrigued me, as it suggested a clinical mind and not one wholly reliant on the rigid foundation of religion, further appealing to my sense that all can be questioned and little should be taken at its face.

I asked if he would join me, and we walked then, to the banks of the Maas, where we continued discussions and watched the current run from past to future. He told me that his name was Bastiaan, and in the course of our conversation he described the particular pain that drove him to the gate where we met.

Bastiaan's sister had taken ill, acutely so. In the last week, she had not left her bed and seemed to wither before his eyes. They were alone in the world, their parents and a younger sister dead from the flu, an epidemic that swept Maastricht five years before. As a student of disease, I pushed for details of her decline, but Bastiaan told me little beyond his sister's shortness of breath, a general lethargy, and the lack of appetite, resulting in a rapid wasting.

Naturally, I offered my services to the boy; I would gladly visit his sister and render a diagnosis, but he declined my offer vehemently. Though I pressed and assured him of my expertise in such matters, going so far as to make list of my many studies, he remained resolute in his refusal.

"She's beyond nature, now."

"Nothing is beyond nature," I told him.

"I should go," he said, abrupt and anxious. "Adda will be waking soon."

"Then I propose we meet again. Tomorrow at the gate?"

"No," he mumbled. "Too many have already been stained."

Such a curious word that was to use. *Stained.* I questioned it.

"The actions of a child's weakness and stupidity," he told me. "Unspeakable."

Sensing that I might never understand the mystery of this boy and might indeed be denied the company of one with whom I had made such quick kinship, I said, "I'll be at the gate tomorrow. You come see me if I can help."

But he didn't seem to consider this possibility. He repeated his concern that "Adda will be waking," and hurried up the slope to vanish beyond its ridge.

I RETURNED HOME in time for lunch with my wife and Wouten, our twelve-year-old son. The sight of him warmed me, as it always did. Annetje doted on the boy; her motherly concerns fierce and consuming. I'm sure that all parents feel that their children are fragile, fine pieces of blown crystal, irreplaceable and delicate, but Annetje, perhaps more than others, felt the particular burden of possessing such a treasure.

Together, we conceived four children that never saw birth, taken by God or nature. Wouten succeeded where his siblings failed in the simple act of coming into existence, and Annetje pained herself with his every movement.

Candles lit the table and a fire roared on the hearth. Annetje fussed and served, while Wouten bounced in his chair like an anxious babe, but my mind was with the solemn young man, who seemed convinced that God had forsaken his family in punishment for some undisclosed misdeed.

"Stew. Stew. Stew," Wouten exclaimed when a bowl of that very dish was placed before him.

I smiled at the boy, wishing he could have become more, but loving the presence of him. It is my supposition that Wouten suffered from a trauma while in the womb, something that occupied or damaged his mind and kept his focus on things, not around him, but within. Few distractions of the world bore the power to draw him out, and of those, only the simplest – a rainbow, a sweating icicle, a stew – were cause to rejoice.

"And how was your walk?" Annetje asked, finally taking her own chair after serving her family. At her elbow, Wouten slurped loudly, devouring his lunch.

I looked at his round, simple face, and a terrible thought occurred to me: what if Bastiaan was our son and Wouten had emerged into that other family? What would it have been like to have a handsome, strong and intelligent boy, who might come to facilitate tremendous events sitting at my table, instead of a boy whose body would grow into manhood while his mind had brimmed to full at the age of five?

"Abraham?"

"Exhilarating," I told her. "I should think tomorrow, I'll have another."

"And what about your book?"

"Stew," Wouten shouted, spraying a good amount of broth and bits of carrot to the table. Annetje leaned across the table and dabbed at his mouth and chin with her napkin.

"The book is much like a stalk of corn," I said in answer to her question. "It needs nourishment and light, and though you watch it, and think it does not grow, it does indeed rise and spread with every passing moment, though imperceptible in its maturation. Yes?"

Annetje smiled and nodded her head at me as she often did when I spoke to the nature of a thing. Next to her, Wouten coughed, giggled and then spit up a barely chewed wad of lamb, which hit the table like a small dead bird.

I RETURNED TO the Helpoort the following morning, earlier than I had that first day. At the wall, I waited and recalled the various ailments I had researched the night before and their respective symptomologies so that if Bastiaan returned, as I so hoped he would, we might find solution to his sister's degenerative condition. After an hour at the gate, however, I told myself that it was time to abandon this folly. Bastiaan would not return.

And, so convinced, I stood from the rock on which I sat and straightened my coat. My legs had taken me no farther than five steps when I heard my name called from a great distance. There, behind me far outside the city gate, Bastiaan raced; his weathered shirt whipped behind him as he made haste toward the shadowed arch separating Maastricht from the greater world.

"She's so sick," he said, his breath coming in harsh gasps. His hand went to my shoulder for support as he doubled at the middle, clutching his stomach. "Adda...she can't breathe...she's...you understand medicine and science...please."

"Of course."

He led me through the Helpoort and along the river to the south. Bastiaan said little as we left behind the neatly packed city, trading it for the tall grasses and marshes of the farmsteads. He looked very young to me then, truly a boy who was frightened and alone. Again paternal notions unfurled in my mind and heart, like the wings of a guardian hawk, and I urged to wrap my arms around this boy but understood the impropriety of such action. Instead, I made attempt at words of comfort and strength, but they did little to assuage his overwhelming despair.

After much walking, we paused near a squat, stone shed. The exterior walls wore bands of mud to insulate from the wind, and lichens, bright green and white, peered through the unwholesome coat. Beyond this small shed, I looked for a house of some sort, but saw only long fields of waist-high grasses and weeds. At the horizon, clouds foamed like frozen surf, and I knew that if we didn't get to Bastiaan's home soon, we would lose considerable light.

But of course, we were already at Bastiaan's home. The dismal stone shelter, hardly acceptable for the keeping of livestock, served as manor to the tattered boy and his ailing sister.

At the door to the hut, I grew cold. Something awful, trapped in the stone walls, exhaled and covered me in foul breath.

Long I had read of the existence of evil, but never had I actually believed it to be a tangible entity, and yet there on the threshold of that unwelcoming hovel, I became certain that evil was as real as the sky, the air. Even if I could not touch it, evil did exist; its breath was covering my face and neck and burrowing into my skin to take root on my bones like the lichens feeding from the house's foundation.

Bastiaan felt my disquiet but it did not stop him from opening the door.

Evil exhaled again, and I took a step back, away from the viscous, pungent atmosphere that emerged from that opening. My skin by this time was ice cold, and I trembled.

Even from the threshold, I saw that Bastiaan's beloved Adda was taken on to her Lord. Her skin was so white it seemed to glow in the shadowed recess; eyes stared at me without fear or gratitude; her arm draped over the side of the small cot on which she lay, her primary finger pointed at the corner of the room as if trying to send attention away from her tragic state.

Next to me Bastiaan gasped and turned from the door. Sobbing, he stumbled into the grass at the side of the shelter and collapsed to his knees. I went inside to the cot and grasped Adda's hand, which met my skin like an icicle. Touching her then, kneeling on the stone floor, I felt a presence in the gloomy chamber, as if her soul had not quite moved on. I felt her gaze on me, or more accurately, I felt *her* on me, since the observation I sensed came from the shadowed air and not the flat, faded lenses of her eyes. Of the dozens, perhaps hundreds, of corpses that had greeted me over the years, Adda's was the first to alight me with fear. She showed no overt signs of disease, no lesions or blisters to indicate advanced fevers or pox. If anything she appeared remarkably lovely and content in her quietus, and this fact, if no other, chilled me.

Upon finishing my examination of Adda, I went to Bastiaan. He clutched at me as if drowning, throwing his arms over my shoulders and burying his head in my chest where he sobbed violently for several minutes. I accepted his grief gratefully and harbored some pride in knowing that I might still tend on him, if not with a physicians' skills, then simply with my presence. He mumbled incoherent passages into my shirt, again making reference to a stain he had brought to his family, stating that Adda's was only the most recent life it had ruined.

I did not question him then. Instead, I lent him my support and sincere regret. After a time, we sat on the ground and watched the clouds approach. I invited him to come stay at my home for any length of time he wished, but he declined, again declaring himself guilty and in some way deviant.

The severity of Bastiaan's emotion faded with the morning, and his thoughts moved to more practical matters.

"She'll need burying," he said with a dry, spent voice.

"I can summon the church, if you like."

Bastiaan shook his head. "God won't have her now."

"That is a matter for God to decide. Her soul deserves prayer."

"She is unholy," Bastiaan told me, and he uttered a word I hadn't heard in years, not since my university days. "*Nosferatu.*"

I must admit that I laughed then. I meant no disrespect to Bastiaan or the memory of his sister, but to hear that antiquated term of folklore and fairy tale spoken aloud broke apart my solemn considerations.

"Have you no respect, Abraham?"

"Do you think that I am not sad, though I laugh?" I asked.

"You're mocking me."

"Bastiaan, I assure you, I'm not. But why this belief in monstrous mythology?"

"I saw it," Bastiaan said. "I saw the thing come for her at night, but I couldn't stop it."

"You're distraught."

"It came through the fields on the backs of rats," Bastiaan whispered. "It rose from their matted hides in a blood-tinged cloud and poured into the room. I'd try to stop it, but I couldn't move. When it stepped out of the shadows, it was a woman, all black and white, except for her horrible burning eyes. Every night, I'd tremble and scream, but my legs and my arms wouldn't move. She made me watch it. She made me watch it all."

"You must come with me," I told him. "You're overwrought, and it plays with your memory. We'll speak with the ministers and have the groundskeeper come out to collect Adda, but for now you need to be away from here. You'll come to my home…"

And with that suggestion, Bastiaan leapt to his feet as if the ground beneath him had suddenly grown hot. "You have to leave here."

I stood then and approached the tattered boy. Again, I wrapped my arms around him in a gesture of comfort and, though he tried to shake off the embrace, I continued to hold him until he calmed.

Eventually he accepted my wisdom and agreed to allow his sister a proper burial. I made the arrangements with the church and gave them more than enough money for her care. Bastiaan would take no money from me directly, so I paid for tea, bread, meats and cheeses at the market in Maastricht and left instructions to have the foods delivered to Bastiaan's modest home.

He refused my invitation of hospitality outright, however. He would not even entertain the possibility of visiting, let alone staying in my home.

Though I could not know it, Bastiaan's refusal of my roof and hearth would one day change, and everything I had thought as solid as the walls of the Helpoort changed with it.

As I had promised Annetje, I spent my afternoons in the study working on my book, or at least occupying time at my desk. Occasionally I observed the map of Amsterdam, framed on my wall. I still found Johann Murray's map to be of exceptional rendering, but more and more, I was stricken by the unwholesome resemblance this chart of my heart's home had to a feeding bat. On those afternoons, I considered Bastiaan's claim of *nosferatu* and recalled bits and pieces of the stories told me at university, stories that made mention of vermin and magic and blood. In the evenings when light waned, I joined my family for supper. Annetje questioned me on the book's progress, spoke eagerly of our impending return to Amsterdam, and related the stories she had heard in town while shopping. I listened, or perhaps it is better to say that I heard her words so that I knew where to reply and when to make the proper gesture with my head. Through these meals, Wouten splashed gravies and sauces with his spoon, giggled and every now and again interrupted his mother with an excited noun that seemed important in his world, but held no great bearing on our own.

More and more, I looked forward to morning, when my strolls took me through the Helpoort and into the marsh and grasslands to the south. Though solemn, Bastiaan greeted and welcomed me to his stone hovel with an embrace and an offer of tea from the supply I had paid the market to deliver. We sat inside, on the cot where I first met his sister, now covered in clean linen, another gift, and crowned by a down pillow. The exhilaration of being in this place with him brought back sensations of youth and vitality, feelings that I once cultivated from the eager faces of my students before the soil of that field was oversown and sapped of nutrient. Here the ground for such emotional and intellectual fruit was fertile and nourished further by the crudeness of setting.

"I envy your fortunes," Bastiaan said on the fourth day as he held a stein of tea and gazed through the open door of the shack. "Your family and students. My past and future are this cell of rocks and a field of weeds."

Can I tell you now that Bastiaan's complaint wounded me? Though why, I could not be certain. I thought much of this young man, and believed he felt the same of me. Though our time together had been brief, our words were often intimate and caring, and yet, there I sat on his cot, feeling the warmth of him at my side with his declaration contesting all that I supposed. He said he had nothing, but did he not have me?

More than ever, I felt a need to express the kinship I felt for him, if only to assure us both that my presence was valuable.

"The future is a black place," I said. "It is lit only as we approach it, never knowing what our candle's flame will reveal until our next steps bring it within the viewing cast. Do you think that I cannot help you? Do you think my coming here is a whim, a curiosity?"

"It is the action of a kind gentleman, but it stretches no further than these walls. Soon, you will return to Amsterdam, to your hospital and your students. For me, there is rock, weed and crosses in a cemetery to visit and mourn."

I reached out and took his hand in mine, patting it as if obliging a patient with comfort, only sensing far more in myself than obligation. "You'll take my house in town when I leave. You'll make it your home and be so comfortable there that, before I return with my family, we will be your guests, and then in time, we will be your family."

Bastiaan's hand went rigid in mine, and in his eyes, I saw a concoction of gratitude and defiance, boiling like a potion. He wanted to accept my offer, for surely it presented him with a far more satisfying future than any he had yet imagined, but something within him struggled to deny this offered happiness.

Sensing his refusal, I took a different tack. "Perhaps you would consider Amsterdam. I could assist in your studies. A lady friend of mine has rooms for let very near the hospital, and I could tutor you mornings until you're prepared for University."

"You're being cruel, Abraham."

"Only if you think me disingenuous."

I was resolute in my determination to free Bastiaan of his cell and his field of dead grasses, but this boy, this tattered child, had known little sympathy and less generosity in his life, so who could find blame in his doubts of me? "You'll think about it," I said. "You'll find an answer for me in your own time."

He startled me then with an act of intimacy. Looking back, I see that it was this act, or a sin of similar composition, that had stained Bastiaan in God's eyes, and in gratitude, ignorant and damnable gratitude, he drew close to me for its sharing.

His face filled my eyes, and then his lips were on mine in the way that only Annetje's lips had ever been on mine. My body pulsed as if nothing but heartbeat, except this thunder paled the organ behind my ribs as a cannon pales a rifle shot. The taste of him on me, and the roar of my heart's quickened efforts, were, for a moment, the stuff of wizard's work.

But soon I considered the open door of Bastiaan's home, and I imagined, with more than minute clarity, a passerby witnessing this uncommon embrace. Fortunately, it was as these thoughts took on the distress of panicked phobia that Bastiaan released me.

He gazed on me with worried eyes, but any legible response was absent from my face, just as it was most assuredly absent from my mind.

"Thank you," I said.

Still cautious, he reached out his palm and touched my cheek, and I let the touch rest there, but this gesture of acceptance was as much a lie as it was truth. Beneath his touch, I wrapped myself in logic's armor for the sake of my soul, but its thick plating was brittle and could not long repel. My body and blood wanted nothing but for more. I was in a moment of such profound intimacy, his taste lingering and sweet with promise, that logic seemed a scratchy, burdensome attire to be removed and cast aside without regard for my soul's protection.

The discord of thought and of blood deconstructed me. His face drew me. His intent repelled. All I wanted I could have, said his river-rich eyes, but whether this was a gift or a snare, I could not determine.

I removed his hand with mine and held it for a moment.

Now, it was I that played the lost child. Though aware of all that I felt, I was in no way able to identify these feelings. With distance I might better ascertain the specifics of this oh so unfamiliar land's topography. So I said my goodbye with a promise to return.

I have damned myself every day since for keeping that promise.

THE TANGLE OF thoughts that knotted my mind as I returned to the gate of my butterfly-city was perhaps the greatest I have ever endured. I thought of sociology and science and poetry and theology, and none of these disciplines provided a clear and concise philosophy to which I could attach my emotions. I imagine that is the very nature of emotions; though they can be examined, dissected and studied, it remains my belief that they exist as a pathology that defies understanding.

Once back within the walls of Maastricht, I felt compelled to buy a box of chocolates for Annetje and a sweet candy for Wouten, both of whom accepted these gifts with bright glee and much fanfare. I spent the rest of that afternoon entertaining Wouten, who slurped at his candy with slobbering tongue and lips and complete joy on his face, while I read to him from the stories of Hans Christian Andersen, a man I had met some years before and who had graciously sent me a bound volume of his works. Wouten paid me little mind, though I imagine he took great pleasure in the sound of my voice. After supper, once Wouten had been put to bed, I sat before the fire with Annetje. I held her hand and threw my tangle of mental knots at the flames, hoping to burn them away and leave me with some little comfort.

This was not to be.

Science teaches us to explore, while religion teaches us to accept boundary. If these two disciplines can find a balance, it must certainly be in the heart of a stronger man. For me, they war.

THE NEXT MORNING, instead of passing through the Helpoort and wandering across fields to Bastiaan's home, I remained in my study and buried my face in books, taking notes and thinking of many things in an attempt to rid my thoughts of the tattered boy who had granted me some dreadful wish, and in so doing condemned me to tortured dissonance. But the great thoughts of greater men proved insubstantial distractions, easily torn away by gusts of embattled logic. For every argument I made on my soul's behalf, another I argued for the nourishment of my flesh.

Disturbed, I remained in my study through supper and late into the night. The following day, the same.

But after so much time of consideration and exploration, I found myself no more learned, no less perplexed. All I knew with any certainty was that I had to see the tattered boy. Perhaps in so doing, I would find revelation.

THE SO COMMON rain of this region was falling that morning in a light mist from rot-black clouds, which smoked above in promise of greater, perhaps even torrential, downpour. I rose and left the house before Annetje or

Wouten woke and paused many times along the city streets, standing for an inordinate time under the arc of the Helpoort, fancying that a step through the stone arch would remove me, wholly and forever, from the familiar resonance of family and self. In fact, my first step into the diseased light on the far end of the arch brought a bolt of shudder that quaked in my veins and nearly paralyzed me. But being determined, I took another step and another, and while the thrumming disquiet remained with me on the road and in the fields and right up to Bastiaan's door, I never again faltered.

Yet when my knock of introduction on that door was met with a low call of "Yes?" I was truly halted, because with that word came the exhalation I had felt on my first visit to this place, that breath of evil that clutched for purchase on my skin. I looked to the fields running from this stone box to the cloud-bruised horizons and was instantly struck with a child's fear of being lost, or worse, trapped. The rain was indeed coming down in greater sheets, and I stood in the drench of it, the urge to flee this terrible place not unlike that which had sent me away days before.

"Abraham?" Bastiaan called.

And so I was discovered, but this was of no surprise. Who else would it be at his door? What other visitors might he have had?

"Abraham?"

I reached out and pushed on the door, bracing myself for the grasp of the tainted atmosphere within. Oh, it was worse, so much worse than my imagination could have conjured. The air that fell over me not only clung, but it pulled, dragged at my coat and hat and legs, fighting to usher me over that threshold, and I would have run then, would have hastened myself back to the walled city, were it not for what I saw within.

Bastiaan lay unclothed, his skin luminous in the cave of stone, and the beauty of him there replaced the blood in my veins with opiate. I stepped into the room, assisted by the vaporous fingers, and Bastiaan sat up in the bed.

"You came back," he said, exhaustion adding a drugged sensuality to his voice. "She said you wouldn't but you did."

My gaze followed his form, rolling from his weary face to the nest of his sex and back to the river-rich eyes, the examination of him bringing lightness to my head as if the motion of my eyes were the rocking of a cradle. He had taken ill, I could see this, but his malady played beneath a costume of ornate and exotic stitching that made the pallor of flesh and protuberance of bone inviting.

"She said that I disgusted you, but you came back to me."

The ill quality of his voice was not lost on me, but it played so well into the daze filling my head that it was not initially disturbing. Indeed, the sin of my thoughts unnerved and unhinged my medical judgment as the thundering pulse conquered my body as it had with his kiss. What did skin that white feel like, I wondered. Would it be cold like sculpted ice or warm like fresh milk? How would it taste on my mouth?

"I told her you'd save me," Bastiaan said. "I knew I wasn't alone in love, but she just laughed."

And it was in those words that my sense found purchase and struggled back into the current of my mind. The love of which he spoke, I could not fathom, but that it had been mocked by a woman, I understood.

"Who laughed?"

"Adda."

"You dreamed of Adda?"

"Not a dream," Bastiaan whispered. "She's an angel and she comes to me. She said you couldn't love me, but you came back."

Why did I not leave then? Why was I not chased from Bastiaan's terrible shack by his lunatic ramblings? Excuse I can make, but explanation is beyond me. I know that I was looking on something exquisitely beautiful, and this simple superficiality conquered logic.

"I came to see..." But no words followed to finish that lie.

"To take me away?" he asked.

"Perhaps when you are recovered," I told him. "First, we have to make you well."

He smiled then, and again, my gaze was drawn over the length of him.

"She said you'd not sacrifice your position or family. She said you'd use me as a toy and cast me aside in time, but she lied."

"Bastiaan? What is this you're saying?" Because surely, I did not know, or perhaps it is better to say, I would not let myself know. "What intent have you read into me?"

A shadow flickered over his brow as if a swallow had flown between his face and the source of that which gave it light.

"You said you'd take me from this place. Have you lied to me?"

"I hoped to better your circumstance, but I said nothing of sacrifice, not of family or of soul."

"Soul," he whispered and again the sparrow flitted across his brow. "Adda was right, then."

"You're very sick, Bastiaan. Your thoughts are fevered, uncontrolled. You're in no state to understand."

With this statement, he rose from the bed. The bird's shadow now permanently affixed to his brow, cheek and chin. "Lies," he spat.

"I should go," I said, and by way of excuse, I added, "My family."

"Now you're leaving me alone with rocks and weeds and lies." He stepped forward, a lithe rippling of leg and hip that brought further agitation to my distress. "Your family doesn't know you, Abraham. They can't make you feel what I can. They can't show you what I can make you see."

I backed away from the fever-dazed boy, and I would have made to run back into storm and mud had he not leapt forward and grasped me by my jacket's lapels. He kissed me again, harsh and angry. His hands grasped the side of my head and held me tight as he pressed his body to mine and began a slow rhythmic dance against me.

My physical reaction to this embrace was immediate and humiliating, but before I understood the fluid warmth on my skin, I threw Bastiaan away from me, toward the corner of the stone box. He crumpled there, again a broken and lost child.

"They don't know you," he muttered. "They can never know you."

But his nonsense had no effect on me. Shamed and angered by the brutality of what I can only describe as sexual violation, I backed to the door. Feeling the clean, wet freedom to my back, I gave what I hoped was my final look at Bastiaan and fled.

I STUMBLED HOME through the pepper and chill of storm in search of the secure walls of my uncle's house. Once there, once I had again put myself within the resonance of my family, I brought them to me with tight embraces and adoring kisses. Even still, the nightmare of Bastiaan and his perverse adoration proved unwelcome companions in the days to come. Sleeping or awake, I felt his breath on my cheek, his taste on my lips, and his body against mine, with the sinew of youth writhing against my trembling, anxious skin.

Bastiaan had found and manipulated something dark within me, and I hated him for it. I hated his youth and his stupidity and his contagious lust, which infected and spread and sickened me.

But how, after so many years of knowledge and experience, had I been weakened and made such a victim?

The answer came to me one afternoon, three days after I left Bastiaan with his rocks and weeds. I examined all I knew of myself and of Bastiaan, and found myself wanting for explanation. But then, in my study, looking at the sketched map of my heart's home, the answer emerged from the shape of a bat.

Adda, Bastiaan's sister, had indeed succumbed to the dark intentions of nosferatu, and then took her place among the undead. I had, after all, felt her presence in that stone house, though her body was truly deceased. Naturally, she would seek to influence the brother she left behind. Wanting sole possession of Bastiaan and fearing my interference, she forced us to actions that would upon unhindered evaluation repel me, thus leaving him to her manipulation.

And so I found the purifying bath of logic that cleansed both the tattered boy and myself; we were under a cursed influence, brought from the devil on the lips of the damned Adda.

Such thoughts occupied my mind as night fell. Annetje knocked to alert me to supper, but I declined in favor of pursuing my study of this matter. None of my texts offered insights, but never before had I reason to collect volumes with such content. I made note on paper of what I experienced and the general series of events that led me to my final visit to Bastiaan's house.

Did an hour pass since Annetje's interruption? Two hours? So lost in my thoughts, I could not be sure, but it was while noting my last moments with Bastiaan that I felt the breath on my neck. The evil atmosphere descended on me as it never had before; it did not cling or grasp, but rather it pushed with palpable force, and I found myself unable to rise from my chair.

Annetje screamed from the room below, and my heart shot through with lightning. I doubled my efforts and struggled to my feet. Though able to move, walking across my study and into the hall was akin to pushing against a river's current. On the stairs, I waded against the evil exhalations as tides of sick desperation crashed in my stomach.

The stair and hall below were dark, but light from the stoked hearth spilled from the mouth of the living room. Annetje shrieked a prayer. I threw myself against the thick atmosphere, toward the light.

And the sight awaiting me in that once comfortable room, which had to my knowledge never known anything but contentment and normalcy...

Annetje hugged herself and cowered against the wall beside the fireplace, her body looking to have bloated and shrunk. This trick of the dancing flames taunted my eyes as I attempted to find my wife in the dwarfed body of the screaming woman. What met my eyes in the opposite corner was an abomination so profound that it stole the planks beneath me, leaving only vast descent before I crashed to the floor of Hell.

Bastiaan held Wouten in his arms; my son's startled eyes, made bright by firelight, saw nothing; his mouth lolled open to reveal the innocent pink tongue within. Where Wouten's throat had been was a ghastly crater with a ridge of stained skin. My son's blood poured over the bib of his shirt in a horrible cascade, and the fire's light revealed similar wounds on his exposed arms and his hands. Bits of my son lay on the floor in abattoir scraps, spat from Bastiaan's horrible, painted mouth. Across the room from this atrocity, Annetje cried for her God, not understanding, as I certainly did, that it was my offense of this God that had brought such misery to her home.

"Welcome home, love," Bastiaan said, in a voice so high and childlike that it settled in my stomach like glass shards.

"Bastiaan," I whispered, trying to keep my tears in my eyes, praying that their sting might cleanse me. "What have you done?"

He released my tragic son's body, and it crashed to the floor. "I've come for you, Abraham."

Amid the flickering light, I looked for signs of the undead on this boy, but was further sickened to find that his brutal insanity was wholly human. Adda had been at him. Of this I was certain. But while her taint was in him, it was not the entirety of him, and this made his actions all the more horrible.

"We'll finish these," Bastiaan said, stepping forward. "And then we're free."

"Abraham!" Annetje cried from the corner.

I backed toward the hearth with heavy feet, shaking my head in protestation of Bastiaan's presence. He moved quickly, as he had that last day in his hovel; his face filled mine and his lips pushed forward, their red stain reeking of my son's ended life and Bastiaan's lunatic need. Those lips settled on mine and I tasted Wouten's death, felt it run through me in a lightning bolt of grief.

As to what happened next, I'm sure I managed to strike Bastiaan or somehow cause him pain, as the next thing I remember was him kneeling before me on the carpet, sobbing, begging, clutching at the hem of my jacket with insane desperation. I kicked him then. My knee landed squarely against his nose, and he collapsed on his back. I snatched the tongs from beside the fireplace and cracked him across the brow with the weight of the iron rods until he wore a crown of blood. When his eyes closed I used the tool to lift a narrow, burning log from the hearth; this I dropped on the murderous boy's belly. The flames leapt to his shirt and his trousers in a flash, the burns reviving him. His screams filled my house, joining Annetje's prayers as I looked on.

Bastiaan squirmed and flailed as the fire devoured his body; his voice reached a shrill pitch that I thought would ring in my ears for the rest of my earthbound life.

Only when his struggles ended did I allow myself to move. I went to the sofa and retrieved the heavy blanket from its back and attempted to suffocate the flames, while shouting at Annetje to fetch water from the kitchen. But my wife did not move from her place in the corner.

I consider our salvation the only miracle I have ever witnessed. Already the quilt in my hands was catching fire and surely the house would burn down around us in minutes if it continued unchecked. But instead of licking outward and continuing over the carpet to the furniture, the floor, the walls, the ceiling, the flames crept inward, toward Bastiaan's charred body. The fire rolled into him as if pulled on the wake of a great wind.

It flickered.

It died.

Staring at this impossible consumption, I allowed myself a moment of peace, my arrogance assuring me that God meant for my punishment to end in the immolation of this tattered boy and with him, the sins we had sewn to us.

And perhaps God did forgive me, or He simply shrugged and turned away.

In the corner, Annetje squatted close to the ground, her bosom resting on her knees. The fisted knuckles of her left hand were jammed between her teeth and her right hand pointed at our murdered son, and she cried and giggled with shattered sanity.

OVER THE YEARS since those terrible days with Bastiaan, I continued to tell my students, colleagues and friends that each failure brings with it a lesson.

I hope this is true, but I'm not as certain as I once was. What lesson have I learned?

Upon returning to Amsterdam, I took sabbatical as professor and returned to the role of student. I studied the dark inhabitants of what I once believed a fairyland. My philosophy had failed me once, proving all that I knew was not all that there was to know.

I lost much in my failure, but I pray that some good might still come from it. I have faith. I have knowledge but still have so much to learn. I can only pray to prove myself a devoted and attentive student. For Annetje. For Wouten.

YOURS IS THE RIGHT TO BEGIN

Livia Llewellyn

I NOVEMBER
OUTSIDE BISTRITZ
SUNSET

"...darkness, lapping water, and creaking wood."

TICK, tick, tick at the end of the chain swings the watch, and back against your fireside bed of needles and furs you collapse and drift away, sweet sister Mina, your thoughts unmoored by the doctor's trick twitch of his mesmerizing wrist, your mind free to wander the wild woods, gleaning the lingering scent of your captive beloved, reporting back to that fierce, relentless Helsing demon all the secrets hidden within our master's untamed kingdom of night. Or so we make him believe.

Drip, drip, drip go the sounds of my thoughts under each little tick of the watch, each unspoken word welling plump from the dark woods and rushing waters and starry void of my mind, staining red all the untouched pink flesh of your soul. In this manner I speak to you, as did the First, who spoke to me a century ago, who plucked me like turning fruit from a long-forgotten tree. Out there in the cold crisp dying of the sunset's flaming light you speak of inconsequential things to your doctor, visions of trails and pathways and roads unseen. Inside, your thoughts drift to the man you love, directing my desires away from your unbroken velvet neck, and yet even as your supple mouth silently wraps around his name I slip into your visions beside him, unheard and unseen, nestling like a buzz just beyond your ear, a warm vibrating hum whispering warm against the rising hairs on your skin. That flush on your pale cheek, my innocent Mina, that effervescence coursing through your blood, is that not also a pure and perfect love? Can I not give you the same?

I am the youngest. I am the Third. What the others have long forgotten, what dark centuries and the monotony of undying time have scrubbed away, I remember still. Traces in the air and against my tongue, like the remnants of a last unforgettable meal. The swelling valleys and hills of the Mittel Land, vast expanses of bright green fields under brilliant sun, the snow-capped mountains but a hazy suggestion at the horizon. Pears and cherries, hard red apples dropping to the warm earth. She came from these lands, the First told me, and to them she returned in the low mists of one early summer some half a century ago, burrowing her way through the warm brown earth, her gold hair and fair limbs entangled in the soft roots of tall grass and vegetables. There as the season quickened did she take both rest and power, soaking up the heat of the sun, small insectile life and fragile boned burrowers that heard her lovely, low call. And above the ground, as the season ripened, we heard her silent song, and we came, too.

Rumors of a mist, sparkling like crushed stained glass, swirling around dusky plums that couples stole and ate before they sank into the grass, into each other, into the earth itself, their bodies found at daylight, hollowed and open-eyed, dry cavities packed with sticky stems and stones. Young girls from neighboring farmlands wandering down roads in the early hours of the morning, covered in beads of dew, pale and feverish, their shaking fingers scratching at wounded necks as they asked which way was home, the words dribbling out of their split lips in slow crimson waterfalls. Mothers sleepwalking newborn babies into the fields, leaving them under the fruit trees like offerings, only days later to awaken in horror, unable to remember what they had done. Circle of cats and dogs, bloodless, beheaded and neatly arranged on the grounds of a local church cemetery. In the center of each circle a pink newborn's hand placed upright, a cold supplication, a decaying plea.

The village slipped into paralyzed silence as the summer bloated and crept toward its autumnal end, cobblestone streets emptied out, windows shuttered tight and rooms darkened, clusters of crosses and garlic swung at every door.

It meant nothing. She fed on us all, and left the seeds and cores and skins of her human crop to shrivel away. I remember my father coming to me during the day, thick ropes of iron dragging from his worn, broken hands. He stopped, stared up at the ceiling, and began whispering replies at the shadowy corners to questions I never heard. Eventually he dropped the chains and left the room. I never saw him again. Outside, insects chattered and buzzed incessantly in the heat. So many creeping things, and not a single bird left to cull them. Cows dying and crops fallow in the fields, and only that one lush mound of the valley blossoming like a poison-soaked paradise, whilst all the land around it cowered and waited. Every night I dreamed, thrashing away the soaking sheets, ripping off my bedclothes. In the stifling dark, my hands crept across my body, and my brown skin was the valley, and she was there, in the center, under the folds of the earth, calling out my name, waiting for my touch. And though I held out longer than the rest, so, too, like the others in the village, I found myself drawn to her as well, making my way through a late-summer village drained of all people and life, walking through rotting and flyblown orchards and fields in the star-studded hour before nightfall, a bouquet of dead, dried flowers in my shaking hands, flowers that exploded into life as I neared her ground, bursting with sticky pollen and green water. And there on that hill in the vast rolling Mittel Land, I, the last of my village, the last of my valley, slid my fingers inside the rich damp loam of the world, teasing her out little by little until she unfurled over me and inside me, gold wheat hair and milk skin, plum sweet lips and a tongue of sharp, sour wine. And there was pleasure, unlike any I had ever known, wave after wave of rich red desire rising up to crash abated against my body's shores, and she pressed my head against her breasts and throat like a hungry child. And a single lap of her blood took it all forever away.

Our bodies are dead, our souls are dust, and decay cannot desire. So she says. My mind cannot forget her, though, cannot shed the memories of her on me, inside me, as she did before I was undone. Like a tickle, a silvery shiver against my skin, the maddening ghost of a touch never truly realized, a desire never fulfilled. The First floats above us in the night when our master has not allowed us out to be fed, and we, the Second and the Third, open our mouths like helpless birds. She bites her fingertips like a cat, and we catch the trickling of blood running off her sharp nails with our snapping teeth and pointed tongues, lapping up more air than sustenance. In each drop I remember the sensation of summer, the crops and fields and lap of the midday sun. I remember her tongue, the smell of the living earth on her breasts and hands. I remember, but my body is cold. I reach up for her, but she is always too far away. And I would go mad at the memory of it all, except for the blood, those few drops of thick plum from her hands that abate the hunger and pain. And so I scrabble greedily about in a cold barren room in a castle that has no name, for a few exquisite sparks of a long-lost summer. Endless winter in these mountains, endless desiccated life, two lovers, and no love at all.

Will this be your existence? Will this be you?

What is it that I say and do here in the cold, in the snow of a country that it not my home? I do not wish to know.

Full of beauty of all imaginable kinds this country is, and every woman, delicious Mina, is a country. Terrible is the country that you travel to. She reaches out to you even now, and you will live forever in a land pregnant with dead branches of desire, continually consumed in hunger's red wave. I do not think it is there that you belong. And the first tendrils of purple morning swell up through the thick trees, and I rise with them, exploding and scattering like floating seeds. Later, when you awaken, your wet clothes will still glitter with the spent remains of that which once was me.

2 NOVEMBER
THE CARPATHIAN SPURS
SUNRISE

"...darkness, creaking wood, and roaring water."

NIGHT SWELLS AND peaks, and still you sleep. I grimace and ride the hours with it, even to the painful razor edge of it, until dawn begins to push its way up through the thin membrane of the horizon, anxious to start the day. Only then does your good companion take out his watch, and so begins your inevitable turn on the Catherine wheel of my thoughts. I waste no time.

I am the Second. I was there at the beginning, I watched the First die and unbecome, and then she cleaved unto me and once again we were brought together in all things and through all things, I once again her willing servant ready to give her my undying life and love.

There are rules, stubborn little Mina. Just as there are rules that govern the entirety of nature, rules that dictate the passage of that water you think you hear, the swaying of those wind-blown branches you think you see, so there are rules that govern his entire world, which is this entire world. As I did, as we all did, you will become a servant to each and every one. No man or mortal shall do your unnatural bidding again. You will be Fourth, and you will drink last, never first. You will be last in everything, you will be the Least. Unbecome by her blood, you will finally learn to submit.

You must never again pay heed to the words and actions of the Third.

You must never leave our chambers unless by his command, through the First.

You must never raise your head in his presence, or look him directly in the eyes. As he is in all things above you, so in all things must you forever remain below.

You must never speak in his presence; and throughout all of the castle confines and the world itself, for all time, you must never speak, or even think, his name.

You must never mention his long-dead sons, though you will be made, as we all are, to dress in their rusting armor and place their helmets over your bound and braided hair. You must show no fear when he drags us to barren fields of skeletons and stone, and under storm gray skies mounts us upon petrified pikes and crosses, crying out *betrayers, betrayers all* with every hammer blow, black gouts from your body squirting against ragged pike and steel, impaled flesh firing white-hot bolts of pain into your shrieking, shrinking soul. You must pay no heed to his laughter when the rays of a feeble morning sun curl the edges of your skin, burn wet layers of your eyes away like autumn mist. All our wounds heal, eventually.

You must not pass out when he nails your clothes to your breasts, when he drives a spike through your tongue. You must learn to lick your lips and pant for more.

In every moment of your existence, you must remember that the physical world is his domain, and no longer yours to command. By air alone, you must travel backwards and never forward, never touching ceilings or floors or walls, whether he is there to see you or not. Always you must travel with your ruby eyes seeing only where you have been, never where you are going, because your destination is nowhere. There is only the past, he says, and we must never forget it. We live forever, but for us there is no future. We are dust, and we move as such.

Books are forbidden, as is music and all the forms of the arts. You must learn to find stories in wind, knowledge in thunder and rain. Your thoughts will no longer be yours to write down, your little diaries and letters shredded and burned. Every transgression will be paid to him with a finger, which he will place in a thin glass bottle and display on our chamber walls. You are not allowed to touch these bottles or take them down. Centuries will pass, and you will gaze upon the forest of fingers you have lost and regrown and lost again, ageless and perfectly preserved in their transparent reliquaries. Unnecessary, useless, broken, replaceable. You will learn that this is us. This will be you.

Once a year, he will dress you in the remnants of a four-hundred-year-old gown, lead you backwards up broken stairs, floating over toothless gaps in the stone, until you find yourself in the highest crooked tower, perched over the deepest ravine in the Carpathians, staring half a mountain's length down to a river so ageless and relentless and hard it has split the very heart of the land in half, never again to be whole. You must not resist his spider-hard grasp at the small of your back as he sends you flying over the edge, nor must you allow your flailing limbs to claw for purchase as you plummet unstoppable into the ravine's crooked maw, bones breaking and snapping with every outcrop of jagged rock. He will fly with you, twisting and turning with every spiral of your breaking body, fingers grasping your neck as he watches all the moments of your life rise and fall like oily tides on your grimacing visage. Do not ask what it is he looks for, what undiscovered truths he seeks in the dark calligraphy of tears penned by your horrified eyes. The ice-black currents will not stop or slow your descent, only push your ribs up through breaking skin like snowy mountain peaks, red mist rising from your body like a distant summer dawn. And when the raging waves vomit your ravaged body from their foamy grip, you will not plead for death or mercy as he rearranged the wet velvet folds of your gown against the iron shores, whispers in your ear the name of a woman you do not know, then leaves your split corpse to gather the first feathers of midnight snow.

And I will come for you, gentle, broken, fearless Mina, as I came for the First so many centuries ago, when I witnessed her fall, the first fall. I will collect your body and carry you backwards all the way, backwards and up through crevices and caverns and passages, no guide except all the ghosts of my former journeys through lost centuries, the worn grooves in the packed earth, the smooth hollows in the stones. And to our chambers I will deliver you, and outside the thick castle walls seasons will pass and change as we lick your wounds and the ivory of our teeth clicks against the white of your ribs, pushing the destruction back inside, back down. Our lips against yours, hot kisses in the darkness, fingers crawling and stitching, swollen folds of flesh closing and opening, the wet of our blood and desire a crucible to transmute and banish all pain: until the following year, when he throws you off the tower once again. And he will be there, at all times watching over all your deaths and rebirths, because all that you do will be for him. All that you experience will be his, over and over, for all eternity.

You must break, and you must heal, and you must break, and you must heal. Sisyphus, never at rest at the summit. Icarus, never reaching the opposite shore.

Is this you, pretty finger in a jar? Will this be you?

Except. I feel it on your breath, against the rigid curve of your spine, in the beat of your steady heart behind such cold, small breasts. There is nothing wax about you. And the watch on its chain slows and stops, and you slip away, toward the mysterious country of daylight I can no longer travel through. And night flows on across the mountains, dragging with it the ominous grays of another relentless day, indistinguishable from any other before it, or after.

3 NOVEMBER
BORGO PASS
SUNRISE

"...darkness and the swirling of water."

THOSE GLASS-CASED FINGERS embedded in the castle walls, Mina: they are not hers. Flesh of my flesh, each one severed from my hands. A forest of defiance and insurrection, thousands of markers pointing every way in every direction, proclaiming at once, I am everywhere, and here. *He catches me looking at them, running my newly grown fingers over the filthy vials, pinpricks of blood coalescing in my eyes. He mistakes the look on my face for sorrow, for resignation, for ruin. Everywhere men are surrounded by life, and see it not at all. Malformed, grotesque monstrosity, he drags his loathsome remains to the center of the web and thinks himself safe as he hallucinates away his years, dreams and schemes of his former self made whole, an immortal conqueror striding across an impaled and broken world as he blots out the sun with the crimson letters of the ancient, unspeakable First Name.*

He does not realize the name he writes is mine.

"This is the way."

4 NOVEMBER
BORGO PASS
THE RED OF THE DAWN

"Why fear for me? None safer in all the world from them than I am."

IN THE BLISSFUL black silence of the woods, beneath the hiss of wind and snow, you hear them. The faint suck and suction of their mouths, the swift rush of life down their transparent throats, the soft sighs of steam rising off the fallen horses entwined in their smooth brown arms. Life: never extinguished, simply traveling, from one perfect creation to the next. Pale flakes drift up around the undead and the dying, all of them heedless to the rising drifts, the pressing cold. Stars wheel and gyre mindlessly in the heavens above us. Branches dislodge their heavy wintery burden, anointing the heads of wolves with silver crowns. And all the terrors of the night have vanished, valiant Mina, deep into the obsidian oblivion of a sudden sleep. Is this not the most beautiful of all countries? Is this not the most wondrous of all nights?

Twice have I come to you in the valleys and mountains of this kingdom, moving the mindless bodies of the Second and the Third as the rosemary honey of my words poured from their puppet mouths. Twice have I watched as you stood trembling but resolute, and refused. Trails of salty blood now crack and flake against my sister's cheeks, yet already they no longer remember that less than a winter's breath ago, they gnashed their teeth at you a third time, wept and rent their garments and breasts as they screamed. That is who they are, and what you might have become. No less animal than the helpless animals they now suckle at, no less mindless in their destruction like winter storms. They speak and spin stories of such aching beauty and pain, yet the words and emotions that pour from their fang-tipped mouths, the shifting forms of their flesh, the touch of their pliant hands are mere traps to catch flies. Bereft of me inside, their actions are nothing but the hunger, taking what revolting shapes and sounds it needs, the quicker to fell the prey, the quicker to feed. They forget what they are, what they used to be. United in infinite confusion and pain, they exist as much on blood as the ever-changing fantasies of what I tell them their meaningless lives could have been, could still be.

To the Third I came in the dregs of a plague-laced summer, the crops and animals already long dead, the villages of that distant valley festering under disease and endless sun. I imbued and impregnated the overworked earth with the corruption of my presence, and rose from flies and fumes hissing from poisoned ground, from slick green ropes of mossy decay bubbling from stagnant pools. I lingered in the blackening veins and mottled skin of all living creatures who lapped and nibbled away at the fruits and flowers and leaves of my sweet false call. A vegetable husk of life she was when the Third succumbed to my song, when she dragged her withered breasts and brittle bones across the soft black pulp of her lands and family to fall apart in my arms, aching for release. Death alone is release. My embrace gives none.

To the Second I came in the mirror shards of soured celestial visions, an iron-maiden angel born from the fevered blood mists of suppressed perversions and misplaced belief. Beneath the revolting excess of vaulted stone ceilings, golden crucifixes and diamond-studded monstrances, far below the scratching swirl of incense, the smoke of white wax and blue flame, under layer upon layer of monotone, miserable lives lived in fealty to a long-dead god, I burrowed up from pagan foundations and writhed against crumbling mosaics, feeding on plump, lost novices and fucking ossified bones as I howled my song of songs. It was there she crawled to me, whip-lashed and pierced, begging for my mortification of her sin-choked, naked flesh, begging for a pain-filled path to a virgin monstrosity. And under the unblinking watch of the skull-studded ceilings and walls did I eat the lids off her wondering eyes, and reveal the darkness and emptiness of faith, the vast insignificance of the human soul, forever in the cosmos falling and alone.

And at the last, undisguised by guile and sorrows and dreams, I come to you. I am the First and am in all things the First, which is my eternal right. I alone bestowed that power and privilege upon myself a hundred hard lifetimes ago, and no man or creature fashioned or forged me. I am a creature of my own making, as all women are. Even to him, I was the First, making him who he was, though he no longer remembers and has usurped my place, rewritten his history and calls himself my Master. And yet even this betrayal shall eventually serve me, for I tell truths to few women, and to no men. I am the Queen of Lies. I live and breathe in the black cracks of doubt and terror that spread vast and malignant throughout all life. I am the mother of flesh rebirthed beyond perfection; I am the devouring furnace of the soul.

The low horrid laugh of my sisters, moving slow against the silence and cold. Satiated, content for an eye-blink moment of time, they drift up, float and dance with the thinning flakes of snow. I feel them at the corners of my mind, casting about for me, heads swiveling for a glance of a presence they have always known yet have never truly seen. You see me, Mina. You see me and you do not look away. The cosmic motes of my incorporeal being slide through your clothes, rippling over the curves of your cream skin, curled hair, warm lips. You breathe me in, and I stream past the hot crimson slick of your tongue into the velvet chambers of your heart, settle against and under the most secret curves of your swelling flesh. Searching, rushing through the hot motes of blood, riding the tender trembling contractions of muscles and lungs, drawing out one lingering, delicate contraction of pleasure after another and mining it for purchase. There are vast pristine skies within here, colors and landscapes and light I have not seen for centuries, achingly full with memory and promise. I could live in you for lifetime after lifetime until the heavens bled stars, and never feed. In you, I have no need to be First. I have no purchase. In you I am contentment, nothingness, alone.

The only darkness within you, inviolate Mina, is me.

Outside our bodies, outside of dreams and sleep, the beautiful sun is breaking across the jagged mountains, golden light creeping through slender trees and sparkling snow. Streams and strands of me pour like the morning mists from your limbs, minute shards of ice that settle against the branches, burn away. Later you will wake, you will rise, you will turn your face upward into the light of a world that is the mirror of your soul, and you will continue your descent into my kingdom, swelling like the great and gentle ocean until there is no more darkness, no more water, no more lies and dreams. Until only you remain, and your right to begin.

SELF-PORTRAIT AS JONATHAN HARKER

Ed Madden

"Sex is a box built by Stoker"
–John Barton

Sex is a box with a lid, something built by Stoker –
keeping the light out,

or keeping the darkness in (which is not the same thing) –
a few years before Freud

would stake his own claim to stories of how things work:
a child with a ball on a string,

or a child being beaten, a girl who lost her voice,
a boy afraid of rats,

a child forcing a kitten's nose into a saucer of milk
compelling it to drink.

Eating is never hunger; desire is a shiver of symptoms.

I could hear the churning

sound of her tongue as it licked her teeth and lips.
Always the problem is elsewhere,

waiting to be exposed, like a box of dirt in the closet,
a book hidden under the bed,

a nightshirt smeared with blood, something for CSI
or the priest's dark offices.

The tongue thickens like a leech, wet thing.
It wasn't her I wanted.

The jewelry box is not a box. The woman is not coughing.
The mouth is not a mouth,

I could hear, far off, confused sounds – men
talking in strange tongues.

SEVEN LOVERS AND THE SEA

Damon Shaw

I. CHRYSOPHILE

Do not struggle. You will not break free. A sailor knows how to tie knots. And nobody can hear you so far from shore. Do not strain your voice. You will need it.

We will be... companionable. We will talk like friends. I will tell you of my life. And you will tell me of yours. Afterwards, perhaps, I will let you live...

I WAS never a good man. The fracture in me, the weakness, was gold. I loved it, as all men love their addictions, deeply, faithfully, and utterly in secret.

The old man on Varna Quay promised me a coin, heavy and yellow and warm in my palm. Enough to take me back home to Saint Petersburg and to eat well for a year should I be foolish enough to squander it so. I should have known not to trust him, this nobleman in filthy clothes. As he took my arm, I felt a chill all the way to my neck. I tried to pull away, but he held me like iron, leading me to the boxes piled on the quay. With his walking cane he scratched an X on the side of a crate.

"This is the one," he said. "It must not be opened, not by crew nor customs. Do you understand?" He withdrew a purse. I caught the smell of him then, musty, like rotten wool, and had to fight to keep the distaste from my face.

The gold coin he offered winked with a promise of more to come. I gave him a nod and slipped it to lie heavy against my thigh. I did not think of warning the Captain we carried some unknown contraband. No, I worried how to give baksheesh to the customs officer in Constantinople when all I had was my one, fat coin. I could not break it like a biscuit. "I need more money," I said. "For bribes."

The rich man grew without moving. Taller than the mainmast, he seemed. He turned on me and his eyes flashed a dark red, like old blood. I tensed to run, but his hand whipped forth and held my chin. He lifted my head until I could not but look at him.

"You have a strength in you," he said. "Open the crate after the last customs inspection and not before. You will find your reward."

I could not pull away. I nodded and felt his fingernails break the skin on my neck. A warm thread ran down inside my shirt. At this, he threw me back. I fell to the cobbles and banged my head. White light flashed as my teeth closed, sharp on my tongue. When my sight cleared and pain permitted, I looked up. Amongst whirling stars, I saw my own blood glint on his fingertip. He put the finger in his mouth and he swelled up, like the wind in a mainsail. He tore into jagged, black pieces and disappeared.

My heart crashed in my ribs. An echoing spike of pain pierced my temple. I blinked and swore. The blow to my head must have brought on visions. I crawled to where he had stood. There, I found silver coins scattered on the cobbles, like stars.

I filled my pockets. With every chink of coin on coin, my courage returned. The man surely had slipped between the crates of cargo. The night was dark. He had thrown me down – here I burned with anger at his arrogance – and while I was stunned, he ran. The lid of the marked crate stood an inch loose on its nails. I slammed it shut with the heel of my palm, and turned to look up at the warehouses and the far-off lantern of a tavern. I saw no-one. Only a skin of mist over the empty quay and a rat that fled even as I gazed upon it.

No matter, I decided. I was young and rich and full of life, and tomorrow we sailed. Ahh, gold, how its steady light blinded me to the monster in full sight.

2. ANDROPHILE

You die and find yourself at a doorway. No angel awaits to judge you, only a mirror set above a door handle. Stare at your face. Judge yourself. Will you open the door to paradise and let yourself enter? Are you, in your own heart of hearts, good...or evil?

ALL SHIPS HAVE their goat. Their fool. The man you blame when a halyard is coiled the wrong way. The man upon whom you cannot bear to look after a month at sea, for his filth and inadequacy remind you of your own.

I saw at once the new man, Olgaren, would be our fool. He was inexperienced and clumsy, and worse, he smiled without cease. He got the worst work that day, under the hoist, to guide the crates into the hold. Obviously, I had to go too, to hide the box with the mark.

The crew laughed at me for volunteering. Petrofsky said I was after Olgaren's arse already. Almost we fought for my reputation, but the mate held both our arms.

"Got a month at sea, boys," he said. "Save your passion for the sails." He winked at me.

I would not back down until Petrofsky swore it was not true. When he swore, we shook hands and I climbed down to the hold, content. I did not want Olgaren.

Or perhaps I did. I did not know. His aspect was not fair to me. He was short, though well muscled, and very pale. He always wore that half smile. You will pardon my frankness, but the men I loved did not smile. They were dark, and taller than I, and I never knew their names.

Olgaren's hair shone white in the gloom of the hold. He had in his eyes the look of a dog you kick, to stop the guilt it makes you feel, but I could not cease to notice how his strength shifted under his clothes as he pulled the swinging boxes across the deck. We lowered them together and fell into step. Away from the crew, he relaxed. His smile faded.

He raised one eyebrow when I caught the marked crate and slid it to the back myself. I did not hide it completely. I had to be able to open it after customs in the Dardanelles. To divert his attention, I said, "Stand up for yourself early on. Petrofsky likes to play with weaklings."

Standing in the light from the hatch, awaiting the next crate, he said, so quietly I had to strain to hear, "*The greatest rebellion is absolute submission...*"

I did not understand his words, but I saw him in that moment. He had circles under his eyes and bruises under his collar. I did not think he would last long at sea.

We loaded the cargo and did not speak further. The wooden crates chilled my fingers and made me clumsy. I was happy to climb up into the sunshine to find the *Demeter* tugging at her halter, eager to take to the sea. At noon the Captain blew his whistle. We cast off, and let her have her rein.

3. PHOTOPHILE

We have taken your ship. I, Amramoff, am first mate now. Olgaren here is captain. He renamed your ship the Pochemuchka - the Asker of Questions. He aims to judge every cabin boy and captain from here to the Americas. I believe, with a crew of those such as us, he can do it. You, too, could be a part of this scourge. You could be one of us. If you convince him of your worth…

FOR FIVE DAYS the wind was favourable. We saw only blue skies, while off to starboard, the Bulgarian, then the Turkish coast slipped in and out of view. The sails took up little of our time, so we trimmed and tarred and made the *Demeter* a thing of clean lines and sharp edges. This can bring joy to a crew. The first days of a voyage are always full of promise. But though the sun shone, a cold crept from belowdecks. Our bunks grew damp. Tinder would not kindle in the galley until we laid it on deck to dry. In the hold, our breath hung in plumes before our faces.

Olgaren had nightmares.

He woke us three times a night, but would not tell us what he dreamed. Two hours before dawn on the third night, he woke us again. Petrofsky boxed his ears until his head hit a beam and he dropped to the deck. When he hit the boards, I saw he smiled. I remembered his words. *Absolute submission….* His smile was his shield. Even unconscious, he did not let it drop.

Perhaps he was stronger than I thought.

On the fifth morning, we entered the Bosporus and soon came into the city of a thousand names; Stamboul, Constantinople, Konstantiniye, Islambol, Istanbul…. Her yellow-walled city and seven hills shaded upward into the dusty air, in a hazy stench of spices and cured fish. The crew was divided into two. The larboard watch – myself, Olgaren and Petrofsky – were assigned to stay aboard while the starboard took three hours ashore. This was fortunate for me, as I thus did not have to scheme to ensure I met the customs officers as they made their inspection. More fortunately still, the Turkish officer was lax. He did not open any of the crates in the hold and I did not have to hand over the silver coins from Varna Quay to distract him. When he had left the ship, we played at dice on deck, and though the Captain returned and saw us, he let us play on. Olgaren lost his coin and stretched out, clearly loving the sunlight. I took two more silver pieces from Petrofsky and felt myself a rich man indeed.

That night I needed sleep early, as I had the three-bells watch, long before dawn. But I had hardly dozed when a cry woke me, so full of terror it had me on my feet before my eyes opened. Even in my anger, I feared for Olgaren's safety. I leaned and shook him awake, but the men had had enough. They wanted to tie him upright to the fo'c'sle steps. Petrofsky wound rope around his wrists, and throughout Olgaren blinked and smiled as though his dreams were full of light.

I could not see a man so treated like a dog. "He can sleep in the hold," I said, untying his wrists. "I'll ask the second mate. I'm relieving him on watch."

"We'll still hear him screaming," Petrofsky said.

"And so will the captain," I said. "So none of us need be seen to complain."

The men nodded. Petrofsky clapped me on the shoulder and grinned.

"I won't scream any more," said Olgaren. "Don't make me sleep in the hold. It is too dark."

"Come on." I took his arm as three bells sounded. "My watch. Sleep well, shipmates."

But Olgaren would not stay in the hold. He did not beg again, but would not sleep in the shadow of the crates. He followed me on deck with a face like an abandoned dog and I cursed his company. The second mate, too, swore on seeing him, and sent him to sleep in the galley, which, to my relief, he did with no complaint. Alone, I watched the shore until the moon disappeared. I heard only the creak of the masts, and the whine of mosquitoes. Something splashed in the water nearby. Once a seabird called, low and sweet.

Then Olgaren screamed. The sound echoed back from the whitewashed buildings on the shore, a wild howl that raised the hairs on my arms. The once warm breeze chilled my neck. I should have left him alone for the Captain to hear, but the cries went on and on and I could not bear to hear such pain. I pushed open the galley door and ducked into the gloom.

Olgaren thrashed on the deck between two sacks of grain. I knelt and took his shoulders, at which his eyes flew open. He clutched at me with desperate fingers.

"Save me," he gasped. "Protect me from the dark."

I could not look away from the terror in his eyes. "I am here," I answered, without thinking. "I will protect you. Everything is well. I am here."

Awareness was long in returning to his gaze. "Amramoff," he said. His voice surprised us both. It left behind a silence, in which I became aware of his grip on my biceps, and the closeness of his mouth to mine. From the fo'c'sle, the bell sounded five. Below us, the water lurched in shadow. Olgaren's eyes were wide and silver-blue. They closed as our lips touched.

We only kissed that night. I stumbled back on deck, confused, and terrified I had been caught, but nothing stirred above. Only the night bird, half a mile away on shore, cut the silence before dawn with its hollow cry.

4. AUTOPHILE

Did you think your cargo human? Did you think of them at all, chained in the hold? Why are they here? What were their crimes? Olgaren and I will not judge them on the legality of their actions. No – many break laws to feed those they love. Here, today, we try to find a deeper judgement, not of laws, but of worth...

THE NEXT MORNING, I woke full of fear this would mean too much to Olgaren. He would reveal our kiss to the crew by favouring me. But neither did he seek to catch my eye while breaking our fast nor when we reefed the main sails to steer a course through the Marmara Sea. The sun shone hot but the breeze was fresh. As we were making such slow speed, at noon the first mate let our watch fish overboard with lines and feathers.

Petrofsky and I caught several fat mackerel while Olgaren tangled his line and lost his hook overboard. Finally, we set him to gutting. Three worries beset me as the hours slid past. The first: How was I to ensure I was kept behind this afternoon so the customs in Çanakkale did not open the marked crate? The second: What did the kiss with Olgaren mean to him? It meant nothing to me, of course, but I feared he might desire some terrible, clinging romance.

My third worry overshadowed all: How in all the hells could Olgaren gut the fish without slicing such clumsy fingers on the sharp knife? I could not bear to watch and had to turn away.

I should have known he had no experience with fish. He cut them into chunks, leaving the scales on, then tried to clean the pieces one by one. The fish were only fit for soup or the gulls. Petrofsky picked up a handful and threw them overboard.

"A morning's work wasted!" he shouted. "Why not ask if you knew not how?"

Olgaren blinked up at him, the knife loose in his palm. Fish scales glittered in his eyebrows. "I thought it would be easy," he answered.

"The fish are biting," I said. "We have time to catch more."

But Petrofsky had an audience, and the men were bored. "It is easy, if you do not slice them up first." He threw another handful of fish. It bounced off Olgaren's chest. "What will we eat tonight?"

"They would make a soup," I said. Why was I trying to protect the man? I wanted to hit him myself.

"Make him eat them," someone shouted from the rigging.

Petrofsky bared his teeth like a shark. He reached out a thumb, red with blood. "Clean it," he said.

Olgaren reached with his shirt, but Petrofsky waved it away. "Lick it clean," he said.

A seagull cackled above us. Nobody looked up. Olgaren narrowed his eyes. His smile did not fade.

"As you will," he said. He opened his mouth.

I looked away as Petrofsky leaned forward. I heard the crew laughing.

"Now eat the fish," said Petrofsky.

"As you will," I heard Olgaren reply.

I turned back to see Petrofsky's hand now clean up to the palm. Olgaren knelt before him. He smiled, raised a chunk of grey, translucent flesh to his lips and began to chew.

Petrofsky nodded. "Is it good?"

"No," said Olgaren. He coughed. I thought he might choke on a stray bone, but he forced a swallow. His smile returned.

Petrofsky grew annoyed. He grabbed for more fish and tried to stuff it down Olgaren's shirt, while the crew whooped and jeered. Olgaren shook and flopped in Petrofsky's grasp, but did not retaliate or try to prevent it.

When Petrofsky stepped back, flushed and breathing hard, Olgaren settled back onto his knees, the same ghost of a smile haunting his lips. The jeers of the crew faded.

The greatest rebellion is absolute submission. Petrofsky swiped at the deck for the gutting knife and at that moment, I saw the captain emerge from the hold behind him. As Petrofsky rose, I threw myself upon him.

He yelled as my weight hit, and we fell. His head thumped off the deck and I saw his surprise turn instantly to rage. Luckily the knife had tumbled aside or he would have stabbed me, I am sure. Instead he twisted and threw me free. His fist flashed. My temple exploded with stars. I managed to land three punches of my own, before firm hands tore us apart.

"What, boys?" The captain spat on the boards between us. His eyes flashed. "Who began this?"

I shook off the hands that gripped me. "He had a knife," I said, staring at the deck.

"I was not going to cut him," Petrofsky said. "I was going to show Olgaren how to gut fish."

The captain frowned and looked to the men for more answers, but, of course, nobody had seen anything. We were punished by cancellation of shore leave for the larboard watch. Despite the blood trickling from my brow, satisfaction made it hard to hide my smile.

Petrofsky glowered at me. "Are you mad? You know I would not cut him."

I shrugged, touched my brow, and winced.

In the smaller port of Çanakkale, the starboard watch ran to change into shore clothes, while I pretended to sulk. At the dock, the captain went off first, followed by the laughing, shouting crew. Olgaren dreamed on deck, supposedly splicing line, while Petrofsky glowered at me as he mended sails.

"You will go down in the hold," he said. "Not I."

When I only nodded in response, he spat. Twenty minutes later, I heard the boots of the customs officer and his two men on the gangplank. I led them down to the hold, keeping my hand against my thigh to stop the clink of coins. The officer shrank from touching the handrail. I noted his polished leather boots, his perfectly creased uniform, his neat moustache and smooth skin, and I relaxed. A man who loves himself always needs extra coin.

Our hold stank. Worse than other boats. We had all noticed the streaks of mould on the timbers, that returned, hours after being scrubbed away. I hoped the officer would stay back when he turned pale behind his moustache and held a white cloth to his nose. But though his men cursed, he led them down the hold, pointing out crates. He opened one in five, keeping an eye on me as he chose. I tried to hide my tension when he neared the marked crate, but his eyes glittered in the gloom. He actually showed his teeth at me as he pointed at the box I was charged to hide. I stepped close and pushed past, leaving a pile of silver on a crate at his hip without the clink of coin on coin. When I turned back, the silver had gone and he watched me with a half-smile.

His men neared the crate and lifted their tools to slip the top. Still he did not stop them. I raised my eyebrows and shook my head only the smallest amount, but his mouth twisted into a sneer. Hearing the sound of metal on wood, I took out the rest of my silver, snapping it into a neat pile with my thumb. I laid it on a crate before him, and again looked away while the money disappeared.

The men slipped the claws of their bars under the lid. It creaked and began to lift. They twisted away and swore again. I smelled rot, sweet and sharp.

"Stop," the officer said his Russian was crisp. "This ship stinks too much to bear. Leave it." He turned and stumbled away.

For no reason I understood, dread, not relief, settled in my chest as they left the hold. I stood by the crate, wishing to run after them into the light. Something glinted in the blackness under the lid. My gold. Should I claim it now? I could leave the ship today, rich enough to buy a boat of my own. I reached into the chill of the crate, stretched my fingertips into the darkness –

"What game are you playing?"

I jumped back in shock. Petrofsky stepped from the shadows behind the stairs. "What's in the box?"

"Nothing. Customs didn't close it behind them, is all." I hammered the lid closed with the heel of my hand, and made to leave the hold.

Petrofsky gripped my arm as I tried to push past him into the light. "I saw you pay the Turk. Baksheesh, eh?"

I pulled free, but he followed me up on deck.

"Where'd you get the coin?"

I turned to face him, my heart knocking so loudly I feared he must hear it. "Captain's business. Speak to him."

Petrofsky grunted, but I kept my eyes cold and still.

"When did the captain ever deal with you?" he said.

It was true. The captain never spoke to the men unless it was to punish. But for that reason I knew Petrofsky would not ask. I stared at him until he turned away. The first mate set us to store provisions in the galley. The ship seemed only half alive with her crew ashore. Petrofsky watched me under half-lowered lids, so I could not sneak back and claim my gold. Halfway up the mast, Olgaren lifted his blond head to the sun, his eyes closed. What dreams played out behind his eyelids? What terrors haunted his sleep at night? Why, if I was so rich, did I care?

5. HEMOPHILE

Listen to the cries! Your cargo freeing itself. Did you treat them well? There were two dead in your hold before you even left Albion's waters. No, no, of course that is not your fault. The law is bound to hand them over to you in fit condition to voyage and if it fails in that respect, you are not to blame...

I COULD NOT return to the crate that day. Shore leave had not calmed the rest of the crew. They seemed nervous and constantly scanned the deck for some unnamed threat, leaving me no chance to slip away. Three days passed, and my imagination filled the crate with treasure, enough to buy a ship, a palace, an entire town. The urge to possess my gold grew with every strike of the bell until I could resist no longer.

That night, with the wind dropped, we anchored in the Grecian Archipelago. The crew slept. I had the midnight watch, and knew this to be my best opportunity. As soon as I was alone, I pushed open the galley door. Olgaren slept, his neck bare in a splash of light from the porthole. I sought not to think about kissing him, failed, and whistled him awake.

"Take my watch for ten minutes," I said.

Olgaren stood, blinking. I felt a wave of heat from his body and smelled the sleepy, dark scent of him as he pushed past me into the open air. He looked out over the rail. A wide, bright moon cast cloud shadows on the sea. Dark slivers of land to larboard. A low easterly offered no challenge to a novice watchman.

"Only ten minutes," I said. The faintest scent of rot wafted up from the nearby entrance to the cargo hold.

Olgaren inhaled. He shivered. The moon reflected in his eyes. "Do not go down there," he said.

"I was not – " I began.

"*Please.* A beast waits below. I dream of him."

I scoffed, but Olgaren did not look away. "How will you protect me if you are his?" he said.

I shook my head. "Protect you?"

"As you did with Petrofsky and the knife." His hand strayed to my sleeve. A moment.

"Take the watch," I said, a sudden anger making me brusque.

"As you will," he replied. "I will not beg you."

I turned away. "Whistle if you hear anyone."

"As you will."

I spat over the rail but the sour taste did not leave my mouth. Then the clean desire for gold overwhelmed the fog of anger and confusion. I took the steps down into the hold with relief, despite the stench.

I had half a tallow candle in my pocket, but now that the gloom surrounded me I did not dare light it, as only thin planks separated the far end of the hold from the crew's quarters, and I fancied I could hear the murmuring of conversation from where I stood. The hold darkened as a cloud covered the moon. The hairs rose on my arms. I fought not to shiver.

I remembered Olgaren's words: *A beast waits below.* He was a superstitious fool, but even so fear feathered the back of my neck. I moved silently, despite my thundering heart, counting crates until I reached the box that held my gold. It was damp and chill beneath my fingers. Should I risk my flint to check the marking? I did not dare. Instead I waited until the moon returned and the hold brightened about me. This was the correct crate.

I felt some of my fear fade. It was a work of moments to find the loosened board and force it upwards again. The sweet, high scent of rot surrounded me and my gorge rose. What could this crate contain? Almost I turned away, but the thought of my gold held me still. A faint red glow brightened in the darkness of the crate, as of a pipe's ember seen far away. My heart lurched. Rubies? Treasure to be sure. I leaned forward. Another light kindled beside the first. They brightened.

Eyes, I thought. Eyes! Before I could fall away in terror, a hand burst from the crate and gripped my throat. Stinking soil filled my mouth and eyes but I could not choke. I clawed at the arm that held me. Knotted muscles flexed, taut as iron, under filthy, black cloth. As I fought to breathe, the moon slid behind a cloud. The hold went black. Boards creaked, then lifted free, and a cold air licked my face. The eyes approached. They did not blink. Fire boiled through cracks in the iris, tinting the entire eye crimson, lit from within.

A deeper darkness sparkled black in my vision as I began to lose consciousness. Then the moonlight returned. If I had the breath to scream, I would have split the main mast with my terror. The old man from Varna Quay grinned at me and his mouth was laced with fangs. Flesh hung loose on his bones. He looked older, dead already, but a mad vitality burned in those red eyes.

"Good prey," he said in a voice dry as a broken board. "You came." He loosed his hand from my throat.

I took a roaring breath to scream for help. The old man, the monster, lunged at me, his mouth wide, and his teeth pierced my neck in a spike of pain. And then...

...everything changed.

When a man is taken by another, the pain of the assault turns to richest pleasure in an instant. My fear turned to shocked excitement, my agony to a sensual burn. My limbs weakened further. I would have fallen but for the kiss at my neck that pinned me upright. Waves of gooseflesh rippled across the small of my back, up my thighs, down my arms. The monster called my blood to him like a lover and I felt it flow from me, felt his body swell against mine. When he drew back, his teeth scraped against some tendon deep in my throat. The pain brought clarity and I saw him anew.

Years had fallen from his form; he looked younger than when he had stood on Varna Quay. Tall and dark, with high cheekbones and full lips. "Sweet," he said. He frowned. "You do not struggle. Do you...want this?"

At the distaste I read on his face, any last remnant of fear turned to anger. "No." My voice, though, wavered and I struggled still to breathe. "I want my gold."

He hissed, and I thought he would kill me until I realised he was laughing.

"Ahh, single-minded men." He pulled me close. "Not a one will survive this voyage. You will not disembark alive. But..." He licked his lips. "You may do so...*vampir*."

I gulped. The word had no meaning to me, and, in my confusion, only the steady glint of gold stayed true. "And rich."

"Gold will not interest you after you drink of my blood," he said. "You will have other wants."

I wanted both to run for help and to have him bite me again. But under both those desires, that from a younger age burned brightest. I wanted that soft, heavy metal in my palm. I lifted my open hand.

He let me go. I slumped against the crate in which he stood. Now was my chance to flee, but my legs trembled just to hold me upright. Reaching into the soil at his waist, he lifted out not gold, but a double handful of dark loam.

"Take this," he said. "Leave a trail from here to the deck and thence to the Captain's cabin."

Filled with disappointment, I frowned. "Why?"

He hissed. "I should kill you now."

I folded my arms and did not take the soil. I do not think I was truly sane.

The monster sighed, though he seemed amused. "A ship is of the sea," he said. "I am of the land."

I shook my head.

"I cannot walk the naked boards. A ship is of the sea," he repeated. "I need land beneath my feet. My native land, where my body lay…in death."

In the silence, a voice in my head screamed at me to run, but his eyes held me fixed.

"Spread the soil. Free me to walk the ship and I will give you what you desire. Take it." The last of the humour left his voice and I trembled to obey.

I took the soil. Our hands did not touch.

"You will keep my presence a secret." His eyes glowed brighter. "Send a man down to me unknowing, tomorrow night, and I shall be pleased."

I lifted my chin. "I…will try."

"Good." He turned from me and sank back down into the blackness of the crate, leaving me gasping and alone.

I pressed the planks of the lid down flat and took my handful of soil, leaving a thin trail along the hold and up the side of the steps to the deck as the monster had instructed. The cool, sweet, night air shocked me into one last moment of clarity. Olgaren stood at the wheel. I held the soil in my cupped hands, and could not look away from him. He shook his head. I saw sorrow in his eyes. More, I saw myself. Self-disgust rippled in my gut. I had brought the monster aboard. I was his slave.

I staggered to the rail. Perhaps I would have thrown myself over, but I slipped and the soil fell from my hands and pattered into the sea. I wiped my hands on my trousers. I feared they would never feel clean again.

"Amramoff, are you – "

I turned to Olgaren and fell into his arms. I trembled like a child. He held me until I calmed.

"Shh," he whispered. "All will be well."

But how could it? I already burned to return and collect more soil to finish my task. Worse, tomorrow night I had to send a man down to the hold. With the calm in Olgaren's arms rose a stupor, filling my mind like fog. I cannot remember waking the next man on watch, nor returning to my bunk....

6. ANTHROPOPHILE

You left Portsmouth, what? Four days ago. Already prisoners have fresh whip cuts. Already I smell them on your loins. You have used them, more than one, and more than once. I fear you are losing my good opinion. Pray that your story redeems you...

AND NOW I lose the straight line through my tale. I remember little and only in brief snatches. The monster's kiss had loosened my mind. I spoke and worked as hard as the next man, but was asleep. Only near Olgaren did voices rise to shriek warnings within me, so I avoided him as we threaded the Hellenic Isles and made our way westward...

Midnight. Rain patters on deck, though the wind is light. I shake drops from my hair and make my way to where Petrofsky shelters at the prow under a stretch of sailcloth.

"Nothing to report?" I ask.

"All well." He turns to leave for his bunk.

"Wait." Under the lantern's glow, I show him the warm glint of my golden coin. "There's more. Down below. Enough to share."

His eyes gleam.

Dawn. The *Demeter* rings to the sound of booted feet and calls of alarm, but Petrofsky cannot be found. Olgaren grips my arm, so tight he leaves bruises, but I will not meet his eye. I shake him free and my terrors subside until he requests to speak to the captain....

Dawn again. The sea is rising. Slabs of turquoise water shatter across our bows. We search the ship again, this time for stowaways. In the hold, I see black soil rubbed between the planks. I do not think I did it myself. The ship is declared clean and something inside me breaks. I laugh and laugh and cannot stop.

Noon. Dark as night. A storm has blossomed above the *Demeter*. The ship lists hard to starboard. The captain screams orders while ropes crack and waves sweep the deck. I climb rigging and untie knots and tie them anew and sleep and climb again for an eternity. Lightning illuminates stark moments –

Flash! Black mud slicks the deck. Ropes and rungs are caked and treacherous. The first mate is screaming, but I cannot hear his words. More men have disappeared. It was not me. It was not me –

Flash! From the top of the main mast, I see sunlight on the horizon. A strip of blue sky and calm sea. Thunder shakes the mast and I reef the topsail. When I look up, the strip of blue is there, unchanging, five miles ahead. Always five miles ahead. The storm races with us. We cannot leave its shadow –

Flash! Teeth strike and sink deep. I moan in pleasure as the monster drinks of me. He croons and whispers.

"I love you all," he says. "You are so sweet." But he does not give me of himself to drink. "Send them down to me first," he says.

I nod and forget to ask about my gold as he draws me close again –

More men have disappeared. I have not slept for three nights. I weep and shake as Olgaren pins me against the galley wall. He stands braced against the heaving deck. He has found his sealegs. He is poised and intent and will not let me free.

"Wake up, Amramoff." He bites my ear. "Come back to me."

I shake my head and find his lips on mine. His stubble grates my cheek. Our tongues meet. Clarity slaps me like a wave and I cry out at what I have become. "The things I have done, Olgaren!"

"It was not your will," he says. "You are a good man." His mouth silences mine, but breaks away too soon. "I could not trust you otherwise. You will protect me." Spray plasters his hair to his head. His face shines blue-white in the lightning's stuttered flare. I see his exhaustion and his fear. I see his faith. It crushes me.

Who am I to protect him? I cannot even care for myself. Worse, I am the cause of his suffering, and of this voyage into nightmare. "Olgaren, I cannot – "

He turns within my grasp and pulls my arms closer around him. I feel the hot length of his body through his wet clothes. The back of his neck smells of nutmeg from the galley. I trap the scent against his skin with my lips, to save it from the lashing rain. I do not lower my arms as I feel him reach around and undo the buckle of my belt.

I take him there, in the heart of the storm, while the *Demeter* heaves under our feet. The men I like are taller than I, and dark. They take their joy from me and I find my own. But here, against the galley wall, I find I am solid, older, a man of weight and purpose. A man I do not know. I am responsible for Olgaren's pleasure and for his pain. I will not take without giving. I will not hurt him or see him hurt. We move together while the wind shrieks about us, and though the watch might see, I do not care.

7. NYCTOPHILE

If you join us, you will open your eyes, and a liquid fire will burn in your veins. It will thread your flesh. Every nerve will sing, and as suddenly – quieten. In the silence you will hear, not your heart, never that, but the heartbeat of the sea. You will know her, will be of her, and her touch upon your skin will tell you of faraway shores and deep currents. The blue depths will call as much as hot, red blood. Poised between both, you will see the balance. The fine line we walk....

I HAD THE wheel. This was rare, but the last steersman had disappeared the day before. I had not sent him below. The monster was free. I had not seen the captain in days. We no longer anchored at night, but fled where the wind took us. I held us clear of the coast as the sun set, my arms numb with exhaustion. Was that black shore Portugal, France, even Belgium? I am ashamed to say I did not know.

Venus shone above the darkening horizon. North. We flew north. The sea, still high, was slow in calming, though the storm had broken hours before. Curls of spray swept the deck. From the wheel, I saw two silhouettes take shape at the prow. They leaned together, pulled apart and closed again. Upwind, I could not hear their words.

I lost concentration on the sea and the *Demeter* struck a wave with a shudder. The figures staggered. I saw them clearly then.

"No!"

The monster ignored my cry. In his grip, Olgaren struggled, then slumped, perhaps unconscious. The beast lifted his limp form to its mouth.

My heart thrashed in terror, but I could not move. The monster's hold on me was as strong as ever. To disobey him was unthinkable. But Olgaren needed me. I had promised to protect him. I could not stand by and let him die. Other crewmen remained. Let the beast take them.

I almost left the wheel, but they were forty paces away, the beast already drinking from Olgaren's neck. Instead, I heaved the wheel to larboard, feeling the deck surge and lift as the prow swung out. Then we slid from the crest and fell lengthways into the deep valley between waves. A wall of water slammed the hull and broke in a sweep of rushing foam across the deck. The two figures fell, and I lost them in the gloom. Searching the racing shadows, I swung the wheel back as fast as I could to help the *Demeter* lift her prow. Water streamed from the deck as she heaved herself clear, and at last I saw him, wrapped around the mainmast, unmoving. I strapped the wheel in place, ignoring the shouts from the fo'c'sle, and ran.

Even after the storm, the deck was treacherous. Mud oozed from the joins between every plank. I skidded to a halt at Olgaren's body. He was cold and white, his eyes rolled back, his teeth chattering. Blood, his own or the beast's, smeared his jaw and darkened his lips. As I leant to touch the pulsing wound at his throat, a shadow slipped from the prow and slid along the deck towards us.

I stooped and swung Olgaren over my shoulder. He seemed light as a child. Where could I run? Where would be safe? Upwards, I thought. At the top, there would be a stretch of rigging free of soil where the beast could not tread. I clutched Olgaren to me and began to climb the mainmast, lunging one-handed, upwards from rung to rung. I climbed until my limbs weakened, until I feared I must fall. When I looked down, the monster hung, scant feet below me. His eyes burned red.

"Drop him," he said. I heard him clearly, though the wind shrieked in the rigging all about. He grinned. "It is time for your reward."

I gripped Olgaren tighter and forced myself upwards, while the monster's voice followed me into the swinging, empty sky.

"You want me," he said. "I shall be your master. You will have no uncertainty, no doubt. Your station will be absolute. You need never struggle to define yourself again. Leave him. Come to me."

Behind his eyes, the red glow grew bright. It drew me downwards, more than the weight of Olgaren on my shoulder. Even up this high, the ropes were black and slick. I pulled us upwards, dreading to feel the monster's jaw clamp on my heel. The deck swung past under me as the *Demeter* heaved herself up onto the next wave. For one small moment, if we had fallen, we would have landed on the wet boards. Around that instant, the dark of the sea crashed in foam-streaked chaos.

I reached the boom. There was no higher to climb. I could edge out along the horizontal beam, but to what end? It, too, was smeared in mud. Olgaren twisted and slipped a handsbreadth from my shoulder. I tightened my grip and when I looked down, the monster was flying towards me, his arms outstretched, his hands crooked into claws.

My body seized. Every muscle locked. My heart clapped once, louder than lightning – and the beast struck. He caught the boom with one hand, causing the entire mast to shudder. The boom swung out and back, whipping the monster's cloak out behind him. He hung below, grinning at me, then in an impossible movement, pulled himself up one-handed, to stand on the narrow, wooden beam. He reached out a claw.

Olgaren screamed. He writhed and fell. I lunged for him. My shoulders almost tore from their sockets as I caught his shirt. The sea swept beneath me, then the brief flash of the deck, then the sea again.

"Drop him," the beast said. "In England, you shall be my hand and I your will." He stood, hardly swaying on the beam, so high above the deck. He was young and strong and dark, having drunk from many men. *He was taller than I, and I did not know his name.*

Yearning built in my chest to be free. To be free of choice, and of duty. This beast could wrap me in his cloak and I would not feel the cold. I would not feel anything at all. *Absolute submission....*

Olgaren moaned. My arms cramped with a distant pain. The beast waited, as again the deck swept beneath me. I would not feel.... *The greatest rebellion –*

No, I realised. There would be no rebellion under the beast. Olgaren was mistaken. Absolute submission was the minimum the monster required.

I let go of the mast. For an instant, we hung, high above the waves. The smile whipped off the face of the beast. He fell away upward as the wind built to a roar about us, foam flashed, and we plunged into the black water.

The shock woke Olgaren, who kicked and struggled free of my arms almost immediately. A slap of salt water filled my mouth. When I had finished choking, the *Demeter* was nothing more than a receding shadow against the silver-streaked horizon. High above the deck, two glowing red eyes faded with distance. Not once did the beast look away before the wind bore the *Demeter* out of sight, but with her passing a heaviness left me. My limbs grew bright with motion in the chill water. I scoured the surrounding waves. At last I spotted Olgaren clutching a length of dark wood, and swam his way.

More under the water than above, the sodden spar tipped as I grasped it. Olgaren gasped. His lips trembled. As I watched, his grip on the wood relaxed and he slipped under the surface. Once again I lunged and found his shirt. I pulled him against me and tried to hold his head above the waves. But the spar rolled, and Olgaren could not help, and my new-found strength ebbed fast. The gold coin banged against my thigh with every stroke of my legs. Its weight seemed to pull me down. With numb fingers I held it above the water. My payment.

I threw it high and far and did not hear the splash.

All night I fought the sea. When at last dawn silvered the eastern horizon, I blinked myself from a dream, to find I had let Olgaren slip. He hung in my arms, below the surface of the water, his eyes closed, unbreathing.

I howled, pulled at him, tried to force the water from his lungs, but he had left me. I had refused the security of the beast. I had hefted responsibility onto my shoulders, only to fail before a single night had passed. I wept at Olgaren's cold features hanging in another realm, inches from my own, and at last, I resolved to join him. The sky lightened above me. I took my last look at Olgaren's face and found his eyes wide open, gazing at me from under the water. His grip in mine strengthened as he pulled himself from the sea. Water streamed down his skin. His eyes glowed, not red, but deepest green. He had drunk from the beast.

He smiled when he saw me, a feral stretching of his face that chilled me more than the freezing water. The emerald glow in his eyes shone bright. "Amramoff!" He reached a hand and cupped my cheek. Only then did he recognise his state. He turned his palm to his face and his smile faded. A wave slapped sea-water into his mouth. He let it drain, uncaring. "I submitted too far," he said. "I drank from him. Will I ever see the sun again?"

I could not but recoil, at which his eyes cleared and the glow faded. "I will not take you," he said. "I will not…do evil."

A wave lifted us. Over his shoulder I saw a strip of shoreline, black against the brightening horizon.

"Swim, Olgaren," I said. "Take me to shore."

In this state, he was stronger than I. His legs churned the sea into foam behind us. I slept, and woke to find him weeping. He had dragged me almost free of the tide, but now huddled behind, attempting to push me further up the shore.

"It hurts me, Amramoff," he said when he saw me awake. "I cannot leave the sea."

I grasped his hand and fought to pull him further, but he writhed in my grip. His hand darkened and shrivelled in mine. He howled. I had no choice but to let him go and watch as he pulled himself back into the surging waves. Separated by only ten paces, we watched each other.

"What am I?" he asked.

At that moment, the sun lifted a golden edge above the horizon. Before I could answer him, Olgaren sank beneath the water. He floated under the surface, his arms crossed over his chest. I could only find one answer to give his unbreathing form. *You are dead, Olgaren. You are of the night. And of the sea.*

I pulled him to a tidal pool. Once assured the receding sea would neither sweep him away nor leave him high and dry, I dragged myself up the beach and collapsed. My last thought was this: of course he could never leave the sea. Just as the monster aboard the *Demeter* needed its own unholy soil under its feet, Olgaren needed the water that had witnessed the passing of his life. The open sea was his grave and tomb, his consecrated realm...

The sun warmed my bones. I awoke with fine sand pressed against my cheek, to find the day passed, the sun not far above the horizon. A desperate thirst dried my mouth and cracked my lips. I must drink soon, or die. I stood and stretched my limbs. The tide had returned. Olgaren floated near the shore.

I had sworn to protect him. How could I do so now? Did my word still hold? Should I aid him in finding blood? The thought repelled me, all the more for having sent Petrofsky down to the beast myself. As the sun lowered and reddened, and seagulls arced overhead, I fought my conscience. I should leave him, and head inland in the hope of finding water. But if I broke my promise to protect Olgaren, who would I be? What was left of my soul? On that nameless beach of white sand and black rocks, I struggled until my mind at last fell silent. Beneath it I heard the steady voice of my heart.

Stay, it said. *He smells of nutmeg....*

I had no plan in mind when the sun slipped away and Olgaren awoke. His face had thinned and he hissed at me, waist deep in the water, before consciousness blinked back behind his slitted eyelids.

"You did not leave me." A wave broke across his back, but he did not fall. "I am hungry, Amramoff."

I nodded.

"I do not know how to be this thing."

I could think of no answer to the anguish in his voice. "I must find water," I said. "Let us walk."

Olgaren drifted beside me as I stumbled along the shore. The reflection of his eyes glinted green in the rock pools. No streams broke the shoreline. No lights twinkled inland. When we rounded a headland and I saw a five-mile stretch of white sand in the moonlight, I fell to my knees.

"I can go no further." My voice caught and cracked.

"I shall go ahead – "

"No, Olgaren." I swallowed, but my throat was made of sand. "How will you bring me water? You cannot leave the sea. I am done. You must drink of me, now."

"No! I would never – "

"I have failed," I said. I felt the weight of it in my bones. "I could not save you. Drink of me and you may survive."

"This is not survival," he cried. "This is not life!"

I crawled towards the waves. Closer, I saw the hollows under his cheekbones, the skin drawn tight over the tendons in his neck. I rolled into the sea, gasping as the chill water soaked my clothes yet again. Olgaren stepped deeper, shaking his head. I fought to keep my chin above the water against the pull of my clothes, spending the last of my strength to reach him. I gripped his cold hands and tipped my head to one side. "Drink."

He lunged in a blur of movement. His hand suddenly gripped my throat. He pulled me close. "There is enough evil in this world," he said. "I will not add more."

And in that instant, I knew what we had to do. "Olgaren."

"Do not ask me again." He dropped his grip and turned to swim away but I grasped his arm.

"Olgaren, I know how we can survive. I see how to make peace with what we are." I took his face in my hands while he kept us both afloat. A wild laughter bubbled in my throat. "It only requires that I die. By your kiss."

He shook his head, but I pulled him closer. "Shh. I am ready. This life is over. Listen, let me explain...."

Silence fell after I had spoken. Olgaren's eyes widened. Emerald light boiled from his pupils. He licked his lips over teeth that lengthened as I watched. He pulled me closer, and his lips brushed my own, then swept past. Twin spears of pain sank into my neck. His legs twined about my thighs and we sank below the waves. A burning heat grew in my throat. I felt his tongue probing the skin. He drank from me. Waves of hot and chill pleasure rippled from his bite along every nerve in my body. My head grew light. I opened my mouth to tell him to stop, and salt water poured down my throat. I struggled then, and tore his teeth from my neck in frenzy.

Strong arms pulled me to the surface. They held me until I ceased to cough and turned me to face an Olgaren renewed. Red flushed his cheeks. His lips were full and dark. He had stolen my strength and I could not break his skin when he held me to his neck.

"Here," he said, and sliced himself with a fingernail grown long and sharp.

His blood tasted of salt, of fire, of whiskey and moonlight. It left me thrilled and sensual in the embrace of the waves. But I did not change. First, I had to die.

"Now," I whispered. "You know what you have to do. Do not tarry."

He pulled me close, while dark tears fell from his eyes. Our lips touched and again we sank beneath the water. I would like to say I did not struggle, but mortal life is determined and will not give up easily. I fought him while my weakened lungs ached for air and my thinned blood thundered in my temples. He did not let me free but watched with infinite sadness in his eyes as the last of my life fled. My vision darkened. I was for one moment a child, warm, wrapped in my mother's arms, then something left me with a snap – and all fear ceased. I opened my mouth and let the sea enter freely. It washed through me, chill and clear. I opened my eyes. I was reborn.

8. THE SEA

THE SHADOWED WATER glowed blue and full of promise. Something slid over my naked eyes, and the seabed came into clear focus. Moonlight-dappled kelp shone a rich purple. Fish glittered like gems. I pulled the blood-dark sea into my lungs and felt myself part of her. Whale song shook my bones. Icebergs calved in echoing rolls of thunder, half a world away. I heard children scream with laughter, heard men drowning, felt entire villages afloat on rafts of flowers. The vast sea contained all, and I loved her and all her loves.

I grinned and felt my teeth grow sharp behind my lips. My muscles burned. My heart had stopped but I had never felt so alive. I turned slowly. Olgaren hung before me. His eyes glowed with worry, with fear, with love. We kissed. His cool lips sent shudders of ecstasy down my spine. His yellow hair lifted about our kiss in a halo, and the halo was gold.

We sought the currents of the sea and sang to them and they took us to the wallowing belly of a ship, bound for Australia. Her hold ached with the moans of chained convicts. I feared we could not mount aboard, but a ship is of the sea, not of the land, and our feet stood firm upon her deck. Surely within this boat, of all vessels on the sea, would rest someone evil enough for us to kill?

We have not killed yet.

We are both hollow with hunger.

And this brings me to you. I have told how I came to be here. You know I am not a good man. Now it is your time to speak. Three fates await you. You may convince us of your worth, and we may set you ashore, free to begin your life anew. We may judge you not worth the soul that animates you, and we shall drink your blood to the death. Or perhaps we shall see a kindred spirit in you. Perhaps we shall offer you our blood in return and allow you to join our crew. The result will be a world slightly better than before. We will not be a force for evil.

I am filled with anticipation. Any one of the three endings will satisfy me. Olgaren will decide which is yours. Watch his face as you tell your story. If he smiles, even once, we will take you. I need not say how much I hope to see his smile again.

Be sure to tell the truth. We can smell a lie.

You may begin. . . .

THE CALM OF DESPAIR

Jason Andrew

"No man knows till he has suffered from the night how sweet and dear to his heart and eye the morning can be."

— BRAM STOKER, *DRACULA*

28 SEPTEMBER 189-

A SHARP wind brought the faint scent of brine from the North Sea along the pastoral green fields that surrounded the ruins of Whitby Abbey. Billington, the solicitor, circled the outer stone archway and ducked under the ramshackle roof where birds nested and squawked their disapproval. He meandered along his favorite place to stroll during slow afternoons while his scriveners handled mundane office affairs and copied contracts.

While the sun remained in the sky, he could pretend that darker memories of the ruins were but a lingering nightmare. Crowded around the fireplace late at night, old fishermen whispered tales of a white lady who occasionally appeared in one of the windows in Whitby Abbey seeking unfaithful husbands to punish...or, he supposed, lost women to protect.

Billington had neither the time nor the inclination to marry, so he resisted the urge to look upward. There could be no heavenly guardian angel peering down at him from the windows of Whitby Abbey, unless one considered the weeping shade of one Miss Lucy Westenra.

It was amongst those arched ceilings and forgotten pillars that he had done unspeakable things in the name of the Count. Sleep had come all too rarely since that accursed Russian vessel crashed upon the sandy shores near Whitby. When he surrendered to nature's demands, Billington dreamed only of the Count's eager lips and the sensual reality of teeth that were not the least gentle.

Billington looked across the soft grass fields towards St. Mary's Church. The old parish had the appearance of an ancient stone fortress perfectly suited for the stormy North Sea weather. The soft cries of the invading hosts of seagulls were muted by the blustery wind and the delightful cheers of children playing under the watchful eyes of mothers and nannies lifted his spirits.

He swore upon his dearly departed mother's grave that he would never return to the cemetery. Any cemetery, for that matter. Yet he found by the light of day that he simply could not keep himself away. It was there that he first caught sight of the *Demeter* crashed upon the shores of Whitby. A strange fever took hold of his mind the whole night of the storm.

He felt that similar burning sensation in the pit of his stomach that morning when he dressed for work. The fears, the ache, for the Count's arrival would not be pushed away. An adolescent should have such feelings, not a grown man, not one of his station, yet he had regarded his reflection in his looking glass as if a young lady awaiting her paramour's visit with unseemly anticipation.

"Mr. Billington!" A tall, slim man with curly hair and warm brown eyes waved from across the graveyard. He was a handsome clerk more than a decade his junior and still bristling with the chaos of life. "Mr. Billington! I'm so sorry to bother you, sir. You received an urgent telegram."

"Thank you, Jeffery." Billington enjoyed their late-night conversations at the office over brandy and cigars. Jeffery wore an Arbutus dashingly in his lapel, signaling his interest. The secret language of flowers was quite in vogue amongst the young and fashionable men of London. His eyes flashed with the same message. *You are the one I love above all others.* "I appreciate you running all the way here. I'm sure it wasn't necessary."

"The telegraph boy offered to run here after you, but I thought it was best for all concerned to attend to this matter personally." Jeffery's voice dripped with jealousy and with good reason. Billington regretted the necessity of excluding him from his affair with the Count. He couldn't risk the handsome young man catching the attention of the fiend. "He said that it was a matter of life or death, sir."

"I appreciate your vigilance in this matter. Thank you." Telegraph boys often doubled their income by plying their delectable lips to a completely different trade. "I am quite glad to see such a friendly face on a beautiful day such as this."

Billington turned his attention to the envelope and opened it with care as though it might contain a tiny viper. His father had once told Billington that urgent missives were never good for business, health, or a good continence. Amazingly, this telegram had been sent by Jonathan Harker. He knew immediately what the poor bastard desired most without reading the rest of it. Could he dare to oppose the Count?

"Are you well, Mr. Billington?" Jeffery asked, daring to rest his hand upon his shoulder. Such open affections were rarely exchanged during daylight hours lest the offenders be arrested for gross indecency. If the famous playwright Oscar Wilde could be sent to prison for private affairs under the Labouchere Amendment, what chance did a mere solicitor from a minor village have? "You look as pale as the White Lady."

He ignored the faux pas over concern for Harker. Should he, could he act on behalf of the better angels of his nature? "Jeffery, please cancel all appointments for the foreseeable future. I'm feeling unwell."

Jeffery nodded, disappointed. "Yes, sir."

"Oh, one more thing, if you please. I'll need the file on all of the Count's London holdings by the time I return to the office this evening." Billington wasn't exactly certain what could be done to resolve things favorably, but he would feel better if he looked. "Just leave it on my desk."

"What will you be doing, sir?"

Billington glanced towards the gravestone where he had left Lucy for dead at the orders of the Count and shivered. "Making amends."

8 AUGUST 189-

A SOFT YET deep voice whispered Billington's name. It lingered in his ear like an extended kiss from a long-lost lover. "Samuel." He kept his eyes closed, but moaned contently under the heavy winter blankets. Like a somnambulist, he strode the path between dreaming and waking ready to fall towards either side with the slightest push. "Samuel. My arrival is nigh. I have need of your services."

He opened his eyes confused and dazed. The voice brooked no argument that Billington was anything but a drudge under its dominion. A slave who harbored hope for his master's caress like an old mistress who missed her man's dying ardor. His stirring arbor vitae and the quickening of his heart provided nothing to dispute the claim.

In bed, he reached out for Jeffery to satiate his hunger before forgetting that he slept alone that night. Young Jeffery had left by train to London that afternoon to deliver the new contracts for the shipping concerns for the Count.

Loud clashes of thunder punctuated the constant howl of the strange storm roaring inland from the sea. He blinked and turned his head as though he could hear his name whispered once more upon the wind.

The embers of the fire simmered, casting a faint amber glow against the walls of the room. Long sinister shadows seemed to stretch across the room to the canopy bed. His breath heated the very air around him, creating white wisps of fog that rose upwards and then dissipated. He was quite glad that he had insisted that the maid bring down the heavy winter bedding this afternoon before the storm.

The weather had been quite sultry as was typical for early August until there was a subtle shift in the wind. The locals plying their trade at sea warned of an oncoming storm of great potency. Sunset had brought forth a display of gold, purple and orange clouds. It stirred Billington as if he were some artist.

Billington remembered his astonishment when the rains and wind took a sinister turn. Some of the houses in the village were ill-equipped to stand such gale forces and a number of the residents took shelter within the safety of Saint Mary's stone walls. He heard tell that the wind had turned quite frigid with power enough that even strong men found it difficult to resist it.

When he camped out in the bedroom with a number of files he needed to read by the morning, a thick, white sea-fog swept over the coast during one of the lulls in the storm. Billington peeked outside past the curtain. The sky straddled the black of night and the early dawn's light. Why were there so many lights near the bluff, he wondered?

The cloister bell rang three times, indicating danger to the entire village. The coastguard ordered all local craft tied down and the entire pier. Billington found it difficult to believe that any captain would be foolish enough to attempt circumnavigate the reef to reach the pier in the storm. What else could cause such a commotion?

Billington dressed, slipped on his greatcoat, and started towards Saint Mary's. Men from the village poured out from the various buildings to lend aid. A tall gentleman who served the village as a doctor walked alongside him. "Do you know what has happened, Doctor Mitchell?"

The grim-faced gentleman shook his head. "I've heard whispers about a ship that sailed into port with a dead crew."

Billington remembered dreaming of the taste of blood and fog such as this morning. He felt ill. "The whole crew? How did it make it into port without a navigator?"

Doctor Mitchell shrugged as though he didn't quite believe the story. "The man that roused me from my bed said that the captain tied himself to the wheel clutching onto a cross. His neck was broken in the storm."

They were joined by other men from the village. It was traditional for every able-bodied man to search for survivors. Billington knew that he was closer to forty than he'd ever wish to admit, and his years had formed some padding around his waist despite his active walking. He was determined to do his part, promising himself that he would walk more and sit less. "Do you know what ship it was?"

One of the men in the crowd answered. "The crier named it the Russian ship *Demeter*."

BILLINGTON WALKED THE path in silence wondering what might have happened to his interests on the vessel. He felt guilty for the selfish thoughts upon seeing the *Demeter* moored to the pier. He had seen a number of ships, having spent the majority of his adult life in Whitby. The *Demeter* had once been a fine tall sail, reliable and well maintained by the crew. Rigging dangled haphazardly as clearly discipline and the storm ensured that the ship had seen better days.

The constable waved across the assembled crowd to catch his attention. He was a large, stoic man, his nose quite red and his eyes wrecked from horror. "Mr. Billington, I was hoping you would answer the all-call. Mind if I ask you a few questions, sir?"

"Yes, sir. I came to help out as best I could."

"If you don't mind, I'd like to show you something on the ship. It isn't for the faint of heart."

Billington nodded his consent and then followed the constable aboard the *Demeter* to the spot where the brave, dead captain had been covered with a bit of the sail. The deck was stained crimson with blood. What fresh hell happened on this ship? Did it have anything to do with the Count's cargo?

The constable tapped a thick ledger with his finger. "It says here in the manifest that there are fifty boxes that belong to you in the hold."

"More specifically my client Count Dracula," Billington explained. "I am his agent in this matter."

The constable coughed uncomfortably. "You'll understand that we need to open the boxes."

Billington blinked. "Why?"

"The log says that ten days after the *Demeter* left the port of the Varna with this cargo a man disappeared from the crew. Someone spotted a strange tall man not known to be amongst the crew. It might have been a stowaway." The constable tapped the manifest once more as though the point should be obvious. "It seems that the only cargo in the hold is your boxes. At the end, the captain seemed to think that the first mate had gone mad. It could be that he wanted what was in these in these boxes?"

A tall strange man? Could that be the Count? Billington nodded his agreement and then watched as men from the village lifted a long rectangular box from the hold onto the dock. One of them pried it open with a crowbar to discover mound after mount of silvery sand mixed with strange mossy mold.

"Why would the Count go to the trouble of shipping dirt?" The constable asked as he had his men dig around the box for hidden treasures. "This seems rather peculiar, Mr. Billington."

Fearing some sort of illicit activity in this strange matter – the constable could charge him with an accessory to the crime – Billington found his tongue quicker than normal. "The Count is famous in his homeland for an interest in unusual botany. To be honest, I hadn't considered the matter closely, as nobility, in my experience, possesses unusual tastes and whims."

Once the men could find nothing amiss, they sealed the boxes. "Where do you want them, Mr. Billington?"

"Excuse me?"

"Where do you want the boxes?"

Billington hadn't thought that far ahead. He looked about the ship, dumbfounded by the destruction and blood. "I have a small building near the pier. The men that work there know it. I'll pay the usual wages plus a bonus, of course."

"Poor bastard." The constable said gesturing to the dead Captain. "Who knows what might have happened if the ship had been allowed to run free. Might have capsized a small vessel or worse. Pity we'll have to bury him at sea."

Billington shook his head. "No, I'll see that he is buried at Saint Mary's. I'll cover the cost personally if needed."

"It looks like we'll have things in hand, Mr. Billington, shortly. If you don't mind, I'll stop by your office this afternoon with any additional questions I might have."

Billington nodded. He couldn't look away from the captain's corpse. "Whatever I can do to help."

"Good man."

Was he a good man? Billington had doubts.

10 AUGUST 189-

SLEEP DID NOT come that night for Billington. Each time he closed his eyes he thought of the tragic fate of the captain of the *Demeter* or the strangely similar horrific death of Mr. Swales. A viciously brutal murder had not been committed within the village of Whitby since the Danes burned the abbey a thousand years previous. Could it be that one of his neighbors had been so disturbed by the mad fate of the *Demeter* as to throttle poor Mr. Swales?

He couldn't escape the queer feeling that they were brothers in fate. There were no survivors of the *Demeter*, unless one counted a black dog that some of the coastguard witnessed escaping the misfortunate ship. A pet? Or something more sinister. England adored its legends of Black Hounds as much as it did White Ladies.

A mighty gust of wind shook the windows as though the breath of hell weighed down upon the house and then there was a deathly silence. Faint scratching sounds inched along the outside of the walls and then to the windows. It moved from window to window across the house, bringing the strange sound closer and closer. Hushed whispers speaking gibbering inhuman languages surrounded the house. The sound grew louder and more desperate. Trembling hands and clattering teeth overtook Billington. He tried to keep quiet, despite his panic-filled breaths. "Go away. Please go away."

A gentle knock replaced the scratching. Curiosity and his dreadful imagination warred for a moment until Billington simply had to know what was out there and pulled back the curtain. A pale handsome face with long pointed nose, large thoughtful blue eyes, and a long mustache peered through the window back at him and greeted him with a toothsome smile. "Samuel, I have come for your services at long last. Open the window and invite me in."

He knew the Count's visage by reputation and portraits. Yet he had envisioned an older man. Was this another dream? "Why don't you come in through the door?" Billington asked, quite perplexed. His bedroom was on the second floor of his cottage without a proper foothold for a man to stand upon. "How did you get out there?"

The Count's only answer was to smile as though to suggest that any of his questions were useless. There was cruelty in such beauty. "I have come here for you, Samuel. Invite me inside."

Rational questions faded from his brain. Billington thought of the Count's hungry eyes and he wanted to be consumed. He unlatched the window and opened it. The Count shook his head coyly, like a playful lover. "You must invite me into your home if you would enjoy my presence."

"Please, dearest Count, come into my home."

The Transylvanian smiled and then stepped into the bedroom with a grace that suggested his feet were unencumbered by gravity. He smoothed his clothing. It was a charming gesture that humanized him. "You did well to keep the boxes, Samuel. I have tasks for you to complete."

Discussion of mundane business matter woke Billington's conscious mind and his fears. "You must have heard of the murders onboard the *Demeter*, Your Lordship? The constable will want to question you when he discovers that you have finally arrived."

"Yes, the murders were required to sate my hunger during the voyage." His eyes shined like black stars. His teeth gleamed. Billington opened his mouth to scream, but his voice would not escape his throat.

"Thankfully, I have other needs at this time that you shall serve. You have talents for obfuscating certain matters and hiding in plain sight. You will obey me in this matter."

In the weakest of voices, Billington uttered, "W-What in the name of Heaven are you?"

"Heaven has stricken my name. Now this: I am your master. Obey me and pleasures subtle and gross shall be yours to enjoy…perhaps for eternity."

"Lord preserve me!"

The Count laughed, a cruel sound. He reached out with surprising speed, to clutch Billington's shoulder with a strength that could crack stone. "I smell your lust, Samuel." He pulled Billington closer and nuzzled their cheeks together while sniffing his neck with as much ardor as a predatory wolf would a lamb. "Would Heaven think your lust any more natural than my own?"

The Count's blue eyes grew wide with hunger and darkened. Billington felt dizzy as though exhausted from fever. They kissed, slow at first before a ravenous desire filled Billington's mouth with the taste the copper. He opened his eyes to see the Count's lips dripping crimson and realized that he was bleeding. The Count ripped Billington's white nightshirt from his body and then thrust him upon the bed. "You are *mine*."

The Count unbuttoned his own shirt. Billington blushed at his own nakedness and his own weakness, the visible excitement of his body towards this monster. "What will you do with me?"

The Count brought a finger to his own chest, sharp and jagged like an animal's claw, and then cut a thin swath across his pale flesh. He lifted Billington's head like a baby's and brought it to his chest to the black wound. "Drink of me and live like no other man."

Billington hungered for this new forbidden drink but shook his head with the weakness of a poppet. "No, I would not sip from a demon – "

"The Turks once called me demon." The Count laughed as he grabbed Billington by the hair and pulled his face against the bared chest Billington could not resist. He tasted the seeping blood. Cold on the tongue, yet it burned as he swallowed.

He barely heard the Count's boast. "I learned much about pleasure and pain while the Turks' prisoner. You will find me an exacting instructor in this matter."

12 AUGUST 189-

THE WORLD FELT muted and faded during daylight hours. He barely noticed that the day had ground to a halt and that of his employees only Jeffery remained attentive to his needs. "Jeffery, your services will not be needed this night."

"Mr. Billington, I don't mind staying until the end." An equal mixture of concern and disappointment cracked in the young man's voice. "Are you feeling well? You look as pale as the dead."

Billington checked his pocket watch. The Count would arrive soon to examine his progress on the requested property concerns. "I must insist now that you leave. I require...privacy. A personal meeting."

Jeffery pursed his lips, but said nothing. He collected his overcoat and hat and then stopped briefly at the door as though hoping Billington would change his mind. But Billington turned away and heard the door shut behind the young man.

He made an effort to look down at the papers until the Count made his presence known. "Samuel, your discretion is admirable, but I think I need another agent for certain duties in London."

Billington flushed and slammed his fist upon the oak desk, scattering the Count's ledgers. "No! We agreed that he would be left out of it, Master."

The Count smirked and placed a hand over Billington's fist. The grip tightened, threatened. "Very well, you will have to come with me tonight. I require privacy. You will ensure that I have it."

"Where shall we go?"

"Follow me and you will soon discover."

Billington walked the streets often in the evening, but the Count seemed to know secret paths between buildings that he had never imagined existed. At length they reached the shadows of Whitby Abbey. "What possible business could we have here, Master?"

A woman stepped out of the shadows clad in a white dressing gown that appeared in the moonlight as a bride's dress. Billington soon recalled her name, Miss Lucy Western. Despite his own tastes, he admitted her beauty, beauty that had earned the formal proposals of three men.

The Count pointed to the stairs that led to the top of the tower that provided a full view of the surrounding environment. "Her family is searching for her even now, Samuel. My needs require concealment. You will keep watch until I call for you and alert me should anyone approach."

A small groan escaped Billington's mouth. To think that he had been so envious of Harker's triumph in securing the Carfax Abbey contract. What a fool he was! Men like them were but slaves in a complex scheme that none would ever comprehend until it was too late. Lucy was merely the latest victim.

"If this is too difficult for you, I imagine that Jeffery would serve my needs."

"No. No." Billington ascended the stairs and turned towards the window. He watched the distant lights from the window. Lucy and the Count disappeared into the shadows, but every sound of their activities echoed around him. Every cry, yelp, and bestial howl was a lash upon his heart.

He lacked the courage to resist the Count, to help himself. How could he rescue the poor child?

17 AUGUST 189-

BILLINGTON ADJUSTED HIS life to serve the Count. He slept late in the mornings and napped in the early afternoon to work as needed into the evening. The Count did not greet him in the customary fashion, but instead appeared behind his desk and issued orders. Tonight it was: "You will have the boxes delivered as instructed."

There was an urgency in the Count's voice. Had something changed? "I shall have the matter arranged by first light, Master."

"Rouse men from their taverns or beds this night. Pay well for strong backs and silence." The Count's moods could shift like a tempest at sea. Billington could imagine them becoming deadly if the Count were displeased.

"I shall attend to this at once." Billington paused a moment, trying to discern if it was safe to ask the questions rising in his mind. "With such short notice...it will be difficult to ensure the deed is done unobserved."

"Tonight. My betrothed are returning to London." Was that a hint of desperation in the Count's voice? "I aim to follow and claim what is mine."

Billington's rational mind wanted the beast gone from his life, but his appetites pained him so at the thought of the Count's abandonment. "What of me?"

"You are becoming too familiar, Billington. Complete your duties. Should I need you, I shall call for you."

21 SEPTEMBER 189-

BILLINGTON WOKE THAT morning with a pain in his stomach. He stumbled out of bed onto his knees and crawled to his water closet where he vomited a putrid black bile. Jeffery carried him back to bed and summoned Doctor Mitchell despite Billington's weak protests.

"Whatever happened seems to have a good effect upon you, Mr. Billington." If Doctor Mitchell found anything unusual about Jeffery's presence, he said nothing. "If anything, the color of your cheeks seems better than I've noted in weeks. You are breathing better and your heart sounds strong. Stay in bed today and I'll check in on you this evening. I trust that Jeffery will remain with you. Consider it doctor's orders."

Jeffery nodded, the gesture of a doting wife, not a clerk. "Of course, Doctor."

Billington didn't feel up to disagreeing. The cook brought up a plate of eggs and toast. He ate quietly while reading the London periodicals. The world always moved forward even when he was ill, after all.

A minor article caught his eye. He read it a number of times and felt as though he would vomit once more. Lucy Westenra had died of anemia. That poor girl! Her death was as much on his hands as those of the monster he willingly served.

He held Jeffery close and wept.

29 SEPTEMBER 189-

BILLINGTON WAITED IN his office while Jeffery built a fire. He felt his age very much in the cold weather. The file waited on his desk. Jeffery walked past and gingerly touched Billington's back. "I can stay. Everyone else went home."

"There are some things in the world I want you not to have to experience, Jeffery."

"I'll withstand any experience as long as it is with you." He took hold of and kissed Billington's hand. "Let me stay."

"If you promise to stay out of sight and not be seen, you may stay. I want your hands clean on this matter." In truth, he was afraid that the Count might be nearby to punish him. Billington kissed the young man on the lips and pulled him close. "I will tell you all tonight."

Jeffery accepted the kiss and the requirements. Billington released his hold and swatted him on the bottom. "I need to prepare. Let in Mr. Harker when he arrives and leave us be until I summon you."

He compiled the shipping manifests onto a new ledger. He looked at each of the addresses. The Count had been quite exact in which properties he wanted to secure. The beast had rejected a number of perfectly respectable properties for some unknown reason. Hubris? Perhaps. A weakness? More likely.

Six of the boxes had been transported to the east end of London near Mile End New Town, surrounded by Spitalfields. He remembered that the properties had come quite cheap as they were just off Brick Lane in the heart of the parish where the Whitechapel murders had occurred a decade previous. What manner of evil did the Count plan at those vile locations?

Harker arrived late in the afternoon, haggard and terrified with streaks of white in his hair. Billington knew then that the Count's murderous attentions had come to rest on Miss Mina.

"Mr. Billington, I apologize for the lack of niceties, but I was hoping to look at your papers regarding Dracula."

Billington opened the folder, not wanting to reveal how much he knew. Harker blanched at the sight of the some of the papers. "Forgive me but I saw these papers upon the Count's desk. How much did he plan so far ahead? How can we fight him?"

The man's tone held only despair.

Billington knew that feeling well when the Count threatened Jeffery. He poured them both a drink. "The Count well knows how to find the weakness in those who would cross him. I've felt the same hopelessness that you must suffer these nights."

"What did you do?"

"By dawn, with some semblance of willpower, I kept track of everything he has done upon our shores in the hope that one day someone would have the resolve to fight him. I am no academic or occultist, but the Count's demands concerning his crates of native soil suggested a desperation, perhaps even a weakness. I know where the earth was delivered." Billington offered to Harker the accountings of the properties sheltering the crates. "I knew you would come this morning and prepared these papers for you."

Later, when he sheltered Jeffrey in his arms, he would tell him what Harker next said: "Morning always comes."

BLOOFER LADIES

Elka Cloke

JOURNAL OF MISS MINA MURRAY
21 NOVEMBER 1884

THIS is yet another entry that will take up many days' space in my journal. I am not sure how the binders of these diaries think that one half-page is enough to put down all of the things that happen to one in an eventful week, and in an uneventful week why one would wish to record anything at all. One thing I am grateful for about this journal, especially today, is that however small and inexpensive it may have been, it possesses a lock. The source of my thankfulness to that little fastening is that what I am obliged to protect within these pages concerns my very closest friend Lucy. I have mentioned before her somnambulism and that the headmistress is becoming quite accustomed to finding her in my bed by morning regardless of where she had lain down the previous night.

Author's Notes:

The dates of these documents place them before, between and after the entries in *Dracula*. Therefore the reader may, if desired, read both texts alongside one another.

"Though Lucy is described as dark-haired, on page 147 Van Helsing is described as having 'brushed Lucy's hair, so that it lay on the pillow in its usual sunny ripples.'" – Leonard Wolf, footnote 3, page 189, *The Annotated Dracula*.

The room all the girls share is large and cold, surrounded by dark wood paneling from floor to ceiling carved with an egg and dart motif and broken only by the lamps high on the walls at regular intervals. The small iron bed frames are painted white and stand each beneath its own dormer window with a lace coverlet, one pillow and one woolen blanket. Each girl is allowed one chair for dressing, one trunk and a small washstand.

The fire is at the far end of the hall, closest to the elder students and farthest from the newer ones. Brass andirons with round knobs at the top and a fireback with an embossed galleon in full sail complete the fireplace. There is a picture rail along the wall but the only thing hanging from it is a silver crucifix over the door.

In the late spring months it can be quite comfortable to sleep with a dormer window propped open, lace curtains gently billowing in the breeze, listening to the sounds of birds from trees on the school grounds. By winter it becomes cold despite the coals. Moonlight through the lace casts patterns on the walls which shift whenever a cloud passes over. This particular November has been bitter with rain and wind and the moaning of the wind around the roof seems to excite Lucy particularly to sleepwalking.

It therefore was no surprise to me to wake in the low firelight with Lucy's warm pale limbs around me, her small bare feet between mine and one of her hands clutching a lock of my hair. Her eyes were open, gazing directly into mine. They were nearly black from the dilation of the pupil with scarcely a ring of pale blue to separate black from white. The expression on her face was tranquil. I wondered for a moment if she had taken to sleepwalking with her eyes open.

Then she leaned forward and kissed me on the mouth with surprising passion. Her kiss was deliberate and sensual. I felt pulled under by it by a rising tide of longing strong enough to border on pain. I became acutely aware of how little separated the two of us; mere muslin threads and my own sense of civility. That was all. I admit to a thrill that ran all through me as I trembled despite the warmth of her body. I pulled away, not without a moment's hesitation. Lucy had not missed that hesitation or the frailty of will it implied.

"Do I frighten you?" she whispered, her warm breath on my neck causing my pulse to quicken alarmingly.

I was frightened and overcome by thoughts and sensations, acutely aware that she was still so close to me, still wrapped in my bed sheets, still clutching my hair. I wanted to hold her again, to feel the sweet softness of her. I shook my head no, not trusting to my voice. Yet this was not enough to reassure her as to my reaction.

"You have nothing to fear from me, dearest Mina." There was still something in her manner, a tension, a tone of possessiveness that was more than ordinary. It must have shown on my face that I thought so, for she went on. "What we do is our own affair, you see? We can pretend we are spinsters together who have only each other for company. Who would question spinsters? Please say we shall be very old together, you and I!"

"Spinsters?"

"Like the Mrs. Lakes," she replied enigmatically. I again suspected she might somehow be asleep, that her dreams had begun that kiss. I knew that in the midst of one of her episodes it could be harmful to wake her, so I waited. "They were friends who knew each other at school, and then they were married women and could not be together for their husbands' sakes, and then they were widows who lived together and even shared the same bed. Like sisters, my mother says. Could we not be like the Mrs. Lakes?"

I saw then what her thoughts had been in the moments she had been watching my face whilst I slept. Lately she had begun to ask what my plans were after the spring. She and I had been nearly inseparable these last five years. She had begun to speak bitterly of the year she would spend here without me after I left and to question me with a sort of desperate persistence as to my marriage prospects afterwards. Once, in a fit of crying, she tried to make me promise that whosoever I married would not live too far from her.

I dared not tell her that the Headmistress had already come to me to discuss the possibility of my staying on to teach etiquette, since Lucy's mother was planning on giving the school a charitable endowment and no doubt Lucy in her current state of mind and with her characteristic charm would induce her mother to make my position a requirement of the gift. I wanted to know that I had been given my duties on my own merit and not merely to please Lucy's family. It was likewise pointless to suggest to Lucy that her beauty and good breeding would make it very likely that she would be married before me, if in fact I were ever to be married at all. She wouldn't hear it said that I was anything less than a great beauty and my station was as meaningless to her at age eighteen as it had been at twelve.

"You will never have to worry about being alone, sweet Lucy," I reassured her, pressing my forehead to hers, "you will attract the fancy of all you meet. Of that you can be sure."

"I don't want the fancy of all I meet!" she stated petulantly, "I want to be with you!" She took my face in her hands and gazed at it with disquieting intensity. "Swear to me that you will not get engaged," she begged.

"Oh, Lucy!"

"Swear to me…or I don't know what I'll do." This was the child Lucy talking, not the young woman. Whenever I disregarded a demand from her during our early friendship she would respond with the vague yet somehow sinister threat of "I don't know what I'll do." I was determined lately not to be won over by this tactic.

"But how are we to be old widows together if we never marry?" I countered, appealing to logic. "Like the Mrs. Lakes? They were very good friends when they were married ladies and spent many happy hours alone together. I am sure of it."

Her eyes looked me over in the firelight gently and longingly, her breath still the deep, soft breathing of sleep. Her hair in the firelight was like a halo of spun gold with wisps escaping from under the white linen cap. Although it was all blonde no single strand of it was exactly the same color as any other. Her cheeks were flushed despite the cold of the room. Her face had shed its childhood plumpness and become, just in these last two years, the face of a beautiful woman. Nevertheless each time I looked at her there was a moment where I saw her exactly as she had first appeared to me when she arrived at school in a lilac velvet traveling cloak with a matching bow in her hair so large that at first she had seemed to be just two extremely large periwinkle-blue eyes and a bow with scarcely a girl at all attached to them. Now even the dull school uniforms could not wholly conceal the fullness of her figure.

"You shall have your choice of prospects, Lucy, but think of me. I must marry where I can and hope that the match is good enough to allow me to continue to associate with you. I could hardly remain your friend and a penniless spinster, not when you are a lady, now could I?"

She looked startled, and tears sprang to her eyes. "Oh, Mina, I have been terrible to you! I have been cruel!" I felt sorry for having mentioned any of it then and I held her more tightly, pulling the duvet more closely around her and wrapping the two of us together. Something came together in her eyes and she nodded. "I see now that you must marry," she said resolutely. Her somber manner in regards to this possible future happy event was too much for me and I confess I laughed softly, but she took no offense. "And if you marry then I must marry too, for it wouldn't do for just one of us to be a married woman, but, Mina, please tell me you know that I would never cease to be your friend, were you the poorest and most pitiful person in all the world!"

What could I say to that? "I believe you, darling," I replied, kissing her. She fell asleep some time later but it was many hours before I could close my eyes. I lay there watching the coals flicker in the grate, the iron galleon seeming tossed on seas of fire and the large round tops of the andirons reflecting the room upside down and in miniature like gazing balls. I stared at them as if I could indeed see the future there, hoping that I would soon be offered employment at the school and thus defer parting from Lucy for another year. Even after a year, to stay on would mean holidays in which I could see Lucy, which a governess position might not allow. I believe that she truly has no idea what it would mean to be poor or a spinster, not from selfishness but out of a type of innocence which never fails to move me when it makes itself apparent. She believes that good people are rewarded and also that everyone is good and therefore to her it is impossible that she or anyone she loves might not get everything that their heart desires. She is too good herself to believe otherwise.

As for the manner of her kiss, I cannot believe that any harm can come of it. If it were not for the lock on this diary I would hesitate even to write of it but I know there is no perversion her There cannot possibly be. I pray only that I will always be so blessed as to have a friend in Lucy even when we are very old, like the Mrs. Lakes.

LETTER FROM MISS LUCY WESTENRA TO HER MOTHER 21 DECEMBER 1885

DEAREST "MÈRE,"

I hope this letter finds you in the best of health and that the cough which bothered you when I visited last is completely gone! My studies are going well. I have made more of an effort to work hard this year and I fancy I shall be the most devoted pupil in the whole school. Even the French Mistress is impressed with my improvement and says that I shall not have to put up with a tutor over the holiday which is good news indeed! We shall have all our time for each other!

My favorite class, you will be proud to learn, is Etiquette. There is "no more important skill for a young lady of quality to possess," or so Mina is always saying. Oh, but I have said too much! You will have the whole story at once, then, since I am all happiness! My dearest friend Mina Murray, whom you remember was to finish last year, has stayed on to teach us Etiquette and Decorum and she is the most delightful of all the teachers. Certainly she is a good deal prettier than Miss Vogel, our German Mistress, who is nearly ninety if she is a day and is always calling me "Lizzy."

Mina has been so helpful to me this year, even spending hours in the evening speaking to me only in French so that we can improve our accents. She is like a savior from a fairy tale, rescuing me from ill manners and worse pronunciation!

Oh, *do* say we can have her to Christmas with us! She is such a good influence on me. She will be no trouble at all. You need not even make up the spare room since she can share a bed with me as we did when she was still a student, before she went to stay in the staff quarters which are very drafty I am sure and where she will no doubt catch cold if she stays in December. And you know, she has nowhere else to go. We will entertain you in the evenings if you like or if you would prefer to rest we will amuse ourselves and be quite out of your hair, so to speak.

Write to me today and tell me if I can invite her. Every hour I wait for your reply.

Your loving "fille,"
LUCY

P.S. If you send me some new pink thread I will embroider a rose on a Christmas ornament for you. I have learned a new way to do a rose so that it looks wind-blown, which I know you like.

LETTER FROM MISS MINA MURRAY TO MISS LUCY WESTENRA 22 AUGUST 1886

DEAREST LUCY,

I am writing you with the most wonderful news! Jonathan and I are engaged. It was over the recent trip I took to Exeter. I'm sure you have expected something like this since I began to correspond with him, but I never sought it. I wanted only to assure myself that what little income I had from my position at the school would be safely cared for, oh, but he was so helpful that we became good friends.

He took me to tea at a little shop on High Street and afterwards to Bicton Gardens. We wandered through the Italian Garden which was designed in 1735 by André Le Nôtre, whose plan of Versailles earned him his reputation.

It had been recently updated with lovely floral borders but, the sun being nearly blinding there, we did not stop to admire them. We were talking of his future plans and the warm weather, as it was rather a hot day, until we came to a little glade entirely filled with large ferns where we were afforded a measure of shade and solitude. I would have felt quite nervous if I had thought for a moment he intended to propose on this walk but I thought he was only being kind to me for old times' sake and perhaps out of his own loneliness. He directed me to sit down on a stone bench but then remained standing with his hands in his pockets as if he did not know what to do with them.

"I have something of great importance to discuss with you," he said then, and his voice wavered a little. I assured him that he could discuss anything with me and that I would be honored to have my opinion held in such high regard by a man of his integrity and good character. He then confided in me that he had been told his clerkship would end soon and that he would be given a position as solicitor in the company, working closely with his mentor Mr. Hawkins. He then told me that he had been advised to chose a wife suitable for his future position and that Mr. Hawkins, that dear man, whom I had no idea I had so impressed, had advised him to choose me!

He, Jonathan that is, told me I was both beautiful and honorable, both hardworking and kind, and that he loved me and would have no other. At first I was completely overwhelmed, unaccustomed as I am to such lavish praise except from you. And now you can say "I told you so" a thousand times because it was you who said he sounded like an admirer when he first wrote although I could not bring myself to believe you.

I have accepted him of course, and now I can look happily forward to the years of having you and your certain-to-be-fine future husband to my table with dignity and pride! Oh, Lucy! I did not think I was so expectant of this day. I have always been taught to rely on myself and indeed I have become quite capable but there is something about being able to depend upon a man which makes one feel as though everything will be all right. I am sure God is preparing for you a day not far off when you will know what I mean!

The wedding will not be until at least a year from now since Jonathan wisely wants to wait until we can afford to have a home together immediately afterwards. It would not do to marry now and afterwards each come home to our separate lodgings and employment in separate towns! So it will be a long engagement. I shall need you to help me with my wedding dress and am so looking forward to shopping with you. Perhaps we shall go to London if your mother is well enough to travel?

Congratulate me, my darling,
Your loving MINA

LETTER FROM MISS LUCY WESTENRA TO MISS MINA MURRAY 23 AUGUST 1886

DEAREST DARLING MINA!

Please I beg of you do not read any letter which may come from me from yesterday! I was in a bit of a "state" as Mother sometimes calls it because I was feeling somewhat ill although I am much better now. Mother says I am not to have more than one cream pastry and puts it down to acidity in the lemonade which I confess I drank three of since the pastries were so sweet and I needed something with which to temper the overwhelming sugary-ness! I wrote you a letter in that state which I have since told the footman not to deliver but he says it may have gone out anyway. Now I regret that letter and hope against hope that you will never receive it but I cannot be certain!

I felt at the time quite unable to be happy about anything and foolishly I wrote to you telling you not to get married, that if you did you would not be *free*, you see, to come and visit me here whenever you pleased and that if you did you would have to stay in a room with Jonathan and not with me and would not be able to sit up with me at all hours as we are wont to do.

But of course we have a whole year before any of that comes to pass, perhaps even longer! How terribly selfish of me to write that awful letter when I should be only happy for your happiness! I cannot think what made me do it! Please forgive me!

I think it is not the lemonade but rather that I am mostly bored to near hysteria here with only Mother for company. She is a dear, but she so often has to go and lie down in the afternoons. The doctor has been several times and has told me sternly that she needs peace and quiet and to be insulated from all possible shocks, so I am tiptoeing around at teatime and cannot go out in the evening unless someone else arrives to chaperone me.

I should love nothing better than to go shopping with you in London! I have told Mother your delightful news and she sends her Congratulations as well and is so pleased to see that you have *done well.* She loves you very much, you know. Mother says she will take you to her personal tailor, when you are ready of course.

I have also been given the strictest instructions that I must make you come to visit us in Whitby next summer! This summer I'm afraid I spent all day talking of you to Mother. Now she says it will do me good to be with you and to that I most wholeheartedly agree! Please say that you will come to Whitby! The salt air will do wonders for both our complexions and you might put on a little weight so you will be nice and plump for the wedding. You cannot possibly refuse!

Looking forward to seeing you in Whitby, and to your future joy,

Your Devoted LUCY

LETTER FROM MISS MINA MURRAY TO MISS LUCY WESTENRA 7 SEPTEMBER 1886

DEAREST LUCY,

First of all so that you do not feel troubled I will tell you that your second letter arrived before the first and I did not read the first. I did not even open it, and I shall not. My sweet and constant companion! I would never do anything to hurt you, and I know that you must understand me. I will confide in you, although I admit I would hesitate to say such a thing to Jonathan, that one of my chief reasons for wanting to marry was that I knew you were certain to do so and I did not want to watch you move, as I know you shall, gracefully into your true life as I sadly remained behind.

You are the most beautiful girl I have ever encountered. I know I have told you so before and you have never truly believed me, but it is so. It is not merely your rosy cheeks or sweet and fair face which make you beautiful. Your beautiful heart, so full of joy and life, shines out through your face and makes all who see you love you.

One day a man will come and ask you to marry him, as Jonathan has for me. He will see you as I see you and love you with his whole heart. He will be everything you admire and he will take good care of you. You will have a fine house, servants to care for you, beautiful clothes and jewels and of course the love of a family. Do not say that you would remain an old maid with me, for you know that is so much less than you deserve. I want you to be as happy as you can be.

When I marry Jonathan I shall not be as fine a lady as you are, but I shall be an honorably (and I hope, happily) married woman, the wife of a solicitor. As such no one should wonder that you and I remain friends. We shall be married women together, have tea together and watch our children play, grow old together and always be a part of each other's lives. Then I shall never be without your sweet smile or gentle voice.

One day, when you are engaged, you will understand these things. For now I will urge you as I have before to put your faith in me. My love for you will not be altered by time, distance or any change in our situations.

And of course I will join you in Whitby next summer. I am counting the days!

Yours Always,
MINA

JOURNAL OF MISS MINA MURRAY
5 AUGUST 1887

I AM SURE now that Lucy's restlessness at night is simply from missing Arthur. Since I arrived in Whitby it seems to be getting worse. At first I thought my presence in her room would calm her, but ever since we began locking our bedroom door at night she has been watching me when she thinks I am asleep. I can hear her breathing change and feel her eyes on me. Once or twice I opened my eyes a little, without raising the lids, and glanced at her from under my lashes and she was there, wide awake and staring at me as I slept. Last night I determined to call her out on it and opened my eyes fully to look directly into hers.

Her cheeks colored and she looked away, ashamed. Instantly I felt I had done something wrong to call attention to her staring although I am not sure why since she was trying to get my attention. I crept out of bed, went over, sat down on her bed and put my arm around her. Her skin was flushed and she felt warm all over and taut with emotion. Her arms were around me quickly and she kissed me on the mouth, over and over, slow kisses like those she would give to a lover.

"Kiss me as you would Jonathan," she whispered into my ear.

I nearly laughed out loud. I did not have the heart to tell her that I have not kissed Jonathan and he has certainly not tried to kiss me. I can't imagine his whiskered face would feel as soft as Lucy's dear mouth. Kissing her is like kissing the smooth skin of a child.

"Is this how you would kiss Arthur?" I asked.

"I don't know!" she cried, "I don't know how I would…." Her sweet brow furrowed. Then she seemed to come to some sort of decision. "I might hold him like this," she said, throwing the blanket off and wrapping one leg around my hip. Her body was pressed against mine and the curves of her neck were silver in the moonlight from the window. "I might touch him like this," she hissed, her voice taking on a cloying sweetness and her hands sliding under my nightdress.

Her touch sent a little thrill through my whole body which frightened me. I knew I must not get carried away or I would never be able to govern her and she was clearly treading on dangerous ground. I knew why she acted in this way. She was simply nervous about Arthur and how to please him. She wanted practice.

It could not be allowed to happen. Not for her sake, for I am sure her desires were all innocence, but for my own. For so many years now I have watched her dress and undress, brushed her lovely hair, laughed with her, embraced her. I must admit to myself that I have wanted her to touch me just like this. I must admit it so that I can suppress it. Is it not enough that I have the extraordinary privilege of being her closest friend? Is it not enough that she and her family have been so generous to me? Even were I a man I would not be worthy of her, so much the less since I am a mere woman. Lucy is meant for better things: for a man who will be her protector and provider, for the admiration of all society, for the continuation of the honor of her family name, for all these things and more, but not for me. Not in that manner.

Gently, I put her hands aside. "My darling," I told her, "it is for Arthur to show you these things! He will teach you. Don't deny him the right due to him as your husband, and don't fret if you are unsure of how to act or what to do. You will not have to act. He will act for you, as God intended."

She looked up at me for a moment and then turned her head aside and laid it on my breast. She did not try to continue, but stilled her breathing with some difficulty as if she were trying not to cry. I smoothed her hair and held her until she became calm, then returned to my own bed.

I could not sleep for some time, but lay awake with tears of my own silently wetting my pillow. I know that when we are married these childish fears and longings will pass away, transforming into the bonds of holy matrimony, but somehow I suspect that I will not love Lucy less even then, or indeed ever.

JOURNAL OF MISS LUCY WESTENRA
10 AUGUST 1887

I HAVE NOT felt well of late. I cannot tell anyone what I feel for fear that I may be going mad, but I shall commit my thoughts to this journal so that perhaps one day I can look back on them and know that I have been very silly indeed. I shall hide this journal, I MUST! If Mina or Mother were to find it I'm sure it would only worry them needlessly. Oh, I am afraid, afraid all the time, but I do not know of what!

The thing I fear most at the moment is to dream, for my dreams are so…I don't know what. I wake up full of intense longing so that I want to run or scream and it is all I can do to lie quietly in my bed and calm my beating heart. I dreamed that I was on a ship traveling under the moonlit sky. Oh, but that is not quite right. I was not on the ship but ABOVE it, flying if you will, and I could feel my wings beating around me like a great black cloak in the wind. There was a young man on the deck below me. At first he merely gazed out at the water but then he seemed to hear me. He looked up and cried out, something not in English, Russian perhaps, and then I swooped down upon him and he nearly died of fright! I awoke and Mina was still asleep. I could not fathom at first how she had slept through all the screaming and then I recalled that I was in my room and that I must have been dreaming.

I tried to get back to sleep but I was so afraid to dream again! I have bit my lip as well, since when I awoke my mouth was full of the taste of blood. The worst part is that I feel no remorse for what I do. I can feel the joy of flight. I smile as I fall onto the poor helpless young man and the taste of blood is sweet to me!

I told myself these were merely nightmares although they were nothing like any nightmare I have ever had before. Then came the news of the shipwreck and when I saw the ship there on the strand it was the same vessel I had seen in my dream! What can it mean?

Then we went to the funeral of that poor brave sea captain yesterday and something so odd and frightening happened. Mina and I were walking our usual path up the cliff to sit in the little graveyard overlooking the sea with its tumbledown tombstones and all their quaint inscriptions, so as to listen to the funeral from that lovely spot. There was an old man there with whom Mina likes to talk but he was found dead with his neck broken, in exactly that spot. It was so sad. Perhaps that was what made me so afraid, but then there was the dog, but I get ahead of myself. There was a grave there, Mina's

Ancient Mariner said it is the grave of a suicide which should not bother me now since it never did before. Today there was a little dog who was also there for the funeral, with its owner, and was staring at me in a most upsetting way. The dog was barking and barking. I looked at the grave and for an instant I felt PRESSURE in my mind, as if someone were staring at me from inside the grave. I could hear a wicked whispered laughter of which no one else took any notice! At the same time as I heard the laugh the little dog became so frightened he trembled all over! It was almost as if the dog had heard it as well!

Now that I put it down into words it seems so silly. Am I really afraid because of a few bad dreams, a sound which on that cliff could simply have been the wind and the fact that a dog was barking in a graveyard? Oh, it is foolish! And yet I cannot shake it. If only Arthur were here. He would tell me I was imagining it all so convincingly that I would believe it as well and then everything would be back the way it was.

Mina has tried to calm me. She took me for the longest walk in the sunshine to Robin Hood's Bay and back. We had cream tea and rested in the shade of a fairy glen. Mina looked almost like a fairy herself, with her dainty face and masses of dark hair above the brown traveling coat she wore, floating in between the trunks of trees. The afternoon passed in a pleasant way. We sat together on a rock at the side of the stream exhausted by our exertions and I nearly fell asleep on her soft shoulder listening to the distant boom of the waves. I lay looking at her white neck. Her pulse seemed to beat very slowly in time with the distant ocean sounds and the worst aching feeling came over me as if I had to hold on to Mina as tightly as possible or she would slip away from me forever and yet I felt so happy – a happiness full of the sharpest pain. To have been any happier I feel would have brought on some terrible fate! Oh, I cannot explain! If only I could have remained there forever, I know I would have done so in perfect peace.

When we got home the pleasant exhaustion of the day began to wane and as night came on the longing for this *unknown thing* came upon me again and made me feel so restless! I excused myself as soon as I could under the pretense that I was tired but when I was alone I regretted it. I have the sense that Death approaches me, so close that I can feel the breath of the Angel of Death on the back of my neck! I must be brave, for Mina's sake, and smile and be gay if I can. I shall try.

JOURNAL OF MISS LUCY WESTENRA 11 AUGUST 1887

How can I ever express my gratitude to my darling, brave Mina for the actions she took on my behalf last night? Truly, in her place I do not know that I could have done the same. But she is so Strong! She is so Good! If it were possible for two women to marry, I would break it off with Arthur instantly and marry Mina! It is to Mina that I owe my life, though I know I can never repay her in kind I will be all my life ever so grateful and give her all my love and perhaps that will be enough!

I again had one of my awful dreams, I was walking through the ruined Abbey on the cliff and all around me was darkness, storm clouds and wind. I was wearing a light sheet of some kind and the wind and mist blew right through it until it clung to my skin. I felt more than ever drawn towards Death, and yet I felt no fear and only an overwhelming calm and a longing for The End. There was a noise, a howling all around as if all the dogs in town had begun baying at once.

Inside the Abbey it suddenly stopped and all was silence and stillness. Even the wind seemed to have stopped. All the way in the back, where the chancel would have been, I saw two red lights. I thought of the candles that would have been on the altar there, but they were too close together. They rose up and up until I had the feeling that they were looking at me from the height of a man.

Then there WAS a man there, a stranger to me whose black hair and glossy black satin cloak had hidden him from my sight except for the eyes. The folds of the cloak came falling slowly open then like two great black wings, revealing a silk lining of darkest red which was almost black itself in the shadows of the Abbey and a pale face with full dark lips. The mouth smiled at me under those red eyes and Oh! The teeth in that mouth! The whiteness of the teeth!

I wanted to run then, to scream, but I was utterly drained of all vital force! I could only stand there as he glided towards me and folded the cold smooth silk of his cloak around me to hide me forever in his vile embrace! I must have been suffering from the terrible shock of it for I remember only a pang of sharpness at my throat and the sound of water and then I felt as if I were being lifted off the ground....

Oh, but I cannot bear to describe it. I think of it now and wish I had died truly.

I thought of Mina then, as a last farewell and as if my thought of her had brought light out of darkness there suddenly was a shaft of moonlight which struck me. In that moment it seemed a sort of Omen. I felt my soul being pulled out of my body. I felt cold inside and knew, distantly and without hope, that I would die.

Then the man was gone and Mina was beside me, shaking me awake and wrapping me in a warm shawl! She half carried me home and in my state it was only when we reached the pavement that I noticed that she was wearing only her nightdress, having used the shawl she was wearing herself to cover me and that she had not even put on any shoes! Her poor feet were getting cut by the gravel in the road, but she would not stop for a moment nor show any pain. Her only thought was for me.

How dear and how brave she is! To have run out into the night unshod, in only a shawl, thoughtless of her own safety! My dear Mina! My most darling and wonderful Mina!

I cannot speak of this to anyone, and yet I know she will ask. I will try to make light of it if I can so as not to worry her and will say nothing of dying and nothing of the Red Eyed Man! She must not know that I was seen and certainly not that he touched me in any way. I will be brave like Mina, and keep my despair to myself. Oh, but I am so tired. I will sleep a little more today, and then perhaps I will be strong enough to play the part.

JOURNAL OF MISS LUCY WESTENRA 20 AUGUST 1887

I SAW MINA off at the train station today. I felt so miserable and afraid, and she was so happy. I didn't have the courage to cry out "Mina, don't go!" as I so wanted to. But it is for the best of course, since she is going to Jonathan whom she is to marry in Buda-Pest. I will not even be able to go to the wedding and when she comes home it will be to her own home with her husband and not to me.

My only consolation is that she has left her trunk with me, so I know I will see her again when she comes to London to fetch it. Hopefully she will fetch it and not merely send for it. No, she would not do that! She would want to see me.

I cannot shake the feeling that I will die and never see her again, but I know it is selfish of me to keep her here out of my silly fears. After all, Arthur is coming and Mina says he will protect me and make me well.

Buda-Pest! It sounds so far away and foreign! God keep my darling Mina, and God have mercy on me!

JOURNAL OF MRS. JONATHAN HARKER
24 AUGUST 1887

TONIGHT IS MY wedding night. I am up alone in my room, Jonathan being too ill to spend the night with me despite our being just married. Some might think I should be sad about this, but truthfully I am all joy! Jonathan is alive and that is enough for me. I am in no hurry for anything else. The minister who was to marry us in England did take me aside and tell me what a woman should expect on her wedding night. It sounded unpleasant, although he assured me I should come to enjoy it in time. I am certain he couldn't have imagined anything like this – a quiet night in a convent!

I do not know what to make of the tale the Sister told me concerning Jonathan's ordeal. I long to return home, but it will be some time before he will be strong enough to travel. When he is sleeping I take long walks. The city is very picturesque and has a haunted feeling about it especially in the mist as Buda Castle, which has been recently restored, rises out of banks of the Danube. I look out my convent window and see Turkish architecture mixed in among the massive churches, the remnants of ancient wars. It is easy to imagine that the city is named after a relative of Attila the Hun, as the guidebook says. It feels like the capital of the edge of civilization. I wish Lucy were here to see it with me, she would love the way it all feels like an adventure.

I shall endeavor to bring Lucy back some of the unique lace they sell in the market here if I have the time. She might like it for her trousseau. I hope Lucy is as happy with Arthur as I am now with dear Jonathan. And now, to sleep. Jonathan will need me tomorrow. Oh, happy night.

JOURNAL OF MISS LUCY WESTENRA
24 AUGUST 1887

I WILL HIDE this journal in Mina's trunk, at the very bottom where Mother will not think to look for it. She saw me writing in it on the train and talked for so long about how "admirable" my keeping it is that I became worried she might look into it, just to check on my state of mind. I cannot allow that! I have read over the things I have written and she would have quite a terrible shock.

Instead I shall start keeping a new one. The new one shall say most things, but I shall keep this one in case I should want to write true secrets down somewhere. Oh, I must go, Arthur is at the door. Good-bye for now, little book!

JOURNAL OF MISS LUCY WESTENRA 2 SEPTEMBER 1887

THIS AFTERNOON I had a most upsetting talk with Dr. Seward. He came for lunch with Mother and me and I knew right away he had not come for a social visit. How he knew something was wrong I do not know, but he arrived looking for it. I felt his eyes on me from the moment he entered, all sincere and serious and concerned in that way of his, but for a while I had thought that if I pretended hard enough to be happy he would believe it and go away.

Well, he did no such thing. After lunch Mother went to lie down and we were left alone. I went up to my bedroom but he followed me even there. The way he looked at me made me quite nervous and I went and opened a window just so he would not see the look on my face. I wasn't going to tell him about the dreams, because I just know he will tell Arthur and then Arthur will be worried and all on my account!

I did tell him, though I stopped myself from telling all, because he would question me so and he simply would not go away! I was so tired that the pressure of the sunlight in the room felt like a weight all over my body and all I wanted to do was sleep. It has been like this all week. Fortunately the moment the sun sets I seem to get back some energy. Perhaps I am walking in my sleep again. Oh, if only Mina were here!

Thankfully Dr. Seward has gone and I am alone. I believe I have fooled him for now, since he agreed to meet with me at the stores tomorrow as if nothing were wrong. Twilight will be here soon. I know I should get up and close the window so as not to catch cold, but I cannot. I will sleep a little, wake later, and see how I feel.

JOURNAL OF MISS LUCY WESTENRA 3 SEPTEMBER 1887

YESTERDAY I SAID I had tricked Dr. Seward, but it appears I did not. Today he came to the house with a very old man from Amsterdam whose heavy accent amused me at first until I had got to know him. His name is Dr. Van

Helsing, and I can tell he knows what is wrong with me, but not if he is friend or foe.

He came into the parlor and sat across from me and talked of his journey, the weather, how lovely the fall is here, until I thought him quite harmless. Then all at once he asked, no, commanded that I send Dr. Seward out into the garden so that he might talk with me alone. He did it in such a manner that I was taken off guard and obeyed before I could think why.

Once we were alone he questioned me in a most curious manner. He asked about the dreams and seemed to know exactly what I had dreamed. He even asked about the red eyes and the dark man who I saw that night! He knew about the howling of the dogs, which I have told no one but Mina, and about the bat by my window although I have told no one about that!

Several times when I answered him he got up and paced about the room and once he shook his head and said, quietly under his breath "*Nee, niet heer en England.*"

He then looked at my neck, which was covered in a high collar today because the pin pricks Mina says she gave me when she fastened the shawl about my neck have not yet healed. I was oddly thankful that he did not see the marks, although I do not know why. It was almost as if I felt *something else* in my thoughts, like I had in the dreams, and that something told me to be ashamed of the marks and never reveal them. I wanted to tell him, but the compulsion was so strong that I found I could not.

Dr. Van Helsing then brought me in front of the mirror, examined my teeth, took my pulse and went out to speak with Dr. Seward in the hall. The look that he cast back at me as he left the room was full of anger! It frightened me.

The result of all this medical stuff is that I shall be watched daily by Dr. Seward who is to telegram Dr. Van Helsing if anything changes. I feel both afraid and comforted by turns to know that I shall be constantly watched. If only I could have someone in my room with me at night, but to ask that of Dr. Seward would be most improper. If only Mina were here! I shall try to keep the window closed for several days and see that I do not catch cold. What sweet friends I have to make such a fuss over me. There are still times when I feel the coming of death but I shall get well, I must get well, for everyone's sake!

LETTER FROM LUCY'S MOTHER TO HER SOLICITOR, 13 SEPTEMBER 1887

To Mr. Barton, Solicitor

My Dear Mr. Barton,

I hope this letter finds you well. I am writing to tell you that despite your misgivings I have decided to go ahead and make those changes to my will. Lucy is simply not well, I am afraid. Our dear friend Dr. Van Helsing has come from Amsterdam and is assisting Dr. Seward with her care. He is taking such excellent care of her and of me. I know that he has our best interests at heart and that he would never suggest anything that would harm poor Lucy.

As per his instructions I am ordering you to make Lord Godalming my sole beneficiary. Lucy will be in his care as his wife and I have no doubts as to the good fortune of that, thanks be to God! Dr. Van Helsing has instructed me to make sure you know that absolutely no assets of any kind are to be released to Lucy without Lord Godalming present. I am certain that his reasons are sound and that it is all for the best.

If you will send someone around with the papers I will sign them today.

Sincerely,

Mrs. Westenra

JOURNAL OF MRS. JONATHAN HARKER 21 SEPTEMBER 1887

So much has happened in so few days. I regret that I could not steal away from Mr. Hawkins' funeral even for a few minutes to visit with Lucy. I feel as if I need to see her, the way one needs food or sleep. I cannot go so long without her. Patience must be my teacher, for we will be together soon and then afterwards we will be together always. My one consolation in such a sad homecoming and the loss of poor dear Mr. Hawkins is that our (that is, Jonathan and my) social position has greatly improved. It will now be not only possible but quite simple to continue to see Lucy at least once per week and sometimes more often than that. Exeter is not so far from the Godalming estate after all and we shall also be able to afford to summer in Whitby together every year. I shall no longer be dependent upon the kindness of Lucy's dear mother.

I comfort myself by imagining all the days of my life entwined with hers, two properly married women, inseparable, going forward with responsibility and propriety into motherhood and then old age together, sharing all life's joys and burdens. Our husbands will be by our sides to love and provide for us and we shall both be so happy. No sadness, even the loss of our dear benefactor, could take from me that sweet dream. Lucy, soon I will see you and we shall embrace each other for the first time as two married women!

JOURNAL OF MISS LUCY WESTENRA 26 SEPTEMBER 1887

THE EVENTS OF the last few days seem like an awful nightmare but in my heart I know that they are all too real. I shall set them down here so as to keep some link to who I WAS, which is slipping away forever! My last memory of life was in my own bed. The tall dark man with the red eyes had come again, and again he defiled me! He held me down to the bed and pierced my neck with his wicked teeth, then – Oh, Horror – he forced my head to his breast where he had cut himself with one sharp fingernail and held it there until I was forced to drink his blood.

I must have fainted then, or rather I thought I fainted but now I know the truth. I have died. There, I have written it and now it must be true. I am dead. And yet, here I am with Mina's trunk in the churchyard in Whitby, writing in my little secret diary, wearing Mina's clothes (Mina, forgive me!) and remembering.

I awoke in a tomb, all lit with candles and surrounded by garlic. There was a sheet over me and that was all I had with which to cover myself. I thought there must have been some mistake, so I went out and tried to get into the church so as to seek help. I was stopped, I know not by what, but the threshold of the church was like a wall of invisible iron! I walked until I came to Hampstead Heath and climbed up the hill in the growing dusk. I was so hungry! Never in my life have I been so hungry, but to smell food cooking sickened me.

There were a group of little children playing at the top of the hill. One stopped, looking up at me with large innocent eyes under thick dark lashes. His hair was dark as well and his skin was fair. He reminded me a little of Mina. He seemed so sweet and gentle. I wondered if he could tell me where I was. I called him to me and he came, smiling and running with that almost falling run that very young children sometimes still have. He came up to me without any fear and put his arms around my neck.

"You're a beautiful lady," he said shyly, hiding his face on my shoulder, only because he was just a child and the word "beautiful" was too difficult for him it turned out "You're a bloofer lady."

I turned to him to kiss his soft neck and cradle his little body in my arms, to stroke his silken jet black hair and smell his sweet child smell. Then, oh God have Mercy on my Soul, I was overwhelmed by the awful hunger and bit the poor child! I felt my teeth sink deep into his neck and his sweet blood swelled into my mouth as I drank and drank! A pleasant sort of calm came over me as I drank and stroked his darling little limbs. Only when I began to feel his pulse slow and the blood flow more weakly did I realize that I was about to kill him! The most horrible thing was that it would have been so very easy to do!

I threw him down and ran home, where I saw a "for let" sign in the window and all of the household things being loaded onto a truck. I tried to go into the house to get my clothes and coat but the smell of the garlic flowers was so repulsive I actually couldn't stand it. Mina's trunk was among the things already outside and I took it. I dragged it into an alley and it came quite easily although it must have been very heavy. In that alley I threw away the sheet which I had been wearing like Persephone and dressed myself as best I could in Mina's clothes. I thought of sending a letter to Arthur. Surely he would help me. Then I realized that I had no money.

I hid the trunk in the alley, taking this diary with me, and ran to the solicitor's office, which was still open since they do keep some late hours. I was shown in, but given the rudest reception with which I have ever had to contend! The clerk there told me that his records showed that I was dead, which at the time I believed to be obviously untrue, and also told me that Mother had made Arthur her heir and left me nothing, nothing at all! I was not allowed to withdraw so much as a farthing! It seems she did this at the advice of that Dr. Van Helsing, curse him!

There was nothing for me to do but wander around the town all night then. I was still very hungry but determined not to hurt any child. I made my way to Whitechapel. The streets were empty but for the mist and a few old drunks. As I walked around someone took me by the shoulder, and then when he saw my hair was blonde under the hat said "Begging yer pardon, Miss, but you do look just the girl who works at the bakery on this corner. Other than she has dark hair, that is." After he walked on I went to the bakery window and saw my doppelgänger there, already baking. Indeed she and

I were very alike, of the same height, figure and shape of face. Even our eyes were a similar color. Watching her I felt I was looking into a mirror. The effect was heightened by the fact that I could not see myself in the window glass, only her. It was very odd since I could see the whole street but not myself. It was as if I did not exist.

Then I began to think that if I did not exist it did not matter what I did or did not do. If nothing I did was real, then could I not do anything I wanted? I had always wondered what it would be like to kiss myself. I have kissed my own face in the mirror many times, but the cold glass was not like my own lips. I wanted to know. I wanted to kiss her mouth and tangle her dark hair with my blonde hair, somewhere out of the light.

I watched until she came out the back door of the shop to toss the rubbish and then grabbed her, placing my hand over her mouth so she could not scream. She bit me on the hand and even drew a little blood but then she went limp and then just quietly moaned as if too tired to move. I drained her as near death as I could, to sate the hunger. Then, when she was quiet, I kissed her lips. There was blood on her mouth and mine, mingling together, tasting so thick and sweet. I fell into a languid dream in which her softness and the sound of her heart were all there was in the world. The warmth of her blood took the chill from inside me. Then I heard her heart begin to slow, and I became afraid that I had killed her. I got up from her body, wiping the blood on her apron and hurriedly went out into the street to tell the first constable I passed that a girl was hurt. I hoped I had done her no lasting harm.

Then I felt a bit better, for a while, but as dawn began to come closer I felt unbearable pressure and it got worse the further I got from the churchyard and lessened as I approached. It drove me on and on! I remembered my dreams of flying and with a small effort of will I flew up over the lamps and through the mist, with the terrible pressure growing all around me. I think I got back in just in time for as the sun came up it was like a knife in my eyes. I lay down in the coffin and pulled the lid over myself so that all was dark. It was only then that I thought to take my own pulse, as Dr. Seward once did, to see if maybe I was ill and this was all a fever dream. Imagine my despair to find that I had none! What Devil was the man with the red eyes? What did he do to me? Oh, God in Heaven, what kind of devil am I?

JOURNAL OF MISS LUCY WESTENRA
29 SEPTEMBER 1887

IT HAS BEEN three nights since I died, and all whom I knew are gone from me for ever! Never again can I speak to Arthur, no, nor to Dr. Seward or Mr. Quincy Morris! Dr. Van Helsing who fought so hard to save me is now my worst enemy, and, Oh, Mina! How can I face you?

The poor baker girl has been sleeping with me in my coffin for the last several nights. She saw me in Whitechapel on the night after her death and followed me back to my tomb. At first she tried to attack me, blaming me for what she had become as I blame the man with the red eyes. I held out my hand and she stopped still as if commanded by my will. It turned out that in fact she could not harm me, held in thrall by the same dark curse which falls on both of us! Since then we have lain in one coffin with our arms around each other like lovers or drowning swimmers who will not go down to the deep alone. I have kissed her many times, told her all of my woes and she has told me hers but neither of us can comfort the other. To look on her face, dead, with her terrible red eyes, is to see my own face and weep!

Tonight she tried to bring back another child, though I have told her that she may not. We fought over it. If I cannot have a child then she certainly cannot have one. I was watching for her to be sure that she did not disobey me and saw her gliding through the trees with the child held to her breast. I was going to go take it from her but then a movement in the trees caught my eyes and I saw them! It was my Arthur and the others including Dr. Van Helsing, who stepped out in front of her and stopped her. She saw Arthur and smiled at him most improperly, holding out her arms. She spoke to him, and though I was too far away to hear I could tell she called him by name. He thought her to be me! Then Dr. Van Helsing held out a crucifix before her and she fled from it, trying to reenter the tomb but jumping back as if she could not.

Dr. Van Helsing drew closer and closer, shoving the crucifix in her face even though he saw it caused her pain. It was clear that he also thought she was me. I crept up until I could hear better.

Finally he asked Arthur, "Answer me my friend, am I to proceed in my work?" and Arthur replied "Do as you will, there can be no horror ever like this anymore."

Dr. Van Helsing went to the door of the tomb and removed something from the edge so that she could enter, and she did. He then sealed it up behind her. After he left I tried to get in but I could not.

I am a horror. Yes, I am! But I am still myself, even if I am cursed! They have all turned their backs on me, and more, they plan something for this coming evening. Oh, I am sorry I made the baker girl like me! I am sorry I cannot even enter my own tomb to warn her. I will fly back to Whitby and see if I can seek out where the man with the red eyes slept among the graves on that tumbledown cliff and perhaps I will be safe there. Safe and Alone. Goodbye, all, and Goodbye to all hope!

JOURNAL OF MRS. JONATHAN HARKER
29 SEPTEMBER 1887

I HAVE JUST finished transcribing all of the accounts that are before me, including Jonathan's diary from shorthand, Dr. Seward's records via phonograph and the entries in *The Whitby Gazette*, *The Pall Mall Gazette*, *The Westminster Gazette* and *The Dailygraph*. What a tale of venomous evil they reveal! It is very late indeed and I have been up almost all night, but I cannot sleep.

I am too full of grief and rage to be calm. When I first heard of Lucy's death I lost all. The dreams of future happiness which I have labored to make a reality for both of us were gone. My life, which many I know would consider blessed, seemed made of tedium and colorless days without her laugh or her kiss, days which stretched out before me to my own grave in a gauntlet barely to be endured. I cried myself to sleep in a separate room from poor Jonathan who has enough to deal with without needing to comfort her who should be comforting him. I thought then that nothing could be worse.

I thought then that she had fallen ill but I know now the terrible truth! I know that she was murdered, and I know by whom. Her killer is none other than Count Dracula, whose crossing to England Jonathan tried so hard to prevent. The Count is a monster. He has been the death of the mother of that poor Gypsy child who was torn apart by wolves and of the child who was feasted upon by worse than wolves. Surely he has caused the deaths of countless others, without remorse. He has nearly broken Jonathan. He has taken from me my darling Lucy, whom I loved! He has robbed her of life at the moment when she should have been so happy. To think, she was to have been married yesterday if not for the Count. To think that she and I....

I have had to leave off writing for crying, but I am better now. Soon Jonathan and the other men will be awake and then perhaps I will be able to add their courage to mine and put manly action to this cause where as a mere woman I fear I could not prevail, but for now I will swear this as an oath before God who punishes the wicked and gives strength to the just: I shall do whatever is in my power to avenge Lucy. If it costs me every penny that is at my discretion, if it costs me my reputation, if it costs my life, Yes, even if it should cost me my immortal soul, I will make the Count answer for his crimes! If it takes a lifetime, if I must go to the gates of Castle Dracula alone and face a thousand wolves alone I will do so if there is the slightest chance that I might rid the world of the Count! Lucy, for your memory, which is sweeter to me than life itself, This I swear!

JOURNAL OF MRS. JONATHAN HARKER
21 DECEMBER 1887

THIS IS THE first time I have written in this journal since I returned from Transylvania and I know it shall be the last. At the time I felt my life to be over. I had lived for Lucy until she was taken from me and then I lived for revenge. Once that revenge was satisfied I thought I would live for my marriage but I know now that I could never have loved any man. I have been blessed to be married to a gentle and sympathetic man, but he is still a man and I cannot love him. Now that I am married I can admit that to myself, but too late, much too late.

When I see other women in the street, walking arm in arm, I know I am a widow although no one acknowledges me thus. I have lost my one true love. I shall not leave Jonathan nor shall I break the vows I made to him in friendship and devotion. I could go back to my little room, my living as a schoolmistress, but what good would it do? I cannot bring Lucy back and I know I shall never love another, not even another woman, as I loved her.

If only I could have stayed in Whitby with her and not gone off to be married in Buda-Pest perhaps she would still be alive! If only I had known what I know now I would have run to her and joined her even in death! I damned myself once to avenge her and would have been damned a thousand times more to be by her side forever! No, that is not to be. I have chosen propriety and now it is all I have left.

This journal shall remain among my private things. Someday if I am very old I may want to take it up and read it and remember the love I had for Lucy, the beautiful and good, before I too am dead. Until then I will not torment myself by looking at it. There is nothing more that I wish to write in it, not now.

JOURNAL OF MRS. JONATHAN HARKER
22 AUGUST 1927

TWO DAYS AGO I came back to Whitby to take the sea air. I felt drawn to the cliffside, perhaps by my memories of Lucy and happier times. Thoughts of her have always been with me. It felt strange to return as a widow, forty years after Lucy's death and more than fifteen years after Jonathan and Quincy both died in the Great War. The last time I was here I was a young unmarried woman and the contrast in how I was perceived was quite striking.

I suppose I looked like some relic from the time of the Her Majesty the Queen as I walked dressed in black lace with a black lace veil and black parasol along the strand between these cavorting young women with their short hair and even shorter swimming costumes. Dress has certainly changed in modern times! The changing tents set up all along the shoreline were continuously disgorging what seemed to me in my old age to be happy half-naked children. Ladies played together at the water's edge and fell, laughing, in each other's arms into the soft sand. I felt the bitter sting of jealousy. I could not help but think that in another life that would have been Lucy and me, had it not been for Count Dracula. We were born too early for that delight, that freedom. Behind my black veil, stifled under my layers of dark lace, I shed salt tears in the salt air for all that I could have had in a different life, in a different time. It felt good to cry over it, even if I did draw a few pitying stares. I walked so far, lost in thought, that by the time I had begun to walk back I knew I would return long after dark.

The Abbey sits on a headland overlooking both town and sea and is large enough to be a landmark for sailors. It has three tiers of ornately carved lancet windows and, when it was home to Benedictine monks, a painted roof which is now wholly missing, leaving the structure open to the sky. Where once there was a stone floor there is now only grass with here and there a ruined set of stairs spiraling up to rooms which no longer exist and fallen masonry from the damage it suffered during the War.

In the setting sun the tall stone ruins of the medieval Abbey glowed on the promontory and I walked up into the steep winding stairs towards it. All at once a white figure flickered into view in one of the openings, gliding over the ground the way I had seen the Count's women do that night in the Carpathians so long ago. I felt cold and afraid but I told myself that it could not be. There could be no vampire women here, since I had heard the report of their destruction from Dr. Van Helsing himself. I decided I must be seeing the White Lady, the ghost of the Abbey, and crept closer to investigate.

I came to the place where the path up to the Abbey branched off and took it. I was unarmed, which gave me pause, but I was hoping to see for myself what the White Lady was without being seen by her. If I were wrong and the figure had indeed been a vampire, then all we had been through, even Lucy's death, would have been for nothing! Although I despaired of my chances of destroying such a creature with no stake and alone as I was, yet I needed to know the truth. If I could learn her resting place and escape tonight there was a chance I might be able to confront her by daylight tomorrow. The closer to the top I got the colder the air was. I could hear the distant cries of gulls. Small bats were moving through the twilight above the Abbey as the last rays of sunlight faded away.

Then I saw her—a lovely slim figure in a one-shouldered heavy white satin dress of modern cut which clung to her down to the hips before flaring gently out in a rippling cascade of satin which fell to the ground. She wore slippers almost the same color as her skin, which made her look barefoot at first glance. Her hair was blond, although each strand of it was a slightly different color and it was cut very short in that style that is called the Eton crop. She carried no purse and wore no jewelry. Even before she raised her face I knew her, and she was no ghost. It was Lucy!

At the first sight of her a pang of joy pierced my heart! She was here! Then I caught the gleam of her eyes, red as Port wine, and despaired! She was not my Lucy, but a vampire. She might not even know me, indeed, she might have no recollection of what I had been to her in another life.

She saw me then, and her face was dear to me even with the red eyes which glowed like embers in the dusk. There was no way for me to escape on that exposed hillside in the deepening night. For a long time I stood still, looking into those eyes. They glimmered, as if with unshed tears.

She stared intensely at me, taking in my widow's black.

"Mina?" she asked, "Mina, can it be you?"

"Stay back," I commanded and my hand went to my throat where I wore a little silver cross on a chain. She stayed where she was, her hands at her sides, and made no attempt to approach me.

"You are Mina," she said in an agonized voice, "and you hate me just as I feared. I can't fault you for that. I've done so many terrible things. Only, please, Mina, believe that I would never, ever harm you. I swear it."

She seemed sincere. I wanted to go to her, to embrace her! It was difficult to remember that this thing could not be Lucy. Apart from the dress and hairstyle she looked exactly as she had when I had last seen her some forty years ago.

"You did not..." I hesitated, unsure how to ask how she was standing here with her head still on her shoulders, her mouth not stopped with garlic and no stake through her heart. " You did not die?" I asked.

"No, they staked another dame in my place."

I stood there with my mouth open for a long while, in shock. It was more than merely hearing slang, the new vernacular, coming out of Lucy's mouth. This was Lucy, but the innocence she had once worn, her belief in the goodness of the world, was gone and in its place was a mixture of regret and resignation such as one finds in the very old. It was odd and tragic to see it on such a young-looking face although I knew she had lived as many years as I. She was half turned away from me when speaking, as if ashamed.

"But you must drink blood to live, mustn't you?" I remembered how it felt to turn. The mark on my forehead was gone, but it was a long time before the nightmares were less frequent.

"Oh, I do, but not enough to kill and only from the strongest lads, too plastered to care, those who can spare a pint for a poor thing like me. And during the war, but that was only Huns. I used to fly out to the ships and pluck them off the decks at night." She smiled a bitter smile. "The sailors said it was the Abbey ghost taking revenge for the damage to Whitby. That's when I took to living there."

She took a step towards me and I startled. "You don't believe me," she said, "but it's because of you that I can live like this. I think if you hadn't killed the Count," she shuddered as she said the name, "I would've been just like him in time. I felt it when he died. I felt his hold on me break." She put her hand on her heart. "I read your account. I know all that you endured for me. Since then I've done my best to stick to the straight and narrow. I am sorry I never came to you, but really how could I? Would you have come away with me? Would you have let me live with you and Jonathan, trusted me with little Quincy?"

"But, Arthur..." I protested.

Lucy laughed ruefully. "Unholy matrimony, that would've been. Arthur found another, in time. I couldn't have been married to him like this, the hunger would've prevented it even if it didn't make me barren. I never found another. Not like you, Mina. It took a lot for me to leave you alone, but I made myself do it for your sake. I wanted you to have a human life. A normal life, like you always wanted." She paused and I could see she was gathering her courage for something. "I adore you, Mina. Always. Since we were children together, I have wanted us to be lovers." She moved as if to take a step towards me, then seemed to think better of it. "I never planned to see you again, but I promised myself that if I did I would tell you truthfully of my love for you. It is, after so many years, still my worst regret."

Her words shocked me and undid the last of my reserve. I could stand it no longer. I ran to her and embraced her. "Lucy, I am a complete fool! All these years I loved you and never once did I think that my love might be returned. I expended so much effort keeping my love hidden from all the world that I never stopped to consider what secrets your heart might be hiding, or what damage I might do to you by keeping silent. I love you, Lucy. Oh, can you forgive me?" I brushed her hair back from her face, wondering at the familiarity and newness of her. Tears sprang to my eyes. "My poor Lucy! To think of you all alone for all this time, afraid to come to anyone because to confess what you were, even that you existed, would have put you in danger. To have fought the hunger alone and learned alone to control it as you have. To have fought during the Great War, like a man, and never be called a hero for it." I looked at her, my Lucy, seeing all that she had endured for all of these years and I knew in that moment that even if she bit me, even if she took my life, I would die gladly in her arms. I kissed her pale lips as we both wept.

"Will you come with me, Mina?" she asked me. "I know I'm asking too much. You'll be cursed with me if you say yes. Never again will you see the sun. Never again will you enter a church to pray. You'll have to sleep in graves and swallow blood, but we'll have each other and it will be forever. You'll look young again, and you won't have to bump anyone off. It's a new era for women now, with so much more to come. Mina, I want to leave here and go to New York. I've got enough dough saved for passage for both of us if you'll have me." She glanced down. "I wouldn't ask, but I can see that you are alone and," then looked up again, her eyes wide and dark as pomegranate seeds, "since you do love me."

I held her to me as tightly as possible for a long moment, then kissed her gently on the lips. "I lost you once and never thought that I would get a second chance to hold you in my arms. I never want to lose you again, not ever. I was willing to give up my life and my soul to avenge your death. How much more do you think I would give up for a life with you? There is nothing to keep me from you now, I have neither the need nor the desire to be proper if to be proper is to part from you. To be with you is not to be cursed, Lucy. You are my sunlight. Your bed, be it even in a grave, is my church and to be at your side forever is my only prayer."

Lucy looked up at me, tears upon her smiling face, and then rose and led me up the steps into the Abbey. There in the ruins we stood face to face, the moonlight through the empty arches casting a silver light over her white satin dress. Slowly, gently, she lifted the dark veil from my face, letting it fall to the ground at my feet. She glided around me and undid the laces of my bodice. Layers of black fell stiffly from me as she let the bodice and then the skirt fall to the grass. I could hear my own heart, beating with fear and desire and my own breath, louder than the sea, but Lucy was silent in every move that she made. My crinoline and its underpinnings she lifted off me with hands as cold as ice and gentle as the wind then gracefully undid my corset and lifted off my shift. I stood there in the moonlight as Lucy plucked my clothes from me one by one like the rind from a fruit, until I was bare as the stones of the Abbey itself. She took a moment to caress me then, taking my hands, bringing them up behind her head and trailing her hands down my bare arms until she was cupping both my breasts, running them down over my trembling ribs and belly then over my naked thighs and hips. I rolled down my stockings, stepped out of my shoes and stood with bare feet on the grass, naked as a Roman goddess. I was beyond shame or pride. I knew what I was about to do was beyond anything I could ever have thought before this night that I would do. With Lucy at my side, returned to me from the very grave, I could believe it was possible. I could believe it was right.

Light mist began to fall, carrying the smell of the sea, and I felt so alive and aware that I could have counted each drop on my skin. Soon I was slick all over with salt rain and every inch of my skin felt as if it were on fire. My whole being vibrated like a plucked bowstring with the need for Lucy's touch. She came around to face me, continuing to caress me as she circled me, her fingertips trailing down my back and over my buttocks and the backs of my thighs. The moon was still low in the sky, enormous and golden in the summer night. She placed her hands in my hair and pulled out the pins that held it up one by one until my dark curls fell about my shoulders and floated around my head in the wind.

She bent forward to place her lips next to my ear and did the one thing Count Dracula would never have done. She asked my leave. "Mina, do you want this?" she whispered.

"I do," I answered. I had never wanted anything more.

Her lips lowered to my neck and hovered there a moment, allowing me to feel the points of her sharp teeth against my skin. I was in an agony of anticipation. All the world contracted to those two points in that instant, then she bit down and in single swift motion buried her teeth in my flesh. I gasped with surprise and my knees bent under me. Lucy caught me and held me to her as if in a vise, bent over my naked body with her mouth to my throat. It hurt only for an instant. Then I felt her mind touch mine and the dreamlike state began in which there was no pain and thoughts passed between us like water between the sea and the river. Her loneliness and her longing met mine in that tide and were one with our joy and the wild power of our transgression.

"Mine," we thought together, "You are mine."

There was a sudden warmth upon my neck and I knew it was my own blood. I could sense Lucy keeping back her need for blood for fear of hurting me. I was beyond caring if she hurt me as long as she did not ever break the bond between us. I felt her tongue slowly pressing back and forth across the skin of my neck to catch each drop and I placed my hands to her head to hold her there, comforting her. She gathered me in her arms, lifting me as easily as a child while she fed. It took a great effort of will for her to take her mouth from me and when she did there was a sensation of emptiness. For a moment I missed her teeth in my neck. She laid me down where I knelt, trembling, and drew back. Her white dress was stained with blood all down the front and there was blood on her mouth and breasts.

She raised her skirt in both hands and I could see that she wore no underclothes at all. The escutcheon of her sex was dark blond. She stood, bending one leg like a dancer and pressed the tip of a long fingernail against the crux of her leg and thigh. Blood welled up as she raised her head and beckoned to me. I crawled towards her and in one long motion licked the blood from her leg and placed my mouth at the edge of her thigh. The moment it touched my lips I was suddenly thirsty as I had never been before. Blood filled my mouth and I drank. There was a pulsing in my ears and a howling as if we were in a storm but the air was still. I felt my mind reach out for her and find her thoughts a whirlwind of ecstasy. It seemed only a short time before she pulled my mouth away but when she did I saw that I had weakened her.

"Did I drink too much?"

She shook her head and laughed softly showing the glints of white teeth in her bloody face. "It will be my turn again soon," she whispered, gripping my hair in both her hands and smiling down at me, "if you want to die tonight."

Many hours later I woke not in a coffin but in Lucy's arms. When I arose I was as young looking as she was, my hand in her hand was alike in youth. Together we flew out over the sea and as I marveled at the moonlight on great expanse and way the clouds felt against my skin I could tell that she was seeing the transformation she had undergone taking place in me but without violence or fear. We cast my old clothes into the sea, so that if they were found people might believe that I had drowned. I felt as if with the corset and crinoline I had cast off all the confining influences of my life and become free.

We easily found two large drunken young men, stumbling home from the pub, and she showed me how to drink without taking a life. I am sure we did neither of them any lasting harm, but we must have looked quite astonishing with each of us carrying one of them unconscious and setting them lightly down outside the hospital as if they weighed no more than a feather. I shall never again fear that any man may do me harm if I venture out alone at night, for to be sure they have a great deal more to fear from me than I do from them!

We slept that day in a tomb beneath the Abbey and the following evening set off for the ship. I astonish even myself to think it, but I have no regrets. In the small round glass of the ship's cabin I went to wash my face before going above deck and in the mirror there was no one. The glass reflected back at me an empty room. I know now why the vampire casts no reflection, for how many of us can say we have looked into our glass and failed to see ourselves? I certainly have never known myself till now. Lucy is the only one who has ever truly seen me as who I am, not as what the world thinks I should be. When we reach New York I shall leave this record and the small account which Lucy kept during her early days as a vampire with a solicitor there, with instructions that they should not be brought to light for at least eighty years. By then perhaps the world shall be ready for creatures like us, and if not we shall be well hidden or long gone. I can only hope that it will be the former. As Robinson has said: "Let us, the children of the night, Put off the cloak that hides the scar, Let us be children of the light, And tell the ages what we are". I will step out into the world in my new body, both dead and more alive than ever. I find it only fitting now that the one place I can still see my reflection is in Lucy's eyes, where it is reflected not by obligation but by freely given love.

THE POWERS OF EVIL

William P. Coleman

I long to go through the crowded streets of your mighty London, to be in the midst of the whirl and rush of humanity, to share its life, its change, its death, and all that makes it what it is.... True, I know the grammar and the words, but yet I know not how to speak them.... Well, I know that, did I move and speak in your London, none there are who would not know me for a stranger. That is not enough for me.

– DRACULA, to JONATHAN HARKER
in BRAM STOKER: *DRACULA*

DR. SEWARD'S NOTES

MONDAY, 30 OCTOBER 1893; EVENING. – Mina Harker's ability to join with Dracula's mind and under hypnosis to read his thoughts, along with her careful reasoning about the facts she learns, have told us his location and plans. He is in his coffin, carried upriver to his castle by Slovak boatmen and guarded by his Szgany retainers. There is a law of nature – and even of the supernatural – that everything must be paid for. The mental link the vampire would use to control Mina is the one we use to trap him.

Our band of vampire-hunters has agreed to split into three pairs so that, by one method or another, we can catch Dracula and kill him, strong as he may be. Arthur Holmwood and Jonathan Harker will chase his boat in a fast steam launch as far up the Sereth and the Bistritza towards Borgo Pass as the mountains permit. Quincey Morris and I will be on the road, riding horse-back, in case the vampire leaves his boat. Professor Van Helsing shepherds Mina Harker along by train and carriage. We must reach Dracula before he reaches his castle and awakens.

This evening we shall set out.

LATER THAT NIGHT. – Strange, but among the things disquieting me is having watched Arthur depart on the launch with Jonathan. Not strange that I would worry about Art, my old and dear friend. Not strange that I, a psychiatrist, would worry about his state of mind. Still, perhaps strange-seeming that, at this momentous turn when the efforts of our small group may decide whether a prepotent monster remains at large, I concern myself with our personal emotions.

They say that on the battlefield, away from the parade ground, a soldier will risk himself and die not for the sake of his country abstractly, but for his comrades concretely. We – my friends and I – risk ourselves for Mina Harker, that she should not suffer what my beloved Lucy Westenra did. We do it for ourselves too, that we should not be the ones to do to Mina what we did to Lucy.

So, in this personal way, I am uneasy about Arthur. He goes at Jonathan's side, sharing the work of their boat, meeting the uncertainties of travel, and preparing for the enemy. Art's history shows that these are circumstances in which he would become closely involved with his companion, especially one as resourceful and attractive as Jonathan. He has never come to peace with himself as a man who loves men or recognized that I understand and support him in being so.

Impossible as it is to guess the outcome of our mission, one fact is certain: if Jonathan remains alive, it will be his wife, Mina, whom he loves and not my friend. Art is already unsettled, and I wish not to see him baffled in that way. Despite his native predilection for men and not women, he followed Quincey's and my examples by proposing to Lucy. Successful in his suit, he had little time to compose his feelings. Then he abruptly lost her with no chance of redeeming his pledge to love her. Will his inner struggle over Jonathan bring despair? or clarity to accept himself as I accept him?

These are notes I should not share.

MINA HARKER'S JOURNAL

TUESDAY, 31 OCTOBER 1893; LATER. – Professor Van Helsing and I sit on the ground by the open fire. He managed to buy a carriage and a team after we left the train at Veresti, and it is now our first night stopping in the open.

He is across from me, thinking his thoughts, glancing at me protectively from time to time. I sit writing my journal, recalling the conversation we just had. It is cold, too cold. Even the furs in which he has wrapped me cannot keep the cold from my bones. The protective magic circle with which he has surrounded me cannot keep the cold away. I fear sleep, which is the monster's special time and no longer brings me oblivion. I am exhausted. So I escape by talking, pestering the professor about matters he already has explained.

"Tell me again," I asked, "who is Dracula?"

"He is a *voivode*, a prince. His given name is *Vlad*. His father, also *Vlad*, was called 'The Dragon,' or *Dracul*. So our Vlad is the Dragon's Son, *Dracula*. His father was made a dragon in 1431, the same year the son was born."

I was surprised. "Made a dragon?"

"Sigismund of Luxembourg took the father into the Order of the Dragon. The son became a dragon too when only five years old. The dragons were ruling knights sworn to oppose the invading Turks, who – unlike the feuding, crafty Europeans – were unified. The dragons didn't succeed. In thirty years the Turks engulfed the Balkans."

Then I remembered. The vampire recounted this to Jonathan last May as history, though to him it was memory. Dracula burned to fulfill his dragon oath because he hated the Turks with a bitter, personal wrath. Time and again, he fought them back, outwitted them, defeated them – whilst also tangling with the allies, including his own relatives, who should have fought by his side. But there were too many Turks and too many supposed allies.

The professor continued, his voice arising from the near-darkness beyond our fire: "Nobody knew how or where he died. He was believed to be buried at the monastery on the island of Snagov, but that tomb is empty. All that history records is that, perhaps in December of 1476, Prince Vlad disappeared somewhere on the road between Bucharest and Giurgiu, south of here on the Wallachian Plain. He was thought to have died. You and I know that he didn't."

I remember the disappearance too – but only as brief, jumbled flashes, enigmatic until Van Helsing just spoke. The story is not mentioned in Jonathan's journal. It was dark as we traveled the flat road, cloud-covered and starless. A hooded man leading a spare horse rode slowly toward us on a path from the neighboring woods. The Count took out his knife and used it on his attendants, then changed horses and cantered off as men and horses lay screaming, moaning, bleeding out onto the cold, hard midnight earth.

It has become difficult for the professor to hypnotize me and extract information from my link with the Count. Conditions have changed. Impressions from the Count leak across to me continually, not just at sunrise and sunset. Van Helsing's questions are too direct to let those impressions explain themselves, but sometimes a waking story or a thought shows me subsequently what they mean. I resist letting the professor know. The vampire's mind and mine draw closer. We must kill him soon, before he can take me over altogether.

ARTHUR HOLMWOOD'S JOURNAL

THURSDAY, 2 NOVEMBER 1893; DAWN. – He sleeps. Last night, during my watch, he would not allow himself sleep, as much as I implored him. His worry over Mina is too strong. I worry for Mina too; I would in any case, but there is that about Jonathan that makes me sense his worry directly, poignantly, before my own worry arises.

This night I deceived him a little. He was so fatigued he must needs fall asleep, willingly or not. I offered to take the first watch, then wake him for the second. But I didn't wake him. It is a small enough sacrifice for his sake.

I sit near the stern at the rudder, and Jonathan lies along the bench, covered by a blanket, his head near my lap, one hand unconsciously reaching to me. There is no cause to disturb him by tending the boiler and engine. I've put them in good working order thanks to my love of fitting machine parts – just tinkering with them, really – that has led me to own two steam launches in different parts of England.

The river – we have passed Fundu and are in the Bistritza, still with no sign of the fiend – is calm and broad for now. Little steering is required. We make good speed, faster than Dracula's double crew of boatmen can. They are, I am certain, less than half a day ahead. Even if they land, they will be slower since they must pull his coffin in a leiter wagon while we can hire mounts. We shall catch them up.

The dawn rays fall softly over Jonathan's face and eyes. I would adjust the awning to shade him better if I didn't fear troubling his sleep by mucking about. We have not shaven for a few days. Numberless short bristles push slantwise from his cheek and downward, especially from above and below his soft lips. They form a rough stubble that makes vivid the thick, recently-sunburned flesh at his strong neck.

It outrages me that such a noble being should be in danger.

MINA HARKER'S JOURNAL

FRIDAY, 3 NOVEMBER 1893. – Now that the professor has agreed to let me take my turn driving the carriage, we have ridden all night and all day, straight through. Stopping at last to make camp, we built a fire. The professor would neither allow me to venture into the woods alone to fetch wood, nor was he willing to desert me to do it himself. So we went together, never leaving the horses unwatched, and gathered as much as we could – enough, we hope, to warm us and to ward off the simpler predators of the night. He has again constructed a magic circle to protect me from other predators. What he cannot do, until Dracula is killed, is to prevent me becoming my own enemy.

Sleep should have been easy to obtain, but we both had too much nervous energy built up in our exertions during the day. We could only wait until that had drained off.

Van Helsing told me, "Even without knowing him as a vampire, people remembered Prince Vlad in succeeding days for his cruelty. They called him 'Vlad the Impaler.' The subject is a murky one. Those were cruel times, inconceivably so to our modern sensitivities – not that we have ceased being cruel. In some countries, the penalty for stealing was to have your hand cut off. Why that should be thought productive of any good, I do not know. The only considerations seem to have been retribution and terror, rather than social benefit. Torture was the usual method of interrogation, despite hundreds of years of prisoners confessing to what their captors wanted them to say without regard for the truth."

I said, "Still, even in that era, Dracula was regarded as cruel."

"Yes. He was. There was the evidence of too many victims impaled – tens of thousands in Vlad's lifetime. There was evidence of too much relish over each one. On the opposite side, many Romanians and Bulgarians regard Dracula as a hero for fighting the Turks – for attempting to restore order and civilization amidst ceaseless war – for doing what needed to be done, without hesitation. When Sultan Mehmed II invaded, he was met by a forest of Moslems impaled on stakes – so many thousands that the sight made Mehmed turn back rather than meet an enemy so monstrously cruel."

That provided enough thought for Van Helsing and me both. We were silent for a while, staring into the firelight, still awaiting sleep.

Then he continued, "Of course, Vlad was instructed in betrayal by those closest to him. After Mehmed turned away from his attempt to conquer Romania, the commander he appointed to do it was Dracula's younger brother, Radu the Handsome – *Radu cel Frumos*."

"What a name! 'Radu the Handsome.' But how was Mehmed able to make him fight against his own brother?"

"As children, Vlad and Radu had been sent to the Ottomans as hostages. Radu became the playmate of Sultan Murad's young son Mehmed. Later, Radu chose to stay on with Mehmed even when Vlad was allowed to return home. After the Turks took Constantinople, Radu was invited to live in the New Palace they have now begun calling *Topkapi*. It was Radu the Handsome who conquered Vlad on Mehmed's behalf and took over Vlad's throne as *Voivode* of Romania."

ARTHUR HOLMWOOD'S JOURNAL

SATURDAY, 4 NOVEMBER 1893; MORNING. – We came near to disaster yesterday. It has taken until now to put the launch – and myself – enough to rights that I have time to describe it.

We seemed to have the Count in our grasp – almost, I imagined, we were able to touch him. In the afternoon, we entered one of the Bistritza's rapids; after all, we are climbing from near sea level at the mouth of the Danube as far up to the passes of the Carpathian Mountains as we are able. Jonathan was in the stern at the tiller whilst I was forward, attempting to guide our progress by pulling on the ropes installed in the rocks there for the aid of boats. As I did I kept a close eye on the machinery. Any loss of headway in water like that would be fatal to our mission and possibly to us.

Just ahead, on and partly below the river surface, a log had one end wedged by the current between two boulders, caught there precariously. Jonathan and I were aware of the danger if it should work its way loose and strike our vessel. Then it did come free, and we maneuvered with all the means we could to avoid impact. It glanced off the launch's side, though with a worrying thud.

What we did not see until too late was that – with the log gone – the water it had been diverting around a rock only a few inches upstream from us would able to flow over it. Hundreds of gallons of freezing mountain runoff poured across the top and flooded into our boat. I was soaked by it, almost knocked off my feet by its force. Worse, it inundated the engine.

The pipes carrying steam from the boiler were scalding hot. Now drenched with icy water, they were stressed by the difference between the expanded metal on their inner surface and the rapidly contracting metal on the outer. If more strain were needed, the descent of one piston was no longer merely impeded by a pliant mixture of steam and air but stopped absolutely short by the incompressible water with which the wave had filled its cylinder. This impossibility of movement was transmitted instantly back to the weakened pipes that were trying to force steam to the piston. The pressure burst them, and they ripped from the joints holding them together.

There was a tremendous bang, and pieces of metal scattered. One fragment of hot pipe tore a chunk from my upper arm, and another grazed my cheek.

"Jonathan," I yelled, "the ropes!" With the engine no longer driving the propeller, they were our sole means of escape from the river's fury. I had only one good arm to use on them.

He leapt to my side and pulled on the lines heroically. His eyes were big as he saw the blood tricking down my cheek and coursing along my wounded arm, but he did the work of several men.

We – or he – got our boat to the shore.

"Run us up as far as you can," I told him.

Eventually, with the kind help of local villagers who had seen our mishap, we had the launch mostly out of the water – resting, careened at an angle.

Jonathan faced me, not thinking of our mission – only appalled at my condition. I didn't agree. My cheek was wet, but with river water – I could feel that the blood flow there had stopped. Some blood still issued from my arm, but I was occupied with other concerns. We must not let Dracula lose us now.

He said, "We have to get you bandaged at once. And we must change your clothing before you freeze in this air."

"No. I don't know if I can repair the boat, but – if I can – we mustn't waste time about it or afterwards getting underway. If I can't, then we must look quickly to finding horses. Later we can tend to me."

He started to reply, then looked into my eyes. "At the very least we must stop that blood."

Using gestures, he got a villager to help him remove my soaked, heavy coat and then to apply pressure to the artery. He cut away the arm fabric from my wet shirt, cleaned the wound, and applied a cloth to bandage it.

I clambered, one-armed, over the lower rail of the boat, avoiding the water that overtopped the bilge on that side. Then I went around the launch to inspect the bottom. The propeller was whole and unbent and its shaft was true. If either had been damaged, then there would be no point in repairing the machinery inside. The hull was bruised where the log had struck, but intact.

Returning to the inside, I sat next to the engine and asked Jonathan to bring me a wooden crate stowed out of the way in the forward compartment. It contained spare parts I'd had the shipyard pack for me. Jonathan was right, though. With lessening of the previous excitement and exertion, I was becoming cold. Still, until I knew what materials I had available, I could hazard no guess about our best course of action.

Jonathan already had villagers at work bailing the water from the boat using hand-driven bilge pumps supplemented with buckets. A few of them spoke a little German. I inventoried the crate. The result was better than I feared, but not good. I had all the pipes and connectors I would need except a certain elbow joint. The one in the crate was for pipes a size larger in diameter.

I called Jonathan over. "You'd better ask them where we might buy or rent horses."

He conferred with the men and came back. "We can obtain nothing locally save plow horses. We'd need to go more than thirty miles further upriver to buy anything better – the same town where we already intended to leave the boat."

"Jonathan, I can repair the damage – in a few hours – but not completely. Part will be a jury rig that should allow us to run in smooth water. Any roughness may cause it to work loose and we'd have to stop until I can fix it – and God save us if the engine fails while we're in rapids. I'll help hold the pipes together by hand, using rags to protect myself from the heat."

"Will it work and be faster than riding the plow horses, do you think?"

"I think so. Meanwhile – while I do the repairs – you have to get them to clear the water from the crankshaft and cylinder compartment – and dry out the firebox and stock us with dry tinder and wood. We must have steam up the instant the engine can work."

As I'd talked, my body was lightly shivering under its wet clothing in the cold November air. I hid this from Jonathan. More worrisome, my fingers felt too numb to make any careful repairs – and now they developed a tremor. I tried to hold them out of sight, but the shivering in the rest of my body overcame me with uncontrollable spasms and Jonathan saw this.

He called to two large villagers.

"Arthur, we must get you undressed and dry," he told me. "Do you understand?"

I nodded, and he had them strip me completely. By the time they had wrestled the wet clothing off me, he had cloths to towel me off. He gently dried those parts that need gentleness, and did his best to warm every other inch of me by brisk rubbing. I didn't mind being naked in front of the villagers, but was shocked to be so in front of Jonathan. Back in school, I'd been nude with other boys. In the wilderness of different, far parts of the world, Jack Seward, Quincey Morris, and I had swum together many times. This time, with Jonathan aware of me so closely, tending me so solicitously, I was upset – helpless to stop him looking or to quell my confusion. Finally, he and the men dressed me again in warm, dry flannels and then boots and a layer of furs.

It was only a few hours until I had the boiler reconnected to the engine. Jonathan had faithfully organized the remaining tasks so that we were prepared to haul the launch back over the mud and into the water. Steam was up and we set off at once. As predicted, the repair I'd improvised – so very neatly and with such precision attaching the pipes to the oversized elbow by means of rags and wire – worked loose several times underway and we needed to stop the boat and redo it. Eventually, I got it so that it stayed put.

We've lost precious time. Yesterday morning, the vampire was almost within reach. Now – after a night of sleeping little and fussing over the engine and with one arm in pain and partly useless – we must race if we are to save Mina.

MINA HARKER'S JOURNAL

SATURDAY, 4 NOVEMBER 1893; MORNING. – And so, Mina, you would like to talk about my little brother, Radu the Beautiful.

Ah, do I surprise you, Madame Mina? the lovely, much-admired Mrs. Harker? What is the difficulty? You see your own delicate fingers grasping the pen – and your arm guiding it. And yet it is my words that appear flowing across the paper. How can that be possible? I even compose in shorthand, which I myself do not know – but your mind provides me its shapes.

When I was eleven, the Dragon was forced from his throne by the Hungarian János Hunyadi and his puppets. Stealing from my father was more important to Hunyadi than joining with him, a fellow dragon, to fight the Turks. To get the throne back, my father simply forgot that he was a dragon. Despite his oath, he asked the Turks for help. They agreed. Their requirement was that my father send the Sultan a pledge of good behavior. He should send us, his two youngest sons: Vlad, his namesake, and Radu the Desirable. This was not a high price to him.

Are you shocked, Madam Mina? You English believe that living virtuously is a guarantee that others must be virtuous in turn. My father delivered me as a child to the mercy of people who wanted to be my jailers. But I was a dragon too, and I would not submit to Turks. I defied them; I fought back; I attempted escape. They beat me; they whipped me; they kept me in an underground cell. You English under your Queen, Victoria, live such comfortable, upholstered, overstuffed lives. You really have no idea.

Did my little brother – Radu the Complaisant – suffer the same? No. Mehmed, the Sultan's son, liked Radu. Mehmed, a year younger than I, took the seven year old to his side. They grew up together. When I was seventeen and Radu fourteen, we had the chance to come back to our home. I returned, but Radu the Friendly chose to stay with his Mehmed. Later, as Radu became adult, Mehmed took youths for his pleasure. Radu did not mind being cast aside. He became Mehmed's soldier and eventually my enemy. It was he, in command of Sultan Mehmed's Janissaries, who pushed me off my throne the second time. That is what life is like outside the wishful moral fantasies of upholstered Englishmen.

My winsome Wilhelmina, you imagine you can use the link between our minds to plot against me. Remember, it was not you who made that link: it is mine. Your pedantic Van Helsing may surround you with garlic and accouterments that prevent my body touching you, but my mind can cross over and enter yours anytime I wish. You are indisseverably mine, more completely, more closely each day.

LATER. – The professor and I have both slept intermittently all day. We try to take turns on watch, but neither can help falling back asleep. I thought before to write a little in my journal as he slept – with the result that is now evident in the previous entry.

It took some time after the vampire left me to be able to move, or think, or write. I am only relieved I did not cry out to Van Helsing in my shame, my rage, my helpless terror at being so invaded and used.

I finally slept again afterwards. I do not know if the professor awoke then, but he sleeps now and I try to write.

Dracula must be killed. He has just now violated me quite directly. Not satisfied with forcing and humiliating me, he means to take me over; his control increases, and too soon he will have me completely.

What distresses me is that he must be killed and I, a woman, depend on the men around me to do it. I remember laughing and teasing Lucy Westenra about the "New Woman." That was in happier times, not long ago – when Lucy was alive, at Whitby, and in love with her tall, handsome, curly-haired Arthur Holmwood, whose father's death had not yet made him Lord Godalming. It was in the time when I was not marked by the vampire.

Arthur, Dr. Seward, and Mr. Morris have trained for this all their lives; they have hunted together and explored the most untravelled reaches of the globe. My dear Jonathan, trained only as a solicitor, yet proved himself at Dracula's castle. He makes an equal partner with the other three. Men are trained from birth in courage and readiness; we women are trained to imagine we fear venturing into sunlight without a parasol.

Physically, I am too weak to fight against the Count. But so is Van Helsing now in his old age, and he is not helpless. Even my four strong men are physically weak in comparison to the Count. They rely on their knowledge and their resolve. I may be small and slender, but I have the intellect and the moral courage to fight the vampire. And I will fight him.

STILL LATER. – The professor was awake for a time and we spoke together. I was more calm than I could have been a few hours before.

"Why is it," I asked him, "that our enemy has such unlimited powers in his evil?"

He replied, "Do not say that, my child; never think such a thing. Evil has no power. That is not its nature. Evil exists only as a disease upon good. It is rust eating metal, cancer eating an animal. By itself, it cannot subsist or grow. It continues only to destroy.

"Evil may not have power, but it has real effect. Rust can ruin; cancer kills. But, in an ontological sense, evil has no being at all. It cannot create. Only good can do that."

ARTHUR HOLMWOOD'S JOURNAL

SATURDAY, 4 NOVEMBER 1893; AFTERNOON. – The engine has continued to run reasonably well, and we have almost arrived at the town. Jonathan are I are packed, ready to leave on the instant. We must push ourselves and our horses to the utmost in our final effort. The Count's Szgany drag his casket in a cumbersome wagon whilst we will be on swift horses, but they are ahead of us – with our delays. He could reach his castle on Monday afternoon. If we are to save Mina, we must get to him before he does!

First, though, we have yet another two hours of enforced idleness as the launch chugs imperturbably up the remaining few miles of river.

"I've been thinking," Jonathan said earlier. He gave a little laugh and smiled to me, then continued, "How weak Dracula is."

This apparent dismissal of the Count's formidable strength made me laugh in return. I said, "Explain."

"Well, he is weak for a creature with supernatural powers. Here he is, for example, running for his life from half a dozen quite ordinary mortals like ourselves. If he hasn't left his boat, then – during daytime, at least – he hides in his coffin like a rat. And from what? a crew of Slovak boatmen."

"You aren't forgetting..."

"Not forgetting anything."

This made me think. I answered, "From your journals, he must have laboriously cherished his plan of moving to England over the course of a century. Yet we six were enough to chase him off the island."

"Yes. We should not be foolishly confident, but objective thinking does clear my head."

I asked, "How did he become weak? He was a kind of a prince, wasn't he? Ruled most of Romania? Captained armies? Fought the Turks? Now – with four centuries of knowledge and with his special abilities – now he's sometimes invincible but sometimes helpless."

"The men in those armies, the individual people he ruled, the Turkish sultan he struggled against – they all continued to flow onward with time and eventually arrived at death. He stood still in his immortality and was left behind."

"What do you mean?"

Jonathan replied, "Think of the books I saw in his castle. You or I could barely finish the ones about England in a century, but he might survive forever to do it. Suppose he wanted to learn Chinese poetry, or the complete history of the Peruvian Inca, or Maxwell's theories of electromagnetic energy. How little it would cost him to use a century for each! But there is a price to be paid. How little difference those things would mean to an immortal once he learned them – after a hundred such centuries had passed and all of eternity still opened in front of him."

"You sound intellectual – like Jack Seward."

"No, I'm a solicitor, a practical man. How practical would I be if I didn't accept the evidence presented me and reason to its meaning, however strange?"

I followed up his thought: "You said he stepped out of the flow of time and was left behind. Remember, he told you he wanted to be in London, 'in the midst of the whirl and rush of humanity, to share its life, its change, its death, and all that makes it what it is.' That was his motive for removing there, not the anonymity or the sheer availability of more lives to kill. He could not himself be alive, but he wanted to reawaken to people who are."

Jonathan became excited at this. "Exactly. Those who lived with him in his own time left him, one by one. Finally, dead but not dead, he was helpless, alone, deprived of the power of those who lived to do his will and made him terrible. I remember his castle – empty even of the servants he didn't need. He had to prepare my dinners himself and secretly carry away the dishes afterwards. He has no one but his equally outcast Gypsies."

I saw an additional side to this. "Those Londoners whom he coveted make choices. Not necessarily the best choices – not always so or perhaps even often. But, once acted upon, choices remake reality. That new reality works, in its turn, to change the people who made it. They make further choices. This continual leapfrog jumble is 'the flow of time,' which eventually breaks up everything. The Count refused any longer to abide choices other than his own, solely his original wants. By terror, he could enforce his will within a circumscribed realm. Events became uniform for him, so time slowed and stopped. He wanted to see it move quickly, vividly again, even if he must be only a watcher, a drinker, outside its stream. So he came to London."

A FEW MINUTES LATER. — We are almost there. According to the map, we should see the town after the next bend.

Thinking over Jonathan's insights as I was writing them down has led me to another thought.

I must stop ignoring that I am fascinated with Jonathan. He fills my mind, especially at irrelevant moments. I thrill to his voice, a raspy note slightly above baritone. I find myself listening to its male pitch and not to his words, watching his lips, tongue, and teeth as he forms the sounds. There is his accent. Many people from Exeter likely have exactly the same accent, but his is beautiful, ceaselessly intriguing in its oddities of intonation. If he stands close to me as he talks or as we work together, I am aware of nothing but him.

He has become my friend — and I want that — but I must admit that I want more. He mentioned the importance of accepting evidence, reasoning to its meaning, however strange. All right, here then are my conclusions, three simple facts that are true but cannot exist together: I want to be Jonathan's friend and more; he wants to be my friend but not more; he instead wants that more with Mina. Indeed, the whole endeavor he and I are engaged in has a single purpose — to restore Jonathan and Mina to each other.

If I am determined to follow Jonathan's advice by thinking objectively so as to clear my mind, then I admit two further things. First, he is not — in an age when men cannot love men — the only man I have felt this way about. When I proposed to Lucy Westenra, I admired her well enough; but I proposed because I knew Jack Seward planned to. I wanted to be like him, to be normal — or what the good opinions of society and the need of continuing my title of nobility and my Godalming family lineage would coerce me to think was normal. Lucy accepted me, and she would not have been sorry. I would have loved her and been a husband as honorably, as faithfully, as any man ever has. What makes me ashamed — bitterly so — is that I didn't think of Jack. He loved her as I never could have. I destroyed my friend's happiness, although the vampire killed Lucy before either of us would have married her.

The second thing I must admit is that, among the men I have felt this way about, there is one who is really the only one. And that is John Seward himself. I have known from the beginning that he cannot feel for any man the way I feel for him. That knowledge – that I cannot obtain the man I completely love – is doubtless why I go along in life aimlessly, blundering into proposing to Lucy and into infatuations with excellent but unavailable men like Jonathan.

Perhaps I can begin to live in the real world.

MINA HARKER'S JOURNAL

SUNDAY, 5 NOVEMBER 1893. – By now, Mina, you and your protector Van Helsing have met my three brides.

Yes, we met them. We turned them away.

I wonder how well you did with them? Can there be any doubt of the outcome?

You see, you foul thing, I am able to answer you back. I cannot prevent you writing, not yet, but neither can you silence me. I am not yours. You cannot defeat me.

I sympathize, Mina. Stronger people than you have suffered from those three women. People do not survive meeting them, but I made sure they understood my intentions for your longevity – and so here you still are.

What is the matter with you? I just told you we turned them away. They did nothing to us. Or – this is amazing! – is it possible you cannot read my replies on the paper?

Your sweet Jonathan was destined to die under their care.

Perhaps, Count, this writing is in my physical space – on my side of the mental boundary – so I can read it directly but you cannot. In your space, it is the same for you as for me in mine. You receive only fragmentary glimpses – impressions that may perhaps be understood only in light of later knowledge.

Does that idea torment you, Wilhelmina? knowing that your Jonathan was in my hands before he was in yours? There was that one day when I saw him shaving – I know he wrote about it and you have read it. Think how I felt. He was shaving his cheeks. I had been looking at them as I listened to him talk every night at my request, planning out how I would touch them. I felt his daily growing uncertainty and fear; I could sense his exquisite emotion and I longed to take him. Then I saw blood dripping where he nicked himself with the razor in his surprise at finding me behind him! Desire overwhelmed me, and I almost took him too soon – too soon. But I waited.

And what did you wait for, monster? for him to mark your forehead with a blow from the edge of the shovel he swung at you as you lay paralyzed in your grave?

ARTHUR HOLMWOOD'S JOURNAL

MONDAY, 6 NOVEMBER 1893; JUST AFTER DARK. – It is over, and I must recount how.

The sun was low in the sky as our horses galloped. We would have feared that the Count had escaped us if we did not hear, from time to time, the voices of the crowd of Szgany higher above us on the twisting mountain road as they labored, perhaps to help their horses pull the wagon over the next ditch. They were close to us by a direct route, but might be far by horseback. An attempted shortcut through the thickets across the loops in the road might cost more in time than it saved in distance.

The descending sun was the clock that measured our fate. At sunset the monster could change form. Once he awoke to the night, he would be strong again. He could escape beyond our reach and imagination, leaving Mina Harker marked by him and obliged then to join him forever once she eventually died. He must be destroyed in the next few minutes, no matter what.

Jonathan and I thundered around a turn and saw them ahead of us. Jack Seward and Quincey Morris were riding fast toward them from the other side. We would meet in the middle.

The Gypsies saw us and took up positions to defend the wagon, but their knives and pistols would be no match for our powerful rifles.

Jonathan stood up in his horse's stirrups. "Stop," he yelled to the Szgany, as Quincey commanded the same. Then Jonathan asked me to cover him. He dismounted and strode toward them fearlessly.

I pulled up my horse and took out my Winchester. In the corner of my eye, I could see Jack taking a similar stance to protect Quincey. Without firing yet, I looked down and pointed the rifle rapidly at each Szgany in turn, taking aim and letting my eyes make contact with his to ensure he knew I had him in my sights. They bunched up closely to prevent Jonathan from passing, but he pushed his way through them.

The sun had come so far down the sky and was so close now to the ground that the speed of its fall became readily perceptible. Jonathan leaped up onto the wagon and pushed the coffin to the ground. Its lid was dislodged in the crash and clattered away. The vampire's eyes opened in anticipation of the setting sun, and his mouth made some arrogant, sneering movement.

On the other side of the wagon, a knife stretched toward Quincey. I could not take my rifle sight from Jonathan's besiegers, could not allow my hold on their attention to break, however briefly. Jack aimed through the dense crowd and made a clean shot into the knife-wielder's head. He was too late. Quincey, bleeding now and grasping his side with his left arm, shouldered through more Gypsies and reached Jonathan.

Dracula's body – all but his mouth and his eyes – remained immobilized by the sun for yet a last instant. He grinned, poised for immediate physical release and victory. Instead, Jonathan's kukri knife whirred above him. The long, outward curve of its bent steel blade sliced through the whole width of the monster's neck at once, severing his head whilst Quincey's bowie – showing a glinting, orange flash of the setting sun – drove straight down into his heart.

And thus we gave the same healing grace to Prince Vlad as we had to Lucy Westenra – as Van Helsing had to the three brides. Entering again the flow of time, his ages-dead body crumbled straightaway into dust.

Mina Harker rejoined Jonathan. Their love, whether to be long-lived or short, has the same chance as any young couple's.

Time however brought an end to my brave and much-mourned friend, Quincey Morris. He died on the spot from the wound inflicted by the Gypsies.

DR. SEWARD'S NOTES

TUESDAY, 14 NOVEMBER 1893. – We remaining five made our ways to Galiti, returning the horses to the liveries and the steam launch to its owners. Now we travel on the train back to England.

When Art had set out on the launch, I'd hoped his time with Jonathan would bring him clarity as a man who loves men. And, whatever emotional turmoil his self-recognition may have cost him, he has won through. I can tell from the way he now treats me, whom he has stubbornly, if erratically, loved since school. His regret toward me is more open, but so is the pleasure he takes in our friendship. He is at ease with me, decisive and confident.

Art talked with me this morning early.

"It must be hard for you," he said. "I don't wish to intrude upon your grief, but hard for you to see Jonathan so relieved – so relaxed – I mean, simply happy – with Mina – when you miss your Lucy."

Strange that he, the successful suitor for Lucy Westenra's hand, should console me, the unsuccessful one, on her death. He sees himself well enough that he sees me clearly too, the strength of my love for Lucy, my doubled pain in losing her when I never had her.

I replied gently, "Thank you. Jonathan and Mina don't take away from my love for her. They show it was a possible reality, and that is a comfort. I will have other chances."

"Yes."

"Jonathan and Mina love now in a deeper way. They know who they are, what each has gone through for the other. We six have rid the world of the vampire and refashioned ourselves and each other doing it."

For Art, it must be like the moment of waking from a dream, one that you partially remember so it slips out of your conscious grasp as you work frantically to recognize it. It's gone, and you regret its loss intensely – even more so because you can't remember quite accurately what it was. Arthur at first denied what he felt for Jonathan – as he'd previously, for a far longer time, denied what he felt for me. Now, he has awoken from his muddle to recognize both at once – in the same split instant he recalls that both Jonathan and I love women and could never return his love. It must be painful. Yet he's not defeated; he's grown too much for that.

I studied his face, his familiar blue eyes that studied me in return.

The train steward knocked on the door to make up our compartment for the day. He excused himself for interrupting: "Doctor Seward, Lord Godalming – a moment, please."

We waited at the long row of windows in the corridor, watching the snow lying on deep-green foothills in the rising sunlight, warm inside the moving train, feeling keenly the cold beauty outside.

When we returned to our seats, I continued, "Art, I wish I loved you the way you need."

"Don't apologize, Jack. I treasure the love you do give."

"You are happy?"

"Happy? No, not happy," he said. "No more so than you. At least, free. Able to be happy."

MY ARMS ARE HUNGRY

Traci Castleberry

LIKE all the other children I thought the woman in white was beautiful, or "bloofer," as the youngest called her. The nickname caught on. Our bloofer lady would appear each evening on Hampstead Heath and choose one of us to lift into those milky arms and take on some unknown adventure.

This night, like those before, I waited, half hopeful, half terrified she would choose me. The sun had been gone for some time when she appeared, hair and shift flowing as if she was an angel. *Pick me,* I silently begged. *Take me with you.*

Some of the children pointed, shrieked and ran away at her approach. I didn't.

Take me. Please. Not that I expected my prayers to be answered. They hadn't saved Mama.

The bloofer lady studied the remaining children, her gaze at last coming to rest upon me. I was transfixed, held in place by such a sudden rush of love and desire that I could not have moved had a horse been about to run me down. She floated toward me and a moment later I was caught up in her arms, my head against her breast. She pressed her lips to my neck. So warm was she, so tender, that I didn't mind the sting which followed. I thought it strange how she suckled my skin but I didn't care. I'd discovered in her the maternal warmth so recently stripped from me and I would do nothing to risk losing it again.

The rhythm of her mouth against my neck lulled me into a stupor. I was lost in her softness and sweetness, utterly uncaring of where we went as long as I was safe within her arms.

I was aware of little else until we arrived in the churchyard high up on East Cliff above the bay. The light breeze carried the salty scent of the sea. As we passed amongst the lane of yews, four men stepped out to greet us.

All illusion of motherhood vanished as soon as the bloofer lady laid eyes upon them. She thrust me from her breast and against the unforgiving stone of a tomb. Agony shot through my back and legs. I cried out, more for the loss of the attention I'd cherished than physical pain, but she snarled, as vicious and territorial as a wild dog.

One of the men groaned. This one she advanced upon, arms wide and bearing the same smile which had charmed me and so many others. Her words fell like chimes upon my ears. "Come to me, Arthur. Leave these others and come to me. My arms are hungry for you. Come, and we can rest together. Come, my husband, come!"

Though we were separated our connection hadn't broken. I *felt* her. Her passion for Arthur became mine, lustful and all-consuming though I was far too young to understand the implications. My gaze, like hers, focused on *him*. Arthur. I wanted him too, but small as I was, trapped in a body broken after she'd callously tossed me to the ground, I could do no more than twitch and moan.

Arthur moved as if spellbound. She had nearly reached his arms when one of the other men, an old man with reddish hair swept about his face, sprang between them wielding a little gold crucifix. Her face twisted with a rage and an answering fury erupted within me. She sprang toward a tomb but stopped as if some invisible barrier prevented her from entering.

The beautiful lady's face twisted and warped into so horrible a visage I wondered that we were not all struck dead from the sight. Unholy wrath flooded my body and I moaned anew.

The old man held her thus for some time. He made a demand of Arthur, who dropped to his knees and gave his consent. With alacrity the old man set aside his lantern, dabbled with something on the tomb's door, and the beautiful woman vanished through an impossibly tiny slit.

As she disappeared so did the fierce emotion which had gripped me. I was left in pain and confusion, as if the body I inhabited was not my own. Only when I gazed upon Arthur did I find any sense of consolation and safety.

The man with the crucifix lifted me, said I was not harmed and should be left for the police to find. Arthur objected. It was his fiancée who had left me in such a state and I wore such tattered rags he wondered if anyone cared for me at all. Surely no detriment would be caused by seeing to my warmth and comfort for the night. The first man objected, citing his wish to keep these incidents between the four of them, but he must have decided that Arthur had already endured enough torment for the night and gave in to his pleading.

And so we went to Hillingham, the estate, unbeknownst to me at the time, my beautiful lady had once called home. Likewise, I didn't know what an extraordinary man Professor Abraham Van Helsing was or how talented a physician until many years later. All I registered then was how his dark blue eyes gazed kindly upon me as he carried me inside. He dosed me with laudanum and I lay in a dreamy haze while he assessed my injuries. "He, too, is suffering from the same blood loss as the other children. He needs a transfusion at once."

Thus Arthur gave me what his fiancée had taken. The part of me belonging to *her* rejoiced at being filled with something of his. Then Van Helsing set my broken arm, all the while admonishing my caretakers to keep me as motionless as possible lest the terrible bruise on my spine grow worse and leave me paralyzed.

I slept, though not well. My dreams were filled with visions of *her* face, eyes sparking with hell-fire, mouth wide and glistening with blood.

My blood.

DURING THAT FIRST day in bed, the awful dreams would not leave even with the warmth of sunlight spilling across my coverlet. The only comfort was when Arthur, wearing the deep black of mourning, came to greet me and rest his hand upon my forehead for a few precious moments.

Van Helsing entered, declared me to have a fever, and since no one as yet had reported a child missing seemed in no great rush to hurry me home. He gave me a gentle pat. "In a few hours you will be back to your old self, dear child. Your tribulations will have ended."

I did not understand what he meant but was too ill to demand an explanation. He took Arthur and the two other men from the night before – Dr. John Seward and Quincey Morris – and left on some errand.

Just after three in the afternoon I was overcome by the sensation of something thick and sharp was being driven deeply between my ribs one terrible blow at a time. I let out a wail that brought two maids, the steward and my nurse running. Hands held me down as I flailed and shrieked. From inside my head I heard Van Helsing's accented voice chanting a prayer in a language I could not understand. The words tore at me as if I were being devoured by a wild animal.

And then, abruptly, it was over. The hallucination faded and I was tired, so tired. My throat burned from screaming. When the men returned Van Helsing was rushed inside where he examined me once more. "He was her last victim and torn from her amidst wrath and agony. The wound from her wicked mouth is gone," he said, removing the bandage on my neck to show his companions, "yet some part of her lingers within him." Worse, my thrashing had worsened the injury to my back. I could neither feel nor move my legs. Van Helsing prescribed rest with a cheerfulness I did not quite believe.

Arthur, Dr. Seward and Mr. Morris went outside and spoke with Van Helsing in a low voice, then Arthur returned to sit at my bedside. At first glance he seemed only a normal man, an adult like any other save for his gentle manner and fine clothes, but I saw in his eyes the same horror that visited me in my dreams. We were bound, he and I, both of us bespelled by the beautiful woman and falling afoul of the beast which had overtaken her soul. He grasped my hand which appeared so small and powerless in his. "Poor child to have been so ruined by the dreadful creature my Lucy had become. Rest, now. I shall look after you."

The moment his tender lips rested upon my brow love and longing burst within me. My craving for the bloofer lady had gone.

Now I wanted Arthur. Her husband.

Being the good man that Arthur was and despite the great grief and distress weighing on his mind, he took me round the neighborhood in search of someone to claim me. "Someone must be looking for you," he insisted, "beautiful child that you are."

Cleaned up as I was, freshly scrubbed and in brand-new knickers and my first pair of shoes, no one recognized me. He had to carry me since I could not walk but he didn't seem to mind. I wrapped my arms around his neck and breathed in his verdant cologne. The scent triggered memories and feelings I couldn't possibly have. Until a few days before we had never met and yet I *knew* this man liked his eggs poached, not fried. He was fond of the dark blue akin to the evening sky. His favorite mount was a sorrel gelding who was always sure-footed during a hunt.

In truth, Arthur was as reluctant to let me go as I was him. Because it was his fiancée who had crippled me he considered himself responsible for my welfare. No one in my poor, decrepit neighborhood in Whitby had the means of looking after a child unable to walk and he could not bear the thought of seeing me turn into a beggar on the street. After several fruitless days of trying to discover if I had any family left, he gave up his search and told me of his intention to see to my care and education himself. I was ecstatic at the thought of having him always nearby, but within a fortnight he came to me with unhappy news. "I must leave for a time. We're going after the beast which befouled my Lucy."

I embraced him and cried, but other than causing him more sorrow my tears had no effect on his plans. For nearly five weeks he was gone, traveling with Doctor Van Helsing and their companions into the godforsaken lands in search of the beast which had stolen the beautiful lady's soul. I missed him unbearably, and despite my nurse's devotion I begged and cried for him and would give the nurse no peace. My strength and health returned, but my legs remained limp and useless. I cried all the more, certain Arthur would find a way to forget about me once he knew for certain I would not walk again.

My worries were in vain. The night he returned he swept me into his arms and clasped me with the strength I'd longed for. "It's over," he whispered in my ear. "The beast is dead. We're free."

I kissed him and slid my cheek against his unshaven face until our tears mingled in shared relief.

SOME TIME EARLIER, Arthur's father had passed on and left him the title of Lord Godalming along with the estate in Ring. We moved there together and he spared no expense, paying first for a fine wheeled chair to give me some measure of freedom and then, when I'd gained some strength and height, sending for Van Helsing to fashion me a set of braces for my legs. Some feeling eventually returned and we were both determined that one day I should be able to walk on my own. I had a tutor, a young, Oxford-educated man who drilled me in mathematics, science and geography and berated me when my handwriting was not as polished as he believed it should be. Words were difficult and though I hated the exercises I persisted, wanting only to please Arthur and make him proud of me.

While we often shared a congenial tea and supper, our nights were not always so peaceful. For months I awoke screaming at the sudden, unearthly rage filling my chest to bursting. In the darkness I saw those hell-fire eyes, disembodied orbs hovering in the air. In a panic I fell to the floor. With neither chair nor braces, all I could do was drag myself in a futile attempt to escape.

Arthur never failed to rush to my rescue. "It's all right." He held me to his breast, rocking me and wiping my tears with his thumb. "Hush, child. She's gone. Her soul was freed. The creature cannot harm you." Then he carried me back to bed and lay with me, his body warm and protective against mine until I was at last able to sleep unhindered.

His dreams were little better. On the nights I didn't awaken him he would appear at breakfast red-eyed despite his otherwise cheery appearance. Our gazes met and silent understanding passed between us. Miss Lucy's soul might be at peace and the foul beast vanquished, but the memory of their torment remained something only a precious few could comprehend.

The days, largely, were happy ones. Arthur taught me the running of an estate. He bought me a handsome pony, a mottled gray gelding, and had a saddle specially fitted for my crippled legs. We rode together often, greeting my lord's tenants and neighbors and sometimes making the long trek to visit his dearest friends. Both of us enjoyed visiting Dr. Seward at his asylum, especially when he found a forthright young woman to become his fiancée and soon his wife.

My favorite afternoons were those when, lying on a blanket in the woods while we devoured whatever luncheon the cook had packed for us, Arthur would wind a finger around one of my dark locks and gaze at me. "You remind me of my Lucy. Such a delicate face and your hair falling like so…"

I smiled at his happiness. My arms hungered for him though I was too young and uncertain of what, exactly, my longing meant or why I craved him so. Despite Arthur's attempts to shield me, I knew something of the ways between men and women and had the strangest image of myself clad in a dress with Arthur paying me the attentions he might give to a lover. I said nothing, knowing not what my strange notions meant and afraid to broach such a delicate subject.

I gained some inkling when, seven years after Arthur and his companions had slain the beast, I accompanied them to Transylvania to the very location where they'd accomplished the deed. With two physicians, Van Helsing and Seward, we were able to accommodate my physical limitations with little issue and no one complained of the occasional slowness. Besides, I was not the youngest on the journey. Mr. and Mrs. Jonathan Harker had brought along their young son, Quincey, to show him the place where his namesake had died.

In the shadow of a castle crumbling high atop a cliff, I watched the child play with boyish energy and innocence. A chord of regret struck within me. At such a tender age it was already apparent he would be a rough-and-tumble boy like his American namesake, but I felt none of the same masculine impulses and wasn't sure if I ever had. I took great care over my appearance, fussing over my hands, complexion and hair with the same obsession as – yes – a woman.

That night we made a bonfire to honor the dead and lay the last of our memories to rest. In a quiet moment alone, Van Helsing sat beside me both to adjust the damnable braces and to inquire after my health. When I mentioned my jealously of young Quincey, who even now forged a mock battle with toy cowboys and Indians, Van Helsing nodded.

"You received a terrible shock when, as just a child, you were the victim of a great and insidious evil. You have undergone a sore trial, entered bitter waters and survived them. The time for mourning is ended. Your path, your future lies ahead of you."

My attention turned to Arthur who sat, head bowed, before the flames. Van Helsing followed my gaze.

"The sweet Miss Lucy made a great impression on you, I think. You felt both her love and the unnatural hatred of the creature in possession of her." He grasped my chin and turned my face toward his. "I see her passion in your eyes. I believe a piece of her soul touched yours and stayed there that night she tasted of your blood."

"But..." My heart hammered within my chest. If that was true, my adoration of Arthur was a morbid, deviant thing not of my own making.

Van Helsing seemed to read my mind. Sympathy and compassion creased his face. "I am a doctor. I have seen a great many things, some of which many of my fellow man would deem unnatural or a sin. Nothing is unnatural if love is a part of it. The greater disgrace is to keep that love to yourself out of fear."

"But this longing – is it mine or hers?"

He squeezed my hand. "Dear child, that is something you will have to discover for yourself."

WE RETURNED HOME, all of us light-hearted and much improved for our travels. As the seasons turned I was able to leave my wheeled chair for good, relying solely on the braces. Difficult and sometimes painful as they were to maneuver, I nonetheless made circuits of the house, traveling farther and farther in an effort to regain strength and coordination. Lord Arthur encouraged me in my efforts and often rewarded me with a kiss on my cheek or forehead. Every time he did, the heat and hunger within me flared until I thought I would go mad with unquenched desire.

One summer we traveled to Whitby and stayed at Hillingham, which Arthur had inherited from Miss Lucy's mother and which had been thoroughly redecorated at his request. We had not stayed there yet as Arthur's poor heart remained tormented by his memories, but between the need to see to business in the area and my unashamed begging we went. I was delighted to have a new area to explore, though, wise to Arthur's mood, I waited until he went out on an errand to nose around the house in earnest. Most of the rooms were richly furnished and lacking a personal touch, so it was the storeroom which held the greatest interest for me. Inside was a wooden chest carved with a pastoral scene, the most feminine item I'd seen in the house so far. With great curiosity I flipped the latch and lifted the heavy lid. Inside were layers of carefully folded dresses and a box full of jewelry and a small bottle of perfume. I froze, shocked at the cache of items long hidden away from sight.

So Arthur had not been able to part with everything belonging to Miss Lucy. The faintest hint of perfume clinging to the fabric assailed my senses with memories of that night when I'd clung to her and she'd so cruelly flung me away – the same night my yearning for Arthur had enveloped my entire being.

With trembling hands I withdrew the topmost garment, a white lawn dress that would have complemented her complexion. A sudden, mad desire overcame me and I stripped off my boy's jacket, shirt and trousers. Slender and slight as I was, the dress slipped easily over my head and waist. Some deep part of me recognized the feel of the fabric and the soft swishing as I walked. Though I had never touched a dress before, my fingers knew exactly how to do up the multitude of buttons and laces. I had not cut my dark hair. Usually I kept it tied back but now I loosened it so it lay in a most unmasculine fashion.

A scratching at the door caused me to turn. Arthur sagged there, his face taken by a ghastly paleness. The sight of him concerned me. If he collapsed I had not the strength to move him.

"Lucy?" The name was strangled as it emerged. Before I could speak he was upon me, shaking me with violent force. "How could you? These are *her* things. *Hers.* How dare you..." Tears slid down his face. "Is this why you begged to come? To shame her memory?" He raised a hand, his face so twisted with grief and pain that I flinched, certain he would strike me as I deserved.

Yet the blow did not fall. Instead he took my face betwixt his palms and placed his tear-dampened lips upon mine not with the usual chasteness of a peck to brow or cheek but with a deep overpowering lust. I closed my eyes, the better to absorb the ecstasy growing within me.

Then Arthur drew back and stopped just short of propelling me away. His features were a mixture of yearning and pain, grief and desire. "See what you have become."

He pulled the dust cloth from a mirror leaning against the far wall and stood me before it. The resulting image robbed me of my breath.

It was as if Miss Lucy had been recalled to life, for it was her luscious lips and passionate eyes that appeared in the glass, the same sunny locks flowing about my shoulders.

Arthur trailed his hands down my cheeks and shoulders. He encircled my waist, pausing just under the place my bosom would be if I had one. How many times he must have done this with Miss Lucy, and how natural it felt to have him hold me so.

I shuddered, suddenly uncertain. The image was undeniably myself – yet it was also her, and I was frightened by the uncanny likeness as well as my intense attraction to Arthur.

"Take these things off and don't ever come here again." His fingers fumbled at the buttons and he stared in wonderment as I nudged him aside and easily stripped the garment. Clad in naught but my underclothes and braces I shivered before him, frightened, confused, and wanting the reassurance he could not give.

Abruptly he turned and left without saying anything more. I sank down onto the edge of the trunk. By rights I should do as he said and repack the dress and leave everything be but I could not. Some devil took my hand and I sifted through the rest of Miss Lucy's belongings. Most tantalizing was the silk nightdress which caressed my bare skin with the same gentleness I wished Arthur would use. My member hardened and grew, which both shamed me and filled me with a need I did not know how to sate.

The most wicked idea entered into my mind. With haste I reclaimed my masculine apparel, which now seemed ill-fitting despite having been made by the finest tailors, and replaced all but a few choice items in the trunk.

I COULD NOT bathe myself, as it was difficult to lift myself from the confines of the tub, but once finished I sent my manservant away and told him he would not be needed the rest of the night. Barely able to contain my impatience I waited until the hall clock struck midnight, then swapped my shift for the silk nightgown that had belonged to Miss Lucy.

I wore nothing beneath. Mindful of gossip I'd overheard regarding how a young lord on a neighboring estate had been caught *in flagrante* with the footman, I reached for the jar of ointment meant to treat the sores left by the leather straps on my braces but which I now put it to a different use. My last preparation was to dab the tiniest amount of Miss Lucy's perfume on my wrists and neck.

With the servants all asleep I made my slow, laborious way down the hall to Lord Arthur's bedchamber, using walls and railings to keep my balance. I'd left the braces in my room, unwilling to let the clunky devices ruin the illusion.

It was far easier to blame this madness on whatever essence Miss Lucy had left behind than to face the remotest possibility that I could want such a thing.

At Arthur's door I twisted the knob and entered silently except for the scrape of my bare feet against the carpet. I stood at the foot of his bed, naked save for the silk sweetly torturing my heated flesh. Either he heard or sensed my presence because his eyes opened and he stared fixedly at me.

I held my arms wide. "Come to me, Arthur."

"Lucy..." Before I could draw another breath he had me on the bed and crushed to his chest as he sobbed. "Lucy." His hand tangled in my hair and pulled my head back. He kissed my throat, right over the spot where two scars from Miss Lucy's teeth remained.

A shudder ran through me. The brush of his lips in that same place brought back memories both terrible and wonderful. I groped at him, eager to feel the flesh I'd longed to touch. I peeled off his nightshirt and breathed in the scent of his skin. My body was at last mature enough to respond to him and accept his attentions, but I had no idea if this plan would be followed through to the end.

"Lucy." His voice was raspy and hoarse, so unlike the man I was used to – and so endearing. Starved of intimate companionship for so many years he lost no time in laying me down and raising my nightdress above my waist. I froze, knowing that there rested the organ which could bring the illusion to an abrupt demise – but Arthur paid it no mind. He climbed atop me, his breath coming in gasps as his lips once again sought my flesh.

Whether I clutched him because of my desire or Miss Lucy's I didn't know and it no longer mattered. Our bodies met, tangled, joined. Within each other's embrace we found a way to quench the fire and torment which had plagued us for so long.

I hadn't known such bliss – such release – was possible. I'd scarcely caught my breath after the first wave of pleasure crested and broke before he began the whole process anew, driving us both to greater, more frenzied heights.

When exhaustion claimed the last of our energy he lay with his head on my chest. I stroked the silken strands of his hair, entirely at peace for the first time I could remember. The moment was perfect. "I love you, Arthur."

He rose up on his arms and shook his head as if disoriented. The fevered passion his eyes vanished. Panic distorted his face as he gazed upon my scarcely-clad body. He shoved me away and spoke with a harshness which had never before brushed my ears. "Out. Get *out*, you foul thing! You have tricked me, besmirched her name and ruined every sweet memory I have of my Lucy. I have damned us both..."

Hurt and horrified I fled, tripping and stumbling because of my weakened legs. I cared not that I wore only a thin layer of cloth or that the heavens had chosen to release a downpour. Crawling and slipping I made my way to the stable and the pony who, usually so patient, was not inclined to venture out into the wet. I managed saddle and bridle but mounting the poor creature took some doing since I could not mount in a proper manner but had to drape myself across his back and haul myself upright.

There was only one sanctuary I could think of where I would be accepted without question. A strange apparition I must have made pounding on the wooden doors at the asylum, but Dr. Seward was used to oddness of all kinds. He opened the portal himself, wearing a thick dressinggown to brace against the weather.

Seeing my condition, he immediately draped the dressing-gown about my trembling shoulders. He sent a man to tend the pony and helped me into his study, whereupon his pretty young wife found me a dry nightshirt and thrust a cup of hot tea into my hands. When she returned to bed and the doctor and I were quite alone he asked, "What has happened to send you all but naked into the night?"

My teeth did not cease chattering for some time. When at last I was able to relate my woeful tale he listened in companionable silence. He nodded as I finished. "There is much to think about but this is a matter we will discuss at a more forgiving hour. Sleep," he said, and fashioned me a warm nest upon his sofa.

He turned out the lamp and left. Exhausted as I was I could not rest. Now that my body had tasted of Arthur's it would not rest. My arms – and other, more delicate parts – remained hungry.

IN THE MORNING the good doctor sent a telegram to Arthur informing him of my whereabouts should he be worried. I listened, mute, while Dr. Seward made a few suggestions, but during the night there occurred to me only one possibility, which I expressed at the first opportunity. "Lock me up. I am certain I am quite mad."

To my surprise, he laughed and gestured toward the hallways filled with his patients. "Those out there, they are the truly mad. They turn away from truths they cannot bear to face. Madness is far easier a thing to live with. They end up here when there is no place left on earth to them."

So had I come to the same madhouse, alone and desperate. My bodily impulses had caused me to disregard everything polite and proper and had sent Arthur into a paroxysm of anger. Worse, I had *enjoyed* the sin.

The doctor must have seen my consternation. "One night when we were quite in our cups I regaled poor Arthur with tales of so-called sinful things. After witnessing two of my patients sodomize each other and noting their apparent enjoyment, I was quite curious about the endeavor." His smile was wry.

I stared, unable to fathom how an esteemed man like the doctor could have fantasized about such things. "And did you?" I asked, knowing how rude the question was.

He stared off into the distance and took his time in replying. "No. I feared the pain. I feared the loss of self." His gaze returned to me. "But you, my young friend, seem to have experienced neither despite your claims regarding gender."

A flush took me from my crown to my toes. "It is a terrible thing, then, to desire to be something I am not?"

Dr. Seward pondered this. "I myself did not find anything clinically wrong with the deeds of either Ernest Boulton or Frederick Park years ago. I was not far from your own age when the pair was arrested for wearing women's clothing. I believe our society is too fearful of vice without thinking of possible virtue in expressing identity."

The good doctor's words made sense excepting for the fact I could not alter certain physical aspects. Social convention, of course, made donning feminine attire a terrible risk. Arthur was a lord and I had no wish to ruin his name with scandal.

Yet Dr. Seward's question caused a dozen brazen ideas to spring forth. I could not return to who and what I was, a creature hovering in Miss Lucy's shadow, subsuming my desires for the will of others. The night's pleasures had opened within me a door I could not shut even if I'd had the will to do so.

I no longer needed Miss Lucy, or the guise of her, either. I now knew what she had given me on that dark night so long ago – not the hatred and vileness of the demon within her but love, courage and strength. These she had laid upon me as a parting gift, perhaps knowing her demise was at hand.

It only remained to see what Arthur would do with my choice. If he thrust me away…well, I would find a means of survival.

Just after lunchtime Dr. Seward received a telegram from Arthur. "He is on his way here. Evidently he is quite concerned and wishes to apologize."

Of all the locations to speak with him, a madhouse seemed an unlikely place despite the presence of our good friend. "I will greet him on the road."

Dr. Seward smiled with great impishness. "Wearing what?"

I MET ARTHUR halfway between the asylum and Hillingham. He drew his gelding to a halt and waited to see what I might do. The animal snorted and pawed the ground with impatience but I bade my pony to take his time as we approached.

Arthur gazed at the jacket and riding skirt Dr. Seward's good wife had managed to find for me, but it was not unhappiness which creased his face. "Are you well?"

In silence I turned my pony round and headed toward Tate Hill Pier and the bridge leading to the East Cliff. Once across I dismounted and tethered the pony which would not be able to manage the steep steps. I wasn't sure I could, but I meant to try.

Arthur followed my example. He said nothing as I struggled to lift my legs and balance, but when he offered his arm for support I did not rebuff him. Together we climbed up to the churchyard and strolled down the lane of yews to Miss Lucy's resting place. Here we had met years before and now would decide our future. With the dead to witness I said, "My arms are hungry for you, Arthur. Mine. Not hers."

I dared not look at him despite the increasing amount of silence. Far below in the bay, ships bobbed on the sea's gentle waves. A slight breeze wafted locks of my hair which I had left loose. Eventually Arthur cleared his throat. "Last night..."

I waited with patience, aware of how overwhelmed he became under great stress.

"Last night it was a grave shock to learn I could lust after another so easily. I lost control and in doing so entered a state of bliss I have not felt for some time. Afterward I was afraid and angry with myself. I spoke harshly, and for this I am sorry." On bended knee, he grasped my hand. I gazed at him, feeling the sincerity of his words. "I love you. *You*, not the shadow of my Lucy. I care not what form you choose, only that you are at my side, always."

My arms curled around his neck, hungry no more.

PROTECT THE KING

Jeff Mann

> *"The leader of the gypsies, a splendid-looking fellow who sat his horse like a centaur, waved them back..."*
>
> – DRACULA, Chapter 27

MARCH 20TH, 1890

A LIGHT snow is falling, yet the willows along the stream are green. Dully, Boldo notes this seasonal juxtaposition as he shovels dirt into his mother's grave.

Today is the first day of spring, but in the Carpathians winter lingers, nipping the new buds, blackening the first flowers. Flurries descend the mountains on a sharp wind – delicate, lacy, killing. *Like the three queens, their long white gowns flowing in moonlight,* the young Szgany thinks, wiping sweat from his dark curls. Their frightful attentions his boyar spared him, those few times Boldo risked his mother's beatings and answered his Lord's call to the castle.

Well, Boldo's escaped his mother now. Forever. No more beatings, no more strictures, no more sour and incessant complaints. At last his life is his own. Now, if the Good God wills, his years of bitter hunger will end. Brown eyes gleaming beneath thick eyebrows, Boldo heaves in the last load of earth and pats the mound down with the back of the shovel. A marker can come later, and perhaps some flowers. No hurry. His mother's needs no longer trump his own.

The flurries have ceased; the afternoon sun's broken free of clouds, rapidly melting the pallid aftermath of the storm. Now that the burly youth's exertions are over, the breeze chills him. He buttons up his dirty woolen jacket, and, shovel over his shoulder, strides out of the graveyard, up the slope, and into the woods. In a clearing among a grove of pines, his *vardo* is parked, the traveling wagon in which he was born, in which his mother died last night. It's still stuffy and smelly with illness. Boldo drags out the mattresses and bed-coverings, spreading them on rocks or hanging them over low limbs to air out. The rear door he leaves open to the sun and wind.

Bone weary, Boldo, after checking on his beloved horses, retires to a nearby patch of sun beneath a great oak, its bud-clusters just beginning to swell with spring. Having cared for his mother all through her last illness, he hasn't slept well in weeks. He leans back against the tree's trunk, pulls out his flask of slivovitz, drinks deep, and heaves a low sigh.

Boldo Gábor is a swarthy-skinned youth of medium height and powerful build. The glossy black hair framing his face is thick and curly. His beard – full, bushy, and black – highlights prominent lips, pursed at present in a thoughtful pout. Years of labor as a blacksmith have blessed him with brawn – big-muscled arms, broad shoulders, a barrel chest – strength that has come in handy during many a battle and brawl. He's known in the tribe as their best boxer and wrestler, not to mention their most agile horseman. His meaty forearms are plastered with the same inky hair that crowns his head; curls of chest hair, a burgeoning wilderness, extrude over his shirt collar.

Despite the naggings of his mother – so recently cut short – he's still unmarried. With sad affection, he thinks of them now, Luminitsa, Nadya, Florica, girls who pursued him for years with no success. For so long, he felt the pressure, not only from his mother but from his tribe, to court a girl and settle down. At twenty-eight, he's far past the early age at which most Szgany men marry, and, to his relief, the tribe seems to have given up its aggressive crusade to push him into matrimony.

Boldo takes another burning swig of plum brandy, closes his eyes, and stretches his aching limbs, luxuriating in the sunlight. Its encompassing warmth reminds him of the passions he felt in his adolescence for older boys of the tribe, young men he furtively studied and adored. Andreas, Gunari, Milosh, Marko, whose rich scents and sinewy bodies he savored as they wrestled, ran, or swam together. Even then Boldo knew: were his feelings ever discovered, were he ever to express his attractions, he would suffer the worst fate a Romany can, to be cast out from the tribe. What yearnings he suffered, long years of stoic repression, before that blessed night of his birthday, when the Boyar of the Mountains overpowered him, carried him to the castle, and showed him another way of loving: painful, sometimes terrifying, but matchlessly profound.

"Boldo!" A shout rouses him from his ruminations. It's his cousin Ion, loping up the hill. He's as darkly featured as Boldo, though thinly built and sharp-featured. He bears a covered crock wrapped in a towel.

"May I join you?" Without waiting for an answer, Ion flops down into a satin-sheen pile of fallen leaves. He lifts the crock's lid, revealing the steamy gold of cornmeal topped with white cheese. "Here's *mămăligă*," Ion says, resting the crock in the leaves. "Your favorite. Mother sent it. You really should find a wife, cousin. Who will cook for you now?"

"You know Mother taught me to cook. Still, many thanks," Boldo says, patting his shoulder. "Thank Aunt Lala. I love her *mămăligă*. Thanks too for helping me dig Mother's grave this morning."

"Why did you usher everyone off after the service? I would have helped you fill it too."

"No." Boldo smiles sadly, stroking his beard. "That I needed to do myself."

"And what will you do now? Continue at the forge?"

"I don't know," Boldo says. "Perhaps I'll take service with the boyar as so many of our tribe have."

"Your mother feared the boyar, you know. She blamed him for her grandfather's death."

"I know, I know, I've heard the story many times. Mother was addled! We all know my ancestor was found in the forest, stabbed to death. No doubt by a goddamned Romanian."

"Who hated him because of his loyalty to the boyar. Surely you know that. My mother distrusts him too, despite his generosity. It's said he attended the *Scholomance*, the Devil's school of sorcery, that he's a warlock whose magic has allowed him to cheat death. I wish you would reconsider."

Boldo sits up. "What would our tribe be without him, Ion? You know how they all hate us, the Saxons, the Romanians, the Magyars. They would have exterminated us long ago if it had not been for his protection."

Ion sighs, waving a placating hand. "Please, let's not argue. You're not moving into our *vardo*, I gather?" Ion gestures toward Boldo's traveling wagon. "You know a place that has seen death is impure. It should be burned, everyone agrees."

Boldo snorts. "Burned? It's all I have left. My father built it. He carved the interior. I was born in it. I shan't be burning it. And, kind as your parents are to invite me, I know how cramped your *vardo* already is. I shall live with the impurity."

"All alone? You're alone too much, Boldo, in the woods or at the forge. That's what Mother says, and I agree. If you were to take a wife, the elders might even choose you as the next leader of the tribe. You've always kept yourself apart, even when you were a child. See? Here you are, camped up here in the woods rather than with the rest of us by the river. Now that you're an orphan, you'll be alone even more."

Boldo sighs. The light is slanting with late afternoon. He stretches out, folds his arms behind his head, and closes his eyes. "Tomorrow, come over for lunch, Ion. I'm going to simmer a pot of beans tonight. I know how much you savor them. Right now, I'm tired. I'm going to take a nap. Thanks again for the *mămăligă*. I'll see you tomorrow."

Ion shakes his head and rises. He shuffles off, kicking dead leaves as he goes. When the woodlands are silent again, Boldo opens his eyes. Shadows are gathering down in the valley and along the river's silvery snaking, falling on the community of Szgany caravans. He lifts his eyes from the lowlands, following the slopes and crests of foothills, up, up, up to the highest mountains. From here, Boldo can just make out, above a band of evergreens, the silhouette of a tower. "Lord," Boldo whispers. Then, knowing how well slumber makes unwanted intervals of time pass faster, he falls asleep.

THE CAMPFIRE, FED with pine kindling, smokes and sparks, wafting the scent of resin through the clearing. Boldo stirs the pot of beans, watching the red sun set over the mountains. By the time he's gobbled a plate of *mămăligă*, followed by a bowl of beans, night has fallen over the forest and clouds have blotted the stars. A light snow has begun by the time Boldo checks on the horses and banks the fire. He stands, shawled in one of the aired-out blankets, staring up at the mountains, and mutters words of welcome before climbing into his *vardo*.

It's chilly inside, yet Boldo strips off his vest, shirt, and trousers nevertheless, eager for what he prays this night will bring. His nakedness, he senses, is a silent statement, a kind of invitation. For a moment, he stands before the little mirror hung on the wagon's wall, studying himself in the light of a single candle. He likes what he sees, the curved muscles of his shoulders and chest, the soft black hair matting his belly and torso, the gold ring glinting in his left ear. Boldo grins, teeth bright white against the darkness of his beard and his olive-hued skin, and flexes his right biceps, then his left. He tries to see himself as his Lord might. With all his heart he hopes that the Boyar from the Mountains will be pleased with him when next they meet. They have been long apart; Boldo's mother has seen to that.

Boldo's eyes fall on the golden cross gleaming in the thick fur between his pectorals, the ornament his mother has made him wear for years, a rueful reminder of his loneliness and longing.

"No longer," Boldo mutters, full lips curling into a snarl. With grim determination, he yanks the necklace off, breaking the thin chain. Turning, he studies the crucifixes his mother was so careful to hang about the small space, and the dusty garlands of dried garlic. Snatching up the protective devices, he tosses the lot into a sack, throws opens the back door of the *vardo*, and flings the bag into the snow-flecked woods with a great heave, a violence born of long resentment and nearly a decade devoid of touch.

Shivering now, the muscled Szgany blows out the candle and slides into his bunk, beneath a woolen welter of blankets. It's his first night entirely alone. He thinks of his mother, of her suffocating love and her casual cruelty – his feelings a confused morass of regret, resentment, grief, and relief – then, weary of ambivalence, shakes his head and shifts his thoughts to the immediate future: what might come to him before morning. Curling up, he tries to imagine the boyar's strong arms embracing him from behind. *Come, my Lord. Come, my Lord. Do not forget me. Please come, my Lord.* He stares into the darkness, aroused and frightened, listening to the wind. He runs his hands over his own nakedness, remembering that summer night when the boyar first took him.

AUGUST 8TH, 1881

THE WOODS ARE dark and the moon is rising as Boldo leaves the forge. Today was his birthday, yet still the master blacksmith kept his apprentice unusually late, determined that Boldo should learn a new technique upon the anvil. Rather than returning immediately to the *vardo* as he'd promised his superstitious and perpetually anxious mother, the bearded youth, enchanted by the warm summer breeze, leaves the Romany encampment. He follows the path through the forest and down to the river, where water is purling and moonlight glints among the reeds. His fingers ache from hours of wielding the hammer, the bellows, and the tongs, and so he kneels by the stream, beneath arched boughs of birch, to bathe his hands and then his begrimed face in the cool plashing. He kicks off his boots and strips off his clothes. Naked, he dives in. The cool water is delicious after a long day spent in the hot forge.

After a lengthy swim, Boldo, relaxed and refreshed, climbs onto the riverbank, stretches out in the grass, and falls asleep. It's nearly midnight when he rises, well aware of the tongue-lashing his worried mother is bound to inflict on him as soon as he gets home.

He belts on his trousers. He's wringing out his hair and beard when he hears a low growl. He turns, only to stiffen with shock. A huge gray wolf, its hackles raised, is barring his path back to the camp. Its eyes glow red. It draws back its black lips, exposing frightful teeth.

Boldo unsheathes the dagger at his hip – one of the few heirlooms his father left him – and brandishes it. At the same time, he crouches, fetching a jagged stone from the riverbank. Wolves are common in these wild mountains, but never has he encountered one so huge.

The wolf regards Boldo's weapons – a gesture so human, one of a combatant sizing the Szgany up. It growls and paces, and then, to Boldo's amazement, it steps back and to the side – in a manner one might describe as courtly – leaving the path free. Boldo moves forward, keeping his eyes on the animal. Then he flings the rock, catching the beast in the side, and breaks into a headlong run. He's only made it a few yards before a great weight slams into him from behind. He falls forward, something strikes the back of his head, and he blacks out.

RETURNING TO CONSCIOUSNESS, Boldo's first sensations are of wind and a gentle sense of swaying. When his eyes flicker open, for a moment all he can see are specks of light, as if he were moving among stars.

It takes him several more confused seconds to realize that he's slung backwards over someone's shoulder. *By the Good God, he must be very, very strong,* Boldo thinks, more startled than afraid. *More than a match for me. Well, I've always enjoyed a challenge.* He flexes, preparing to struggle, only to find his hands bound behind him.

The stranger responds to Boldo's movements by tightening his arm around the youth's waist. "Be calm, boy," he says in the Szgany tongue. The voice is low, hollow, curt with command.

Boldo growls and kicks, only to find his feet bound as well. Angry, he tries to shout, but the sound he emits is muffled. Furious, he bites down into dense softness: his mouth is obstructed with a series of tightly tied rags. Teeth gnashing the gag, the blacksmith begins to squirm and curse.

His abductor chuckles and grips him tighter. "I would advise you to save resistance for later. Look down."

Boldo does so, only to heave a stifled gasp.

Below are starlit treetops and sharp rocks, and, far, far below them, the twining silver strand of the river. Boldo and his captor are hundreds of feet in the air, hanging off the stone walls of a great edifice built on a sheer-sided crag.

The pugnacious Romany may be nigh unbeatable in combat, but heights have always terrified him. Finding himself so helpless, carried so far aloft, his customary courage deserts him.

Thunder rumbles in the distance. The stranger's voice has much the same timbre as he whispers, "Keep still now. It would be a great loss, would it not, if I dropped you? You, so young, so handsome, so full of life?"

Boldo, trembling, nods. With a soft whimper, the distance below claims his eyes. He faints.

A BED. LARGE. Very soft. Musky, like the smell of sweaty men, dense woodland, rutting animals.

For a few seconds, Boldo nuzzles the pillow, relishing the comfort of it, before memory returns and with it his fear. Dark eyes wide, a lump in his throat, he rolls onto his side, stretching his cramped limbs and taking his bearings.

He's in the much same state as before – the rags are still tied between his teeth, and his wrists and ankles are still roped tight. His captor, whoever he might be, is nowhere to be seen. The only sounds audible are the shush and drip of rain.

Boldo focuses on freedom, wriggling and twisting his hands and feet, trying to suppress his panicked pants in case his captor is somewhere within earshot. The rope around his wrists refuses to give, but, after long struggle – wincing, wriggling, and kicking – he manages to free his feet.

Boldo slips off the bed and stands, ears cocked for any human sound. He surveys the room. The chamber is large, huge compared to the narrow *vardo* he's lived in all his life. A small fire smolders in a great stone fireplace ornamented with baronial designs. There is no other source of light, other than two narrow windows that pierce one side of the room, apertures that admit only darkness, a chill breeze, and the steady sound of rain. In the opposite wall is set a great oaken door of Gothic shape. The bed, a side table, and an elegant armchair compose the only furniture.

Frantic, Boldo ranges the room, looking for something sharp on which to cut his remaining restraints. He finds nothing that might serve that essential function. He struggles against the coarse rope till his wrists are raw. To no avail: the bonds are expertly tied, cruelly tight, and unyielding.

Now he leans out the windows, hoping to ascertain how far he might be from possible rescue, only to glimpse the same terrifying drop he'd seen while hoisted on his abductor's shoulder. The wall drops sheer into mountain darkness, a sickening abyss whose depths his eyes cannot plumb. Shuddering, he backs up and turns away.

Now he paces the room, bare feet chilled by the stone floor. Swearing, he flexes his thick arms, maddened by such helplessness, champing his mouth-rags like an angry animal. He backs up to the door, pinioned hands fumbling with the iron handle, only to find it unmoving. He tugs and twists till his fingers ache. It shifts not an inch.

Now he falls to his knees, shaking his head of shaggy black hair from right to left, as if he could throw off despair the way a dog could dirty pond water, as if his repetitive gesture of negation could magically transform the harrowing reality of his circumstances into a bad dream dismissed at dawn. Head bowed, he recommences his desperate efforts to free his hands – with panting pauses to catch his breath and choke back terror – till the chafed skin of his wrists breaks open and begins to bleed.

Now he struggles to his feet and collapses onto the armchair. For a short time, he slumps there, fighting back tears. Now, hysterical, enraged, he throws himself against the door, slamming his shoulder against the wood till his joints ache and his head throbs.

Now he rubs his face against the wall, against the bed, against the door, till his cheeks are scratched and red, trying and failing to dislodge the knotted rags. Now he leans his head against the door and howls, ferocious threats that alternate with sobbed pleas for release. Now, again, he approaches the awful windows, lifts his face into the gusts of storm, the rain a cooling relief against his flushed face, and screams for help.

Robbed of circulation, his hands are numb now, and cold; he can barely move his fingers. Heaving with frustration and hopelessness, Boldo falls upon the bed and breaks down. He weeps like a child, soaking his black beard and the pillow with tears. Exhausted, he curls into a ball and, shivering, falls asleep.

Sounds wake Boldo. The storm is roaring outside, downpour become violent tempest, but, in the rare intervals of quiet allowed when the mingled noises of wind, rain, and thunder pause, he can make out voices beyond the door.

Boldo wipes his still moist cheeks against the coverlet. Rising, heart pounding, he creeps to the door. Hunching down, he presses his ear against the crack along the doorframe.

Women. Several of them, voicing what sounds like querulous complaint. A man's voice, deep and satiny, answering them in tones of courtesy and cajolery.

The women's voices recede. There's the jingle of metal, then a key clicks in the lock. Boldo jolts up and staggers back, eyes on the entry.

The great door opens. There, in the aperture, looms the silhouette of a tall, lean man.

"They are gone," says the stranger. Closing the door behind him, he locks it. Turning, he steps into the firelight. Slowly he moves toward the captive Szgany. "Now we may talk, you and I. I am the boyar Dracula. I knew your great-grandfather, Mircea. And I've watched you for a long time, boy. Tonight, I think, you will grant me a boon."

Once more the young blacksmith's bravery abandons him. He edges backward, quaking with fear, nauseated by his own vulnerability, feeling his fate entirely in this stranger's hands. As the man approaches, Boldo can make out black clothes of an antique cut covering a strong, lean physique. His hair is dark and neatly cut, his skin pallid, his forehead high, his close-trimmed brown beard streaked with gray. His aquiline nose and high cheekbones somehow remind Boldo of a picture book of noble Romans his cousin Ion used to own. Yet it is his eyes that are most prominent, riveting Boldo with their as yet unspoken intent. Beneath arched and bushy eyebrows much like Boldo's own, they seem almost to glow.

Inch by inch, Boldo backs up, till he's pressed against the wall between the two windows. Outside, the storm continues to resound, but the youth, so swamped with terror, can barely hear it. Now Dracula stands before him. The boyar grips his shoulders, a touch both chilly and painfully strong.

Boldo gulps. Unaccountably, desire pervades him, one more profound than he's ever known. Limbs shaking, sex stiffening, confused by his body's betrayal, he bows his head, unable to meet the nobleman's intense gaze.

Dracula gives a low laugh. Cupping the Szgany's bushy-bearded chin in his hand, he lifts it until the two men are staring into each other's eyes. The boyar strokes the younger man's cheek, running his fingers through his thick whiskers.

"Finely favored," murmurs Dracula, squeezing Boldo's biceps, then the fur-matted mound of his left pectoral. "Just like your forebear."

Sudden heat suffuses Boldo; he breaks into a profuse sweat. With a fore-finger, Dracula traces the boy's upper lip, then runs that same finger down his breastbone, then around a nipple, evoking from the lad a shudder and a groan.

"You have never known such touch, I gather. Another man's touch."

Boldo's cheeks burn with shame, and with shock, that a stranger could so easily see into his most carefully concealed secret. Mesmerized, he shakes his head, unable to look away. Inside him, volition dwindles, like an air-starved candle, like drought-struck grain.

"You want it, do you not? My touch? A Lord's favor?" The boyar's grip intensifies. "Have you not hungered for it?"

Boldo nods. Grinning, Dracula wraps his arms around the bound black-smith and nuzzles his cheek. Boldo leans against him, sex throbbing in his trousers. The boyar's lips range over him, kissing now his gagged mouth, now his brow, now his bare shoulder, now his neck. There's a sharp pang at his throat. When Boldo begins to struggle, Dracula only tightens his embrace. The pain at Boldo's neck worsens, and then it recedes, replaced by a burning akin to pleasure.

Weakness floods the boy's limbs; his head swims. He moans and sags, thighs trembling and knees buckling. Suddenly, for all his muscled weight, he is being lifted into his captor's arms as if he were as light as a sheaf of wheat. Dracula carries the youth across the room and eases him onto the bed. Again, for long moments, he caresses the youth's strong body, and Boldo, nodding, so long starved for touch, can only whimper with welcome. Brushing back Boldo's mussed black hair, once more the boyar kisses his neck.

Boldo closes his eyes. His heart races, the sensation like a great red vortex pulling his soul from his body, his self from the world. He presses his face against his master's shoulder and swoons.

FOR THE FOURTH time this night, Boldo comes groggily to consciousness. He's prone on the bed, still bound. He tries to roll over and fails. He tries again, this time with great effort succeeding. His joints ache, his limbs are leaden with lethargy, yet his fear has vanished. In its place are aching ardor and boundless submission.

Where has my boyar gone? The enfeebled youth lifts his head, looking anxiously around for the man who held him so wonderfully close, who touched him so firmly and yet so tenderly. *Has he left me? Oh, no. Come back, Lord.*

There he is, Boldo realizes with deep relief, just across the room, adding wood to the fire. "My Lord?" Boldo grunts against the knotted gag. At the boy's muted words, Dracula turns.

"Awake at last?" He sits on the bed and strokes Boldo's bare chest, then rests his hand over his heart, as if he were a healer feeling for the race of its beat.

"You will obey me now," Dracula says.

Boldo nods again and again, a gesture that begins with blank-eyed stiffness but ends with smiling enthusiasm.

"And do you wish to go home?"

Boldo hesitates. He thinks of the cramped *vardo*, of his mother's querulous domination and occasional blows. He looks up at his captor, meets his glowing eyes, and slowly shakes his head.

"Good, good. You will be quiet henceforth. Your clamor has disturbed the ladies of this house."

When Boldo nods, Dracula, reaching behind his head, unknots the rags, pulling the moistened lengths gently from his mouth. Boldo licks his lips, croaking, "My thanks, Lord." From a table beside the bed, Dracula lifts a goblet to the boy's lips. Frigid water: Boldo gulps and gulps till his thirst is quenched.

"Now for these." The boyar helps Boldo to his feet, turns him, and unbinds the blacksmith's hands. He kneads the numbed digits and bloodied wrists, then lifts them to his mouth. Luxuriously he laps the dried gore there, running his tongue along the oozing grooves the rough ropes made. Boldo shudders at the sensation.

"You will stay here tonight," Dracula says, wiping his mouth.

"Yes, Lord. Thank you, my good Lord," Boldo whispers. Standing on tiptoe, he wraps his arms around the taller man's neck and leans against him, trembling. "Will you hold me, my Lord?"

Dracula chuckles. "You are so eager, so hungry for love." The boyar's arms encircle Boldo's waist, pulling him closer. "Mircea was the same." For a long interval of silence, they stand there, the boyar nuzzling the youth's black hair, the youth breathing deep his Lord's earthy animal scent.

"Do you know your name's meaning, boy? The name 'Boldo'?"

"I do, sir. It means 'protect the king.'"

"Indeed. And will you, boy? Will you protect your king? Will you pledge your fealty? Will you swear to obey me in all things? As your great-grandfather did?"

"Yes, Lord," Boldo murmurs. "Oh, yes."

"Kneel then."

Obedient, Boldo drops to his knees and bows his head. Once – he reflects in what lucid self-reflexive corner of consciousness he has remaining – his considerable strength and pride would have chosen death over such a show of surrender, but now, somehow, ever since the boyar's first touch, submission to one so much more powerful than he feels to Boldo like a golden honor and the purest strength.

"Swear. Pledge your troth," Dracula says, resting his hands on the Romany's bare shoulders. "For one day I will have great need of you, Boldo Gábor, as I once had need of your ancestor."

"Yes, Lord. I swear." Boldo gazes up at the nobleman, nodding. Abruptly, he wraps his thick arms around Dracula's waist and presses his face against his groin. "I am your faithful servant."

Dracula helps the young Szgany to his feet and back onto the bed, where he covers him with a heavy blanket. "I know you are weary, boy. Now sleep. In the morning you must return to your mother. She is Mircea's granddaughter, learned and powerful in her own right, and, as I swore at your birth, I'll not take you from her. But the day she is gone, you will return to serve me. You will be my protector, my preserver."

Dracula lies down beside the youth, wrapping an arm around him, a gesture of ownership as much as protection. Boldo snuggles against him, as he once did against his father, when the man was still alive and Boldo was still very small. Weak with blood-loss, Boldo slips off to sleep, his Lord's cold fingers tracing his face.

MARCH 20TH, 1890

BOLDO'S EYES BLINK open; he rolls over in his bunk. What woke him? *There. Someone is calling my name! No, that is only the roar of the wind, louder than before. But...wait. Yes. Again. My Lord!* Boldo bolts up from the bed and throws open the vardo's rear door.

Bitter cold flows into the wagon, chilling the naked Szgany. A spring blizzard is pouring down from the mountains, enveloping the forest clearing in thick mist and blinding white snow. Shivering, hugging himself, Boldo leans out, peering around for some sign of the visitor he's prayed for.

For a moment, he sees nothing, and his heart sinks within him. The only sounds are a horse's nickering and the wind soughing through pines. Then, there! Stepping out beneath snow-heavy evergreen boughs is the tall figure in black. *At last!* The breath snags in Boldo's throat. Dracula lopes across the hoary clearing and stands at the bottom of the *vardo*'s steps.

"I am here at last, boy. Here to comfort you. To give you purpose. May I take shelter here tonight?"

Boldo knows what to do. He has learned much during those brief visits to the castle, those few times he was able to flee his mother, receive instruction, and pleasure his Lord. "Come in, my master," he sighs, stepping aside.

Dracula does so, striding into the tiny wagon as if he owned it. Sex rigid despite the cold, Boldo locks the door, then falls to his knees.

"You have kept faith then," the boyar murmurs.

"Yes, Lord. I feared you had forgotten me."

Dracula guffaws. "Fool." Seizing Boldo by his shaggy hair, he jerks him to his feet, only to hurl him onto his back on the bunk. Throwing himself on top of the youth, he clamps a hand over the blacksmith's mouth.

"You will keep still and be quiet, little one. Yes? You will suffer for me?"

Boldo nods, dark eyes wide with longing and fright. Acquiescent, he lies unprotesting, arms at his side.

"I must taste you tonight. The blood is the life, Boldo. Well I know how badly you have ached for my touch. How you have yearned for my cruelty and mastery. Tomorrow, you will saddle up your mares and bring your *vardo* up to the castle. No further reason for you to live down here. I have need of you now. I have plans, a visitor from England on the way. And you must help me. All you Szgany will serve me. Your brave tribe has aided me much over the years, in return for my patronage, for my gold."

With that, Dracula runs a sharp fingernail down Boldo's breastbone, scoring the furry flesh of Boldo's chest. He repeats the action, pressing harder. A third time, harder still, this time cleaving skin, leaving a long thin furrow in which Boldo's blood wells. The youth whimpers beneath the nobleman's palm, his groin throbbing. Dracula bends, lapping up blood with a bass growl. Then he jerks Boldo's head to the side and gashes his neck with sharp teeth. Boldo wraps an arm around the boyar, pulls him closer, sighs with rapture, and knows no more.

MAY 28TH, 1890

THE ENGLISHMAN, HARKER, a weakling, has a face like a woman's. Smooth and wan. In other circumstances, Boldo might wonder what it would be like to lie with him. But, as it is, Boldo has never known such violent jealousy. When he imagines his Lord feeding on this effete cretin, his blood boils. He would like to throttle the fool, punch him in the face, break his delicate neck and throw his corpse into the gorge, but he does not, for that would interfere with his Lord's plan. Instead, Boldo smiles, acts congenial and half-witted, and pretends not to understand the man's words. Retrieving the letters thrown through the barred window, he bows like a peasant, places them beneath his cap, and pockets the pathetic bribe of a gold piece. As if he, Boldo Gábor – chief servant to the greatest nobleman in the Carpathians – needs this scrawny solicitor's coins.

For a while, Boldo strolls the courtyard, chatting with acquaintances, enjoying the company of his fellow Szgany. At the Lord's invitation, this morning his tribe set up camp here, to feast and enjoy the boyar's generosity. Soon, under Boldo's direction, they will help in the furthering of Dracula's plan, one the foolish Englishman has inadvertently contributed to. As Boldo strides past the *vardos* and cooking fires, everyone treats him with deference, knowing of his closeness to the boyar. Even his cousin Ion, who once confessed his fear of Dracula, nods and smiles with begrudging family pride.

Now, as daylight declines, Boldo enters the castle, moving through echoing halls. Here's the circular staircase leading to the cavernous cellar, a long descent. Here's the ruined chapel where his Lord sleeps. In dim light, he pauses, breathing in the scent of archaic earth. How old is his master? It thrills him to imagine the many battles Dracula won against the may-the-Good-God-damn-them-to-hell Turks, those smelly Asiatic hordes. That such a great hero would deign to drink from him, to take him into His service!

Here is the great tomb. Boldo pushes back the heavy lid and stands reverentially over the coffin, studying his master's serene sleep. He places Harker's letters in Dracula's hand, kisses his cold brow, and smoothes his gray mustache. "My king," Boldo sighs. "My beloved." Unable to resist the temptation, he pulls open the boyar's shirt, so as to stroke the thick black animal hair there. When he bends to kiss the Lord's cold mouth, he could swear that a smile flickers over the somnolent red lips.

For a while, he watches his master slumber, swamped with adoration verging on agony. *I am a warrior,* he thinks, swelling with pride, *like my great-grandfather Mircea, not merely a blacksmith or castle cook. And I am ready to die if necessary.*

Pulling himself away from his vigil, Boldo returns to the ground floor of the castle and then on out to the breezy courtyard. Here comes the food cart Boldo has been waiting for, bearing provisions he ordered from the village at the base of the mountain. If it were not for generations of Szgany guarding the castle, the bravest of these village fools might long ago have ridden up here and tried to harm his Lord. At the thought of such effrontery, the young blacksmith spits into the dust of the courtyard, then goes out to meet the wagon.

The man there abrades Boldo's ear with his erratic talk of missing infants. *As if I could care about your scruffy spawn, considering how most of you have mocked and abused the Szgany.* Smiling benignly, Boldo unloads beef, onions, cabbages, a sack of cornmeal, a crock of sour cream. *Well, ah, children,* thinks Boldo as the man continues spinning out breathless tales of woe, *the queens must have* something. *Better your dirty village brats than me!* He grins, remembering his Lord's ferocity when one of the pale ladies tried to take Boldo for her own. *Milady will never dare do that again! He called her a common trollop and thrashed her well! Who knows what she was to Him before? Lover, sister, wife? I care not. He cares best for me.*

Back in the capacious kitchen, Boldo unpacks the goods, then begins preparing another meal. Though his boyar has no need of nourishment other than Boldo's own blood – an essence the youth is more than willing to give – the whining English visitor must eat. Boldo would gladly starve him, now that the many locked doors have revealed him to be a prisoner, but cooking for Harker only gives Boldo an excuse to treat himself.

Thanks to Dracula's generous coinage, what fine meals and rich wines Boldo has enjoyed here! After years of relative poverty in the Romany caravan, now, ironically, as Dracula's slave he lives like a prince. Robber steak. And chicken paprikas. Eggplants with forcemeat. Transylvanian sauerkraut, layered with rice, sour cream, and three kinds of pork. Steaming, spicy goulash! Boldo's childhood favorite, *mămăligă*, with feta cheese. Apple strudel, cherry strudel, honey cake. And Tokay, that sweet, musty wine. Every night, full with food, pleasantly drunk, Boldo lies naked on his luxurious bed, waiting for his Lord to join him, waiting for his master's rough touch, his fierce lips and teeth and tongue.

Smiling sheepishly, the youth pats his solid belly, remembering how lean he used to be. With his mother's scrawled recipe on the counter and an open bottle of wine at hand, he begins frying minced beef for tonight's stuffed cabbage, contemplating with great pleasure what terrible things might happen to the Englishman once the boyar wakes to find the letters Harker tried to smuggle out.

JUNE 17TH, 1890

THE SLOVAKS' LEITER-WAGONS, heaped with wooden boxes, rattle into the courtyard. Boldo sighs, watching from a window. He knows what this means: his master will soon depart for England, and Boldo must return to his people. If he stayed in the castle during his master's absence, the three queens would end him, messily, no doubt, and with unimaginable celerity. Begrudgingly, he descends the grand staircase, ready to direct the unloading.

JUNE 30TH, 1890

THE FILLED BOXES are too heavy, complain his fellow Szgany. Boldo – at last their acknowledged leader, thanks to the boyar's influence – tells them to shut their mouths and work harder. And so they do, loading box after box of earth into the Slovaks' leiter-wagons. Though he's wobbly and bruised after last night's bliss – his Lord's ardor was more violent than usual, no doubt due to their impending parting – Boldo nevertheless helps to lug a few boxes. Now he takes up a hammer, and, with his cousin Ion in attendance, prepares to fasten down the lid of the closed box in which Dracula sleeps. But first a glimpse of his master's face, the last he will enjoy till their evening together in Varna, the night before the *Demeter* sails. Face agleam with fondness, Boldo slides the lid off.

He gasps with shock, then snarls with hate. Someone has attacked his Lord! The pallid forehead is gashed and bleeding! The eyes are open, fixed in a glassy glare.

"The English. *Pizdă!*" Boldo swears. "Cunt-munching swine. May the Good God damn him. I'll kill him myself." Fists clenched, the furious Romany strides toward the stairs.

Ion seizes his arm. "No, cousin. You are too weak today. Leave him to his fate. The ladies will punish him, be sure of it."

Boldo stiffens. "The ladies? You know of them?"

"Yes, I do. I know many things, Boldo," Ion murmurs, careful to keep his voice low. "I know you do not want women as you should. I know you love the boyar. Some say your great-grandfather did the same. I know long loneliness led you to that love. Whether that passion is damned lust or the purest of warrior fealties, it is not for me to say."

"You're right, it isn't." Boldo shakes off Ion's grip, grimacing with mingled shame and defiance. He sways, head swimming, and sits heavily on a stone step. *Ah, the English, shrieking like a village lass, being pursued through the long halls of the castle by the voracious trio of queens…suffering unimaginable torments before he dies…*

Boldo sniggers and then guffaws. With Ion's help, he climbs to his feet. With a handkerchief, he dabs blood from the boyar's brow before nailing the lid shut.

JULY 5TH, 1890

BOLDO IS GRATEFUL for the leather scabbard firmly bound in his mouth. To grit it between his teeth is a kind of comfort, when the pain grows too great.

"Again, little one? Tonight my hunger is vast."

Boldo nods. Tonight, loving torment is combined with the terrible imminence of Dracula's departure. Both make him want to sob, but he would rather die than show unmanly weakness in the presence of his Lord.

The *Demeter* sets sail at noon tomorrow. Who knows when the two will meet again? Boldo has begged his Lord to make the precious little time left together last, and Dracula has agreed. He stands beside the bed, red eyes agleam, studying the boy's supine body and licking his lips. In his hand, an ornate dagger glints with candlelight, its curved blade mimicking the curve of the boyar's smile.

The furry youth – tense, suffering, and rapt with thanks – is naked, bound spread-eagle to a big bed in his master's elegant Varna apartment, set high in an octagonal turret over the harbor. The Black Sea is so close that, in between his tortured moans, Boldo can hear the shushing of waves on the shore. The sea breezes tickle his sweating flank, the moist hair in his armpits, the blood trickling down his sides.

For hours, Boldo's Lord has used the razor-sharp blade – with exquisite care – to score the body of his wincing slave, to sip from deep cuts made in smooth olive skin. He began with the boy's fuzzy thighs, then his hips, then the flesh of his upper arms, then his luxury-plumped belly. Now he moves his attentions to the bearded Romany's heaving torso. With the point of the blade he follows the thin scar above the breastbone, the one left by his fingernail during their ecstatic reunion that snowy night in March. Having opened the flesh there, he bends, lapping gently, before cutting parallels in Boldo's pectorals, through Boldo's nipples. Growling low, he nuzzles, feeding lushly from the youth's broad breast.

Boldo trembles, teeth sunk in the scabbard leather, moist eyes awash with reverence, agony, and delight. The touch of the boyar's lips to his wounds, the pull of that animal-fanged hunger: Boldo knows, with absolute conviction, that the world holds for him no greater blessing than this.

When Dracula moves to the wounded boy's neck, the forbearance shown till now shifts abruptly into brutality. It is finally too much. Head lolling, Boldo faints.

He wakes to find himself still sprawled on the bed, but unbound. His body is swaddled in gauzy white. The boyar is wrapping more gauze about the boy's neck.

"Cerecloth?" Boldo mumbles, blinking. Dracula has drained him so deeply he can barely move. "Am I dead?"

"You are not dead. These are bandages, fool," Dracula says, finishing his ministrations.

"Lord, you are hungry still. I can sense it. Drain me to death if you must. The voyage to England is very long."

Dracula tucks a blanket over the dazed Romany and tousles his unkempt hair. "Never fear, boy. The *Demeter* has a more than sufficient crew. Stocky Russians, I gather. I have a better use for you. Here."

Dracula hands Boldo the antique dagger. It's sheathed now; Boldo can see the deep imprints of his own teeth in the tooled leather.

"From the *Scholomance*. Enchanted. Mircea used it to effect. Like your forebear, are you ready to give your life for me?"

"I am ready, Lord. You know I am. Please don't doubt me. Your eyes see into my soul, do they not? I swear to do whatever is necessary." Boldo rests the knife on his chest and covers it with his cold hands.

"I do not doubt you. Now I must leave. It is nearly dawn."

"M-may I, may I escort you to the dock? Please, sir?" Boldo, near tears once more, tries to keep the tone of frantic pleading from his voice.

"No need. Remain in bed and recover; your men can see me off. I've left money enough for you to stay in Varna for as long as you please. Savor the city's pleasures, my lad. I know how much you love your slivovitz, cabbage rolls, and honey cake."

"Thank you, Lord Dracula," the bandaged Szgany sighs. "You are so generous. But there is little of pleasure in the world without you."

The boyar grips Boldo's hand. "When next we meet, perhaps I will have a royal residence in London for us."

Boldo nods, closing his eyes. "Yes, Lord. And while you are gone, I will guard your castle well."

No response. When Boldo opens his eyes, the room is empty. He clambers feebly from bed and staggers over to the open window. Nothing but the susurrus of the sea and a sky full of stars.

Boldo, free of witnesses, gives vent to his sorrow. Crumpling to his knees, he clasps his face in his hands and bursts into tears.

NOVEMBER 6TH, 1890

BUSHY BLACK BEARD flecked with falling snow, Boldo rides his saddled stallion beside the leiter-wagon as his band of Romany speedily ascends the mountain. After months of mourning Dracula's absence, today Boldo's heart is light within his breast, for his beloved boyar has returned, sleeping mere yards away, in the great box borne upon the wagon. *To hell with the English curs who dared to thwart my master's hopes. Cunt-lickers. Jack-offs.* Soon he will have fulfilled his duty and seen his Lord safely back to the castle. Tonight, he will build a fire in the grand bedroom he once enjoyed; he will strip and offer himself. No doubt his master, after such a journey, will be ferociously thirsty. It will be a bloody and euphoric reunion.

"Faster, men," Boldo shouts with hoarse eagerness, pointing to the red sun sinking in the west. "Faster still. Let us make the castle by sunset." Goading his horse into a gallop, he grins with pride, studying the fierce band of mounted warriors surrounding the wagon. To be the leader of men such as these. He has Dracula to thank for that.

If ever there were a question of his men's undivided loyalty, there is no longer. The vicious actions of the villagers have settled that matter, even for Cousin Ion and his ilk, who once dared question Dracula's motives. Ten times since Boldo's Lord left this land, the village men, maddened by the disappearances of more of their children, have ambushed and attacked members of the Szgany tribe. Each time, the boyar's gray wolves drove them off.

They have always hated us. Is it the Szgany's fault that the ravenous queens must feed? Boldo snickers, remembering that afternoon a month ago when ten men cornered him in a glade near the castle. Dagger drawn, entirely surrounded, Boldo feared the worst. At the last minute, a pack of slavering wolves leapt from a thicket, positioning themselves between the young Romany and his attackers, flinging themselves at the shrieking peasants, wounding some, tearing out the throat of one, disemboweling the hindermost.

It is sweet to see foes perish, Boldo thinks, digging his heels into his steed's flanks. *Outlaws, we must care for each other.*

As if in response to Boldo's musings, a familiar feral music catches his ear. "Listen, men," he shouts into the rising wind. "The wolves. Our protectors. Our wild friends. They have come to greet the boyar home!" Amid gusts of storm, he can see them now, descending the highest slopes, converging on the road, a few even racing alongside the Szgany band.

The snow thickens, so dense that Boldo cannot see in front of him, and then the veils of white part. There, against the red sky, the battlements of the castle. "My Lord. Oh, my Lord, tonight," Boldo mutters, sex stiff and throat tight.

"Halt!" A man's voice resounds behind him. Then another voice, shouting the same command: "Halt!"

Boldo reins in, stunned. His men do the same. Overtaking them, two riders to the left, and two to the right! *There, the English, Harker. The three queens should have ended him.*

"Get back, you pig-fuckers," Boldo snarls, waving them away. "Go, men, go."

Boldo's men lash the reins; the horses jolt forward. In answer, the strangers shout, "Stop." This time, the four raise rifles.

"Eunuch! Cunt juice! *Pizdă!*" Boldo bellows, summoning the nastiest insults that come to mind. Now a gray-headed man and a prim-looking woman rise from behind a rock above the road.

An Englishwoman with a gun? On a different day, I might piss myself with laughter. Boldo reins in his mount, mind racing. *Surrounded. Goddamn them.*

"They want to assassinate the boyar, men," Boldo spits through gritted teeth. "Defend Him to the death." His men pull knives and pistols.

"Look," Boldo shouts, pointing to the red west, then the silhouetted castle. "In a matter of minutes the sun will set, and then He will defend us. These swine and their pale sow will stand no chance then. Get the boyar to the castle!"

Too late. The Englishmen already have dismounted, darting for the cart.

"*Stop* them, *slaughter* them," Boldo screams. His men surround the leiterwagon in a tight circle. Leaping from his horse, the *Scholomance* dagger raised, Boldo joins the fray. Here comes a lithe young man with a bushy mustache and a tanned face. Wielding a long knife, he's fighting his way through the living wall of Romany men. Within a minute, he and Boldo are face to face.

"Get back, you gypsy trash! Get out of my way! The scruffy likes of you aren't going to stop this Texan. That monster murdered my little Lucy."

"*Pizdă! Pizda mă-tii!* Go back to your mother's cunt where you belong," Boldo howls, flinging himself upon his opponent.

The foes commence a savage grappling. Boldo is clearer the stronger. He breaks from the American's grasp, punches him in the side, seizes his throat, and sinks his knife between the man's ribs. The Texan slumps, face white.

"You are done!" Boldo takes a deep breath, gathering air for a laugh of triumph, when his opponent rallies, elbowing the Szgany in the belly, then slashing his thigh.

Boldo staggers back. Swearing, he clutches his wound and drops to his knees.

"You aren't going anywhere now, big man," the bleeding Texan gasps, stumbling past. When Boldo turns, through the throng of battling men he can see Harker atop the cart. Now the detested Englishman, to Boldo's disbelief, heaves the great box to the ground. Now Harker and the man who stabbed Boldo are prying at the lid.

"Cousin." Ion heaves Boldo to his feet.

"Help me, Ion," Boldo begs. Blood wells against his palm and seeps through his fingers. "I must save the boyar!"

His foes have the box open. Dracula's red eyes meet his; the boyar's voice echoes in his mind, as it has ever since the Lord first kissed him.

Boldo! My boy, do not fail me.

Then the damned foreigners are upon his beloved with their knives.

Boldo lurches forward, howling with hatred. Ion seizes him around the middle and drags him back. When the murderers part, all Boldo can see atop the boxed earth is a pile of black dust, as if from the ashes of a fire.

"I will gut you. I will gut you. I will feed your steaming entrails to the wolves! Pigs will eat your eyes. Mules will fuck your women. I will plow your firstborn." Boldo reels forward, hands clawing air.

"Quiet, cousin," hisses Ion. "Men, for God's sake, help me get him out of here."

Cursing, struggling wildly, Boldo is heaved belly down over a horse. Ion climbs up behind. Soon they are galloping away into the woods, flanked by retreating wolves. Boldo weeps openly, flinching as the roughness of the terrain jars his wound. He looks back once, to see the castle set against the sky. Then, despite welling grief and rage, he remembers. *I must rest. I must survive. I must have strength for what there is left to do.* He wills himself to relax, to take deep draughts of mountain air.

"Tomorrow," he sighs, slipping into insensibility.

NOVEMBER 7TH, 1890

THE ASH IS heavy and black, like powdered metal or coal. Boldo gathers it all, handful after cold handful, collecting it in a ceramic vase that his mother used to display flowers.

Tears blur his vision. His bandaged thigh throbs and oozes. Ion looks on, brow crinkled up with concern. About them, snow thickens.

"Hurry! We should leave soon," Ion urges. "See the sky. Those wild clouds! A worse storm is on its way. It is nearly dark. Why did we come so late in the day?"

"That is all of it," Boldo says, rising with painful effort to his feet. Ion helps him climb up onto the saddle. They gallop the last steep mile to the castle.

In the courtyard, Boldo, flinching, slides off the horse, clutching his prize. "Thanks for your help, cousin. Go back now. I will take shelter here tonight." He may be wounded, and his boyar gone, but his voice still retains the customary note of command.

"But the queens?"

"They are gone. The English ended them. Now go."

"But you're bleeding." Ion points to the crimson-stained bandage. "You can barely stand! I won't leave you here."

"Yes, you will. I want to mourn my Lord alone."

Ion shakes his head with disbelief. "You're mad, Boldo. Why would you want to stay in this cursed place?"

Boldo's handsome face contorts. "Go!" He points down the mountain. Swaying, vase cradled in his arms, he turns his back on Ion and totters toward the castle.

"I'll be back for you tomorrow, you fool," Ion yells behind him before snapping the reins and galloping away.

BOLDO, SHIVERING VIOLENTLY, peels off his thick coat, then his clothes. Naked, a study in black fur and swarthy muscle, he stands before the open tomb, embracing the vase of ash with his left arm, holding the unsheathed *Scholomance* dagger in his right hand. In the far distance sounds the howl of wolves.

For a long minute, the youth hesitates, remembering green on the willows, thick rich goulash, slivovitz, and the warm, convivial fires of the Romany camp. Then he thinks of his Lord – his touch, his kiss – and, jaw set, climbs into the sarcophagus.

Fah! The pale wafer of the Host. The English must have left it here. Lips curled with contempt, Boldo flings it out as if it were composed of crawling vermin. For a moment, he sits cross-legged in the oblong of freezing stone, gathering his courage. Then he carefully empties the vase onto the floor of the sarcophagus.

"My Lord," he murmurs, smearing a handful of black powder into his chest hair and beard. He lies down atop the gritty ash. He lifts the dagger to his lips and kisses the blade.

"You said the blood is the life. I pray you were right."

Now Boldo does to himself what Dracula did their last night together in Varna. Teeth gritted, he cuts his forearms, thighs, belly, breast, and sides. His life, liquid and crimson, trickles, dripping, dripping, then pooling on the bottom of the sarcophagus. Heart swelling with hope, he waits. He repeats the process, this time cutting more deeply.

Coward! What if it is not enough? I should simply have cut my throat! Too weak to continue, hands shaking, Boldo drops the dagger. He groans, wraps his arms around himself, and closes his eyes. If the magic does not work, then the cold will end him. No matter. He would rather die today than fail his Lord a second time. If the magic does succeed, he might yet die, but his sacrifice will have saved his beloved.

Inside Boldo's head, comets arc and sparkle now, waves break, thunder rumbles. Dazed, he rolls off the pile of blood-soaked ash and onto his side. Curling into a ball, he loses consciousness.

Boldo jolts awake. Heat, not cold, suffuses his body, cozy warmth like that of a woolen blanket. The air teems with smoke. He coughs; he gasps for breath.

Behind him, something rustles. "My Lord?" Boldo rasps. He tries to roll over but cannot. Numbness pervades his limbs, a black river rising.

An arm slips around his waist; a deep sigh fills his ears. Softness brushes his shoulder, then his neck. *My Lord!* Boldo, smiling, drifts off, his last sensation that of fingers stroking his hair.

HUNGERS

Rajan Khanna

DAWN clutched at the English sky and I gave the command. My men jumped from the two carriages and ran for the Winters estate, weapons drawn, senses alert.

Up in front, of course, was Harker, his stark white hair naked to the sky. Flanking him, as protection, were the Farley twins, Frank and Fitz, ginger hair tufting out from their matching newsboy caps. Next came Ajay Bedi, our Sikh companion, wearing a white turban instead of his usual blue.

I followed behind them, my breath fogging the air, conscious of the absence of Bas. My heart ached to think of him. He'd been gone for just over a week, disappeared while carrying out a scouting mission. That I'd sent him on it had been weighing heavy upon me. I missed his reassuring smile, his touch on my hand, his kiss.

Behind me, lagging with his limp, was Jack Seward. I'd tried to talk the doctor out of accompanying us, fearing his infirmities would be a liability, but he wouldn't be dissuaded. I hoped he'd prove me wrong.

Ahead of us, the Winters estate loomed.

I FIRST MET Jack Seward in his office with Bas at my side. "I am Isaac Van Helsing," I said. "And this is Bastian Van Sloane. I am here because of my father."

"Van Helsing?" Seward had said. "I don't..."

"I'd hoped to come earlier, but the ship we took here was delayed by a storm. I'm aware we missed the funeral."

Seward's face was still frozen in surprise. "He never.... I didn't know.... He said his son died as a child."

I flushed despite myself. I longed to reach for Bas's hand. "I'm afraid we had a...falling out." My favored term for my father's rejection of me after he'd stumbled upon Bas sharing my bed. His eyes, their condemnation, had been burnt into my mind so clearly that they were what I saw when I thought of him. That Father preferred to think of me as dead brought the pain back anew.

"I'm sorry," Seward said. "For your loss."

"Thank you." I faltered for a moment, unable to speak, and Bas stepped forward as he always did, closing the door behind us and taking over with gentle confidence. He smiled at Seward to put him at ease. "We'd like to know how this all happened," he said.

Seward told us. About the struggle with Dracula and their triumph. And how unbeknownst to any of them, Dracula had created a cadre of lieutenants, turning an unknown Inner Circle into the UnDead. I did my best to absorb it all but my mind was still reeling as Bas and I headed to our lodging in Chelsea, the separate rooms with adjoining door.

I slipped into bed and Bas lay down beside me. He ran his fingers through my hair. "Quite a lot to accept," he said.

I nodded, enjoying the smooth, steady feel of his hand. "I knew Father had some unconventional interests, but...nosferatu?"

"He never spoke of it to you?"

"He spoke very little to me about anything. Even before he discovered.... I knew he had varied interests, though. Science, of course, but also metaphysics. . I suppose mythology as well. Seward knew all of this."

"It bothers you, doesn't it," Bas said.

I shrugged. "It seems Seward was more of a son to my father than I was."

Bas squeezed my shoulders. "But you are of his blood."

I grunted. "Bad choice of words, I think. Nosferatu? In this day and age of science. They say it's the blood that makes us what we are. A simple liquid, a collection of cells. So small a substance, so tiny a flow and yet its force is like a river, with us caught up in it." I turned to meet his eyes. "Does our blood makes us what we are? Uranian in persuasion. And if so did my father hate what he gave me?"

"He was guided by things other than blood," Bas said with a sigh. "Like his Holy Bible."

Bas was right. My father turned his back on me because of his faith. Then I turned my back on his God. If He found me so distasteful after making me so, well.... Science always seemed a kinder master. More interested in truth than superstition.

"Do you want to return to Holland?" Bas asked.

I grabbed Bas's hand and wrapped it around me. "Soon. I wish to learn a little more of what is happening here, what my father did."

"Out of debt?"

"No." But the word sounded hollow.

THAT HAD BEEN two years ago.

We raced across the estate grounds, the sun warming us as it rose. It meant Winters would be at his weakest, but he was likely to be guarded.

The air smelled of fresh grass as we climbed the fence and followed the hedge around to the back of the house. I froze as a mournful howl filled the air, followed by snarling. "Dogs," I yelled. "Quickly now."

We ran, seeking shelter against the back of the house. Ajay, Fitz, and Seward drew their revolvers while Frank Farley raised his elephant gun, a lit cigar hanging from his mouth. Harker helped me work the door with a crowbar. The snarling had turned into barks and angry growls which grew louder.

"Hurry! They're coming," Ajay said.

Pistols fired. I turned to see the beasts, vicious predators with bared fangs, breath steaming from jaws that could crush bone. Their eyes gleamed with hunger and a savage brutality.

Harker strained at the metal crowbar. I lent my strength to his. Wood creaked and then the doorjamb splintered.

Someone screamed. I pushed Harker inside, then turned and fired my own revolver. One dog yelped and danced back, my shot striking home. The other men ran past me and into the door. All save for one of the Farleys, who lagged, a dog's jaws clamped around his arm.

I saw that it was Fitz, and he struggled toward the door, dragging the dog. I moved to his aid, helped pull him away, and Frank was beside us, battering the dog with the butt of his gun.

Eventually we wrested Fitz free of the dog's grip and over the threshold. I helped lower him to the ground as Frank and Ajay slammed the door and held themselves against it. The wood shuddered as the animals thudded heavily against it from the other side. Ajay was almost knocked over from the impacts, but he bent his legs, steadying his feet against the floor.

The sound of the hounds was loud. Snapping their jaws, scratching their claws upon the door. Harker helped me drag a wooden table over to the door to bar it, then several chairs.

Freed, Frank moved to where Seward was caring for his brother. I followed. Fitz cradled his bloody arm, his face twisted in pain. His breathing was shallow and high-pitched whimpers issued from him. "Let me see," I said, kneeling by him. He held his arm out. It was little more than tattered strips of flesh on the bone. The handkerchiefs Seward had wrapped it in were already soaked through. "He can't come with us," I said.

"What?" Frank said.

"He's in too much pain. And he can't hold a revolver, or a cross."

"I can give him something," Seward said.

"No," Fitz gasped. "No drugs."

"We can't leave him here," Frank said.

Ajay stepped forward. "We'll leave him a shotgun," he said. "He can guard our backs."

I nodded. Frank frowned, said some words to his brother as he passed Fitz the weapon. I doubted that he'd be able to use it. His face was already pale, and I worried that he would pass out from lack of blood. But I tried not to let my worry show. We had only just entered the estate and one of us was already down because of a *dog*. I was reminded of my father's notes: dogs, rats, foul birds. All of these things are at the command of the vampire.

"We must continue," I said. "Come on." We pushed into the Great Hall, ignoring the lavish furnishings, looking about us for the next threat. The house was old and it creaked as we moved. I became aware of a faint scratching and clicking coming from somewhere in the house. "Quincey," I said. "Can you sense him?"

Harker closed his eyes, concentrating, and the tip of his tongue poked out from pursed lips. Not even Seward was able to determine why the youth had these sensory abilities, but they'd been an asset to our endeavors. Harker was still practically a boy, and I regretted the need for his presence, but things would be much harder without him.

The scratching grew louder and, pistol clutched in hand, I scanned the room, trying to see what might be causing it.

Ajay fell away from one of the doorways saying, "My God."

A writhing swarm of black shapes spilled forth through the doorway, flowing like a dark fluid on the walls, floor, and ceiling. Thin wire legs and antennae waved delicately in the air as they moved en masse toward us. Insects of every type and shape from hard-shelled cockroaches to glistening millipedes weaved sinuously across the room. Ants, silverfish, beetles and more, chittering and clicking as they came.

Then the buzzing began.

"Harker!" Seward yelled.

Frank Farley, his eyes wide, fell back and fired the elephant gun at the vermin, and the roar filled the room. But if it had an effect on anything other than our ears and the wall, it wasn't obvious. Firearms would be useless, as would the blades we carried. "Fire," I said. "We must have fire."

Ajay began fishing in his pockets, but insects fell on him from the ceiling. Then onto me. All of us were pelted with hard black shapes that clung to our hair and tried to crawl down our collars, thin legs tickling and pricking as segmented carapaces clicked. My feet crunched down on the first wave of attackers on the floor. I pulled at the shapes on my head, resisting the urge to run madly away.

Already the buzz had grown. The bites of the crawling insects were getting more aggressive, stinging, biting; the winged insects would be worse. A single ant bite or a wasp sting would cause little problem, but a sustained series of them would be venomous. Frank Farley screamed and beat wildly at his own face, trying to dislodge the stinging shape that had attached itself to his eyelid.

Something pierced the crease where my lips met. I slapped at the clinging shapes that clung there. A buzzing filled my ears as small shapes entered and pushed their way in. In a fit akin to madness, I frantically stuck my fingers in after them, feeling the bodies crack and tremble.

A scream bubbled up inside of me. I am going to lose my mind here, I thought.

"How do you stand it?" I asked Seward. I followed him as he limped through the halls of his asylum, listening to the screams and ravings of madmen.

He smiled at me. "I am an alienist. It's my job." He ushered me into his office, leaning heavily on his cane. "And I can help them. Not all of them, certainly, but some. There needs to be some hope for them."

"And the vampires? What calls you to that second occupation?"

His face grew serious. "Need," he said. "Dracula's brood still operates in the shadows here in England. They are still capable of creating more of the UnDead. They are a disease that must be eradicated so that the good people of England can survive."

He took a seat behind his desk and cleared off a box with a hypodermic needle and some vials in it. He flushed. "Sleep often eludes me. I find injections help. And then there is the pain.... Please. Take a seat."

I did so. His office was unkempt, much like the minds of the men at his asylum. I wondered how he could find anything amid the mess of papers and books strewn across his desk alone. . "But Mina and Jonathan, even Lord Godalming saw fit to walk away from this life."

He waved a hand in the air. "Godalming gives us money, and that helps provide us with weapons and supplies. And he has his wife. The Harkers have their son to think about. And they've all already paid a price."

I heard the faintest hint of bitterness in his tone. "Weren't you married?"

He looked down at his hands. "I did marry. Sarah died of consumption, of all things." He looked up at me. "Why are you helping, then? You have someone."

My face burned and I began to stammer a response but he held up a hand to cut me off. "Please. Unlike others in my profession, I see nothing abnormal about inverts. And I do not I share your father's prejudices. That is what caused your falling out, isn't it?"

I hesitated for a moment before answering. So few knew about Bas and me.

"Come now," Seward continued. "I've seen the way you look at one another, the way your bodies move when you are close. I study the human mind, Isaac. You love him. And he loves you."

"Yes," I said, looking down.

"Well, then. Why aren't you back in Amsterdam or wherever, living your life?"

"Partly for the same reasons as you," I said. "It needs to be done. And partly.... My father gave his life to rid the world of these things. And he wasn't able to finish what he started. Whatever differences we had in life, I can help see to it that his labors are ended. We are on the threshold of a new century. I would like to see it cleansed of this plague."

"It's a connection to him," Seward said.

"I suppose so. My father was a man of science and yet he exists more as myth to me. If this is one of the ways I can understand him, then so be it."

"And Bastian?"

I felt a surge of emotion rise through me at his name. "Bas stays because I do. Because he supports me. Because he understands what this means to me. And he is one of the strongest and bravest people I know."

Seward nodded. "Then we understand each other." His face grew grave. "Just...you fight together. You risk your lives to do this. Look out for him. I've lost those I love – first Lucy, then Sarah. I would spare you that grief."

My throat grew tight, and I nodded at him. Then we sat and discussed the business of our hunting group. When we were finished, I headed straight back to my hotel room and kissed Bas passionately before throwing him down onto the bed. I tore at his clothes, my mouth pressed hard against his, my hands finding their way to his skin. We made love before I could strip him bare, garments and fragments hanging off of us in ridiculous poses. When we were finished, I rolled to one side and panted.

"What was that for?" he asked, staring at me the way he often did.

"I needed you. Here. With me." I laced my fingers in his. "I always need you."

THE SCREAM TORE its way from my throat and insects flew into my mouth and I spat them back out again.

Then Frank Farley, his face red with welts and stings, revealed a metal flask and shook it out in front of him. I smelled the particularly harsh whiskey the Farleys favored. I fumbled in my pockets for a match, trying to push away my terror. But I didn't need one. After coating the insect-covered floor, Frank threw his cigar upon it.

Fire whooshed across the floor and walls, and a great gout of smoke boiled off into the air. Insects hissed and popped as the fire consumed them. I ran to Harker and put my mouth to his ear. "Harker. We need you now."

Segmented carapaces littered his head. He dared to open his eyes and nodded. "This way!" He ran through one of the doors, trailing a confetti stream of insects as he ran. Beckoning to the others, I followed after him, feeling the crunch of chitin underfoot. The buzzing was lost in the roaring of the fire. Flames began to lick at the walls and raced up curtains. The whole mansion might burn.

"He's below us," Harker said. "I think there are some stairs ahead." He led the way, his stark white hair bobbing in the darkness. Ajay and Seward followed, both scratching their exposed skin.

"I have to go back for Fitz!" Frank yelled, as the fire spread.

"No," I called.

"Go on! I'll catch up to you."

"Come on, Van Helsing," Seward said. He pulled me into the passageway and down the stairs.

Then, with a tremendous crash, the door at the top of the stairs fell in upon itself, the wood collapsing as its supports burned away.

Frank wouldn't be able to get to us. I felt a surge of grief, but I pushed it away. There wasn't time for this. I felt like a fool for leading these brave men to their deaths. At best I could wrest a Pyrrhic victory. At worst....

My hands were shaking. I pulled out the sharpened wooden cross and held it tight, willing the trembling to stop.

"Van Helsing," Seward said. "We have to keep going."

I nodded and we all followed Harker down a winding staircase into the dark. We lit torches and the light sent shadows over us in the orange glow. The air in the stairway smelled like damp earth and mildew beneath the smell of smoke, and it was still. Very still. "Keep alert," I whispered.

We wound our way down the stairs until we reached a corridor hewn from the rock underneath the manor house. Harker remained up front, sensing or sniffing the vampire through whatever consequence had changed Mina Harker's blood. It was why I had recruited him, against the wishes of his parents. I wasn't certain they even knew where he was right now. One more questionable decision in following the footsteps of my father.

The only sound other than the flickering and spitting of the torches was a far off echo of dripping water. I cocked an ear for more insect sounds but there were none. My heart pounded in my chest, skin quivering from the pulse. You've done this before, I told myself. It wasn't my first hunt. But the voice I had tried to keep silent, that maddeningly enduring voice, bubbled up. Bas could be here, it said. You can save him.

You can right at least one of the wrongs.

"Van Helsing," Ajay said. "There's a room up here off the passage. Should we take a look?"

"Harker?" I asked.

"I don't know – it's difficult to tell down here. The impressions I'm getting are very strong, from all around me. It might be worth taking a look."

"Fine," I said. "Seward and Harker – stay here and watch the passage. Ajay, attend me."

The door opened at my push and we entered into a dark room. The light of Ajay's torch didn't reach all the way into the room, but I could smell rotten meat. Something dark lurked in one corner of the room. I lifted a hand to halt Ajay.

Something sniffed and a shadow moved. Chains rattled. "Isaac?" came a voice.

"Bastian?" The voice was hoarse and strained, but I recognized it as the man I loved. A surge of relief, warm and sweet, flooded through me bringing a flush to my cheeks.

"Give me the torch," I said to Ajay. After he passed it to me, I asked him to wait outside. He opened his mouth to argue but I put a hand on his shoulder, demanding privacy. "Please."

Once he left, I moved toward the corner. Bas was but a dark shape in an iron cage. The torchlight made his shadow seem to shift. "Bas, I thought.... I had no idea."

Bas hushed me with comforting words as he always did. "But you found me."

I moved toward him and a weight shifted from me. The terrible weight of guilt.

Bas sipped his drink. "You are planning this mission?"

"Well, yes."

"You discussed this with Seward?"

I sighed and leaned back in my chair, loosening my cravat. "He was doubtful, but I insisted. We've been part of the last few raids. I think...I know I can do this. Besides, Seward slips deeper into addiction every day. I can't remember the last time I saw him lucid."

"He feels his position being usurped," Bas said. "You've been part of the group now for barely two years and already everyone looks to you."

I felt anger spike up in me. "And what? You don't think I can do it?"

"It's not that, Isaac. But why are you pushing so hard? We were never going to be a part of this. And I support you of course, but…you seem tortured by this. Are you trying to prove yourself a better man than your father? Or just a man?"

"How can you say that? This is good work. We save lives. We protect the future."

"Tell me that your father has nothing to do with it."

I closed my eyes, pressed the bridge of my nose. "I can't. He proscribed me. I have no regrets for having you, and yet…. Here I chase a dead man's blessing. Maybe I'm fit for Seward's house of horrors."

Bas rose and walked to me. He bent down until his face was level with mine. "Your father's failing was not in ridding the world of these creatures but his inability to recognize how wonderful a son he had. I am not going to follow his example."

I reached for Bas' hand, tears misting my eyes. I nodded. I kissed him and quoted Whitman's "From Pent-up Aching Rivers."

Later, when I could think once more of my plan, I asked of him, "I need you to do something for me. The last of the Dragon's brood, this Winters. He is different from the rest. He comes from a background of science. Dracula must have known his vile kind couldn't live in the past forever."

Bas's face grew tight. "What do you need me to do?"

"Seward told me that Winters has not left the usual trail of exsanguinated corpses. He keeps his prey alive. I need to know why."

"I'm to be your spy?"

"You're better with people than I am. Your empathy…they trust you. I need you to see what you can find out about him for me. He might have connections at the university. Or among the peerage. Can you do that?"

He nodded. "Of course."

I remained silent about my other reason for selecting him. Already those in our group had recognized the strength of our "friendship." I believed for them to truly take me seriously, to accept me as their leader, I needed to show that I did not favor Bastian above all others. Not even when lives were at stake.

"THE LIGHT HURTS my eyes," Bas said. I thought of the days he must have spent in the dark. I dropped the torch to the ground and moved forward. My love stood in the center of his prison, a dirty smock draped over him. He looked gaunt, and the smell intensified as I approached. I almost sobbed as I thought of him, starved, forced to share space with his own filth.

"Bas, I missed you so," I said. "I...." My body shuddered as I released the pent up emotions of the past days, my hands desperately gripping the bars of his cell.

He raised his arms, and I saw the manacles binding him, the chains leading off onto the far wall of the cell. "Don't worry," I said. "The others are with me. We'll get you out of those."

"The key to the cell is on the wall, just there." His voice was hoarse. Dry. I followed his pointed finger and saw a key ring hanging upon a hook. I grabbed it and hastily fit the key to the lock and opened the door with a screech of old metal.

"I'm so cold, Isaac."

I crossed the cell toward him, my arms outstretched. His stretched toward me. Then we embraced one another, my arms encircling him. He felt frigid, as if layered in rime. . Up close the smell of rot was overpowering, but I ignored it like I ignored the pain of the insect stings on my naked flesh. All I knew was that Bas, my dear Bas, was returned to me.

Then his arms grew tighter, and he twisted me to one side. I admit I struggled against his grip. "I'm sorry, Isaac. But I'm thirsty. So very thirsty."

I saw Bastian's red, cracked mouth move forward—his fangs extended, inching toward my neck. The world spun away from me then as reality's inexorable weight fell back upon me with crushing intensity.

Then I was falling free, rolling away from Bas and I heard hissing.

My fingers grazed the silver collar I wore. Bas had given it to me. The vampires found the metal repellent.

I scurried back to the bars. "No. No. No."

"Please, Isaac." Bas pouted. His face, despite red eyes, wide mouth and those teeth, his face aroused me. "I have not changed. I'm still myself." He paused. "I still love you."

Tears poured down my cheeks. I could not summon even the thoughts to address him, let alone raise a weapon.

He pulled up the dirty smock. Beneath it, his chest was carved open, his insides bared to the air for all to see: iron bolts pinned two great flaps of skin to the sides of the chest and within the chest cavity, where several ribs and some muscle tissue had been removed, sat his heart, now still and silent.

I gagged, bringing my hand to my mouth in horror. "Oh, merciful God."

Bas chuckled. "You never believed in God. I did. Once. Now, I have a cruel god. He did this to me. He seeks to understand how we work. He is, like you, my love, a man of science." He let the smock cover his mutilated body. "

My mind writhed with troublesome thoughts. I needed him still. Without him I was nothing. And so, I could get him out, keep him apart from the others. It would hardly be different than what we had done most of our lives. I could feed him, slake his thirst. Prevent him from killing. He could control himself for love of me. So that we could continue to be together.

I moved closer to him.

He reached out for me.

But no, I was too much my father's son. And, when offered the opportunity to forgive, I spurned that. Even as I placed my left hand on his face – so cold beneath my touch – my right hand clawed the sharpened cross from my pocket. I do not remember my words as I plunged it through the smock and into his stilled heart.

I wiped my face of tears, swallowed both sadness and fury, and left the room calm. I addressed the men outside. "Winters turned Bastian." I looked at Ajay. "Please?"

He nodded and removed the kukri at his belt. He disappeared into the room to relieve my dead love of his head. I looked at the other faces, all clouded with grief. They had always enjoyed Bas's company, the levity that he often brought to our gatherings.

Tears glistened at the corners of Seward's eyes. "I'm so sorry, Isaac."

I nodded. When Ajay returned, I said, "Let us kill the baron."

The corridor continued on, more doors studding the stone walls. "He's ahead," Harker said. "I can feel him." He led us to a large stone door set into the wall. "This is it."

"Get it open," I said.

A large metal ring hung from the door. Ajay pulled, grunting with the effort, but it refused to move. Harker added his strength, then me and Seward. It wouldn't budge.

"Blow it." I said.

"Dynamite?" Ajay asked. "I thought we agreed that it was a last resort."

"We did, but how else are we supposed to enter Winters' tomb?"

"But the noise, the clamor, it will alert everything in the place," Harker said.

"So what do you suggest?" I snapped. "I'm not leaving here. We blow the door and go in with our crosses out and weapons drawn. The sun is high. He should be in torpor ."

"He's right," Seward said.

Ajay nodded "Get to the end of the corridor." He removed four sticks of dynamite and placed them against the door. "Go. Now."

We crouched at the far end, fingers in our ears. A moment later, a sprinting Ajay appeared and took up position next to us just before the explosion roared through the corridor. A thick cloud of dust followed, showering us in grit and powder. I coughed, trying to wave it away with my hands. "Now, quickly, ready your weapons and let's go."

We set off at a trot down the hallway, gingerly stepping over the ruin of the door which now lay cracked and smoldering, chunks of rock scattered all over the floor.

It was like stepping through an open, smoking mouth, like that of a dragon. Into the belly of the beast, as it were.

The large cavern seemed hewn from the rock itself, a natural formation that must have existed for centuries. I could hear the sound of water running; an underground stream or lake nearby. Objects filled the cavern – tables covered with glass contraptions, large metallic pillars, and metal instruments, all glinting in the orange glow of the torches. It resembled a laboratory, or a hospital, or both at the same time. It was a place my father might have felt comfortable in, if not for the taint that seemed to cling to the place, tight feeling at the base of the neck, the tingle at the roots of the hair.

At the far end of the cavern, upon a shelf of rock, stood a large stone box. I recognized it for what it was, the resting place of the vampire, Winters. I moved forward, my spare cross in one hand, a torch in the other. I felt the others behind me.

I neared the box. So far there had been no response to the explosion. I smiled. Winters' eyes were wide open – he could see, but he looked confused, his eyes darting about, trying to discern what was happening, trying to break free of the trance state, smelling danger, but unable to act on it. I felt an almost predatory glee. I felt the leader of a pack of wolves. And the predator was now prey.

But a true predator was always wary. I learned that lesson the hard way when something struck the back of my head and darkness took me.

SEWARD SLAMMED HIS hand down on my desk. "You must take me with you!"

I glared at him, closing one of my father's journals. "Jack," I said carefully. "You are an important part of this operation and your information has been valuable to the cause, but…." I sighed. "You are too dependent on morphine these days. And your limp slows you down. You would be a liability."

He brought his face closer to mine. "I'll have you know that I was hunting vampires before you ever heard of them. This injury of mine – " he tapped his leg " – was sustained in fighting one of Dracula's brood. I have given more for this fight than you will ever know."

I grabbed his arm and pulled it to me. Rolled up his shirt sleeve to reveal the needle marks. "I can see."

He wrested his arm from my grip and grabbed my arm, rolling up my sleeve. "Don't think I haven't seen, too," he said, his eyes gleaming. I flushed as he bared my own needle marks. "You've got a taste of this now. The toll it demands. Bastian has been gone, what now, five days?"

I turned away from him, blood roaring in my ears.

"You're down a man anyway," Seward said. "I'm going."

"Very well."

He paused at the doorway before exiting. "You're not him, you know."

"What?"

"Your father," he said. "You're not him."

I should have felt happy at the words. But I didn't.

I AWOKE TO blinding light and stinging pain. The back of my head felt like it had been dynamited. I lay on my back, my arms and legs restrained. A bright light shone down on me from above.

When I tried to gain a better look at my surroundings, I found my head restrained as well. I was reminded of many of the inmates at Seward's asylum.

There was a creaking sound, then a waft of cold air. I caught the scent of fresh earth, and old blood. A face, pale and bright as the moon, drifted into view. A man's face, the skin stretched tight over prominent bones, the lips full and red. Long hair hung about it, a blonde as pale as the skin it surrounded. It was a handsome countenance, but a cold beauty, hard and sharp, like that of a mountain peak. It smiled at me.

"Van Helsing. I am Baron Edmund Francis Winters. What a pleasure to meet you."

"I wish I could say the same."

"I understand. You are none too friendly with our kind. Like father, like son? Still, Abraham did me quite a service."

"My father? How?"

"When he killed the Count, I was freed of his influence. Without him, I would be a slave rather than a master."

I snarled "What did you do with my friends?"

"That you even have to ask is a disappointment. You have already seen some of my handiwork. Experiments always need fresh subjects.." Winters lowered his face until it was next to mine. With a start I realized that my silver collar had been removed.

"Name your protector. What did I miss?"

"For a man of science, you fell like the proverbial messiah. You missed a Judas, Van Helsing."

"Judas?"

I smelled his cologne before he neared. "Hello, Isaac," Seward said.

My mind reeled. "Why?"

"I've grown tired," Seward said. "Tired of trying and failing. Tired of being passed over. Tired of the company of madmen.... While you were leading the charge against the Count's other offspring, I came to the Baron and sought the means to end my streak of being passed over.... Lucy. Even Sarah. She wanted to leave me, could not stand my work at the asylum.

"My leg? The limp? Gone." Seward grinned, showing fangs. "All my human weaknesses are gone."

My whole body burned with rage. "You bastard. You knew about Bas."

Seward's grin faltered. "I told you to keep him close. You should have listened. At least now you can join him."

I considered spitting in his face, the only act of rebellion I could manage, but I was interrupted by a howl of pain from outside the room. It had to be one of my men, but pain had distorted the voice into something almost bestial.

"Seward, go tend to him," Winters said.

Seward disappeared from view and Winters once more lowered his face before mine.

"Why are you doing this? Why the vivisections?"

"I might have been given this power, but I seek to understand it. I need to learn everything – why we hunger for blood, why silver burns us. "

"Science will not help you. You are an aberration, an abomination."

"Prejudice from an invert? Winters chuckled. "Science tells us that all things are natural."

Another scream sounded, this one wilder, more desperate. I thrashed about in the restraints. "I swear I will kill you."

Now Winters laughed. "My dear fellow, I'm already dead."

He moved with exquisite grace. drawing a scalpel from a coat pocket. He seemed enamored by the long thin blade a moment, then loosened the strap holding my left arm. His grip might as well have been a manacle, made of steel. He ran the knife down my palm, releasing my blood. I gasped in pain. In almost an obscene gesture of kissing a woman's hand in greeting, or a lover nibbling the soft flesh of his partner's palm, the monster brought my cut flesh his lips and started to drink.

As I knew he would, as all his ilk did, he swallowed greedily before tasting what he drank. I had once said that to Bas, that the vampire's need, its constant hunger was its weakness. What I hadn't told him was that my need for him, just as constant, was mine. Oh, Bas.... I felt myself go lightheaded.

Winters shuddered and dropped my arm. He coughed. "What did you do?" He started to double over, to retch.

Ignoring the blood flowing freely down my freed arm, I began working to loosen the head strap. Quickly I sat up and, using the very scalpel Winters had used on me, I cut myself free of the rest of my bonds and stood over the vampire.

I rolled up my sleeve to show him the needle marks. "You talk of science?! For the better part of a week I have been giving myself injections. A colloidal silver suspension in holy water." I had wanted to try it long ago but Bas had persuaded me not to. He feared the silver would poison my blood. With him gone, I had no reason not to try.

Winters howled in pain as he clawed his chest. His spasms were a delightful tarantella, but I dared not tarry.

I found a wooden chair in the room and broke off one of its legs. It wasn't very sharp, but it would serve. I drove the splintered leg into Winters's chest.

His shriek as the wood pierced his heart drove me on until his twitching ceased.

Before I took the time to decapitate and ensure his final death, I had to rescue my friends and deal with my Judas.

But Seward was nowhere to be found. He must have heard Winters's howls and fled like the coward he was. Poor loyal Ajay. He had been turned. Worse, Seward had sawed off the top of his skull, exposing the man's brain. I disposed of him quickly, staking him and cutting off his head.

I found a few other pitiful specimens as well, some of them made vampires and some of them dead. I dealt with them all.

At least there was comfort in saving Harker. To my surprise, he wasn't dead or turned. I wept in relief when I found him. He was weak from being cut and tortured, but was alive. He muttered that the vampires found him tainted, his bloodline worthless.

Together we staggered out of the estate, following an underground stream that led to just without its limits. I went back for the Farleys but found no trace of them in the burnt shell of the mansion.

I collapsed for a day and a half, and when I woke up I did not want to leave the bed, but the smell of Bas clung to the sheets. I changed rooms. I refused any visitors, even Mina or Quincey. I spoke to my father a bit as a I drank, replacing the colloid in my blood with the Farleys' salvaged whiskey. Abraham and I came to an understanding of sorts.

I knew his disgust in a man. Seward. I, who could be sent to prison, hanged in England for loving Bastian...my crimes, my failures, were a thousand times less vile than a madman now loosed upon the world. One who willingly abandoned humanity with each step he took along the path to Hell.

I asked my father if I were stepping on the very same path: loss, obsession, need. A hunger for love. A hunger for purpose.

My father gave me another. The hunger for vengeance.

I aim to see it fed.

THE LETTER THAT DOOMED *NOSFERATU*

Steve Berman

How frustrating to pen a serious missive while Emrick seeks to distract me by trifling with his false eye on the bed. I believe he has lost two since I made his acquaintance last month. His current plaything is wooden rather than glass as Emrick shares both my poverty of blood and the dearth of coin brought by treatments for anemia. We met at the sorriest of physicians and he followed me to my flat and has truly yet to leave. I consider him an illness I cannot shake.

He whines a great deal. About his poor fortunes – "Before the war, I would have easily earned a spot in one of my uncle's factories. But I am not meant for a life in steel and fumes." About his urges – "The only relief from boredom is to transgress. Biblically transgress. But does Berlin has a golden calf? No." About his impaired vision – "I think the paint on this orb is poisoning my blood. Some nights I glimpses shapes, see motion.... Not from my good eye but through this damnable thing."

I groan. "I swear, either put the bauble back in or stuff a kerchief into the damn socket."

"Always scribbling, Tabner. Why you bother to send scraps of paper covered in your inky webs remains a mystery. There are so many men you can speak to face-to-face at a cabaret...."

"Some thoughts are best shared not with beer on the breath..."

"I don't believe I've ever had one of those."

"...and a letter is addressed to an individual. By name. How often do you ever know the name of your indiscretions?"

"They are only indiscretions if I am successful. Your Irish authors would agree with me."

I do not bother arguing that while Wilde would be proud of Emrick's demeanor, LeFanu I suspect would not, and Stoker...well, before I left university, I heard talk that the man perished from the French disease but not before infecting his widow. That poor woman....

I hear the creak of the old furniture as Emrick leaves the bed and takes the three steps to where I sit by the small writing desk beneath the gap in the wall that once was paned and called a window.

Thankfully he has returned the false eye to its hole. His face would be handsome if I did not often suspect the slatternly thoughts it conceals.

"Let us go out. The sun sets. The cabaret has music. If you are afraid of beer, I will buy us schnapps."

I sigh after staring at the inkwell, nearly as empty as our pockets. "With what? Spielkarten?"

"Charm. I have heard there is a man who stares at many while ordering glass after glass. I aim to captivate him tonight."

"Libertine."

Only as he gets his threadbare coat from the nail on the wall does Emrick think to ask me to whom I'm writing. But because it is a woman, he takes no interest.

THE CABARET MIGHT as well be a photograph with movement and smoke. So much smoke. Colors are muted by what dim light penetrates the hundreds of cigarettes lit in procession. Cigarettes in ebony holders. Cigarettes dangling from ruddy lips. Cigarettes held by nicotine-stained fingertips. Black is fashionable, black is everywhere, black is the only option other than pale skin and shirts and the atmosphere of gray smoke that hides the ceiling.

I cough. Emrick slaps me on the back and I remember the first time he did so, when he was beneath me. A lapse in judgment, an act on the sheets that he read as his papers to stay forevermore in my flat. The sheets, stained by our emissions, were his passport to the country that was my forlorn life.

At the microphone sings a woman in a fine tuxedo. Her hair is short, oiled and dark. Her thick eyebrows and mustache a smear of shoe polish. She gestures to members of the audience during the lyrics of "Heute Nacht oder Nie" as if choosing her partner for later that night:

"Since I once saw you, I cannot withstand you."

Emrick has left my side. I venture to the bar. I lack his talent for looking like a mongrel that will lick rather than bite the hand that feeds it. But then, there are always old men who believe the risk is worth losing a finger. Not that I would snap my jaws. I lack Emrick's insatiable hunger. And there is always someone who needs my talent for translation. My mother believed the only good book was a song book; my father, a lapsed priest, insisted I learn Latin and Italian as he felt Mussolini would end the papacy and I might find work in Trient. I added English to my repertoire because I suspected Hollywood's great producers such as Laemmle or Lasky would do the same.

"Tabner, you must meet this dour fellow I have found to buy us drinks. He shares your obsession with moving pictures." Emrick laughs his coarse and mean-spirited laugh. "And women."

I will admit I prefer the company of a woman's mind to that of a man's. But the rest. Ah, the Creator instilled in me so many needs.

Emrick tugs at my sleeve until I follow him to a table where a single occupant sits with his back to the bar so he may watch the door open to let inside the thirsty, the needy, the lonely.

"You didn't bring me a beer," says the seated man after a swift glance at us. "So much for Berlin's hospitality." His accent suggests one of the outer regions of Germany. He reaches into his vest pocket and pulls out a few coins. "Might as well buy my own. Or three."

Emrick winks at me before rushing back to the bar.

"Sit. Your...friend – I may call him your friend? – tells me you have a fondness for the cinema?"

"For once he tells the truth."

That makes the man laugh. He is not as ugly as most Emrick approaches for money. He is so ordinary. Not a student, not an old man. A bland man, unnoticeable except for the wide-pored skin revealed by being clean-shaven and the gleam of fresh pomade in his hair. He smells a bit rank like he has been traveling a while by train. He's just another man who embarks for the promises of the capital come evening and then returns to mundane life, mundane wife, annoying *kinder*.

He opens a cigarette case. Offers me one but I decline. I am already in his debt for a drink. More and he might expect my ass. "I try to see as many motion pictures as I can. Who is your favorite director?"

A very unordinary question as most filmgoers I meet in bars such as this seem to care only for the faces on the screen rather than the hidden masters.

"Lang. Wiene – "

Acrid smoke roses from his cigarette. "Ahh, how that Jew's Caligari enthralled me. Mesmerism. I often wonder if the large screen is not some great eye that beguiles us all."

Emrick returns with three beers in small glasses. I am sure he will forget to return to the stranger whatever coin remained after such an extravagant purchase.

"You think we're all somnambulists in our seats ready for the dictates of the director?"

The man shrugs. "It is not as far-fetched as *Der Janus-Kopf*? I think Murnau's art is mired in phantasmagoria."

I may set my glass down too hard. Emrick kicks me under the table. The stranger flicks ash in the tiny puddle of spilt beer near my glass. "To enjoy Wiene and reject Murnau is like...." I who regularly pen letters to men and women around the world, find myself at a loss for words. Kind words. Civil words.

The stranger chuckles. "But his latest is of a *Nachzehrer*."

"A film based upon a brilliant novel."

"What book is this?"

Emrick finishes the little beer at the bottom of his glass. "Must we talk of books? Haven't we had enough imagination to dull the sense. Look, friend – "

"The name is Kürten." I hear iron in our benefactor's clipped speech.

"Kurt, dear friend, after drink and smoke, the next delectation is the firm thighs of a woman. I happen to know several that would smother you with perfumed tits, a skilled mouth – "

"It is Kürten. And are you not both Hinterlanders?"

I stand. I have been called much worse but never in one of *our* cabarets.

"Sit, sit, Tabner. There is no shame in the truth." Emrick turns back to this *schwein*. "Who better a woman to trust than a man who has no claim to any of her lips?"

"There are brothels a plenty in Berlin. Some might even take your money," I say.

Kürten turns his head to look at the singer who is in the midst of "Kann Ich dafür?" "I am curious what it would be like to bed a woman who wears a man's clothes to feel whole. Is she still warm inside?"

"Very warm," Emrick says in a low voice. His pose, his tone, everything about him so disgusts me that I resolve to never speak to, or touch, him again.

"I would be amenable to that." Kürten doesn't look away from the singer. And so he misses what I see next: Emrick nodding before his expression changes. As if half his face, the hemisphere housing his false eye, is overtaken with temblors. He lifts a hand and covers the other side, as if blinding, masking, much of his face. He gasps, which brings the stranger's attention, but by then Emrick has stumbled out of his chair and headed back to the bar.

Kürten chuckles, a sound without any warmth or mirth. "I offend. I am from only Düsseldorf. There I catch curs and bitches. Dogs. You are obviously well read. Come, sit back, enlighten a man. Perhaps change his ways?"

I glance over my shoulder at Emrick, who is demanding in a pained voice drink from the bartender. Something is terribly wrong.

"Sit," the stranger commands. I do, because I feel troubled and do not know what I should do or where I should go next. Or is it that his voice has a weight to it that enhances the gravity's pull on my body, which now feels weak like an infant? I suspect he must talk to his wife and *kinder* in such a beguiling tone. And they do not refuse him either.

"This book you mentioned? It is good? What is its title?"

"*Dracula*." I leave unsaid my preference for the original title: *The Un-Dead*.

He nods but says, "I have not heard of it."

"You are only from Düsseldorf."

He smiles and reaches over to my glass, which has sat abandoned, not quite emptied. He downs its contents. I notice an ugly rash along one side of his neck. "Tell me more. I assume that there are beautiful women in this book. And cruelty."

"It was written by an Irishman. A man named Stoker. A nosferatu travels to England and preys upon several women."

"English women? Already I can see this is foolish. Why would he like the taste of their blood? Our woman are strong.

"Then you'll be pleased to hear that Murnau's film is set in Germany," I say. "It premieres tonight."

"I had not planned on staying so long in Berlin but if you are attending I could be your guest."

I feel shame color my face. "I-I cannot afford such a ticket. It is a gala affair at the Primus-Palast." Besides, the thought of spending more time in this man's presence is unthinkable.

He gestures with his cigarette at the singer, as if marking one of her notes in the air. She smiles at him. It is her trade.

"Perhaps you are only afraid to be proven wrong about Murnau. Meet me tonight at this Primus-Palast. I shall pay your ticket. I always feel generous after…." Kürten stands and walks toward the singer. "After," I hear him echo.

I join Emrick at the bar. In the short span from last I saw him he has managed to drink himself into a near-stupor. When he realizes I am standing by his elbow he blinks his authentic eye at me. The other stares wide. "Nothing," he mutters. "Not you, but around him, they all float."

"What are you talking about? Do you enjoy introducing me to these reprobates? If you wish to be my Wotton, at least surround us with beauty."

"He was surrounded." In trying to nod towards the strange man named Kürten, Emrick nearly falls. "They're all around him. They all float."

I hold him steady by the shoulders. Once, I might have kissed him. His mouth is slightly agape with a strand of schnapps-scented saliva connecting those lips. I'm disgusted that part of me still finds him appealing. "Make sense."

He writhes, shaking loose of my grip. Then his fingers reach for his wooden eye and in front of everyone who took to staring at his raised voice and physical antics, he plucks it loose of the socket. "This. This sees girls, young girls, old girls, so many girls…they're like those flickering actors you adore so much. Not on a screen, but they're all around him. M-Mutes. Mute, flickering girls." He then vomits.

Cringing at the stench, a hand covering my mouth and nose to prevent myself from getting sick, I turn to where Kürten was talking to the singer. I see neither.

I help Emrick back to my flat. He is in a stupor as I strip him bare and clean him. The sight of him so helpless is overpowering, and fucking his ass serves as a panacea for the day's worries. For I have decided I must accompany Kürten this evening.

I have read too many tales of the macabre to resist the chance to see phantoms, whether they are real and haunt Kürten or cinematic and haunt Murnau. To be among the elite few that attend the premier of Nosferatu...would both impress and endear myself to Frau Stoker and Frau Holland. Their opinions of me are all that matter these sorry days.

I RENT SOMETHING suitable, something not so old as to embarrass me, arguably wasting my very last mark. If I am even a day late in returning it to the Jew, he will demand a pound of flesh.

Kürten waits for me. He has also changed his clothes but they seem ill-fitting. I watch as he smokes another cigarette. Parallel scratches to the left side of his nose are raw. I think of the singer's hands. Had she worn kid gloves? And then I realize that his suit is the same as hers.

Neither can I repress a shudder nor is he bothered by the reaction.

"I am pleased you came. I thought you might not," he says to me.

"Even my ilk has occasion for boldness."

He nods in mock appreciation.

My free hand accepts the ticket from him. I see beneath his fingernails is filth. How much time must pass before something so vital as blood becomes raff? Less than a day? An hour? Beneath his shirt are there more scars, more ruddy daubs?

My other hand remains in the pocket of my trousers as my fingers encompass the wooden eye. I aim in the darkness of the theater to lift Emrick's eye to one of my own, squint and peer through it as if it weren't wood but a camera obscura. I need to know if Emrick did see phantom girls. The false eye has grown quite warm from my touch. I can feel it is not a perfect sphere. I wondered along the walk to the Primus-Palast from what tree had it been carved and by whom? Both of my favorite correspondents married storytellers with a penchant for the gruesome and romantic. What would their men have conceived of mute ghosts? Alas, I am not so creative but I am anxious, the trait common men possess instead of imagination.

"How do you handle your wife?" I ask.

"Hmm?"

"Does she know about these...trysts of yours?"

A better question I should ask is why I am fascinated rather than frightened. My insides twist, yes, I sense a shiver ready to take hold of my entire body as I remember the words Emrick muttered –

> Mute girls, *even as I fucked him I think the thrust forced his torso to work like a bellows and he moaned* Mute girls *repeatedly. Or have I developed an imagination finally after reading so much Stoker and Wilde?*

– tonight my eagerness to discover the truth behind Emrick's claims rivals my anticipation for Murnau's film. If there is a threat from Kürten, I am inured to it.

"No," he says. "Perhaps one day. I am not so different from a somnambulist; something sleeps within me, even while I work or eat or talk with you. It stirs now and then. I imagine we all stretch and kick when we sleep. A pillow is lost to the floor. The sheets tangled. I have grown to love tangling sheets." Both his hands become fists, crushing his own ticket, dropping the cigarette.

"But this beast still sleeps?"

"Beast?" He blinks at me, as if the word had no meaning. Or the wrong meaning. I repeat the word, more for myself, in Latin and English and then German again.

"Does an expectant mother think the child up her prune a beast? No, they all think it's the next messiah."

I DOUBT I shall ever set foot in a more lush building than our movie palaces and the Primus-Palast might be the finest I visit. My eyes welcome the rows of electric chandeliers on the plastered ceiling that brighten everyone's countenance except my benefactor's. My lungs breathe in a not-unpleasant blend of colognes and perfumes and expensive tobaccos. My feet are comforted by soft carpeting.

A lad grins and takes our ticket and an usher smiles and leads us to our seats. Both wear crimson uniforms with shiny buttons and gold epaulets. Germany has proud soldiers once more, but they escort through rows that can house more than a thousand eager patrons rather than perish in muddy trenches that hide many bloated corpses.

We are in a row not too far from the large orchestra and the stage, which could swallow the cabaret as Leviathan did Jonah, and the velvet curtains that frame the massive screen would be coveted by Emrick as ideal swaddling for every illicit act imaginable.

Thoughts of Emrick brings thoughts of ghosts as does the death of all light in the theater and the commencement of the orchestra. Overhead, an amber ray pierces the darkness. Some in the audience gasp. There are always those who have yet to experience a motion picture. Even I am captivated by the science, which I could easily believe to be occult rather than optic.

The first title card – *Account of the mass death in Wisborg in the year 1838, by* † † † – has Kürten asking me in a whisper where is Wisborg. It is not in Transylvania, I am sure.

I slip the false eye from my trousers and roll it back and forth between my hands. The audience is captivated by the film. And when I read the card *Travel fast, travel well, my friend, to the land of ghosts* I can only think that Murnau himself is whispering to me to look through this wooden lens for the real Kürten.

I rest my head against my hand so as to bring up the orb in as surreptitious a manner as possible. At first I see nothing. Not until I shut the unobstructed eye. Then, I glimpse a pale fluid dripping down Kürten's forehead into his eyes. Immediately the temple beside the false eye erupts in pain; I think I am not meant to see such things, that flesh and blood are allergic to spirit. But I persevere and the fluid coalesces into small hands that are hiding – no, blocking, they are trying to blind – the man's eyesight. But if he can feel their presence, he does not react. Rather, he is chuckling as he watches. At what, I dare not look, because gaunt, white arms and shoulders are coming into view for me.

"Now that is a beast," Kürten says and nudges me. The miraculous – or accursed – eye drops from my grasp. I am blind for several moments. I cannot see his face or that of anyone else in the theater. Not until I turn to the screen do I see the beast he fancies.

No Dracula. No white-maned wolf of a man, no immortal lean and hungry Cassius. Stoker would choke at the sight of this vampire, who is an ignoble and bald rat which has discovered how to dress in funereal garb, walk about on two long legs and taunt the audience with its talons. This is not a noble predator but a carrion-eater. Why does Germany persist in its adoration for the Great War's losses?

I look away. Kürten smirks. I wince at this expression and search the crowd. Surely they must all be aghast, horrified. And by the flickering light above and beyond us, I do see their eyes wide, their hands covering their mouths to keep silent. But too I see the occasional sardonic grin, the rare flush of a man or woman who looks more ready to rejoice than scream.

When Orlok arrives by ghost ship in Wisborg, he easily, comically escapes the notice of the incompetent bureaucrats who seek the cause for the plague. I hear Kürten mutter, "All too true," and I am sure this man is all too familiar with avoiding the attention of authorities.

I yearn to flee the darkened theater but even the lamps outside would be little comfort. I need sunlight. That is what is supposed to kill Orlok. But what will sunlight do to men like Kürten other than let them notice that the filth under their nails is dried blood?

And the final scenes, of Orlok's true death and the mourning of a man over the still body of a beautiful woman? Am I the only one in the theater who realizes this is but a weak reflection of life, that monsters are not confined to nitrate but are seated unbeknownst beside us?

Kürten's grasp on my arm is forceful; but he claims it is only a courtesy to allow the slower members of the audience to clear the row first.

"I am in your debt. Murnau is no charlatan but a black magician," he says.

"I must admit I am less than pleased your opinion has changed."

He laughs and gestures for us to leave. Together. I find that he matches my quickened pace with skill.

"She was like all the others, you know?"

I assume wrongly that he means Orlok's victim.

"Once shed of those manful trappings, she was soft. Too soft. When they are delicate it is too easy to silence them. I dread the day I hear a woman speak in a motion picture. It would ruin the fantasy. Do you know the folk tale of Patient Grizzel? She is the ideal woman because she will not raise her voice to her husband."

He has led me to one of the many alleyways that turn Berlin into a warren. I lean against a stone wall. Gas lamps flicker in the distance. His shadow looms large, reminiscent of one scene from the film, of Orlok ascending a staircase.

"I think I shall head to the train station now," Kürten says. "No need to thank me for this treat. I don't think you want to thank me."

"You trust my silence?"

"I trust your terror. I think you will linger a while at this very spot until you are sure I am far away. Perhaps you will listen until you can no longer hear my footsteps. Then I suspect you will drink whatever you can afford or beg so that you might forget me.

"But you won't." He steps back, letting shadows fall over him. "You will go tomorrow to that very cabaret and hope, like a sick suitor, that the singer will appear. And when she doesn't, will you curse Murnau, because I have drank deep of your adoration for that man and now the bottle is either sour or empty."

I ADMIT THAT he spoke the truth. But before I venture to see if the cabaret can ever again offer me some measure of comfort, I take a circuitous route back to my flat. My mood is dour. How many performances of *Nosferatu* will there be? How many will be comforted, even inspired by it? Despite it being a travesty of Stoker's brilliant novel, caricatures are favored by the uneducated more than the original.

Emrick snores. One eyelid lies limp against the vacant socket.

At my tiny desk, I notice the unfinished letter to Frau Stoker. Has she any idea what has been done to her husband's legacy? I think back to the film and wonder if *Dracula* was even credited as its inspiration. If not then some salvation might be achieved.

I crumple the letter. Tomorrow I will sell her husband's book. I care not what I'm offered; I cannot look at its cover or pages without thinking of the many authentic beasts hiding within men.

I take the pen to my last, virgin sheet of paper and slow my handwriting to ensure there will be no error, no spill of precious ink. If Frau Stoker does reward me for alerting her to Murnau's poaching, I shall purchase Emrick a fine eye fashioned from glass by a real artisan. And we will drink and never talk of books or phantasmagoria again.

As I sign my name and gently blow upon the ink to dry it, the corners of my eyes tear. I think in the darker corners of the room, the ones the candle at my desk cannot reach, shapes are applauding because they cannot speak and what I write must serve as their only voice.

ARDOR

Laird Barron

– Yukon-Kuskokwim Delta, February 9, 1975

What is it Pilot John says right before we drop from the sky?

Where is Molly's body? No, that's my own voice haunting me on account of someone else's ghost, someone else's guilt.

The pilot's head inclines to the left, slick as any disco-floor pro. He gasps and takes the good Lord's name in vain. There's a quality of terror in the sharp inhalation that precedes this utterance. There's rapture in the utterance itself. His words are distorted by electronic interference through the headset. The snarl of a lynx wanting its fill of guts.

Obligingly, The world rolls over and shows its belly –

– I come to after the crash and call Conway's name the way I sometimes do upon surfacing from a nightmare. In this nightmare he is kissing me but his left eye is gone and I can see daylight shining all the way through his skull. He says hot into my mouth, *This wound won't close.*

Now I'm awake and alive. Hell of a surprise, the being alive part.

Snow trickles down through a hole in the fuselage and crystallizes in my lashes and beard. The last of the daylight trickles through the hole too and the world around me resolves into soft focus. Buckets of white light saturate everything until it's all ghostly and delicate. I'm strapped into the far back seat of the Beaver. I close my eyes again and recall low mountains rising on our left and the shadow of the plane descending toward an ice sheet that seemed to stretch unto the end of creation.

Our particular jag of beach lies south of Quinhagak, not that that helps. In the summer, this is a vast circulatory system of bogs and streams on the edge of the Bering Sea. Ptarmigan and wolves, bears and fish dwell here, feast upon one another here. In the winter, it's one of God's abandoned drawing slates. The temperature is around negative thirty Fahrenheit. That's cold, my babies. The mercury will only keep dropping.

"Conway's in Seattle," Parker says. "He's safe. You're safe. Who's your favorite football team?" His breath is minty. He thinks I'm slipping away when I'm actually slipping *back* into the world. Sweet kid. Handsome, too. Life is gonna wreck him. That's funny and I chuckle. He grips my shoulder. His mittens are blue and white to match the stripes on the plane. "C'mon, Sam, stay with me. Who'd you root for in the Super Bowl? The Vikings? I bet you're a Vikings man. My cousin met Fran Tarkenton, says he's a gem. Can't throw a spiral, but a hell of a quarterback anyhow."

"Cowboy fan." I'm remarkably calm, despite this instinctive urge to smack the condescension from him. He means well. His eyes are so blue. Conway's are green and green is my favorite color, so I'm safe, as Parker keeps saying.

"The Cowboys! No kidding? Seattle doesn't have a club. One more year, right?"

"Dad is from Galveston." I haven't thought about my father in an age, much less acknowledged him aloud. Could be a concussion.

"Where's your accent? You don't have an accent."

"Dad does. Classic drawl." I hesitate. My tongue is dry. Goddamned climate. "How are the other guys?" The other guys being pilot John, regional historian Maddox, and our wilderness guide extraordinaire Moses.

"Don't worry about them. Everybody's A-okay. Let's see if we can get you outta here. Gonna be dark any minute now. Moses thinks we need to be somewhere else before then."

His voice is too cheerful. I'm convinced he's lying about everyone being all right. Then I catch a glimpse of Pilot John slumped at the controls, his anorak splashed red. His posture is awkward, inanimate – he's a goner for certain. The engine has to be sitting on his legs. Snapped matchsticks, most definitely. The windshield blasted inward to cover him in rhinestones. I lack the strength to utter recriminations. Abrupt stabs of pain in my lower back suggest my body is coming out of shock. It isn't happy.

Parker strips free of a mitten and there are pills in the palm of his hand. He feeds me the pills.

I clear my throat and say, "Somebody will be along. The posse can't be far." Lord, the aspirin is bitter. A slug of lukewarm coffee from Parker's thermos helps. "John got a Mayday out, didn't he?" But what I recall is John with both hands on the wheel while the rest of us yell and pray. Nobody touches the radio in the eight or so seconds before it all goes black. "Sonofabitch. Tell me it's working." I know it's not working, though. The radio was smashed on impact along with Pilot John's body. That's how this tragedy is unfolding, isn't it? After making a career of fucking over others, finally we are the ones getting the screw job. O. Henry or Hitchcock should be on the case.

Parker says, "I wonder if you can walk."

While he struggles to extricate me from the ruins of the plane, I'm thinking not only is it a damned shame Pilot John failed to transmit a Mayday, he didn't even file a flight plan that accounts for our detour to this wasteland of tundra and ice. We're at least two hours southwest of the original destination. That potentially lethal blunder is on me. I'd gotten greedy and tried to squeeze in an unscheduled stop. Thanks to me we are all the way up shit creek.

A storm is moving in off the sea. Blizzard conditions will sock in search and rescue craft at Bethel. That means three, possibly four days of roughing it for us. If we're lucky. How lucky we are remains to be seen.

I cough on the raw taste of smoke.

"Heck." Parker glances over his shoulder. "Guess she's on fire."

Yes, Virginia, we're in trouble —

— Professor Gander invited me to lunch at the Swan Club in Ballard and laid it all on the table. Entrusted me with a withered valise stuffed with documents and old-timey photos. He endeavored to explain their significance through suggestion and innuendo. Two things I dislike unless we're talking romance, which we weren't. I disguised my fascination with a yawn.

He lighted a cigarette and set it in the ashtray without taking a drag first. "The papers were written by RM Bluefield, allegedly a mysterious Victorian fellow Stoker based the Renfield character upon. Bluefield was an avowed mystic, a fascination he acquired abroad in Eastern Europe and Asia. He possessed medical training…was obsessed with the concept of immortality, but then, so were many others of that era. His particular interest lay in the notion that it might be obtained through certain blood rites or the consumption of animal organs. Stoker, it is thought, perused the fellow's papers and then mocked in print Mr. Bluefield's eccentricity.

"The journals changed hands, most recently belonging to an actor from the 1950s and '60s named Ralph Smyth. Where *he* acquired them is a matter of conjecture, although it's of scant consequence. For our purposes, we simply need to locate Smyth himself."

"Ah, the royal we. There's a booster, I presume."

"Yes, Mr. Cope. I represent a patron. One with very deep pockets."

"God love 'em. And what does this patron want with Smyth?"

"You will locate him and ask a single question. Return with his answer, whatever that may be."

"A question?"

"One question. I'll even write it down for you." He produced a fancy pen and indeed did write it on a coaster. He also wrote his home address and a set of numbers that represented the payment on offer. A nice plump round figure, to be sure.

I lingered over the coaster and then put it in my pocket. "A little more detail, Professor. What's the catch?"

"It is possible the fellow's dead, although we suspect he's very much alive. In hiding, we think. Took a powder into the Alaskan wilderness during the spring of 1967. There are more recent accounts, multiple sightings of a man matching Smyth's description."

"Seven years is a long time to be on the lam. The cops want him?"

"The authorities don't possess evidence to implicate him in any nefarious dealings, such as the disappearance of my patron's daughter. My patron suspects otherwise, naturally. That's where you come in."

"Maybe Smyth's got an aversion to overly aggressive film buffs." I smiled, but he didn't seem amused. "So, I'm going to put together a team and fly all over the ass end of Alaska, hunting for some guy basically nobody's ever heard of..."

"Ralph Smyth, Ralph Smyth, surely you recall..." Professor Gander buffed his signet ring and waited for the light to dawn in my presumably Neanderthal brain. Fucker wore a cardigan and rimless glasses. He'd gone prematurely white like Warhol.

"Surely I do not." I took a gulp of Redbreast. Glass number three. I'm not a heavy drinker, but suffering the good professor required extreme measures.

"A poor man's Lon Chaney, Sr. who eked out a career from getting violently offed in a dozen Hammer films. What he's famous for, however – "

"Nothing, apparently," I said, a teensy bit drunk already.

Gander bared his mismatched and silver-capped teeth. He wanted a taste of my blood, it could be assumed. "Bravo, Cope. The man is famous for nothing. What he's *infamous* for is his final role in a French-Canadian art film. *Ardor*. An exceedingly liberal interpretation of *Dracula*. Ten years ago this spring *Ardor* premiered at a Quebec festival, then sank into obscurity. It is reviled by critics and forgotten by the public. Have you seen it? Amazing work."

"Oh, by art, you mean smut, eh? I dig."

"Yes, a pornographic movie. Rated X for sex and violence. A notorious piece of cinema, even by genre standards. Banned in many countries. Only a few copies rumored to survive, etcetera, etcetera."

"I'm sorry I missed this one. A porno retelling of *Dracula*. What will they think of next?"

"The forces at work in the world are endlessly inventive. Artistic autocoprophagy is here to stay."

I studied him through the haze of his untouched cigarette, preferring not to dignify his comment with a response. I made a mental note to look up *autocoprophagy*.

He said, "Why don't you come by my place tonight and I'll show you the film? I've got a bootleg reel. A few colleagues and some friends of the university will be in attendance. You can mingle, make new acquaintances. A fellow in your line can always use new connections, and a better class of them, too."

"You and your cronies going to gather around the campfire to watch a stag flick, huh?" I said. "A banned stag flick. That's a relief. I prefer the company of miscreants."

"There's another item we'll need to discuss," he said. "The client is a dear friend of mine. That's why he's come to me in the wake of the law's failure to rectify his concerns. Nonetheless, I've reason to believe Smyth went to Alaska on a specific mission. He's a bibliophile and an antiquarian. His home, which he abandoned, was stuffed with extraordinary...items, shall we say? By all means extract the information my patron requires, but if you can bring home any significant papers or relics, or lacking that, photographic evidence of said, you'll be generously compensated."

"Well, in that case, here's another coaster." –

– I DROVE OVER to the professor's house around nine. Late enough that people would've settled in, but before any craziness had gotten started, or so I hoped. Gander struck me as a buttoned-down freak. Perhaps a Wally.

The address he'd scribbled on a coaster led me to an old mansion in the U-District, set back from the street. Parking is hell in the U, so I left the car in a likely spot and walked three blocks. The windows were dark. A housemaid answered the bell and greeted me with a scream.

She fled down a gloomy hall, an ornamental candle bowl flaring in her hand. I wound up in a darkened room – I got the impression of antique furniture and lots of bookcases. A throng of silhouettes was back-lighted by a projection screen. I whiffed cherry pipe smoke and fancy cologne, a hint of marijuana.

A film played for this crowd of rustling shadows. Its frames jumped, were poorly spliced; the scenes were muddy and marred by frequent cigarette burns; the color flickered. Tiny subtitles and a strange, scratchy orchestral symphony accompanied the grunts and cries of the actors, all a half-beat offset from the action itself. Somebody was fucking somebody. Somebody was murdering somebody. Cocks everywhere, thrusting into every opening. A guillotine blade dropped through the neck of a devil clown. Gore splashed the thirteen dancing brides of Dracula and flecked the camera lens. Darkness flooded in. For an instant the gallery dissolved and I became dislocated, a bullet shot into the vacuum of deep space.

The lights came up while the film kept running. Someone said, "Jesus Christ!"

I beheld a congregation of the cream of UW faculty; fifteen or so middle-aged dudes in sweaters and slacks, drinks and smokes in hand, all of them sniffing in my direction like moles. The departments of anthropology, psychiatry, and literature were well-represented.

Horror stretched Gander's face in all kinds of unpleasant directions. "What are you doing here?" He gestured as if to ward away an evil spirit. "What are you doing here? You can't be here."

I wanted to tell him to piss off, he'd invited me, but I couldn't speak. There was too much blood in my mouth. I looked down and realized I was naked and covered in blood. I extended my arms like the Vitruvian Man and the room rotated. Centrifugal force pinned me in place. On the screen, washed out, yet immense and wicked, naked Dracula embraced naked Renfield and crushed the life from him. The camera zoomed in on Renfield's glazed eye, penetrated the iris into the secondary universe, the anti-reality. It was snowing there, in Hell. I was in there, in Hell, in the snow, waving to myself.

A white glow ignited on my left where the doorway to the long hall should've hung. Instead, an ice field bloomed through a porthole. So bright, so beautiful, filling up my brain with fog –

– THE TEAM ASSEMBLED at the Bull Moose Diner in downtown Bethel, Alaska to plot a final sequence of site flyovers. Alaska is a big place. Nonetheless, we were running out of places to search for our quarry. If I couldn't find Smyth in the next few days, that might be curtains for the expedition.

The frigid Alaskan winter wasn't doing my mood any favors. Relocating to western Washington for a vacation didn't sound half bad. I could take Conway to Lake Crescent for a romantic idyll, or hiking along Hurricane Ridge. Or maybe we'd hole up at my house and drink wine and watch the rain hit the windows.

Is retrieving the bones of a person treasure hunting? Or would you call it grave robbing? Conway posed this question with a smile – he could afford to smile because he didn't know the half of what I did for a living. That was the last time I'd seen him in the flesh. He'd spent the night at my place on Queen Anne Hill. The next morning would find me aboard a jet to Anchorage. He lived across town in North Gate; sold insurance to corporations. The job took him out of my life about as often as mine took me out of his. We'd been lovers for three years. I'm tallish and homely; he's shorter and handsome enough to model if he wanted. He's a man of his word and I'm shifty as they come. The arrangement worked, barely.

Grave robbing? Maybe Conway had it right. Over the past decade I'd flown thrice around the world in the service of numerous scholarly profiteers of the exact same mold as Professor Gander. Missions revolved around wresting artifacts of historical significance from the locals, or better yet, absconding with said relics before the locals even suspected chicanery. Sometimes, this job being an example, I was sent to retrieve a real live person, or extract information from said. You just never knew. My chief talents? A willingness to follow orders and endure a not inconsiderable measure of privation and hardship along the way. I don't balk at getting my hands dirty. Runs in the family. Granddad shot people for the Irish mob back in the Roaring

Twenties; made an art of it, or so the legends go. I'm not even close to being that kind of a hardcase, just sufficiently mean to get matters across when it's called for.

The future would take care of itself. Meanwhile, here I sat in Bethel with a string to play out: four sites within striking distance of the village. Gold Rush mining camps abandoned since World War II, except for infrequent visits by tourists, researchers, and ne'er-do-wells. That last was us. My comrades were more inclined to the business of looting and pillaging native artifacts under the guise of academic inquiry.

"A sentient being isn't an artifact separate from the universe," said Moses as he counted out bills for the waiter. None of us had the first clue who he was speaking to. "Sentient beings are the sensors of the universe, its nerve endings. A colony of ants, a gaggle of geese, a city-state, are the places where enough sensors amass and the universe becomes self-aware." He paused with a scowl. "Somebody needs to kick in another two bucks."

That was doubtless Maddox who'd skimped on the tip. I tossed a five-spot on the table to save time and frustration for all concerned. Prior to this assignment I'd not worked with any of them. I preferred the southwest states. My Alaska network was weak, forcing me to rely on a subcontractor in Juneau who'd made the initial referrals. Over the months I'd gotten to know this group, on a superficial level, at least. This line of work doesn't engender intimacy, it heightens eccentricities. A man becomes known by his foibles, his personality tics. Illusions of bonding or brotherhood are perfidious.

Pilot John was a boozy loser who'd washed out of life in Vermont. Maddox was a boozy loser who'd gotten dumped from the faculty at the University of Anchorage for a variety of sordid offenses; one too many coeds had dropped her panties for him, I gathered. Moses, our Yupik guide, was a boozy loser who'd blown his Western State degree and done five years in the pen for grand larceny. Nowadays he guided hunters and hikers and nefarious types such as me, even though his expertise lay somewhere in the area of philosophy and he didn't know an iota more about snow than anybody else schlepping around the Yukon Delta. Parker... Him I couldn't figure. Didn't smoke, didn't drink, so what did he do? Clean as a whistle except for some domestic bullshit with a younger brother. His specialty was photography and he knew his way around the northern territories. The mystery was why a smart, clean-living guy like him couldn't get a reputable gig. Punching his brother in the kisser wasn't a satisfactory explanation for why he'd become persona non grata.

I hate mysteries, but the solution to this one had already suggested itself to me. What to do with my conclusions was the problem –

– I KICKED IN a lot of doors and looked under a lot of rocks to discover five pertinent facts of the Ralph Smyth case.

Fact One: He'd received training as a playwright and dramatic actor and it hadn't helped. His oeuvre mainly consisted of crappy monster flicks that would've mildly entertained my twelve-year-old self. He routinely played second fiddle to the main villain. He chewed scenery as Igor or Renfield in at least half the movies and as an enforcer, arm-breaker, or button man in most of the others.

Fact Two: Smyth had had a reputation as a real sonofabitch. Small-time actor, yet connected behind the scenes. His father had owned majority interest in a lighting and set-making company. Money opened all the right doors. Ralphie baby was chummy with Karloff, Price, and Cushing, and every two-bit producer that came down the pike. He enjoyed conning young, naïve starlet wannabes. He seduced them, screwed them, strung them out on dope and then turned them over to one of the slimeball directors for further abuse and exploitation. Molly Lindstrom, so keen to escape the tyranny of daddy dearest, was just another fly in Smyth's web. She vanished six months after principal photography wrapped on *Ardor*. The authorities looked into it, Burt Lindstrom being important and such. Never came to anything.

Fact Three: The case went cold and Smyth dropped the acting gig and disappeared into the woodwork. His trail wound all over, from Juneau, to Anchorage, to Fairbanks, and west toward the bitter coast. He was a ghost with many aliases: George Renfro, Ogden Shoemaker, Bobby Stoker, and Gerald Bluefield were the popular ones. He had plenty of cash and Alaska isn't the kind of place where people ask a lot of prying questions. There was a long line of secretive white men seeking some grand destiny in the wild.

I grudgingly admitted Gander was correct in his assessment that Smyth was on the trail of something big. He was a man of disconcerting depths. He'd allegedly gotten wasted at a cast party and told a grip that the Dracula legends were rooted in fact. Yeah, Vlad the Impaler, said the grip. Smyth laughed and said, Not the Țepeș horseshit. Think the Devil's Triangle. Think the sailing stones of Death Valley.

Fact Four: Nine people had gone missing in the various regions of Alaska coinciding with Smyth's travels. Drunks, lost hunters, adventurers. Folks nobody would miss unless, like me, one paid attention to patterns. My man Smyth was a pervert and a cad of the worst sort. Sorting the old papers he'd lovingly collected on ritual cannibalism and human sacrifice, I suspected he was also a murderer.

Fact Five: There are six quarts of blood in the body of a man and I'm low, very low. Now I know I should've stayed in Seattle with my true love –

– SPRUNG JOINTS OF the plane seethe smoke. Flames streak from the cowling that's half nosed into the ice. The smoke is black and thick. The column rises several feet, and then spills down over the ground, pressed hard by the frigid temperature. Visages of devils float in the tide and shoot forth hot red tongues. The wind whips it until it boils. Concupiscent curds of death. Where oh where is my shirtless and muscular roller of big cigars? Call that bastard in here on the double! I have my second chuckle of the day in celebration of wit undimmed by the impingement of certain doom.

We've trudged a good distance inland. The plane is a toy. My glove blocks sight of it easily. We are even farther from the brightening stars. The blue-black horizon has enfolded the ocean like a curtain dropping onto a stage. Moses leads. Parker and Maddox drag me and our pitiable remnants of gear on a canvas tarp salvaged from the wreckage. My knee is sprained, my back is in spasms. I can but hope that's the worst of my injuries. We'll know tonight when the universe freezes and the aspirin runs out.

Pilot John screams way back there where we left him in his pyre. I can barely hear him over the rising wind and the crunch of boots in the snow. The men stop in their tracks and gaze back across the flats. Vapor wisps from their mouths. For a moment they resemble a lonely trio of caribou, separated from the main herd and bewildered at a sound foreign to their existence.

"Hey, he's not dead," Maddox says to Moses. His tone is reproachful.

Moses pulls down his hood. His face is broad and dark. His mustache is silver with frost. He frowns. No, he definitely doesn't look like a man who wants to believe what he's hearing. He stares wordlessly into the gathering darkness, into the coal at its heart.

"Oh, no. Moses, you said he was dead."

"That's the wind."

"No, it's him. God help us." Maddox crosses himself.

Parker glances from man to man. "What's happening?" He really doesn't get it. His hat has fur-lined earflaps; maybe that's why.

"Pilot John is frying," I say through gritted teeth. Nobody says anything for a minute or so. The screams have stopped. My hunch is the unlucky bastard woke up to his flesh popping like bacon, then promptly succumbed to smoke inhalation. Here's hoping. I can't help myself; I quote from the poetry of that long dead Yukon sage, Robert Service: "The Northern Lights have seen queer sights, but the queerest they ever did see was the night on the marge of Lake Le Barge I cremated Sam McGee!"

Moses raises his hood again. His coat is a really nice homemade one with a wolf ruff and more fur trim at the wrist and ankle openings. It'll take him a lot longer to freeze to death than it will for everybody else. He starts walking again, toward the foothills of the Kilbuck mountains. I can't help but imagine them as tombstones.

"Shouldn't we stay with the plane?" Parker says this for the third or fourth time. He managed to save his best camera and carries it on a lanyard around his neck.

"We'll die in the open." Moses doesn't glance backward. Shoulders squared, head lowered, he plods on.

"Gonna buy it either way," Maddox says, low and grumbly. Not a protest, it is an utterance of fact.

"Somebody might see the smoke," Parker says. His is the faint and fading voice of reason swallowed by the wilderness and the indifference of his comrades.

"C'mon," Maddox says. A bear of a man, red-eyed from lack of drink. He and Parker grasp the edges of the tarp and begin dragging me again.

According to the maps, long ago there was a village around here. I'd hoped to find Smyth or some clue regarding Smyth's whereabouts. The village has crumbled, or the ice has buried it. No trace of the fish camps or the mining camps either. A cruel wind blows, scouring the ice to dirt in spots and making brick ramps of the snow in others. The wind doesn't ever really stop in this place. It has, like Sandburg's grass, work to do erasing all signs of human habitation. The wind is the tongue of a ravening beast. It licks at our warmth, the feeble light of our miserly souls.

Our company founders and staggers and scrambles onward. It is dark when we tuck into the shelter of a rocky crevice. Nearby, the face of the mountain is glaciated. Water oozes and steams over ice stalactites and we lap at it. My lips are already cracking and it's only been a few hours. This kind of weather leaches a man, withers him to a husk.

By the beam of a heavy-duty flashlight, the men stretch the tarp as a windbreak. They shore and buffer the enclosure with hastily gathered alder branches and rocks. In the end, we cuddle into a hole and pull the lid over ourselves. I'm wedged between Parker and Moses. A rock digs into my spine. It is cold, concentrated cold, and numbs me with dreadful immediacy. The canvas molds over my face in a death mask, tightening, then slackening with the gusts. The wind roars in the absolute blackness. Farther off, a fluting note as ice shears free of its mooring and is dashed upon the rocks.

Tomorrow we'll find a better shelter, build a fire if we can, if we survive the night. I shiver uncontrollably. I am a particle adrift in a gulf. The horizontal fall is endless –

– "WHAT'S GOING ON with you?" Conway says. He's got my cock in his hand, but not much is happening. "You're different these days." A not good kind of different, apparently, because his voice is too flat to mean anything else.

I'm on my back on the bed, staring at the wall, at the Wawal tapestry of a stigmatic Christ that I appropriated from the estate of a wealthy geezer in Maryland. The image doesn't thrill me, nothing does. I am bereft and confused. I am still falling, have been since the night I went to Gander's house. When was that anyway? Before or after the year in Alaska? Before or after the crash?

"Sam?"

I turn my head and look him in the eye. He's whole, handsome. I understand what he wants and choose to play dumb, which is a mistake. Despite his Ivy League degree Conway's not the sharpest knife in the drawer, but he's far from dull. He's intuitive as the devil. Sometimes we're so synched it's as if he's in my head. Cue the persistent whisper in the back of my mind: I came here to the coldest place I could find because it slows everything. The cold. There is no way to explain my experience in Alaska to Conway any more than I could to the investigators or the shrink. Not in a truthful fashion. To the cops and officials I gave lies. With my beloved, I let my smile be the lie. Only, he isn't having it.

"Sam. Where are the others?"

I wish I knew. Except, I do know –

– THE STORM LASTS thirty-nine hours, then there's a lull. Maddox crawls forth, reborn from the stone womb into a new Ice Age. The sun is a crimson blob low on the horizon, Polyphemus glaring through a hole in the clouds. The other two men follow him, creaking and cracking as they move. They are stick men, dry as tinder. It is so cold spit freezes on my lips. It is so cold my tongue is a clammy lump, separate from the rest of my flesh. Thirst gouges my throat. The others stand over me, black silhouettes seething. Maddox and Parker yank me from the hole like I'm a sack of feathers. Parker hands me a snowshoe to use as a crutch. I'm wobbly and in a lot of pain. On my feet and under my own power, however.

Moses says, "There's gonna be another blow." He's covered in a glittery coat of hoarfrost. He resembles a ghost. We all do. I'm thinking we're very close to it now. The abyss that men tumble into when they shuffle off the mortal coil is right here, always present in places such as this one. The bones of the earth are all around us.

We need a shelter, a fire, and water. Moses chops ice with a hatchet and stows it in a bag. We move against the flank of the mountains, searching for a cave or an abandoned cabin, any kind of habitation. The wind picks up again –

– THERE'S A SCENE in *Ardor* that transcends the smut and the schlock. It is the scene wherein dutiful Renfield and the Count repose after a murderous orgy. The count reveals that his body is an illusion, a projection of pure darkness given fleshly form. He isn't a sentient creature, merely the imitation of one, the echo of one. The consumption of blood is a metaphor, larger than sex, more terrible than repression. There's a hole no man can fill, says the count. No amount of love or hate or heat poured into the pit. No amount of light. I am the voice of the abyss.

The idea of Dracula as genius loci is, well, genius. Vampires as black holes, the dull and ravenous points of a behemoth's fangs. Out of place for a smut flick, I admit, yet brilliant. Too bad it didn't clue me in to my imminent peril. By a trick of the camera, Dracula implodes in slow motion, a star collapsing into itself, and for a moment the bed is rent with a slash of radiant blackness and bits of ash.

Then the film skips and it's back to fucking and sucking –

– I EMERGE FROM the bathroom and find Conway naked atop the covers. He's peering through a magnifying glass at the papers from the antique valise Professor Gander gave me.

Valise and contents are dated at approximately ninety years old. The leather is wrinkled, the documents crinkled and yellow as the piss I just took. These items, the curious circumstances of its last owner's flight from civilization, are supposed to convince me. Silly, wicked Gander. The only thing that convinces me is money.

Conway frowns. "Who wrote this? The fellow's penmanship was atrocious. From this passage all I can make out is, *My wound won't close.*"

I don't get a chance to answer because the next slide clicks into place and I'm shot forward in time and back to Alaska. Nobody knows the trouble I see, except my comrades and none of them can do shit about it either.

Smyth emerges from the storm to deliver us from our predicament. His skull is stove in, as if by a hammer blow, so I can make out the petrified coils of his forebrain and I'm trying to remember if Dr. Seward trepanned Renfield in attempt to save his life. Smyth's appearance is more monstrous than any master makeup artist could hope to devise. He is an upright cadaver manipulated by strings of icy vapor.

His song is irresistible, although he explains it's not his, that he's merely a vessel. He speaks of cabbages and kings and how a combination of saline and cold will send a death spike into the depths of the sea, killing everything it touches. He describes a crack that runs through the dark of space and how it bends the light, how it wears faces and how it wails. How it drinks heat. He is a madman. I've never seen a tongue so long or black.

Eventually, he lights a wooden pipe and passes it around the circle. Claims the hash is from a batch made by monks in 1756, so it's the good stuff. Calls it crypt dust, or something like that. Insists we fortify ourselves for the walk, and nobody argues. I don't taste much of anything, don't feel much of anything, and decide it's probably leaves and twigs. I change my tune a few minute later when the sun begins to contract and expand like an iris.

He leads us to a palace he's carved from ice and rock. Nothing lives anywhere around his home. The desiccated carcasses of bats lie strewn everywhere. Hundreds of them. A carpet of shrunken heads and brittle matchstick bones. Rocks for furniture, icicle stalactites for chandeliers, an irregular pit in the tilted floor. The pit is approximately four feet in diameter. It wheezes a foul, volcanic draft.

Smyth says coming down from the experience of starring in *Ardor* was nearly the death of him. In a fit of despair, he went to his dressing room and drank a fifth of bourbon and shot himself in the head. He wore hats everywhere after that incident.

I came here to the coldest place I could find because it slows everything. The cold. It keeps me. While he's talking, we're in a state of exultant exhaustion. We've taken a hit of the dragon and reality had begun to distort.

Parker asks about the hole.

"That's the crack that runs through everything," Smyth says. "I dug it myself." The sonofabitch doesn't even need to move fast, we're all dumb and stuck in our tracks as cows lowing on the ramp to the killing floor. He uses the hatchet that Moses brought along, two or three licks apiece. I'm lucky, it's only my thigh, and Parker's kind of lucky too.

The bodies of the unfortunate slough into the pit that's awaited us a million years –

– My parents are old as the dust that blows across Texas where they've retreated to for those golden years. I haven't spoken to them since Vietnam got cooking. Dad didn't take to his son turning out a faggot, honorable combat service or not, and Mom, well, as her husband went, so did she.

It's been a few months and I've slowed down on the pills and the booze and am sufficiently restored to humanity to report my true findings, the findings I haven't told anyone, not Gander, not the cops, not Conway.

Molly Lindstrom's parents remind me of mine, except a bunch richer. Their house is in a gated neighborhood amid carefully manicured forestland outside of Seattle. Burt Lindstrom made his dough in the engineering division of a certain well-known aerospace company. His is a precise and austere mind. Wouldn't know it from the décor. Antique hunting rifles, swords, and moose-heads on the walls and nothing to do with aviation or aviators. He favors red and black checked plaids, denim pants, and logging boots. Makes Lee Marvin seem soft and cuddly in comparison. His wife, Margaret, a former bathing beauty, has gone thick in the middle. She's in a dress, a blue one. Her eyes are cruel as a bird's.

Their guard, a goon named Larry, stands at the window. He's peering through binoculars back the way I drove in. "Brown sedan, last year's model. Just pulled a U-turn outside the gate. Two guys." He keeps on scanning with the binoculars. His lips move silently. He's got a gun slung under his ugly tweed jacket.

I'd seen the car on the highway, trying to blend with traffic and not quite making it.

"That'll be the feds," Mr. Lindstrom says to the goon while he stares at the brand-spanking-new scars on my cheeks where the frostbite laid its brand. "Got you on short leash, huh? They reckon you kilt that man of theirs. Left him on the ice. I gotta buck says you did. Kind of hombre you are."

Parker's white smile flickers in my mind. "I didn't kill him," I say with real weariness. It's the hundredth-and-first time I've said the words.

"And I don't give a shit," says Mr. Lindstrom.

"A drink?" Mrs. Lindstrom is already gliding toward the liquor cabinet. She's got the grace of a magician's assistant. Lickety-split, hubby and I are each clutching a scotch and soda in front of the hearth. There's a fire in there. I'm sweating in the nice suit Conway made me wear, but frozen at the core. After Alaska, nothing will ever warm me up again.

She says to him, sweet as pie, "Civility, Burt. We agreed how you'd be." Those eyes again. I wouldn't want to be trapped on a lee shore with her and no supplies.

He smiles like you do when you get punched in the balls. "Sure, hon. How's the booze, Cope? Fix you another?"

"No, sir. I'm fine." I'm not fine. I'm minus a leg and I use a cane and I've gone from recreational drinker to hardened drunk.

"Gander says you have something for us. You met Smyth." Mr. Lindstrom's mouth twists and he visibly restrains himself, turns away and says to the goon, "Get some air, Larry." The goon makes himself scarce.

Mrs. Lindstrom moves close to me. I doubt there's much contact between her and the husband, and she's starved. She smells bitter, like winter flowers. "He told you about my daughter?"

I nod and sip scotch.

"You anglin' for more cash?" He gives a snort of contempt. "I'll write you a damned check on the spot. Out with it, man!"

"Easy, dear, easy," she says to her husband. Then to me, "We saw the film, Mr. Cope. There isn't anything you can say that will shock us. All we want is a little peace. Her marker is over an empty plot. I can't bear it anymore."

He drains his glass, seems poised to chuck it at the fire. "She had a bit part. Basically an extra, for Chrissake. Bride of Dracula Number Three. So what? Those rat bastard producers seduced her. Smyth sold her a bill of goods how he was gonna make her the next Monroe. Molly was a good girl. She mixed with bad people." He runs out of steam and stares dumbly into the distance.

"No argument here." I steel myself. "Molly's dead, ma'am. She died ten years ago in Los Angeles. Remember when Mr. Lindstrom flew to LA to help the private dick he'd hired to search? Well, he and this lowlife named Brent Williams found her all right, shacked up with a hood from the projects, strung out on heroin and hooking for rent money. *Ardor* ruined her. Ruined her in every way you can imagine. There was an argument. Your husband killed her and the pimp in a twenty-dollar-a-night motel room. It was an accident, everything simply got out of hand. The dick got rid of the bodies himself." I stare at her, try to project compassion at her blank, shocked face. "It was you who hired me, isn't that right, ma'am? Your husband signed the check, but it was you, because you couldn't have known, and he went along, played the part of the grieving dad. And I guess maybe you *are* grieving, Mr. Lindstrom. Maybe you're sorry for what you've done."

Nobody says anything for a bit. Then Mrs. Lindstrom bursts into tears and flees the room, face buried in her hands.

"You bastard," Mr. Lindstrom says and shakes his head the way a confused bear might. "You come in here and make my wife cry? Bad mistake, son." He takes a knife from behind his back. A big one with a fixed blade that would've done nicely as a bayonet.

The guard confiscated my piece when I came onto the property. That's why I'm standing next to a pair of crossed cavalry sabers. I hope against hope they're sharp –

– SMYTH WROTE THIS in one of his abandoned journals: As a boy I started with bugs and small animals. I accidentally clipped the end of my index finger off at age sixteen while stacking chairs in the school gymnasium. It completely repaired itself within two and half years. Spontaneous regeneration. This was long before I discovered the Bluefield papers. Bluefield was a crank living in the wrong century. Still, his instincts were true. After my last film with Lewton I visited Borneo on holiday and trekked into the brush, learning the old ways. I ate a fresh human heart. The shaman of a friendly tribe told me I'd inherit the strength and the vigor of the fallen warrior. It tasted sweet. There's no returning from that. Sadly, it's only part of the secret. The keyhole you peer through. The dark mystery itself is unapproachable. –

– PARKER IS STILL ticking, still got some fight in him. He's missing some pieces, so not that much fight. He says to me in a tired voice, "I suppose the fact your grandfather was a gangster makes us meeting like this sort of poetic."

"You say poetic, I say pathetic. Wait a second… You're a cop?" I mug at him, best as I am able. He chuckles, horribly. I'm groggy. Haven't had a sip of water in hours. Two days since I last ate. The tips of my fingers and toes are numb and my heart knocks too fast. Besides bumps, bruises, and a back sprain I've suffered an injury that defies my layman's ability to classify. Partial exsanguination might be closest to the mark. None of this bodes well.

Beyond this litany of woes looms a bigger problem.

The others have bled out on the ice floor of the crystal cave. All that life coagulated into a crimson slick. The enormous cascade of blood is too hot to completely freeze. It oozes toward the hole in the floor. The pit that has awaited us for a million years.

Parker and I cling to a rough section a few feet upslope. We've linked arms and combined our waning strength. The ice is damp and slippery. Inch by inch our purchase loosens and we slide toward doom.

The man who once played Renfield on the silver screen throws back the hood of his bearskin parka and laughs. His hands are bare to the elements, fingernails blackened or gone. I try not to consider what he's done, what he's going to do.

He says, "The tragedy is that the Renfield figure wants what the master already has. Immortality. After all my searching, all my supplication, all my obeisance, I have found only a slower way of dying."

The walls of ice molt crimson. They seep and drip.

My grip fails. Parker groans and slides past me, down the bloody ice chute into the shaft that probably goes straight past Hell to China. The groan is just a sound he's making. It doesn't touch his eyes. I'll never get to ask him if he'd gone undercover to bust me or to get a line on Smyth, that alleged murderer of starlets.

A moment later I'm gone too and Smyth whistles to mock my departure –

– And then I die –

– Maybe an eon passed in the void. How would I know? Mostly I spent the time falling like a stone into an abyss. There were interludes when I segued from falling into walking through a vast maze, a hedgerow of obsidian. The sky was also obsidian splintered by jags of white light. The light was so dim and so far away it might've been the inverse of itself. Figures moved in the distance. Moses and Maddox. I couldn't quite catch them to see for certain. Parker paced me by trudging backwards. A bit green around the gills and sickly pale. Breathing, though. I cried out to him and he smiled and drifted away.

Sometimes Smyth's disembodied voice echoed along the twists and turns. "I didn't travel into the wilderness to find the dark. I brought the dark with me. The seed is inside everybody, waiting for a chance."

Another occasion he said, "I went out there to be alone. You got what you wanted, you stupid twit?"

I realized I was probably talking to myself and in those moments of clarity the maze disintegrated and I'd be lying in that grave on the ice between my comrades, or plummeting from the sky in the plane, or kissing Conway at the Phoenix Theatre, or transfixed in a study while *Ardor* squelched and squealed on the wall and stodgy guests gawked at my apparition.

In every case the snow returns, and covers me—

—I WAKE IN the summer to a good morning blowjob, but the ruined nerves in my remaining leg kill me and the vertigo unmans me and I scream and Conway has to hold me down until I stop. I lie there in a sweat and tell him the fog has lifted. I remember everything in Technicolor.

He cautions that I can't trust my recollections, claims I returned to Seattle a night before I ever left and then blinks and says he didn't say anything that crazy. He leaves red marker messages on the mirror: *Where's her body, Sam?* I confront him and he kisses my ear and says I didn't get eaten by the Ouroboros and shit out into an alternate universe. Take your meds and do your physical therapy, Sam. Where's her body, Sam? Where's Parker's body? Where are they, Sam?

If I didn't die, if this isn't Hell, then what has actually transpired is worse. Always something worse. That first night in the storm does for Moses, his fabulous parka notwithstanding. Maddox may or may not have had life in him. Parker is only strong enough to tow one of us and despite my length, I don't weigh much. The good cop drags me back to the seashore and we await rescue near the plane's wreckage. Along the way a diamond-hard sliver of ice or a jagged rock has torn through my overalls and sliced my thigh to the bone. I don't feel it happen and the blood covers my legs like I've a lap full of rubies. We hunker for two days. Parker's face turns black and his eyes go milky blue. He stays with me a while, and then between buffets from the north wind he's gone.

The troopers are able to dig Pilot John's remains from the barbeque pit. They are mystified at the bullet hole in his skull. Bits of glass in there, so the bullet was fired from the ground as he banked the plane for a pass is what they conclude. Helicopter rides, hospital wards, a long white veil over the universe come next. Ice covers the Earth, then recedes and reveals the green. I'll never walk quite right again. I lose an ear, a leg, all my fingernails, my belief in the rational, my sanity.

Night after night I dream of *Ardor* and Renfield in his cell with worms, lice and flies for sustenance. He gibbers and hoots until the Count slips into his cell and maims him, leaves him paralyzed in the shitty rags of his bedding. I follow the camera into his glazed eyeball and come out on the other side inside a cheap motel room in Van Nuys. I'm a fly on the wall during the encounter between papa Lindstrom and his private dick and Molly Lindstrom. The shouts and the tears are flowing freely when the pimp walks in. Bullets don't have names on them. The girl and the pimp get bundled into the dick's Caddy for a long, lonely ride to the landfill.

I don't have a shred of proof, but the fucking imagery is so vivid, eventually it eats away at me, plagues my waking hours. Lately, I'm convinced that nothing is real, so the unreality of this scenario assumes the same weight as anything else. Conway helps me into the suit I usually wear to funerals and drives me to the Lindstrom estate. I leave him in the car, tell him it won't be fifteen minutes and then I hobble inside to say the awful things I've got say.

Here's the test. Here's where I receive validation or comeuppance. Maybe it'll be both. For a moment I hesitate on the steps while a goon named Larry approaches. It is lush and green and sweetly humid. Not a glacier in sight—

—LINDSTROM CHARGES ME with the knife brandished. I'm a step ahead of the game. I drop my cane and snatch the cavalry saber from its ornamental wall hooks. Coming in I'd expected mockery, perhaps indignant outrage, the threat of arrest, and certainly the risk of getting roughed up by one of the old man's goons. Hell, if they'd simply laughed and phoned the funny farm, it wouldn't have surprised me. What I didn't account for was how fast the situation escalates into a killing. In retrospect, I can't blame myself for not entirely buying that the dreams were bona fide. Crazy people believe their own bullshit and so forth.

The snarl, the savage glint in his eyes, this is the murder in L.A. reprised. Man, it's not as if I'm a fencer, or anything. I make a haphazard swing when he gets close and there goes the knife and two of his fingers under a table. Unfortunately for both of us he doesn't take a hint. He leans down and retrieves the knife with his left hand and I hobble forward two steps and swipe at him again, both hands wrapped around the hilt. The sword cleaves through his neck without any trouble and his head plops onto the Persian rug and rolls onto its side so those devil-dog eyes are blinking at me.

"Oh, shit," I say.

The wife doesn't return and there's a hell of a mess in the parlor, so I leave. The goon doesn't intercept me on my way out the door. I do a spot check of my reflection at the car and don't see any blood on my suit. My hair is mussed and I'm sweating, but that's me these days. I smile at Conway and tell him to take us home. He doesn't suspect anything and I retreat into myself with alacrity. My brain wants to shutter the doors and call it a day. I roll down the window and breathe in the smells of grass and leaves.

A cloud swoops in and paces the car. The breeze gains an edge and snow begins to fall. My heart stops. But it's not snow, it's hail and Conway hits the wipers and in a minute or two we're through it and gliding beneath glorious blue skies. I place my hand over Conway's and close my eyes and try not to make that transcendental journey to Alaska, or visualize Lindstrom's mouth working up a voiceless curse.

I figure if this isn't a dream, the cops will be waiting at the house. And they are.

A CLOSER WALK WITH THEE

Sven Davisson

You back in New Orleans?

Yup

you in Amsterdam?

Yes. How was your flight? I slept all the way through mine

Same here all the way back to new orleans

Didn't much sleep the night before

Cool. Too bad we only met on the last night

I know. Right?!

would have been nice to get to know you a little bit more

we didn't allow for much time to talk LOL

not that i'm complaining

neither am I =]

well I have to finish unpacking and get down to the laundry

k

then send me your backstory

you still have my email?

Yes sir. Will do

Cool ttyl

U2

HEY VAN, Don't remember what we did manage to cover. Don't worry I do remember the important (read *good*) stuff. My family is primarily of English background. I'm named after my great great grandfather Quincy who was the one who moved the family across the atlantic. My father passed away when I was young and my mother and grandmother raised me. She bought a winter house in New Orleans a few years back and I've been down here for the past 8 months helping to restore it. It's a classic double shotgun that pretty much survived Katrina but suffered enough to need some attention. I'm a location scout/manager for film/tv (commercials mostly). My last job on a mercedes trade show "image" film ended so I decided to take some time and come down here to swing a hammer.

Time to change the laundry over.

How bout you? Did you grow up in Amsterdam?

DAG QUIN,

Great to hear from you :)

I actually grew up in Rotterdam and my father still lives there. I moved to Amsterdam right after University. Got a job in a small ad agency and have been doing mostly print and online campaigns since. Nothing major. Nothing anyone outside of the Netherlands would have ever heard of. No viral youtube videos yet. Though they are testing me out on a larger, multi-media campaign and that's what I was in New York last week. Meeting with the client's US PR firm. I more or less just have to adapt the North American campaign over to a Dutch context, but it's still something different from what I have been doing. Wish they would throw a New Orleans client at me. It would be good to see you again. Just sayin. Anyway...

Tot ziens, V

VAN, Strangest thing happened to me today. I was walking and killing time getting some sun when I happened upon a "jazz funeral" or a funeral with music as the locals call them. It was coming up Treme st toward Ursulines. It was on its way out from the church. Hearse leading. *A Closer Walk with Thee. As I Lay Down My Burden.* I followed keeping a respectful distance enjoying the music. The procession closed ranks when they reached the tight confines of the cemetery. I had no choice but to press into the back of the group since I'd obviously been walking with them for several blocks. Turned out the funeral was for a guy I know from the bars. Pretty sure his name was Joe but not positive. We only spoke a couple of times, but we had been eyeing each other and flirting from a distance for years at the Bourbon Pub and Oz. Just a few weeks ago I'd screwed up the courage to talk to him at the more relaxed atmosphere of Café Laffite. It was happy hour and the three $2 rail bourbons I'm sure helped. It was a couple of days before I left for NYC. I'd been hoping to run into him when I got back to town, but not like this!

After they cut the body loose I joined the second line back into the Treme. Everyone waving their white handkerchiefs to *Didn't He Ramble*, *Feels So Good* and *Saints* all those NOLA classics in two-four time.

So weird. Makes you think. You could be fucking gone tomorrow. Anyway not to get all Buddhist and impermanent on your ass. How's home? Getting back to the routine? ~QH

QUIN– Wow that is an odd story. Things are good. Getting back into my groove. Went down to Rotterdam and saw my sister and niece last weekend. Always nice =]

VAN, must be my week for oddness. Finally decided to get out this weekend. Remember I was telling you about happening on the funeral for that guy Joe? I was at the Pub and I could have sworn I saw him out of the corner of my eye. You know how it is. That quick passing glimpse in the peripheral vision? Of course it wasn't him. He wasn't there. Quirky how your mind plays tricks on you. Like when you keep thinking you see a particular person on the street and then remember that they moved or went back to school or whatever. Kind of killed the night though, so I ended up grabbing a po'boy at the nelly deli and going home. ~QH

IT happened again. I was walking around the French Quarter last night. Grabbed a to go cup from Laffite's and tried to avoid the ghost tours. At the end of the block I could have sworn I saw Joe rounding the opposite corner from St. Ann to Chartres. Same black shirt, skinny jeans. Spikey robert smith black hair. But then that could be any one of a 100 at that distance. When I got to the corner he had gone inside somewhere. Oh well. It was a beautiful night for seeing ghosts anyways. Cool breeze coming up the Mississippi. ~QH

FUCK. There has to be a guy in town who looks just like Joe. I saw him on the balcony of Oz from across the street at Bourbon Pub. When I made my way across and through the line. I couldn't find the guy. ~QH sent from iPhone

Hey, Van

Hey

What time is it there?
must be 10 or so? So I'm good
I try not to drunk text so I thought it safe to bug you

how u been?

doing good
well
sitting on a bench near Jackson Sq
watching the drunks walk by

just watching?
=]

what r u up to?

Work. Some of us have to be gainfully employed LOL
have a big account meeting this afternoon

oh sorry for drunking in on you

that's ok
always good to hear from you whatever the circumstance

shit

?

it's him

who?

i swear its him
joe
dead guy

ah maybe it's time for you to head home

no really I swear it's him
just came out of Pirate's alley and is heading down chartres
I'm following

Van I think you should start toward home

no I'm good ttyl

VM : Van. It's him. Well it can't be. But it looks just like him. Kind of creepy. I don't know. Anyway. Sorry. You must be in your meeting. Hope your phone was on silent. I swear it looks just like him. Anyway I'm on my way home talk to later.

QUIN, How u doing? Got your voicemail. Hope you made it home ok. Maybe he has a twin. Anyway give me a shout when you're back in the land of the living. Van

V– a twin? maybe. Idk As I said I never really talked to him so I have no clue anything about him really other than he;s dead. Well he should be at least. I mean I was at his funeral. A closer walk with thee and all that shit. I'll just chalk it up to mind playing tricks. I was pretty lit last night. Anyways, how did the presentation go? ~QH

IT went well. I think we nailed down the account. And I got a date for Thursday with their communication director's assistant. I know I'm bad =] as ever, van

VAN, I saw that guy again. Joe. Or the guy who looks just like Joe I mean. This time I was stone-cold sober. Had just stopped by Rouse's to forage for some food. When I came out he passed right in front of me on Royal walking toward Esplanade. I paused then followed at a safe distance. A couple of blocks on he turned down an alleyway. When I got there it was secured by a locked gate and he was no longer in sight. Figure he must live in one of the two buildings on either side. ~QH
p.s. gotta let me know how the date goes!

THE last few of days I've been making a point of walking by that block of Royal. Call me obsessed, I know. But I can't get him out of my head. It's like he's haunting me, LOL. Wow that sounds a little conceited! I meant it's like he's stuck in my brain and I can't shake it. Imagination or twin or doppelgänger. ~QH
ps and your date???!!! So good it hasn't finished?

It was him.
Don't ask me how but I'm sure now

We ran right into each other
He looked up and right into my eyes. Smiled.
I know he recognized me. It wasn't his twin
wtf I don't know how but it's him

DAG QUIN, how are you? You're starting to scare me a little, man. Well maybe not, but sounding a little weird or wired. Later, Van
p.s. date was good. And yes Thursday night did blur into early Monday morning =]

OKAY I know you're starting to think me crazy. I haven't lost it I swear. He was at Café Laffite in Exile last night. He brushed past me on his way out. His elbow touched mine. When I looked up I could see the back of his head as he left. I went outside but couldn't see which way he'd headed. Really not crazy. ~QH sent from iPhone

VAN, now I'm starting to think that I may be going crazy. I asked around and verified that he's dead and that was his funeral I was at. And not his father or uncle's or something. It was his. Aletha and Frank both knew him. Walking myself back off the ledge and convincing me that he does have a twin. Probably a good chance he'd be gay too, right? So no surprise he would haunt the same bars. ~QH

QUIN– Deep breath! Sure you're right. I know statistically the chances are higher. Did anyone you asked mention a twin? Van

VM : Van? Fuck. It's Quin. It is him. I don't know how, but it is! I mean, I saw them cut the body loose!! I was just at the bar at Café Laffite and someone behind me said hi. I turned and it was Joe. I looked around and no one seemed to react. Aletha was talking to Frank at the other end. They both smiled at me but it was like nothing was happening. I turned back around and he wasn't there. Call me!

Hey, Quin?
Van?
Hey man. How are you? Doing better than last night's voicemail?
A little.

Dude, how drunk were you?

I wasn't. That's the thing. I'd just gotten there.

Oh. Sorry.

He came out of nowhere. He was just suddenly there. And then disappeared.

You home now? Good. Stay put for the night. Get a little sleep. Maybe you've been working on that house too much and need a break.

Maybe. But I know he was there. He talked to me.

He did?

Well he said Hi or Hello or something like that. I don't really remember. It happened quick. Maybe it is just me. Aletha notices everything that happens around that bar and she didn't react to a dead guy standing at it.

Well, get some sleep. I don't have an international plan on this phone. Email or skype me later.

Will do.

Promise? I don't want to have to worry any more about you than I already do.

Yes I promise.

OK, take care of yourself.

Thanks. I'll talk to you later.

OK now I know I'm not crazy and am convinced I'm completely insane. Maybe it's this town and all the talk of ghosts and vampire wannabes. He was there again tonight. Or last night since the suns coming up. I knew he was standing right behind me. I could sense him before he spoke. He was standing close. The bar was crowded. His face was close to my neck. He said, hi. That's it like nothing out of the ordinary. Just hi. I could feel his skin near mine. It was like... I don't know really hard to explain... It was like he was breathing me in. I felt this pull to him. I turned to look at him his eyes were half closed. When they opened I felt like I was free falling off a cliff into black water. Everything was caught and the noise of the bar was silenced. Just as quickly he asked how I'd been and the spell was broken. How had I been? The most mundane question like he had just been chillaxin' in California for a couple of months. I didn't respond and he didn't wait for one. We walked outside. He took my hand and pulled me along Dumaine. It was odd. His hand was cold though the night was warm. We hit Rampart and the lights from Armstrong Park's gate was there like a carnival. It was so *there*. I'd never realized how bright they are. We continued across the street and into the

Treme. It was like he knew where I was staying. Not a word. No question. Just two blocks right to the front door of my mother's house. Still without anything exchanging between us, I unlocked the door. We were in the double parlor. The street shut out as the door closed behind us. We just stood there in the dark. His eyes reflected the little light from outside like obsidian. He pulled me toward him and we kissed. It was incredible. I can't explain it. It felt like he was pulling me inside him. Not just close but really inside his skin. Then I realized his cock was so hard pushing against the buttons and denim of his fly. It was a wooden stake between us, my own straining to meet it. I'm rambling I know and starting to sound like a bad romance novel. Fuck me. But it was all so strange and intense and I don't know. It was so real but like a hallucination. Things were razor sharp and blurred at the same time. Then it's dawn and I'm waking up on the sofa just my clothes on the floor. Maybe someone slipped me something in my drink. I know it happens. I really can't explain. It all seems so real and then a blank. Like a vivid dream you can't shake free of upon waking – the emotion and energy carrying on. Sorry for the long email, but I had to get this down before it started to recede to that void all dreams are relegated to when memory eclipses fantasy. I do have a pretty vicious headache this morning, so maybe there was something in my drink. I've got to go and catch some more sleep. I can barely keep my eyes open. Ttyl ~QH

HI QUIN, how you been? Haven't heard from you in a couple of days. Eagerly waiting to hear more of your mysterious stranger… Work's been keeping me busy. The new account's kicked up the level a little. Anyways get in touch! As ever, Van

QUIN, What's up? It's been almost a week! Hope everything's ok…
Van

VM : Hey… Quin… Getting a little worried… saw some strange posts on your facebook wall… ok I'm a lot worried… give me a call!

VM : [This mailbox you have reached is currently full and cannot accept messages at this time.]

QUIN, I can't believe it. I've been all over your facebook and read through all the comments. Fuck, dude, I just can't believe your dead!!! I don't know what else to say. Please please just hit me up and let me know it's some kind of joke or mistake or... idk what. I know it can't be true... As ever, your friend Van

I'm about to board the red eye from jfk

VM : Van. This is Quin. I just landed at Schiphol – that's Dutch for "ship's graveyard" isn't that cool? Anyway, I couldn't sleep on the plane so I'm going to lie low at the Hilton here until dusk probably. I'll meet up with you later. Don't worry. *We'll find each other in the dark* [humming]

UNHALLOWED GROUND

Seth Cadin

GEORDIE Canon dragged his bad leg behind him up all the way up the cliff, lurching his way to the end of his life as awkwardly as he'd lived it. In the last moments, though, he was graceful, balancing and twisting like a mummer as the musket blast echoed down the rocks before his body fell onto them. Swales wasn't there, and didn't see, but many were the times he sat companionably beside the long flat stone – carved with lies – anchoring his friend in the dirt until Judgment Day – with the image in his mind nevertheless.

They still talked almost just as they always had, for with the left side of his face frozen up like his leg, Canon found the sound of his own voice unpleasant, which was not a trait anyone would ever accuse Swales of having. So, season through season as the decade shifted by with another slinking along behind it, Swales chatted away in the dark, always with the sense that any moment now, a quiet, slurred, hesitant voice would come out from the grave. He'd speak when he had something important enough to say. Sometimes Swales could hear it without his ears:

"You do go on a bit, Swales," the corpse might say, its skeletal jaw grinding. "I reckon the world must be more crowded for you than most." Canon rarely explained himself, but mostly there was no need.

"We understand," he'd said once, as they lay tangled on a hay bale, and the low afternoon sunlight came through the barn's high window and made his face into a painting, marked his bare, distorted spine and shoulders with shadows and beams, like trails left behind under Swales's idle caress.

Now only the thruff-stone travesty with the carved lines spoke for him, fetching no true part of who Canon had been, still was, into the minds of visitors passing by. Perhaps that was why Swales had regaled the poor dear lasses – though at the age he'd somehow found himself, the few barriers he'd ever had to holding forth a spell were crumbled. Sometimes he thought he drifted to the graveyard so much because he wanted to get to know his new neighbors. But no, it was Geordie, the lamiter, the hunchback, his lover, who silently drew him there, and left him to mutter aloud under the trees and the stars like a witch-doctor chanting – or an old man rambling.

"I've often heard him say masel'..." he remembered telling the more nervous of the two little lasses. She'd make nothing of it, overwhelmed by the ugly ideas with which he felt compelled to disturb her tranquility. That tense of the present, a confession hidden out in the open: the day Canon's body was picked apart by the clegs and the dowps was not the end of their entanglement, but the end of the beginning, for he'd kenned the man better now in death than he ever had in the moments they'd stolen together in mutual life. Turning every angle, he agitated his memories, stirred them right up until they made all the shapes and sides of Geordie Canon shine clearly in his head.

That was why, when the lasses were gone and he was alone again by the grave and he felt, there, not the sense of a listening silence, but an empty one, a cold and terrible absence where an invisible presence had so long lingered, he'd been the fool and ran and seized the gels again. He was sure his casual talk, the cheerfulness of his dark expressions, had offended the spirit of Canon and sent him through the Gates of Judgment at last. Swales had only badly angered Canon once before, but being as how that took place in the hours proceeding that pirouette of blood and bone made by the gun and the rocks, he was scart to his heart through that his lad would again choose oblivion over strife, in his humiliation, his wrath.

Borned ashamed, the lad had been, and crippled into a tormented mind by that Mother of his – all her vicious, mindless ways.

"You talk to stop thinking," Canon'd told him once in another of his rare contributions. So Swales reckoned Canon just thought all the time, pressed between his mother and his afflictions, just as his mortal remains were now pressed beneath the stone and earth.

"'Tain't so," Swales'd said at the time, as they leaned drunkenly together behind their secret little shack in the woods. Naked as they'd come into the world, feeling the breeze. They knew they'd hear anyone approaching in time to jump back into in the little stream nearby, as if they were just two tramps bathing. They'd clutched each other first like drowning men, and then, later, touched like the butterflies that sometimes floated past on the rough path to their hideaway – lightly tracing each other's outlines, swaying and bumping each other's frames. Geordie was a beanpole, his hips sharp, but with more to him on top than Swales had imagined. At first, like Mrs. Canon and many others, he too only saw the hunch, the lameness, the odd twist to the mouth that the Lord had seen fit to give Geordie, in His unknowable ways.

When Swales seemed to marvel at the strength he found in Geordie's arms and chest, the lad had spoken up:

"I have to push myself more for everything, and I make work what does work as hard as it can." This was a little naughty joke as well, and they both laughed, though soon they were again silent aside from sighs and groans.

Swales was remembering this as he retraced his way to the graveyard after wailing to the dear lasses about feeling the Angel of Death's wings beating the air just behind him. *Lord knows I was born to speak on what others give silence,* he thought as he passed through the gate and made his way to his familiar seat, trying to ignore the dreadful fear that crept along beside him, like a wildcat stalking.

There was often mist on the ground, but tonight it was rising up into clouds of fog, thin enough at the top to be a haze around his head, thick enough to feel like the wispy white sea might tangle his legs and make him stagger like Canon always had, since his first steps on the earth. A film of midnight dew covered his seat, and he wiped it away with his sleeve, watching the drops make the smooth stone seem to glow in the moonlit fog.

Why did he return, even as he was feeling so strongly the push of evil coming from the sea? Why else? If the Lord was calling him, where could he hide? And even if ol' Cloven-hooves offered him shelter, he wouldn't, could not in himself, take that bargain the way Geordie had done. He went back because he wanted to set with his friend one last time, even if doing so ticked off faster the minutes and hours remaining in his long life.

As he settled down, he tried not to think of the awful chill he'd felt before, the pit where Canon's ghost should be waiting. *You'll run flapways like a headless chicken if you get yourself going,* he chided himself. He tried not to think about how strange the mist looked wreathing the tompsteans, making ghostly figures seem to arise and writhe around them. He tried only to breathe evenly, sit in stillness, and look inward for his shield of holy joy. "Lord, make me answer cheerful, when my call comes," he murmured again, prickling with shame as he remembered shouting it at the little lady, bur holding to it just the same.

What rose up with the mists were more images, vivid as a dream is in the moment before it is forgotten. Moments from the time before that *wretch* of a mother to a son christened George Canon had made it filthy in the lad's good heart. From the time when they were so enraptured together, they were fearless, reckless, at liberty to caper and laze without doubt of the simple purity of their encounters.

It started in the winter, with the two of them huddled together in a chilly tent in the woods, and ended in the summer on the cliff. Hardly any time at all, yet it'd somehow stolen from the future to make itself brighter and deeper – like the water was, in the middle of the lake they'd once rowed to so they could float along, wrapped up around each other, under an October sky glowing with reflected oranges and reds from the surrounding trees. The time they'd had together seemed to roll on forever, while the present world faded around Swales as if drained by the parasitical past.

It started in drink and equally intoxicating exchanges of glances, gestures that came too close or lingered too long. They were testing, carefully testing, even as they both, as Geordie later said, *understood* – knew each other's minds without needing words to wrap around them. And they were also sampling, waiting, teasing themselves and each other by delaying the inevitable. Once he had met Canon as a man instead of an acrew'k monstrosity, he knew if any chance presented itself – which seemed unlikely at first anyhow, as being twice Geordie's well-grown age, Swales was fully old enough to be the lad's father, or even grandfather, and thank the Lord his own wife handled the children and let him keep his distance, because otherwise he'd have lessoned them with more truth than they could bear.

As he had done with Canon, that night of the cliff, the lucky carrion, and Swales left standing alone. A few hours, a few months, and nearly twenty long years were present in webs of memory in Swales's reality, always.

"Time is the Lord's way of punishing us for our sins," Canon had slowly proclaimed back on that fresh, cool afternoon on the lake.

"Speak for your own self," Swales rumbled, wrapping their bare calves together as they lay back on the still waters. "The Lord's greatest gift is his worst punishment. He lets us be ourselves."

"Sometimes." Geordie's voice came faster than usual, and he turned his head away, looking toward the horizon.

Swales understood. "You feel like a rabbit besnared. But you're more free in yourself than many fit men."

Only the gentle sound of the boat displacing waves and a few birds calling in the distance came then, until Swales thought they were leaving the subject behind, but then Canon said:

"Every day I think about whether I'd feel anything when the musket shot took my head off."

They held each other even closer, and soon rowed back to shore, as the charm of the isolated setting had faded and the breeze which had been refreshing was starting to give them a chill.

They made it back to the shack's narrow mattress and Swales knew his lad wouldn't want to sleep right away, even after such dark discussion. They understood but didn't *protect* each other. To do so would have been an insult. And that night Swales convinced the lad to try something he had always refused before, seeking to ease the ache they both felt by trying for a more intense experience. It certainly was.

The delicate waves of mist and swirls of fog grew heavier in the graveyard as Swales reminisced, but so deeply immersed in the vivid past was he that he hardly noticed. As for the soft footfalls stealthily approaching, he heard them not at all. Without knowing it, his mind was slowly drifting out of his control, and his senses were befuddled between the bone orchard and his memories.

The old woman'd started to suspect it. Swales had been amazed, as he didn't reckon she could see her son as anything more hideous than she already did. But she could, and she thought they were like animals, just rutting in the bushes, unable to control their deviant impulses, their demonic proclivities. For a long time the difference in age, Canon's deformity, and Swales's natural, avuncular charm with young ladies reflected suspicion when the oddly matched pair of them were known to be vanishing at the same times, and were hip to hip even when in the town. Oh, they'd believed they were fox-sly, getting away with it, but now Swales reckoned half of all the town had known and half again of those had nattered on about it out of earshot. Mrs. Canon had sharp hearing for sharp tongues, though, and soon she was confronting Geordie – who was creeping in past midnight, clothes askew on his twisted body – with a Bible in one hand and a belt in the other, as if he were a small boy again.

She'd lashed him where he stood, one handed, the other arm rigidly holding the Bible aloft as if to exorcize the evil spirits that surely infected her lame and degenerate son. Again, Swales had not been there, but he'd seen the welts and bruises, and felt in himself the ability to do murder, to spit on the Lord's good work and choke the life out of the shrew who did that to gentle Geordie. But he held it back, hunted it down and trapped it in a cage in his heart where it snarled and bit but could not break free.

"See," the lad said later. "You're thinking about it, so you're not talking about it."

"What matter of thing more should I say?" Swales demanded. "I've said it. Leave her, come with me somewhere else, where we can be invisible."

"Invisible!" Canon ran his hands down the front of his own body. "I'm always in someone's line of sight. Maybe Mother is right about me, but I'd rather burn forever than go to a heaven that would have her in it."

"If you truthfully feel that way, maybe she is right." Swales said it before thinking, and he'd never stopped wishing since that he hadn't. He said it *uneasily* – that was what did it. Not in anger, but in a moment of doubt. A betrayal.

"Then I might as well get it over with." The lad started for the shed's creaky door. Then he stopped and laughed, and later Swales would remember it, the last time he heard that sound, so much like a wind-chime, something gleaming and bronze. "Maybe in the next life I will become a rogue, and heist a shipment of gems and spices, and sail the seas forever."

"You don't mean it, do you, Geordie my dear?"

"Who knows what means anything," was all the lad said, after a long silence in which they met each other's eyes, but couldn't understand any longer what they saw in secrets there.

"Stay tonight, lad." Swales tried to make it an order, but knew it was a plea.

"I'm too busted up for acrobatics." Again Canon looked away, unfocusing his eyes.

"It's more than just the circus," Swales said.

Canon said, "Old man, the circus never is."

THE WARMTH OF the July air came into the cabin as George Canon left it, to sulk in his bath or hang himself from the rafters in the barn. If he were determined to do it, Swales knew he couldn't be stopped, and if he were making an empty threat, it was a question looking for an answer. And so Swales couldn't chase Canon, because he had nothing to do and nothing to say.

Swales wasn't there, he didn't know, but he couldn't stop seeing what he believed he was doing when Geordie was making real his wish and damning his soul eternal: he was eating half a bowl of oatmeal the lad had left behind, so it wouldn't go to waste. He was watching the sun, so later, when they told him the time the blast was heard, he decided that was what he'd been doing. It was there before the row, so he'd been wondering if Canon wasn't hungry, or had left it for him, because it was the last of their few supplies.

They were never staying long, everywhere they snuck away together—Swales understood, Canon didn't want to run and couldn't stand to stay. He was cornered like a bear in a dismal zoo, on display, his quiet dignity disrespected by every circumstance of his life.

In the graveyard, as the fog enclosed Swales and his memories, he felt a density in his brainpan, like the pressure of a squeezing hand. His eyes watered, then all at once cleared. The shapes in the fog were not mirages, but entities approaching him—or perhaps one great big creature encircling him diffusely. In a moment, although his neck was held rigidly ahead, he felt the pressure of Geordie sit beside him, and a cold hand ran along his leg from thigh to knee, sending a terrible shock through the pit of his stomach, which lingered as tension in his groin, despite the terror flooding him at the same time.

Then at last the dead did speak, though Swales's mind was so befuddled, he could hardly tell whether the sound came from his ears or his mind, or indeed even if it sounded quite like Geordie had all that time ago. *Well, twenty years in the ground would change a man,* he thought, but uneasily, for in flashes of awareness he felt there was a terrible danger in believing his senses.

"I forgive you," the figure, which was wavering and pale in the corner of Swales's vision, told him, or somehow made him hear.

"I never pulled that trigger," Swales said, his voice tight and short. "Never stood you over that abyss, neither."

"I just want to rest," Canon said, with an edge in his tone, a quiet threat. "All I wanted then was some rest."

"More'n you wanted me." Swales kept staring ahead, unable to look sideways at the figure even when he tried.

"Did you want me to suffer, so you could keep me?"

"I kept you, all right, an' your sufferin' too, because now there's no way around it. We could have killed the old lady instead, and who would miss her. You could have left with me. You could have – "

"Could have killed you instead, Swales." Canon was calm, firm. "Would've. You or me. You think now I chose wrongly?"

All at once, Swales woke up, or came out of a trance – he couldn't tell which. The ghostly conversation was already fading in his memory – it felt like his own thoughts echoing back at himself, now, though it had seemed real and solid a moment ago. Thoughts he couldn't have before, but which lurked at the bottom of his awareness, tainting his spirit.

He blinked rapidly, trying to make his eyes see what was in front of them, and found he could move his neck again. As he did, he saw the corner of the flat rectangular stone sliding closed, half of its width lifted up and pushed aside as if by some incredible force. The mist that had encircled Swales's head was draining away down through the opening in a steady stream. In his shock, he thought his careless words to the lass had been prophecy after all, and soon every stone would tremble and shift, and the dead would come dragging them along behind.

...want to rest... These words stood out in Swales's memory all at once, and against all reason he resolved the real scene into an image: someone was sneaking into George Canon's eternal bed, to lounge with him, take rest with him. Then came an even stronger image of himself stretched out in a real, rough bed, a little cot only half again as wide as the coffin, entwined with Geordie and drifting off to sleep with the scent, the warmth of his skin surrounding him.

"No!" Swales shouted at the open grave, at the intruder invading it. "You'll not take my place, whatever manner of fiend y'are."

With an eerie swiftness, the ribbon of mist reversed direction, and Swales found himself dropping back onto the seat with wrenching force, having not even realized he'd stood up. He was still half-lost in the memory, which uncovered the deep longing he'd had all along to join Geordie again: to rest together again, sprawled out on the bed with a cool breeze coming in from the window, to tussle and play and please each other to exhaustion. He'd been living in the shadow of one idealized moment in the distant past, defying time to keep taking him farther away from it.

The mist began to take shape, this time with much greater solidity than before, when it was Swales's hypnotized imagination defining it. The creature was hard to see in the silhouette created by the moonlight, but the glint of two red sparks and one gleaming white fang was enough to prove it surely a denizen of Hell. Swales tried to rise up, but found himself trapped by those glowing eyes, which burned with a hideous rage.

There was a growing lightness in the sky, black shading to dark grey, and Swales realized he'd been sitting there for hours, until it would soon be dawn. They had often drifted off around this time of day, him and Geordie, having spent every hour of the privacy of night engaging in what Geordie called acrobatics, and talking when they rested – or Swales would talk, for the most part, but they conversed, nevertheless. He remembered those lulls of satisfaction, building slowly back into desire as evening became night and night became morning and they finally slept, out of step with the world outside their bodies, happy to be living upside-down and sideways from the rest of the world.

However long they had to meet together, it played out in the same waves, so if they had hours, the peaks would be sharper and the sleepy interludes more dreamlike, and if they had days they would know it was time to go home when they started to wear on each other's last nerve. The wave turned back on them if they pushed against the tide too long, it seemed.

The first time was such a tangle of sleeping bag, limbs and the need for relief from all the built-up sexual pressure, Swales could hardly remember it, even the morning after when he awoke, before and beside Geordie, as startled as he'd ever been to find he was not dreaming. When he thought of that, he always thought also of their *proper* first time together, the moment and place where their arrangement shifted from being merely a strange companionship and the mutual practicality of sexually compatible met. It was in that little pine cot, with enough room, if not to be acrobats, then at least to tame some lions.

"Why couldn't it be enough for you?" Swales asked the past. But in this world at least, Canon had left no ghost except the one haunting Swales's conscience. He could only ever again answer from memory and imagination. He was, had been, dead since Swales was already old, and now even his grave, already cursed, was going to be defiled by some beast beyond the catalog of Swales's previously firm opinions on the nature of reality, in which all the monsters were human and wore familiar faces.

The hideously twisted and unrecognizable face of this new monster was advancing now, then in a rush was over him, seizing his neck in an iron-cold grip. Even as his face froze into an expression of terror, that part of Swales which had always remained stuck in the unfolded past all at once overtook his mind completely. He dimly heard his own neck cracking, but his attention was on the way the rising pre-dawn light began to fade, not realizing it was his own eyes going dim. The horrible creature shook his body limply like an old withered stalk of celery, and again from afar Swales heard his own bones popping and snapping.

There was pain, but it too came from a distance. The sounds of his body being brutalized to death all became, in his fading mind, the ordinary noises of a boat drifting over a small lake on an evening in the early summer: the slap of the oars disturbing the surface of the water, the industrial woodpeckers drilling into trees on the approaching shore. Then the tiny spark of consciousness remaining as the pulses of thought in his brain finally ran down escaped the graveyard, escaped the burden of lugging around a meager load of flesh and bones in a world where the best life he could ever have had already come and gone.

The past became the present, and the perfect moment was at last fully unveiled, alive to his senses, simultaneously an echo of the past and a flicker from a future that never came to be. He and Geordie rowed to shore and docked the little boat, and walked with their arms slung around each other's shoulders into the deserted cabin they had illicitly made their own. There was half of a moon in the sky, a curve that was fantastically bright until it suddenly stopped at its own rigid edge of darkness. Grasshoppers played their tiny bows in the grass all around them.

Swales breathed in the cool fresh air, confused for a moment – wasn't he choking, wasn't his head twisted until his throat was a useless corkscrew? No, that was just a dream. It was a phantom life, drifting over and through this real life like a fog. Again an image nagged at him, something about fog, and mist, but as death slowly stalked after that last surviving spark inside him, it seemed unimportant, a minor detail forgotten to no consequence. Soon he would be in bed with Geordie – soon they would strip each other down and climb under the chilly sheets and thin quilt, and warm each other with their hands, their bodies, their breath. As he thought of it, he was in it, and the pleasure made little prismatic flashes appear in his vision – or was that the last of his now slow and labored breathing stalling, stalling, as his body became one more corpse in a field of them?

Perhaps the stone pulled itself closed again, leaving no sign except that which a good dog would scent out at the funeral, growling and refusing to go near the seemingly undisturbed grave. In some corner of what was left of his awareness, Swales felt this sealing, but at the same time a wonderful relief – it didn't matter, the living Geordie was beside him in the bed again, and all there was left in the grave over which he had kept watch for so long was dust and bones. The demon could have them. They had never been the man who had lived in them.

Death couldn't catch Swales if he hid somewhere that was not quite real. In the chilly cabin, Geordie Canon's twisted body – all its distortions uncovered, unhidden – awaited Swales's own – aged, frail, softened by time – on the thin mattress held up by the rough pine frame, which they'd made together, shirtless and side by side, working in silence on their secret wedding bed.

"It was enough," the Geordie in his mind belatedly replied, careful but still slurring on the softer sounds. They were chest to chest, naked legs entwined, arms around each other's backs. "But then it was over."

"There's something I never said – " Swales didn't understand the regret that welled up, because he could no longer remember the future of a world that no longer existed for him, or for Canon.

"So you never needed to say it. You talk too much anyhow. We understand. Blow out the candle, old man. It's time for us to sleep."

The Authors

Jason Andrew lives in Seattle. By day, he works as a mild-mannered technical writer. By night, he writes stories of the fantastic and occasionally fights crime. As a child, Jason spent his Saturdays watching the *Creature Features* classics and furiously scribbling down stories. His first short story, written at age six, titled "The Wolfman Eats Perry Mason," was severely rejected. It also caused his grandmother to watch him very closely for a few years. His story "Moonlight in Scarlet" received an honorable mention by Ellen Datlow in *Year's Best Horror*. You can find out more about Jason at jasonbandrew.com.

Laird Barron is an award winning author and poet, much of whose work falls within the horror, noir, and dark fantasy genres. Barron spent his early years in Alaska, where he raced the Iditarod during the early 1990s. Barron retired from racing to better express the darkness he experienced in the wilds of Alaska. He was a 2007 and 2010 Shirley Jackson Award winner for his collections *The Imago Sequence and Other Stories* and *Occultation and Other Stories* and 2009 nominee for his novelette "Catch Hell." Other award nominations include the Crawford Award, Sturgeon Award, International Horror Guild Award, World Fantasy Award, Bram Stoker Award and the Locus Award. His first novel, *The Croning*, was published in 2012.

Seth Cadin is from New York and now lives in California. More of his short stories can be found in the Prime anthologies *Bewere the Night* and *Bandersnatch*, in the anthologies *Willful Impropriety* and *Brave New Love* from Running Press, *Where Thy Dark Eye Glances* from Lethe Press and in Issue V of the annual *Three-Lobed Burning Eye* anthology. He has one partner, one daughter, and many pet mice.

Traci Castleberry is a former saxophone major and Denver native now living in Tucson and serving the whims of her Lipizzan mare, Carrma, who demands rides, exercise and plenty of horse cookies. She's been a fellow at the Lambda Literary Retreat for Emerging LGBT Writers,earned an MA in Writing Popular Fiction from Seton Hill University and has attended the Clarion and Taos Toolbox workshops. She's written a dozen queer erotic romance e-books as Evey Brett and Nica Berry. Traci and her alter egos can be found online at orossy.com.

Elka Cloke is a poet, fiction writer and family doctor. She is the author of "The Adventure of the Poesy Ring" from *A Study in Lavender: Queering Sherlock Holmes* (Lethe Press, 2011) and *Bitter Language* (Lethe Press, 2010). Her poetry has also been published at the front of the novels *Clockwork Angel* and *City of Ashes* by Cassandra Clare and in *The San Fernando Poetry Journal* and *The Santa Monica Mirror*. She is married and is the mother of twin boys. She has always believed in the true love of Lucy Westenra and Mina Murray. She lives in Western Massachusetts.

William P. Coleman is a writer from Buffalo, NY. His novella "The Well-educated Young Man" was published in *A Study in Lavender: Queering Sherlock Holmes* and the story "Paying Alex" can be found in *Pay for Play*. He has completed a novel, *Telémakhos*. His website is wpcwriter.wordpress.com.

Sven Davisson is the founding editor of *Ashé! Journal of Experimental Spirituality* and the publisher of Rebel Satori Press and its imprint Queer Mojo. He received a degree in Critical Theory/Photography from Hampshire College, Amherst, Massachusetts. He studied photography under former Photo League member and noted American realist Jerome Liebling and documentary folklorist Carrie Mae Weems. He resides in Maine.

Rajan Khanna is a fiction writer, blogger, narrator, and graduate of the 2008 Clarion West Writers Workshop. His work has appeared in *Beneath Ceaseless Skies*, *Daily Science Fiction*, Podcastle, and *The Way of the Wizard*, among others. His articles have appeared at Tor.com and LitReactor.com and his podcast narrations can be heard at *Podcastle*, *Escape Pod*, *PseudoPod*, *Wired*.com, *Starship Sofa* and *Lightspeed* magazine. Rajan lives in New York where he's a member of the Altered Fluid writing group. His personal website is www.rajankhanna.com and he tweets @rajanyk.

Livia Llewellyn has been a finalist for the Shirley Jackson Award for her critically acclaimed short story collection *Engines of Desire: Tales of Love & Other Horrors*. At night, she writes about lonely young girls who can speak to engines, Nikola Tesla's secret journals, long-horned demons lost in Northwest suburbia, giant biomechanical insects, mothers who are good monsters, monsters who are good mothers, and lots of consensual human-&-creature sex.

Ed Madden is a poet, political activist, and associate professor of English and Women's Studies at the University of South Carolina. Madden is president of the American Conference of Irish Studies, Southern Region. He has written several critical articles on modern British and Irish poetry and has completed a book on representations of Tiresian liminality in modernist poetry. His poetry collection *Prodigal: Variations* appeared in 2011. His newest book, *My Father's House*, was a finalist for the 2011 Robin Becker Chapbook Prize.

Jeff Mann grew up in Covington, Virginia, and Hinton, West Virginia. His poetry, fiction, and essays have appeared in many publications, including *Arts and Letters*, *Prairie Schooner*, *Shenandoah*, *Willow Springs*, *The Gay and Lesbian Review Worldwide*, *Crab Orchard Review*, and *Appalachian Heritage*. He has published numerous poetry chapbooks and volumes, two collections of personal essays, two novels, *Fog: A Novel of Desire and Reprisal*, which won the Pauline Réage Novel Award, and *Purgatory: A Novel of the Civil War*, which won a Rainbow Award. His erotic vampire collection *Desire and Devour: Stories of Blood and Sweat* was released last year. He teaches creative writing at Virginia Tech in Blacksburg, Virginia.

Damon Shaw lives in the Canary Isles, fifty miles off the African coast. He designs and makes wooden...things, which he sells on a market stall to the endless stream of passing tourists. He has sold stories to *Icarus*, *Daily Science Fiction*, and *AE: The Canadian Science Fiction Review*. His work has appeared in several anthologies, including *The Touch of the Sea* from Lethe Press, and *The Lavender Menace: Tales of Queer Villainy*, edited by Tom Cardamone. To find more of his work, follow his rarely updated blogthing at damonshaw.livejournal.com.

Lee Thomas is the Lambda Literary Award and Bram Stoker Award-winning author of *The Dust of Wonderland*, *In the Closet, Under the Bed*, *The German*, *Torn*, *Ash Street*, and the new collection *Like Light for Flies*. Lee lives in Austin, Texas, where he is always working on a new book. You can find him online at leethomasauthor.com.

The Editor

Steve Berman's favorite actor to play the role of Dracula is Bela Lugosi because his mother encouraged her young son to sit beside her on the sofa and watch the Universal horror films on the television with her during weekend afternoons.

Berman grew up to love scary stories, of course. And Halloween.

He has sold nearly a hundred articles, essays and short stories as well as the young adult novel *Vintage: A Ghost Story*. *Suffered from the Night* is the twentieth anthology he has edited (he has been a three-time finalist for the Lambda Literary Award for such efforts).

He resides in a lonesome spot in New Jersey.

www.ingramcontent.com/pod-product-compliance
Lightning Source LLC
Chambersburg PA
CBHW030406020726
47493CB00003B/961

* 9 7 8 1 5 9 0 2 1 3 9 9 5 *